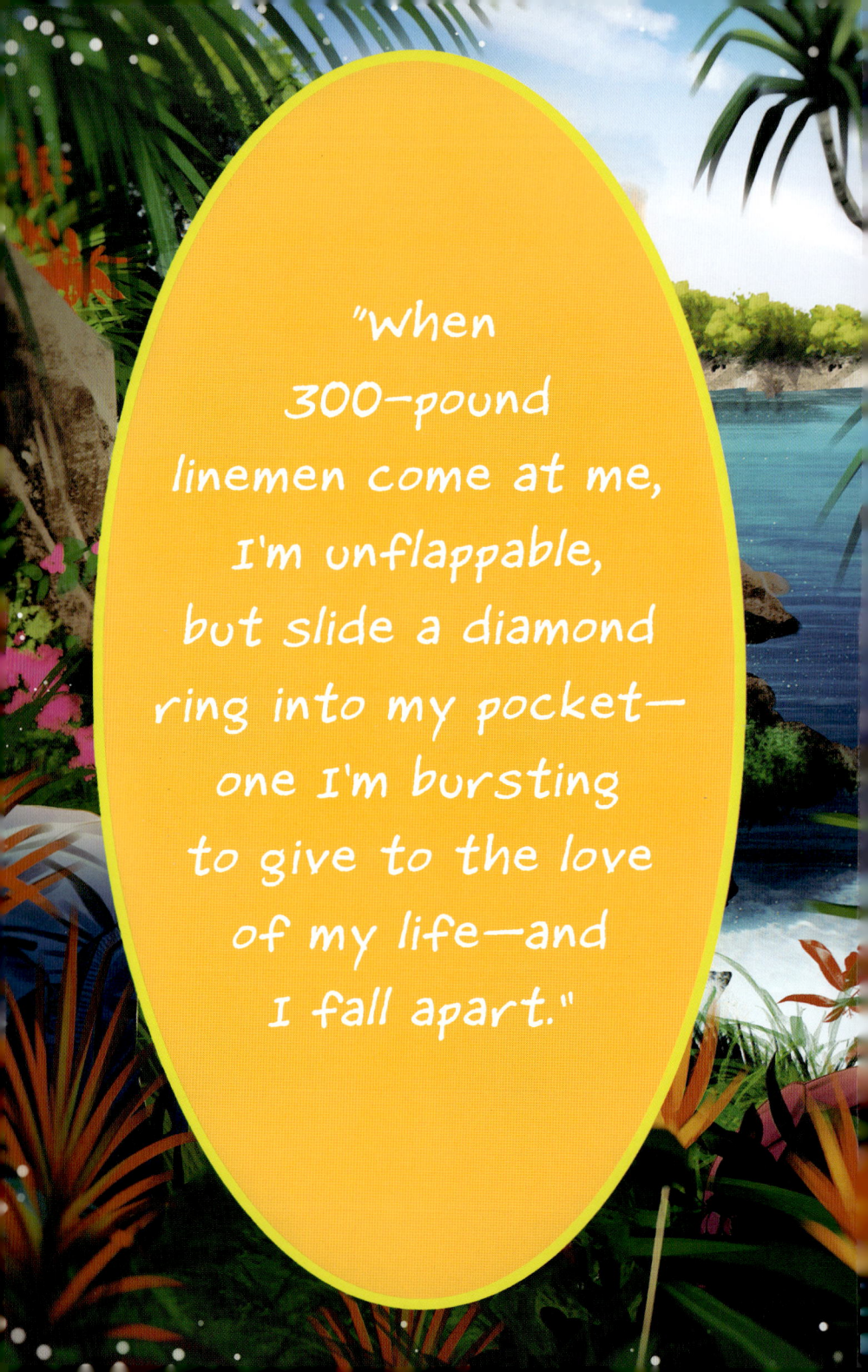

# ALSO BY LAUREN ROWE

**The Morgan Brothers**
*Hero*
*Captain*
*Ball Peen Hammer*
*Mr. Bodyguard*
*Rockstar*

**The Reed Rivers Trilogy**
*Bad Liar*
*Beautiful Liar*
*Beloved Liar*

**The Hate Love Duet**
*Falling Out of Hate With You*
*Falling Into Love With You*

**The Club**
*The Club: Obsession*
*The Club: Reclamation*
*The Club: Redemption*
*The Club: Culmination*

**The Josh and Kat Trilogy**
*Infatuation*
*Revelation*
*Consumption*

**Meet Me at Captain's**
*Who's Your Daddy?*
*My Neighbor's Secret*
*Textual Relations*

Standalones
*Finding Home*
*Hacker in Love*
*Smitten*
*Swoon*
*Spark*

# LAUREN ROWE

kensingtonbooks.com

KENSINGTON BOOKS are published by:

Kensington Publishing Corp.
900 Third Avenue
New York, NY 10022

kensingtonbooks.com

Copyright © 2026 by Lauren Rowe

This is a work of fiction. All of the characters, organizations, and events portrayed in this novel are either products of the author's imagination or are used fictitiously.

All rights reserved. This book or any portion thereof may not be reproduced or used in any manner whatsoever without the express written permission of the publisher except for the use of brief quotations in a book review.

All Kensington titles, imprints, and distributed lines are available at special quantity discounts for bulk purchases for sales promotions, premiums, fundraising, educational, or institutional use.

Without limiting the author's and publisher's exclusive rights, any unauthorized use of this publication to train generative artificial intelligence (AI) technologies is expressly prohibited.

Special book excerpts or customized printings can also be created to fit specific needs. For details, write or phone the office of the Kensington sales manager: Kensington Publishing Corp., 900 Third Avenue, New York, NY 10022, attn: Sales Department; phone 1-800-221-2647.

The K with book logo Reg US Pat. & TM Off.

ISBN 978-1-4967-5772-2 (trade paperback)

First Kensington trade paperback printing: February 2026

10 9 8 7 6 5 4 3 2 1

Printed in China

Electronic edition: ISBN 978-1-4967-5775-3

Interior design by Kelsy Thompson
Interior art courtesy of Noun Project/Aina Puigcerver, Evan MacDonald, iconfield, and Natasha Rose

The authorized representative in the EU for product safety and compliance
is eucomply OU, Parnu mnt 139b-14, Apt 123
Tallinn, Berlin 11317, hello@eucompliancepartner.com

*To my readers, old and new. I'm grateful for all of you and our shared love of love.*

# CHAPTER 1
## Iris

"Who wants the last pour?" As Tatiana asks the question, she holds up a nearly empty bottle of pricey champagne—the third of three she brought as her contribution to tonight's pre-wedding sleepover.

To celebrate my last night as an unmarried woman, my four bridesmaids—my two college besties, Tatiana and Kaylee; my best friend since grade school from here in Orchard Blossom, Harper; and Brandon's nineteen-year-old little sister, Delilah— have come to my dad's house, the modest, cozy home where I grew up, for a good, old-fashioned slumber party.

To give us some privacy for our girls' night, and to free up the necessary beds, my dad and brother kindly went to sleep at our town's biggest and only hotel for the night. Dad and Atlas said they were happy to do it, though, since the hotel is where my groom is hosting a "boys-only" poker party tonight. Classic Brandon.

"Iris?" Tatiana, our bartendress for the evening, says, tilting the neck of the champagne bottle toward me. "As the bride, you've got dibs."

I shake my head. "That's the best champagne I've ever had, but I don't want to risk feeling the least bit hungover tomorrow."

"Well, if no one else is gonna drink it," Kaylee, our resident party girl, says, "then I will."

"Yes, we're well aware you'll drink it, you lush," Tatiana teases. "I figured I'd offer it to the *bride* first."

Laughing, Kaylee addresses Delilah, my shy soon-to-be sister-in-law. "You want to split the last bit with me?"

"No, you go ahead," Delilah replies. "I'm an even bigger lightweight than Iris." To emphasize her point, she rises from the couch with a big stretch. "It's bedtime for Delilah, ladies. Alcohol always makes me sleepy." She grins at me. "No need to be quiet when you come in, Iris. I can sleep through anything, especially when I've been drinking."

"I'll be in soon. I want to get lots of beauty sleep for tomorrow."

After Delilah disappears into the short hallway, my three best friends and I lean in and whisper about how adorable she is and how lucky I am to be gaining a sweet sister in addition to a husband.

"Hey, Iris?" Delilah says, poking her head back into the living room. "Can I borrow some toothpaste? I left mine at the hotel."

"There should be some in my toiletry bag, which is sitting on top of my suitcase for Hawaii." Brandon and I will be taking an early-morning flight to our honeymoon the day after tomorrow's wedding, so we packed separate bags for that portion of our travels.

Delilah thanks me and leaves again, and conversation in the living room resumes, this time about the schedule for the Big Day tomorrow. But midway through our conversation, Delilah reappears with a confused look on her face and a cell phone in her hand.

"Did my brother leave his phone here?"

I don't recognize the device in Delilah's hand. At least, not from here. "No, Brandon's definitely got his phone. He's been texting me all night."

Delilah hands me the thing, which is turned off, and resumes her prior spot on the couch. But even close up, I don't recognize the mysterious device. "Where was it?"

"In Brandon's toiletry bag. I assumed the bag was yours, but when I found a bottle of aftershave in a pocket with this phone, I realized my mistake."

My brow furrowed, I press the phone's power button, and it lights up and springs to life.

"Could it be a work phone?" Delilah asks innocently.

Panic slams into me. After almost seven years with Brandon, the last four spent living with him in a small apartment in his hometown of Denver while he's worked at his father's insurance firm, I'd definitely know it if Brandon had a work phone. My extroverted husband-to-be didn't take his studies all that seriously at UCLA, but once we got to Denver, he became a veritable workaholic. These days, my hardworking fiancé is always on his phone with clients and running off to after-work drinks with potential ones.

*Oh my God.*

Suddenly, things I've always considered innocuous seem horribly suspicious in this context. When we got to Denver and Brandon started working such long hours at his father's firm, I was thrilled to support his newfound work ethic and passion, especially after Brandon proposed last year and started talking about working hard for *us*. For our future. For the family we're both excited to build one day. God knows my salary as a preschool teacher isn't going to buy us a house any time soon. But now, thanks to this foreign phone in my hand, I'm seeing everything through a new lens. Was Brandon *really* out schmoozing potential clients all those nights he came back home late from work tasting of whiskey and bragging about landing a big new account?

*No, don't jump to conclusions, Iris.* There must be a logical, innocuous reason for Brandon not to disclose this mysterious phone. He could be holding it for a friend, for instance. Or planning a big surprise for me in Hawaii, so he got a secret phone to handle all necessary arrangements.

My spirit sinks. For what purpose would Brandon keep a phone tucked away in his toiletry bag for a friend? Also, Brandon's never arranged anything romantic for me, big or small, throughout our many years together, so it's hard to imagine him planning a honeymoon surprise for me in Hawaii. But even if Brandon did do something totally out of character like that, I can't fathom it'd be anything elaborate enough to require a secret phone to safely arrange it.

Even when proposing to me, Brandon only spontaneously blurted the idea one random Tuesday night following our weekly dinner with his parents. During the meal, Brandon's imposing father had asked his son, "So, Brandon, what's next for you two, after all these years? Marriage, I hope?" And the next thing I knew, during our short drive home, Brandon was saying he thought the timing was finally right for us to get engaged and start planning a wedding. "We'll go ring shopping together this weekend," Brandon suggested, at which point I gleefully shrieked, "Yes!" And that was that. We got the ring that very weekend, exactly as Brandon had suggested, and we've been happily engaged ever since. Or so I've thought till a moment ago, when Delilah handed me this mysterious phone. Now, I can't deny I'm rapidly questioning everything.

"Maybe he's holding the phone for someone else?" I venture weakly, hoping the theory sounds more plausible when spoken aloud. But when I look at the faces of my three best friends, it's plain to see they're having worst-case-scenario thoughts about this phone, the same as I am.

"We need to get into that phone," Kaylee says, her eyes fixed intently on mine. She's my most vivacious, passionate friend. And right now, the fire in her eyes is unmistakable.

My stomach churns with my exhale. "It's password protected."

Kaylee's fierce eyes harden. "What's the passcode for his main phone?"

"I don't know," I admit, my voice turning squeaky.

All three of my best friends scoff and exchange concerned looks.

Harper, my maid of honor for tomorrow and my bestie since childhood, mutters, "Gee, that's not a red flag or anything, Iris."

"Let's not jump to conclusions here," Brandon's sister interjects. But it's clear from my friends' facial expressions that horse has already left the barn.

"Does Brandon have *your* passcode?" Harper asks.

I nod. "But mine is easy—my birthday. And I don't have any confidential client information on my phone, the way Brandon does." That's the reason Brandon has always kept his phone confidential—because of some insurance regulation that requires all agents to . . .

*Oh my God.*

Am I the most gullible person alive? I've never thought of myself that way before this moment, but suddenly, it seems entirely possible.

Tatiana, the more reserved of my two college besties, wags her finger at the phone in my hands. "Try his birthday."

I input her suggestion, but no dice.

Harper and Kaylee both offer additional ideas, but again, nothing works.

I'm panting now. Officially freaking out. "I've only got two more guesses before it locks me out, ladies," I say, my voice tight. "And I'm out of ideas." I look at Brandon's sister, Delilah, since she's the only one who hasn't offered a suggestion yet. She grew up in the same household with my future husband, after all, so she's got to have at least one new idea. "Delilah?" I choke out. "Got any ideas for the passcode?"

Delilah swallows hard. "I think you should call my big

brother and ask him about the phone." When everyone pushes back, she shouts, "You're marrying him tomorrow, Iris! Don't you think you should trust him enough to give him the benefit of the doubt, instead of sneaking around behind his back?"

As Delilah says those last words, I feel a lot of things in a torrent. Deflated. Appalled. Offended. But not the least bit surprised. Delilah's always idolized her charming, charismatic big brother, the same way everyone does—only more so, since Brandon is her blood and has always been her family's golden child. What's that old saying? *Blood is thicker than water.* Apparently, Delilah Gladstone is going to prove that maxim today in spades.

Kaylee grits out, "Delilah, the only person sneaking around here is Brandon."

"I agree," Harper offers quickly. "No offense, Delilah, but you're giving Iris some terrible advice."

Nodding furiously, Tatiana pipes in to say, "If that phone really is work related, then fantastic; Iris will find that out when she gets into it. But if not, then why give Brandon the chance to gaslight her about it before—"

"*Gaslight* her?" Delilah booms, shocking me with both her volume and intensity. "My brother would never do that, any more than he would do whatever you all think he's doing with that damned phone."

The poor girl looks like she's having an existential crisis, and I can't blame her. Before this moment, I never would have believed, not in a million years, that Brandon would be capable of owning a secret phone—one he tucked away in the toiletry bag he's taking on our honeymoon. And yet, over the past several minutes, as my brain has furiously connected dots that were there all along, I'm suddenly feeling extremely suspicious my soon-to-be-husband might be capable of doing a lot of things I never would have believed. Is Brandon even hosting a poker night tonight, like he told me? Surely, my father and brother would have told me if not. *Right?* My head is spinning with possibilities—all of them terrible.

"Delilah, please think about this rationally," Kaylee interjects, an indignant hand on her hip. "What's the harm in Iris getting into that phone, if it's only going to prove your brother's innocence?"

"It's about trust," Delilah insists.

"*Trust?*" Tatiana booms, making me flinch. Normally, Tatiana is the more soft-spoken of my two college besties, but that particular retort was delivered in an ear-piercing shout. "Sorry, Delilah, but trust flew out the window when Brandon hid that phone from Iris in a pocket of his toiletry bag!"

"We don't know that he hid it," Delilah screams back. "He put it there—*if* that's his phone at all."

Trembling, I raise my palms to the group. "Everyone, calm down. Please. This isn't productive." I pinch the bridge of my nose and take a deep breath, trying to wrangle my racing thoughts and hammering heart. "Maybe Delilah is right. Maybe I should bring the phone to the hotel and ask Brandon—"

"So he can deny it's his?" Harper yells. "No, Iris."

Kaylee adds, "Or delete everything on it before handing it over to you?"

"Exactly," Tatiana agrees. "Don't you dare do that, Iris."

Delilah visibly bristles. "Wow, you all don't like my big brother very much, do you?"

"It's nothing personal," Kaylee insists. "If Brandon wasn't your brother and this exact scenario happened to your best friend in the world, would you do everything in your power to help her get into the phone, or would you tell her to call the man she's supposed to marry tomorrow to ask him about it?"

Delilah bites the inside of her cheek. Based on her body language, it seems she's seriously considering Kaylee's argument.

I gently lay a hand on Delilah's arm and flash her my most you-can-trust-me facial expression. If I'm right and Delilah's confidence has been shaken by Kaylee's words, I want to land a knockout punch. "Please, Delilah," I say, holding Delilah's anxious gaze. "This feels like a life-or-death situation to me. Like everything I believe about Brandon hangs in the balance."

I wouldn't normally put Delilah on the spot this way or lay it on quite so thick. She's a sensitive soul who's deeply loyal to her brother and their entire family. But given the situation, I have to look out for myself above all others, including Delilah. Mere hours from now, I'm scheduled to marry Brandon, the likely owner of this phone. And not at city hall, with a couple of witnesses, but at the small, quaint church I grew up attending in Orchard Blossom, in front of every living person who's ever loved me. And I can't do that if it turns out my groom has been lying to me about more than the existence of a secret phone.

After what feels like an interminable amount of time, Harper breaks the thick silence by speaking in a pleading tone to Delilah. "If you have full faith in your brother, then you should want Iris to get into that phone to prove your point."

Delilah swallows hard and glares at me. "If I help you get into that phone and we find out there's nothing bad on it, promise you'll tell Brandon what you did before the wedding tomorrow."

"I will."

"He needs to know he's marrying someone who doesn't trust him."

I nod furiously. "If I'm wrong, I'll drive to the hotel tonight, throw myself at Brandon's feet, and beg him for forgiveness."

Delilah's shoulders droop. "What guesses have you tried already?"

*Thank God.* With my pulse pounding, I recount the passcode attempts I've made thus far, and Delilah offers two more suggestions—the second of which opens the phone like Aladdin opening the Cave of Wonders.

# CHASING THE RING

"It worked!" I shriek excitedly. "You're a genius, Delilah. My guardian angel."

They're the last joyful words to leave my lips for the rest of the night—and quite possibly, for the rest of my life. Once I start scrolling through the contents of Brandon's secret phone—his texts, photos, messaging apps, porn apps, and every kind of dating app—nothing but the sounds of wails, retching, and heartbreak escape me, until finally, as the sun rises on my long-awaited wedding day, I pass out on the cool tile floor of my bathroom, feeling like my heart has been ripped open and scraped over endless shards of broken glass.

# CHAPTER 2
## Iris

I stare at my reflection in the full-length mirror.

White gown and veil, both embellished with handmade Italian lace.

Picture-perfect makeup and hair.

My late mother's pearl choker wrapped delicately around my neck.

If it weren't for my red, puffy eyes, I'd be my wedding Pinterest board come to life. Well, also, if it weren't for the fact that my groom has turned out to be a pathological liar. A narcissist, at any rate. Whatever his technical diagnoses, the bottom line is the Prince Charming I thought I'd be marrying today has turned out to be a lying, cheating sack of shit.

With a loud sigh, I unclasp my mother's treasured necklace. I thought wearing it today would help me channel her legendary strength and tenacity. But now that I'm seeing it on me, I can't bring myself to taint her memory this way. If I wind up getting married for real one day, I'll wear this precious keepsake then. Granted, that seems unlikely now. I can't imagine myself trusting any man enough to fall in love, let alone to say yes to marrying him. But time heals all wounds, so they say. I'm only twenty-six, after all. Never say never, I guess.

A rising din in the adjacent chapel jerks me from my thoughts. It sounds packed in there. Which means any minute now, my mother's best friend, Darcy, will come in here to fetch me from my requested moment of solitude. Thankfully, Delilah promised not to give her big brother a heads-up about what we discovered last night. After she saw the phone's contents, she agreed it was my news to break and nobody else's. Poor Delilah. I think she was as devastated as me last night, in her own way.

At any rate, thanks to Delilah's discretion, I've got a decision to make. Am I going to follow through with the juicy plan my friends and I cooked up last night after Delilah fell asleep, or am I going to quietly sneak out of this dressing room and leave Brandon standing at the altar in front of everyone he knows and tries so hard to impress?

If I'd found out about Brandon's betrayals before last night—at least, with enough time to get my father's money back from all the wedding vendors—I'm sure I would have broken up with him back then and quietly cancelled everything. It's never been in my nature to make a scene. But given the actual timing here, I'm not willing to go gentle into that good night. The last thing I want to do is give Brandon the unfettered opportunity to create some false narrative about me in front of everyone we know. Now that I know Brandon's true character, who knows what he'd be willing to say to save face?

A soft knock prompts me to turn away from the mirror. But it's not my mother's best friend who enters the small room; it's Kaylee, Tatiana, and Harper—aka my life support system.

"Have you decided?" Tatiana asks gently.

"Whatever you want to do," Harper adds, "we support you one hundred percent."

A puff of air escapes my nose. "Well, what I want to do is

douse that motherfucker in gasoline and barbeque him with a flamethrower in front of everyone he knows."

Everyone laughs, including me. But nobody more so than Kaylee.

"Sounds like a great plan to me," Kaylee says with a gleam in her eyes. "I'll go get the flamethrower, baby."

"Sadly, I can't do that without going to prison, though," I lament with an exhale. "Not with this many witnesses, anyway. So, I guess I'll settle for torching Brandon's reputation, instead."

"Shoot," Kaylee says, snapping her fingers. "I was so hyped about the barbeque idea."

"Life is full of disappointments, my love." I rub my forehead. "I should warn Delilah. She might want to contract a mysterious case of the stomach flu right about now."

Tatiana shakes her head. "I just talked to her. Delilah said she supports you, one hundred percent. She wants to stand by you today, literally and figuratively."

My heart lurches at the unexpected vote of confidence. "Delilah said that, or that's your interpretation?"

"She said it, just like that. This has been humbling for her. Before last night, she thought Brandon walked on water."

My heart squeezes for poor Delilah. "Brandon fooled everyone, including every person sitting in that church."

"All the more reason to go in there and torch him," Kaylee says. But when Harper and Tatiana glare at her, she adds, "But, of course, we'll support you, no matter what you decide."

"I'm going to do it," I whisper. "I'll regret it if I don't." I look at a circular clock on the wall. "Will one of you grab my dad and brother and ask them to meet me in the hallway? I don't want to blindside them when everything goes down."

"I'm on it," Harper chirps before scurrying away, the long skirt of her yellow bridesmaid gown whooshing glamorously as she goes.

"What a waste," I mumble softly, my heart panging with memories of our ebullient day of dress shopping months ago. "I was giddy about your bridesmaid dresses when we picked them out." I look down at my own gown. "About mine, too."

"None of our dresses will go to waste, honey," Kaylee declares. "We're going to wear the shit out of them while celebrating you dodging the biggest bullet of your life tonight."

I hang my head. "I don't feel much like celebrating."

"Then you'll drown your sorrows while we dance around you," Tatiana insists. "Kaylee's right. Why let all that money go to waste?"

It didn't occur to me I'd go forward with the reception tonight, but I think my friends are onto something. Everything is all paid for, after all—the food and booze and so on. Why not enjoy all of it in celebration of me *not* marrying a serial cheater/sociopathic narcissist?

"Okay, count me in." As my friends express support, I take a deep breath to calm my racing pulse. "I need to get this show on the road, or I'll lose my nerve." I double-check that Brandon's weapon of mass destruction is still nestled inside my bra. When I see that it is, I head toward the door with my shoulders set and my head held high. "This is going to be fine," I murmur to myself. "I'm going to stay calm the whole time, stick with the facts, and torch him with his own words."

"Iris," Dad breathes as I approach him and my brother in a quiet corner of the church's hallway. "You look so much like your mother in that dress."

"You look beautiful, Iris," my brother, Atlas, agrees. He's the only person who never fell prey to Brandon's charms. In fact, my brother has flat-out never liked Brandon, for reasons he couldn't articulate other than to say, "I don't know, he just seems super fake to me." That comment always baffled me as much as it annoyed me. But now I know my little brother had a sixth sense all along.

I look around to make sure nobody can overhear the shocking thing I'm about to say to my family. God knows I especially don't want to say this to my father. He's always loved Brandon like a son.

"I'm not going through with the wedding, Daddy."

"*What?*"

"Let me explain without interruption," I whisper urgently, glancing around. "We don't have much time." I give them a quick summary of what's happened, and with each new sentence out of my mouth, my father looks more and more like he wants to throw up, while my brother looks more and more like he wants to commit an extremely violent murder.

"I always knew something was off about him," Atlas says through gritted teeth.

"Believe me, I wish I'd listened to you. I guess I was too brainwashed."

"I can't believe this is happening," Dad murmurs, rubbing his forehead. "I never thought Brandon would—"

"He would, Daddy, and he did. Repeatedly, and for a very long time." To emphasize my point, I pull out Brandon's burner phone and quickly show them a string of dirty texts from about two years ago—the one where Brandon told some woman he was coming over that night to "rail" her until her insides were "scrambled." "This is just one of many, many examples," I say. "He's been cheating on me since we got to Denver, at least. Probably longer, but this phone doesn't go back that far."

"But *why*?" Dad laments. "When he's got the best girl in the world?"

"It's pointless to ask why. I don't even want to hear his excuses. All I want to do is unmask him in front of everyone he knows so I can get on with my life and never look back."

Dad furrows his brow. "Unmask him? What does that mean?"

I tell Dad my plan to out Brandon at the altar as the lying, cheating scumbag he is, and my father looks like he's on the cusp of a heart attack.

"No, Iris. You can't do that. Please, no."

"That's exactly what she should do," Atlas insists. He pats my shoulder. "Go for it, sis. I'll tackle him to the ground if he starts anything."

"Physical violence won't be necessary. I'm going to say my piece calmly and succinctly, and then walk out with my head held high." I touch my father's arm. "I'm not asking for your permission, Daddy. I'm giving you fair warning so you can brace yourself or choose not to walk me down the aisle, as planned." I pull away and begin to wring my hands. "I would have told you about this last night, but since we can't get any of your money back, I figured I'd take some time to decide what to do for myself."

"Don't worry about the money," Dad mutters, still rubbing his forehead. "That's the least of our concerns."

My heart squeezes with affection for my sweet father. He's not a wealthy man. Not even close. So, the fact that he said that, and with such sincerity, touches me deeply.

Dad takes my hand. "I'm worried you're going to regret handling things in such a public way. You've never liked being the center of attention."

My brother shakes his head. "If ever there was a time for Iris to get out of her comfort zone, this is it. That motherfucker deserves to be publicly shamed, Dad."

"Don't say that word here, Atlas," Dad snaps. "We're in a church."

Atlas scoffs. "So, it's okay for a scumbag to stand in a church and pretend to be the world's most perfect guy, but I can't call him out for it while standing in a hallway?"

Dad sighs. "I can't believe this is happening."

I squeeze my father's hand. "Some of Brandon's clients are here today. Don't you think they deserve to know about Brandon's true character? If he was willing to cheat and lie with me, then what's he been doing with their money? There are weird bank notifications on the phone, Dad—from a bank I've never seen Brandon use. I don't know what it all means, but I think it's possible Brandon's been stealing money at work."

"Jesus," Dad says, running his free palm down his forlorn face.

"Do you remember what Mom used to say about us doing things in secret?" Atlas prompts.

Dad nods slowly before whispering, "'If you're too embarrassed to do something loud and proud and in front of the whole world, then that's your sign you shouldn't do it at all.'"

Atlas and I exchange a nod.

"Words to live by," I whisper.

Dad pauses for an eternal moment. Clearly, he's distraught. But eventually, he squeezes my hand and says, "I'm with you, honey. Do whatever you need to do, and we'll both support you."

"Thank you, Daddy. Thank you, Atlas."

My brother takes my free hand. "Now, get in there and take that motherfucker down."

# CHAPTER 3
## Roman

"Welcome to the wedding of Marco and Nicola!" my younger brother, Luca, booms with enthusiasm, and the crowd reacts like they're once again witnessing Marco diving into the end zone at the Super Bowl.

There are about fifty of us assembled on this beachside cliff in Kauai for today's happy nuptials. I'm today's best man for my cousin, of course, dressed to the nines in a light blue suit that matches what Marco and all his groomsmen are wearing. Standing immediately behind me is Levi, Luca's twin, followed by some teammates of Marco's: a couple from his longtime NFL team and one from back in his college days.

"Eternal love and commitment," Luca continues solemnly. "Soulmates. New beginnings. *Family.* These are the revered things we're here to celebrate on this picture-perfect day in paradise."

I bite my tongue to keep myself from snorting. Luca never talks like this. Obviously, he's doing a bit—role-playing a wedding officiant who takes his job seriously. But come on, what the hell does twenty-six-year-old Luca Maguire know about soulmates, eternal love, and lifelong commitment? Not a goddamned thing, unless you count the lifetime he's spent watching our parents' happy marriage.

Granted, I don't have much more knowledge than Luca about any of those things. I admit I don't have the best track record for long-term commitment myself. But at least I've managed to fall in love a time or two in my thirty-two years, if only briefly. My brother's an even bigger player than I was during my twenties, and that's saying a lot. What was Marco thinking when he said yes to his bride's request to have Luca of all people officiate the wedding today?

Mid-speech, Luca pauses dramatically, drawing out the silence for an inordinate amount of time. Finally, he scans the audience and somberly declares, "*Mawwiage.*"

Everyone bursts out laughing at the gag, including me. But nobody more so than the bride, Nicola. I've never seen *The Princess Bride* all the way through. Only clips of it on the internet. But even I know that's what Luca was referencing, to hilarious effect.

"That was for you, Nicola," Luca says to the bride with a wink. "I know how much you love that movie."

"It's my all-time favorite," Nicola confirms with a giggle. "That was perfect, Luca."

*Huh.* Maybe my little brother's gonna pull this off after all? Could it be Nicola wanted Luca to officiate today precisely *because* he's a loose-cannon weirdo wild card, and not in *spite* of that fact—and Marco's too in love to deny his beautiful wife-to-be anything? Either way, it occurs to me it's a good thing Luca's got something fun to sink his teeth into—something to help him feel good about himself again. When he got cut by yet another team at the end of last season, we all know he took it really hard, despite the smile he always manages in a crowd.

Luca calls out to the maid of honor, "You're up, Cordelia. Delight us with those golden pipes of yours!"

With a little squeal, Nicola's sister scurries to grab a ukulele from behind a floral arrangement. A moment later she's enthusiastically performing a lilting ballad that instantly makes me want to take a long nap. Or maybe that's all the spiced rum punches I've been guzzling all week. I've definitely been overdoing it.

I always give myself some latitude during the offseason to let loose and have fun, in terms of my strict diet and exercise regimen. Life is short. But even I have to admit I've taken the latitude thing too far this week, probably because I've been looking for any way to distract myself from the current precariousness of my career. What team will I be joining next season? It's all up in the air for the first time since the Baltimore Crusaders selected me eleven years ago as the overall first pick in the NFL draft that year.

Nobody but my closest inner circle knows this, but I didn't sign a contract extension with the Crusaders, despite our winning record and playoff run last season. Instead, I instructed my longtime best friend and agent, Cameron, to feel things out with some other select teams.

Apparently, my top pick, the Thunderbolts in LA, are desperate to have me, at least based on what they've been telling my agent—but so far, they've been dragging their feet on meeting my salary demands, so who the fuck knows how things will end up?

My phone in my pocket vibrates as the maid of honor continues her languid song. Is that Cameron texting me with an update on negotiations? My fingers are physically twitching with the desire to pull out my phone and find out, but obviously, I can't do that while standing here as Marco's best man. If my mother in the front row saw me checking my phone at a time like this, she'd leap out of her chair, bat my phone out of my hand, and tackle me to the ground faster than any cornerback.

The thought of my mother springing from her chair and taking me down in her pretty lavender dress makes me smile to myself and glance at her. She's sitting in the front row with my father and my four-year-old son, Maverick, right next to my aunt and uncle, Marco's mother and father.

When my eyes train on my son, my heart skips a beat. Maverick looks so damned cute guarding that ring bearer's pillow with his life. Give my kid a job, and he'll do it with every fiber of his being. In that way, among others, my son is exactly like me.

Maverick's gaze shifts to me, and when he realizes I'm smiling at him, he proudly points at the lace-covered pillow in his lap as if to say, "Look how good I'm doing my job, Daddy!" I can't help chuckling at his exuberance as I flash him a thumbs-up sign.

I can't believe there was ever a time I reacted negatively to Vanessa's positive pregnancy test. Of course, I immediately requested a paternity test, simply because Vanessa and I had only been dating casually. Not even dating, really, in the true sense of the word. It was more of a brief situationship. And when the result came back unequivocally positive—the baby in Vanessa's oven was definitely mine—I wasn't pleased, to say the least. Of course, when Maverick arrived in this world and I held him in my arms and heard his little, cooing voice, I immediately realized he was the best damned thing that's ever happened to me. A true blessing. Which is why I'm now working so damned hard to switch teams next season.

If it weren't for Maverick, I probably would have re-signed with the Crusaders, despite all the bullshit, stress, and personality clashes I've been experiencing there for quite some time. But with Maverick in the picture, I can't stop dreaming of a different kind of life for us. One in which I'd play for a team in Maverick's hometown of LA. One in which I'd get to live within driving distance of my son and therefore get to hang out with him all the time, unlike now.

"That was beautiful, Cordelia," Luca says, yanking me from

my thoughts. The song is over and everyone is applauding, so I quickly join in applauding, too.

"And now, it's time for the vows," Luca reports. "Nico, do you want to kick things off?"

"Gladly," Nicola replies with a beaming, bright smile. She takes her future husband's hands, looks deeply into his eyes, and proceeds to earnestly explain all the ways she loves Marco and always will.

All of a sudden, a strange sensation of yearning settles into my chest, followed by a thought I've never had before: *I want someone to talk like that about her love for me.*

What?

*I want the kind of love Marco's found with Nicola.*

Jesus Christ. Is this another side effect of all those spiced rum punches? I've never in my life felt the urge to get married. Not even when Vanessa told me about her positive pregnancy test. Not for a nanosecond. And yet, I can't deny, witnessing Marco and Nicola's love makes me think there might be something to the whole marriage thing after all. Did Maverick cracking my heart wide open do this to me? Has my relatively newfound love for my son turned me into a greedy bastard who wants even more unconditional affection in his life?

I rub the back of my neck and tell myself to cool my jets. It would be the worst possible time to even think about finding myself a wife, when I'm on the cusp of switching teams and cities to become the father my son deserves.

"You're a lucky man, Marco," Luca says to our cousin, after Nicola finishes her vows. "That's gonna be a tough act to follow."

Marco chuckles. "Nico's always a tough act to follow. No matter what she's doing, she always throws a frozen rope."

*Ding, ding, ding!* It's the first football reference of the ceremony, as far as I know. I've been daydreaming, so in theory

I could have missed a couple before this. If I'm right, however, then I need Marco to make at least three more before this ceremony is through so I can win a cool two hundred bucks—one hundred from each of my twin brothers—in the three-way bet we made last night over a game of pool.

"Evil Levi," as our family calls him, took zero to one football references in our bet. Not surprisingly, since Levi's the most skeptical of the three of us. Luca, on the other hand, took two to three football references. Still a low number, especially for an optimist like him. But given the topsy-turvy path he's been forced to walk lately in his football career, I don't blame him for playing things kind of safe these days.

At any rate, for me to take home the pot in our friendly three-way bet, my cousin's got to make four or more football references during the ceremony today. I gladly took the long-shot position—the one with the slimmest odds. Why not? Go big or go home, I always say. I've always loved a good challenge. Not to mention, the chance to gloat mercilessly about an unexpected underdog win to my two brothers.

At Marco's reference to a "frozen rope"—football slang for a straight-shot rocket of a pass—I covertly hold up my index finger to Luca, signaling the current tally in our bet, and my brother subtly nods his acknowledgement. I turn around and do the same thing to my grumpier brother—"Mr. Grumpy Pants," as my mother sometimes calls him—and Levi nods the same way Luca did before him. Then, Levi, the "evil twin" of our family—at least, according to playful family lore, thanks to his dark humor and generally dour mood—accompanies his nod with a single raised finger of his own.

A subtle *tsk* erupts from the front row, and all three of us Maguire boys instantly straighten up and fly right. Levi should have known our mother would notice his middle finger, no matter how cleverly he held it up to me. I swear, nothing gets past Ava Maguire. We've all learned that lesson time and again.

I return my eyes to my cousin. Marco's only getting married once. There's no doubt about that. So, the least I can do is give him and this ceremony my undivided attention.

Marco's always been more like a big brother to me than a cousin. In fact, he's more like my older twin—a future version of me marching down the same path three paces ahead. Yes, Marco's always played at the tight end position, while I've always been a quarterback; but other than our different positions on the football field, we're basically the same person with the same dreams, goals, and outlook. Until Marco met Nicola, that is; suddenly, he started doing and saying things I couldn't fathom. Things like, "I can't live without her, man" and "Nicola makes everything better."

"Nicola," Marco says softly, his tone awash in emotion as he gazes intently at his bride. "You've given me a spring in my step, both in life and on the football field."

*Ding, ding, ding!* Surely, that qualifies as another football reference? I subtly flash two fingers at Luca, my eyebrows raised, but the fucker shakes his head.

I'm annoyed, but I don't press the issue. Partly because I'm sure our mother is watching, though I'm too scared to look and confirm that hunch. But also because it's now clear my brothers and I will likely need to hash out the final tally after the ceremony.

Still gazing into his bride's eyes, Marco says, "We all know how proud I am of this ring here." He holds up his hand to display the coveted Super Bowl ring on it—the one Marco jubilantly won with the San Francisco Knights last season. "But standing here today," Marco continues, "I swear there's no ring or trophy in the world that could possibly matter more to me than the wedding ring I'm going to wear to mark me as Nico's husband. You're the best thing that's ever happened to me, Nicola Benson, and you always will be."

Is he serious? There's no way.

If I were forced to rank football versus Maverick, I'd put my son in the top slot, obviously. But he's my child. My blood. My legacy. My miniature doppelganger. But ranking a romantic relationship above football? I can't imagine it. What relationship, even a good one, could possibly feel better than the rush of a football win? Not to mention, romantic relationships consume far too much time and attention during the season. Hence, the reason I've always been content to be married to football. To give football—and now, Maverick, too—my undivided attention during the season.

Although . . .

*Hmm.*

Come to think of it, Marco did wind up having his best season last year, despite being engaged to Nicola the whole time. Could it be Marco didn't have his best season ever last year *despite* Nicola being in his life, like I've been assuming . . . but instead, *because* of Nicola? Is that even a possibility?

Everyone laughs and claps, drawing me from my wandering thoughts.

Marco says, ". . . and I can't wait to tackle life with you forever, baby."

*Tackle.* That's definitely another football reference. Which would make the tally at least three by my count, unless I've missed something while daydreaming again. *Come on, Marco, give me one more, cuz.*

As if reading my mind, Marco delivers for me. "Nicola," he says, "I promise I've got your blind side covered forever, baby—through infinite overtimes."

*Jackpot!*

I turn and shoot Evil Levi behind me a wink of victory, and of course, my brother rolls his eyes.

"You killed it," Luca says to Marco. He motions to my son. "You're up, Mav. Bring your daddy the rings now."

With a little whoop, my son slides off his chair and carefully makes his way to the front with his lace-covered pillow in hand. When he reaches me, I pat Maverick's soft hair and praise his excellent work before taking the pillow. As Maverick goes down the line of groomsmen getting high fives, I quickly release the fake, plastic rings and swap them out for the real ones from my pocket. In the end, the ring ceremony goes off without a hitch, without Maverick ever realizing he's been guarding plastic rings with his life this whole time.

Luca bellows, "By the powers vested in me by the State of Hawaii and the certificate I bought online for a hundred bucks—you're welcome, that's my wedding present to you—I now declare Marco and Nicola husband and wife. Marco, kiss your bride!"

As the crowd cheers, Marco joyfully kisses his new wife. And less than a minute later, I follow the newlyweds down the aisle with Maverick's small hand in mine.

When I reach the end of the sandy aisle and all appropriate hugs and congratulations have been administered, I pull out my phone and check my texts. As it turns out, that buzz from earlier wasn't Cameron sending me an update on negotiations. It was from someone far better than that—Coach Hardy, my legendary coach from college and my favorite coach ever—replying to my text from earlier this morning.

Over the years, Coach Hardy has turned down every NFL head coaching job offered to him, preferring instead to continue coaching and building his legacy at my alma mater. Thanks to a longstanding beef between Coach and the asshole owner of the Crusaders, I've always known he'd never consider leaving Michigan for a coaching job in Baltimore, not even for the chance to coach me again. But now that I'm hopefully leaving the Crusaders and going to a new, not-yet-determined team—preferably, the Thunderbolts in LA—I'm hoping Coach Hardy will agree to become a package deal with me and finish out his storied career as my new team's head coach. Hence, the reason I reached out to him this morning to ask if I could fly to his lake house in Michigan for a chat this week.

*Coach: Hey, Rome. It's great to hear from you. Great pics of Mav in his little wedding suit. There's no need for you to come to Michigan. Coincidentally, Marsha and I are heading to Maui to celebrate our fortieth anniversary tomorrow and we'll be staying for ten days. If you're still going to be in Hawaii by then, I could sneak away to play a round of golf with you on Friday. There's a golf club on Kauai I've been wanting to check out, so I'd come to you. Let me know if that works. Looking forward to seeing you and finding out what's on your mind.*

# CHAPTER 4
## Iris

AFTER WANDERING AROUND aimlessly through Kauai's small airport for a solid ten minutes, I find the right rental car counter and take my place at the back of the line. There's only one clerk and several people ahead of me, so this might take a while.

"Gramma!" a little squeak of a voice shouts excitedly, drawing my attention. "We saw a whale in da bathroom!"

The voice belongs to a striking, dark-haired boy of four or five—a kid whose soft curls and blazing smile melt me upon impact. His arms flailing, the boy careens from the bathroom to an elegant older lady a few yards away, while an older gentleman trails behind.

"There's a sea-creature mural on the wall in the bathroom," the older man explains with a hearty chuckle.

"How exciting," the woman replies. "What else did you see in there, honey?"

The kid cocks his head. "My pee-pee."

Both the man and woman burst into laughter, and I can't help but do the same.

"In the painting, honey," the woman amends. "What else did you see on the wall besides the whale?"

"Ooooh," the little boy replies in his heart-melting voice.

Clearly, he wasn't trying to be funny or sassy when he answered his grandmother's question. Like most kids his age, he was likely being literal, as his brain is wired to be during this particular stage of development. "I saw fishes and a sea turtle and..."

Yet another wave of grief slams into me. When I said yes to Brandon's marriage proposal, or whatever that was, I thought I'd one day get to be like that beautiful lady over there: a wife and mother and, eventually, a grandmother. I know I'm young, but I'm scared I might have wasted too many years of my life with Brandon—that because of him, I've somehow missed some sliding door I was supposed to walk through to meet the true love of my life.

"Next, please," the rental car clerk calls out, jerking me from my thoughts.

"Aloha," she says brightly as I step to the counter.

"Aloha," I manage, even though I'm feeling more like dog poop on the bottom of a flip-flop than a happy tourist.

"Name?"

"Iris Benedetto."

The clerk taps on a keyboard and furrows her brow. "That name isn't coming up. Could it be under another one?"

"Oh. That's right." I palm my forehead. "Brandon Gladstone." My stomach revolts. Saying his name makes me realize I'd be standing here as Brandon's wife, Mrs. Iris Gladstone, if it wasn't for Delilah saving the day.

"Ah, yes. I see it now." The clerk gasps and looks up from her screen. "It's your honeymoon! Congratulations, Mrs. Gladstone!" Whatever facial expression overtakes my face instantly makes the woman's smile droop. She clears her throat. "Would you prefer to change the name on the reservation?"

I exhale. "Yes, please. To mine. Iris Benedetto." I shift my weight. "The wedding didn't, uh, pan out. I'm here for a much-needed solo vacation, instead of a honeymoon."

# CHASING THE RING

The rental car clerk's mouth twitches with sympathy, but other than that, she maintains a neutral expression. "No problem," she chirps. "I'll change the name on the reservation and upgrade you to a Jeep."

"Oh, no, I can't afford an upgrade."

"It's on the house, Miss Benedetto."

A lump rises in my throat. "Thank you. I really appreciate that."

We finalize the paperwork, and the clerk slides a set of car keys across the counter. "Honeymoons are overrated, anyway," she murmurs. "You wouldn't believe how many couples on their honeymoons squabble viciously over which car to rent. Nice way to kick off a marriage, huh?"

I don't know what to say to that, so I wordlessly nod and grab the keys. When I turn around, however, I'm shocked to find the pretty older lady from earlier standing before me with my sunglasses in hand.

"I'm sorry to bother you," she says sheepishly. She holds up my sunglasses. "You dropped these a while ago, and I . . ." She shifts her weight. "I didn't want to interrupt your conversation, so I waited."

Crap. Everything about this woman's body language makes it clear she overheard my embarrassing exchange with the rental car clerk. Which means there are now two people too many on this island who know the mortifying truth about why I came on my Hawaiian honeymoon by myself.

"Thank you," I choke out, taking the sunglasses from the woman. "I'd lose my head if it wasn't connected to my . . ." I can't finish the sentence. I'm suddenly too overcome with emotion and embarrassment to speak, partly thanks to this woman's kind, sympathetic face reminding me so much of my mother's.

"Oh, sweetie," the lady coos. "Let's sit for a minute. You can't drive like this."

"I'm okay."

"No, no, come sit with me."

As she guides me toward a bank of chairs, I babble, "I'm not normally this emotional. I mean, yes, I'm an emotional person, but I'm unusually emotional today because, on top of everything else, I'm really sleep deprived." I'm also hungover, thanks to all the tequila shots I threw back at my raucous Iris-dodged-a-bullet celebration last night. But I see no good reason to confess that fact to this lovely woman, when she's already overheard far more about me than I'd ever want her to know.

"Well, if sleep and relaxation are what you came for," the woman says, as we settle into some seats along a wall, "then you're in the right place." She assesses me for a moment before brushing a lock of hair from my face, the same way my mother always used to do. "Hang in there, my dear. This too shall pass. I know it doesn't feel that way. But one day, you'll look back on this horrible pain and realize it was the thing that propelled you to your rightful destiny—a place in life that's going to make you happier than you can imagine in this difficult moment."

*Well, shit.* If this lady is trying to make me cry, then she's figured out the perfect way to do it. As my tears flow, she opens her arms to me, and I fall into them.

"Good girl," she says, patting my back. "Keeping sadness locked inside only makes it harder to heal and move on. Let it out, honey."

Did my mother send this angel to me? That's certainly how it feels in this moment.

The woman calls to her husband, "Edward, honey, take Mav to get a snack by the gate, would you? I'll meet you there."

"Oh, gosh, no," I say, sitting up straight and wiping my eyes. "I can't let you be late for your flight on my account."

"We have plenty of time. Hang on." She turns to her

retreating husband again. "Edward! Get him something healthy to eat this time!"

Since he's holding the boy's hand, her husband simply throws up his free one in the air as if to say, "I've got this!"

"He's going to get him another Hawaiian ice," the woman mumbles. "I swear, our grandson's got my husband wrapped around his little finger."

I chuckle through my tears. "But not you?"

"No, me too," she admits with a grin. "But only to the point where I'd let him have *one* Hawaiian ice per day. Not *two*."

Against all odds, she's made me smile through my tears.

"Your grandson is adorable. If he were mine, I'd be wrapped around his finger, too."

"He's a cutie. That's for sure."

On the flight here, I promised myself I wouldn't tell anyone about Brandon during my stay. In fact, I decided never to speak of him again. But now that this lovely woman has already overheard my situation, I feel the urge to provide some details for context so she doesn't think I'm a sobbing hot mess for no good reason.

"I'm usually a happy, bubbly person," I say through a sniffle. "But two days ago, the night before our wedding, I found out my fiancé has been cheating on me for a very long time."

"Oh no. You poor little thing."

"That's why I came on this trip by myself. To try to have fun and heal, rather than sitting at home feeling sorry for myself."

"Good for you," the woman says. "As hard as this must be for you, I'm glad you found out the truth before you married that man."

"Me, too. That's definitely the silver lining in all this." I take a deep, steadying breath. "I feel a lot better. Thank you. I can drive safely now."

"Are you sure?"

I nod. "If you're late for your flight because of me, I'll never forgive myself."

The woman stands and smooths down her skirt, so I stand, too.

"Enjoy this week to the fullest, my dear," she says, taking my hand and patting it. "Whatever you want to do, whatever it is, promise me you'll go for it."

"I promise. Thank you."

The woman lets out a sympathetic *tsk*. "Shame on that horrible man for hurting you." She pats my arm. "Have the time of your life this week and beyond. That'll be your best revenge."

"I'll do my best."

We share a smile. And then, the kind woman—the guardian angel who was surely sent by my mother in heaven—heads off to reunite with her lucky family to board her flight to who-knows-where.

When she's gone, I take a deep breath and traipse out a sliding door toward my rental car, even though all I want to do is follow that beautiful soul to wherever she's going like a wounded, heartbroken little puppy.

# CHAPTER 5
## Roman

I'M DRIPPING WITH sweat as I amble down the winding, plumeria-lined path from the hotel gym toward my bungalow at the farthest corner of the resort. After that workout, I'm ready for a hot shower followed by a double-decker sandwich and another spiced rum punch, all of it enjoyed while gazing out at the ocean from the comfy couch on the deck.

As I reach the front door of my unit, my phone buzzes with an incoming call from Cameron. My stomach seizes. If he's calling instead of texting, he must have something important to report.

"Good news?" I ask in greeting.

"Great news. I floated the idea of Coach Hardy coming aboard with you, and—"

"I haven't even talked to him yet, Cam." I'm in the bungalow now, but I'm too amped to sit, so I pace around the small living area. "You're putting the cart before the horse."

"Rome, I merely floated the idea, like I was brainstorming. Trust me, I handled it perfectly."

"And?"

"They went batshit crazy over the idea. To be clear, they want you any way they can get you, with or without Coach coming along; but it sure sounds like a package deal would bring them all the way up to our asking price."

"They'd have to pay Coach whatever he wants, too."

"They know that. His salary would be chump change compared to yours, though, so it's barely worth stressing over. They said the two of you together would be a 'dream team'—too big an opportunity to pass up."

"That's good to know."

"No, it's great to know. Are you sure you don't want me to fly out there and join your golf game on Friday?"

"Having you there would only fuck up the vibe."

"But what if Coach has questions about—"

"He won't. Cam, I don't want it to feel like a business meeting, okay? I want the conversation to unfold organically throughout the day."

"Yeah, that's probably the best strategy."

"It's not a strategy. That's my whole point."

"I'm just saying, whatever tack you want to take with Coach is great with me, as long as it gets the job done."

"Would you take your agent cap off for a minute and be my best friend? You know Coach is like a second father to me, so I'm not gonna push him into doing anything he's not completely sure about. He's an institution at Michigan, so I don't want him risking his legacy if he's not one-hundred-percent certain that's what he's willing to do."

Before Cameron responds, my phone buzzes with a call from my mother. "My mom is calling. Keep me posted." Without waiting for Cameron's reply, I end our call and take the incoming one. "Hey, Mom. Everything okay?"

"It's great. We're on the plane, and Maverick wanted to say another quick goodbye before it's time to turn off our phones."

I head into the bedroom. "Put him on."

As I sit on the bed, there's a shuffling noise, followed by the sweetest sound in the world. My son's voice. "Guess what, Daddy? Grampa let me have *anudder* Wyan ice!"

"*Another* one?" I gasp out. The kid devoured Hawaiian ices twice daily this past week.

"Grampa said it was my last hooray."

God, I love all of my son's cute Maverickisms. "Grampa always knows best. Enjoy your last 'hooray,' buddy." As a family, we've decided not to correct most of Maverick's cute mispronunciations. As my mother said, he'll grow out of them soon enough, at which point we'll miss them dearly.

"Gramma said I can watch a movie on her iPad on da airplane, so I'm gonna watch *Cars*."

"Sounds like you're gonna have a fun flight. I love you, Mav."

"I love you, too, Daddy."

*Oh, my heart.* Hearing those magical words from my son never gets old. "Hey, don't hang up. Put Gramma back on."

There's another shuffle. And then my mother's voice. "For the record, I wasn't there when your father bought him that Hawaiian ice. If I'd been there, I would have put a stop to the madness."

"Don't be a scrooge, Mom. It was his last 'hooray.'"

Mom cracks up. "I'll put that in my journal." She's been meticulously keeping a journal about all the cute things her first grandchild says and does, the same way she kept journals about all three of her sons. "Mav said something journal-worthy earlier. He'd just come out of the—" There's an overhead announcement on Mom's end of the call. "Oh! They're closing the doors. I have to hang up. I love you, sweetheart."

"I love you, too. Thanks for taking Maverick back to his mother for me. I wouldn't have asked you to do it if this meeting with Coach wasn't so damned important."

"We're delighted to get some one-on-one time with our sweet boy. Keep us posted about the golf meeting, okay?"

"You know I will."

"Thank you again for booking all those bungalows for the whole family. Everyone had so much fun."

"It was a blast," I agree. "We shouldn't wait for another family wedding to do it again."

"Although I admit I'm partial to the idea of us getting together again soon for *your* wedding."

I roll my eyes. Ever since Maverick came along to show my mother how much she adores being a grandma, she can't resist dropping hints about how much she wants more grandbabies. Preferably, on purpose next time. Even better if the next baby is born in the context of a committed relationship. Best of all, in the context of an actual marriage. But we both know she'll take another grandbaby any way she can get one, as long as it's sooner rather than later.

"I thought you said the doors were closing."

Mom snorts. "I'll text you when we land and when we get to Vanessa's."

"Thanks. Make sure to thank her for taking such great care of our boy."

"I will."

We say our final goodbyes, and I stare out the large bedroom window at the nearby ocean with my phone in my lap. Spending every day and night with Maverick this week made me even more determined to close a deal with the Thunderbolts. But the fact remains, there are too many moving parts for me to make that happen for sure.

Puffing out my cheeks, I get up from the bed, strip off my sweaty gym clothes, and head into the bathroom for a hot shower. I've got several days to myself before my scheduled meetup with Coach on Friday, and I'm determined to spend them relaxing, decompressing, and emphatically *not* thinking about how badly I want to finish out my career in the same city as my incredible son.

# CHAPTER 6
## Iris

A GRUNT HURTLES out of me as I lug my suitcase out the back of the Jeep. Why'd I pack so much?

With the car unloaded, I turn and survey the row of beachfront bungalows before me. They're even prettier in person than online.

As promised, I shoot off quick texts to my family and best friends, letting them know I've made it safely to my hotel; and then, off I go with my rolling suitcase toward my home away from home for the week.

When I reach the front door of unit three, I input a code provided in a confirmation email a couple days ago, but it doesn't work. I try it again, figuring I must have messed up somehow, but I get the same result.

Oh, God. Did Brandon somehow cancel the bungalow? He shouldn't have been able to do that without notifying me, since my email was used on the reservation. But I wouldn't put anything past Brandon at this point. I've been in such a daze since the wedding, it didn't occur to me before now Brandon might have tried to sabotage this vacation for me.

Standing in front of this locked door, it dawns on me how urgently I need to pee. I was planning to go at the airport before making the drive here, but I guess I was in a fog after talking to that nice lady. It also doesn't help matters that I drank a huge bottle of water during the drive. Why'd I do that?

I notice a maintenance guy on a nearby path, so I waddle over to him and beg him to pretty-please unlock my bungalow door. I show him the confirmation email and my driver's license and confess I'm probably ten seconds away from having an embarrassing accident, and thankfully, the man takes pity on me and lets me in.

Once inside my unit, I vaguely register the tropical perfection of my surroundings—elegant, island-themed décor, stunning ocean views through large windows, high ceilings, and a plumeria-scented breeze wafting through it all—as I frantically scan the place for the nearest bathroom.

The closest door turns out to be a closet, so I sprint toward the bedroom in the back, figuring an attached bathroom in there is a good bet.

Thankfully, my gamble appears to have paid off: There's a closed door on a far wall of the bedroom, exactly where a bathroom would be. I fling it open and sigh with relief at the glorious sight of a toilet, before frantically yanking down my shorts and panties and hurling myself down.

As my bladder releases, I widen my thighs, lean back, and groan loudly, feeling supremely relieved I didn't kick off my solo vacation by pissing down my leg in public.

"Thank you, Baby Jesus," I mutter. "Damn, that feels good."

My brain abruptly registers something unexpected in the small bathroom. *Hot steam.* It's everywhere. Covering every inch of my face, arms, and bare legs. Before my brain processes the significance of the mist surrounding me, however, the shower curtain whips open and a dripping-wet, fully naked, tanned and fit Adonis of a man appears before me, his dark hair wet and his large, naked dick hanging low between his muscular thighs.

"Can I help you?" he asks, his eyebrows raised in surprise.

I'm not finished peeing yet, but I somehow manage to stop my stream, mostly, and bolt out of the bathroom without stopping to pull up my shorts and panties.

The good news is, by the time I'm standing safely outside in the sunshine, I've got myself pulled back together. The bad news, though, is that I sprinted out of the bungalow without thinking to grab my phone, purse, or anything else.

After a moment of fidgeting nervously, I try the front door, but it locked behind me. So, I cross my arms over my chest and try to wait patiently for the gorgeous man with the shockingly large dick to come out here—fully dressed this time, hopefully—to explain his presence in my reserved bungalow. I'm thinking he's last night's occupant who didn't check out in time. Hopefully, he'll come out here with his suitcase, apologize profusely for scaring me, and leave the bungalow to me. If not, if it turns out that man is here rightfully—if it turns out Brandon has, in fact, managed to cancel my reservation—I truly don't know what I'll do.

After a while, I knock tentatively on the door and call out, "Would you come outside, please? The door is locked and I left all my stuff in there!"

"Just a minute!" the guy shouts on the other side of the door. "I'm getting dressed!"

The thought of that hunky man getting dressed makes me remember him *undressed* and dripping wet. His dick hanging low. I can't believe a total stranger was mere feet away from me, fully naked, while I was half naked and sitting on a toilet. *Holy hell.* The way my legs were spread, he must have seen everything there is to see between my thighs.

The whole situation should be nothing but mortifying to me, by all rights. But if I'm being honest, in addition to mortification, I'm feeling a sliver of titillation as well. That man was the hottest creature I've ever beheld in my life. In person, at least. And I can't believe I saw every inch of him. The stripper at my bachelorette party in Vegas was fun, but he did absolutely nothing for me, other than making me whoop and snort with laughter. But Shower Guy? My God, my entire body feels like it's going haywire when I visualize what I just witnessed.

A crazy thought makes me gasp out loud. What if my friends sent that hunk of a man as a gift, inspired by that raunchy thing I said at the very end of my diatribe in the church? Nah. As soon as I have the preposterous thought, I banish it. My friends knew I was simply parroting back the same raunchy words Brandon used in a text to one of the many women on his secret phone. They had to know I wasn't serious but, instead, that I was merely trying to piss off Brandon as much as possible.

The front door finally flies open, interrupting my thoughts, and the naked Adonis emerges, fully clothed. His dark hair is wet but towel dried and slightly curled. He's wearing board shorts and a T-shirt that clings to his broad shoulders and hard chest. *And he's tall.* Much taller than I realized while sitting on the toilet. That man's got to be six-four or -five. A full foot taller than me, at any rate.

"Did my friends send you to be my boy toy?" I blurt.

He shoots me a crooked grin. "I'd say you're a bit young to be my sugar mama, wouldn't you?"

I blush crimson. I'm such a dork. He looks several years older than me. So, yeah, "boy toy" was probably a ridiculous choice of words.

When I'm too tongue-tied to respond, the man folds his arms across his broad chest—a maneuver that incidentally emphasizes the sculpted, tanned beauty of his biceps and forearms—and says, "Let's start over. How did you get into my bungalow?"

"I . . . I've got it reserved for the week."

"You should double-check the unit number on your reservation. I've got this place reserved for the week, starting today, and I paid in full."

"Unit three. I have a confirmation email from two days ago."

Mr. Beautiful furrows his dark brow. "Hmm. Yesterday, they let me extend my stay in unit three for another full week. They said I was in luck because someone had just cancelled at the last minute."

Shit. That makes me think Brandon definitely managed to screw me over somehow. "Did they say when this supposed cancellation occurred?"

He shakes his head. "All I know is they said the unit was available when I asked to extend my stay yesterday afternoon."

I rub my forehead, trying not to hyperventilate. Left to my own devices, I won't be able to afford even the smallest room at this swanky resort, let alone this huge, fancy bungalow. My credit cards are maxed out, my savings account is nonexistent, and there's no way I'd ask my father for help after everything he's already paid out.

"I never got notice of any cancellation," I say, with far more confidence than I feel. "The last thing I've got is a confirmation email that gave me an entry code for today at three." Granted, the entry code didn't *work,* but I see no reason to admit that in this moment.

The man frowns. "It sounds like the hotel messed up. Let's call the front desk to get this straightened out."

I motion toward the closed front door. "My phone's inside."

With a tap of his keycard, he opens the door for me with a wink. "After you . . . Sugar Mama."

I roll my eyes as I pass him in the doorway, and he chuckles heartily.

Once inside, we sit on a couch and compare the key paragraphs of our respective emails from the hotel. Quickly, we conclude this unit has, indeed, been double-booked. At least, as far as Mr. Beautiful knows. At this point, I'm fairly certain Brandon figured out a way to end my vacation before it started.

"There's no need to panic," the guy says, probably reacting to my panicked facial expression. "We'll tell the front desk about the mix-up, and they'll give you another bungalow. Easy peasy."

I say nothing, since I've got a hunch it won't be nearly that simple for me. Unfortunately, we used Brandon's parents' card for the reservation, since the honeymoon was their wedding gift. At this point, I'm fairly certain, despite my present state of sleep deprivation and fogginess, that card being on file made it possible for Brandon to unilaterally cancel my reservation without the hotel providing notice to me.

The man picks up his phone, plainly intending to place a call. But I can't have that. I don't know what's happened for sure, but the last thing I need is for this man to become the third person on this island to find out about my embarrassing shit show of a busted wedding yesterday.

"No, don't," I blurt quickly. "I'll call them. You're the one who's already checked in." I run a hand through my hair. "Sorry if I'm a bit frazzled. I'm exhausted from my long day of travel."

His features soften with sympathy. "Why don't you take a seat and relax for a bit? I'm not doing anything, so you can hang out as long as you need while we straighten this out."

"Thank you so much."

"Are you hungry? I was about to make myself a big sandwich and a tall spiced rum punch. I'd be happy to make both for you, too."

His offer feels like a much-needed hug, the same way that nice lady's kindness at the airport did. "Thank you. I'd love both, if it's not too much of a bother."

"Not a bother at all."

While he busies himself in the adjacent kitchenette, I call the phone number listed at the bottom of my confirmation email, and sure enough, a full refund was sent yesterday to the credit card on file—Brandon's parents' card.

I clutch my chest as the hotel clerk explains everything to me, my spirit lodged into my toes.

"But wasn't it too late to get a refund?" I ask hopefully.

"Normally, it would have been," the clerk confirms. "We made an exception this time, given your family emergency and because we happened to have another guest willing to pay in full, right then."

This is a nightmare. I don't know what "family emergency" Brandon or his parents concocted to make the hotel bend the rules, but I suppose it doesn't matter. Not when the money's already been returned and I can't afford even the cheapest room at this fancy resort.

The hotel clerk adds, "We're sorry for your loss, Mrs. Gladstone. Our sincerest condolences."

My stomach revolts. *Please, let that be the last time anyone calls me that slur for the rest of my days.* "Thank you."

Mr. Beautiful returns with two fruity-looking drinks just as I'm disconnecting the call. When he sees my dejected face, his smile vanishes. "They're not giving you another bungalow?"

I shake my head. "Looks like I'm going to have to find somewhere else to stay for the week. They're all booked up."

"*What?*" He places both drinks on a coffee table and sits next to me. "That's unacceptable. They need to give you another bungalow."

"They don't have one to give." I don't know if that's true, but there's no way I'm going to reveal the truth about my situation to this man.

"Did you tell them to at least give you a suite or room in the main building?"

"They said the resort is all booked up. Every single room." Again, I don't know if that's true. But God help me, I don't want him picking up the phone and demanding another room on my behalf, only to find out they've given me a full refund, due to some made-up family emergency.

The man scratches his stubbled chin. "Come to think of it, I think they mentioned something about the resort being at full capacity when I extended my stay. Shoot. This is a pickle, huh?"

Goddamn, he's gorgeous. His sheer physicality and proximity are conspiring to quicken my pulse.

I suddenly remember how I promised that nice airport lady I'd fulfill my every desire this week, big or small, in order to heal myself. Well, I can't imagine something I'd like to "do" more than this gorgeous man sitting next to me. Not to mention, sleeping here for tonight would conveniently solve my current state of homelessness, if only temporarily, in addition to being a delightfully exciting thing to do. Even if it's only for one night, that'd at least give me a place to rest my weary head before setting out to find a motel or hostel somewhere on the island tomorrow. Obviously, I'd never have sex with this man solely to finagle myself a place to sleep tonight. I'd do it because he's hot as hell and I'm in dire need of a pick-me-up. But as luck would have it, sleeping with him would also solve my current housing crisis.

The only problem? I don't have the courage to make the first move on this stunning hunk of a man. Even if I did, however, who knows if he'd be willing to become my first-ever one-night stand. For all I know, he's not even attracted to me. Or to women. Or maybe he's got a wife or girlfriend back home—maybe even one who's somewhere around here at the resort, like at the pool or spa.

I glance around the space for evidence of a woman staying here. Shoes, a purse, a bikini drying on the deck. Did I see makeup on the counter in the bathroom? Were there two toothbrushes or only one? I can't remember any of those details.

"Everything's going to be okay," he says. Whatever he's seeing on my face, he apparently thinks I need reassurance. "I tell you what. I'll make those sandwiches, and after you've had a chance to fuel up and rest, we'll search online together for a nearby bungalow for you."

"Thanks for the sweet offer to help, but I'll search for another room by myself. I don't want you interrupting your vacation."

"It's the least I can do. I feel terrible about the mix-up. I wonder how it happened?"

I don't want to keep lying to his nice man. Lying isn't par for the course for me. How could I teach preschoolers about the importance of being honest at all times if I weren't committed to honesty myself? And yet, in this one unique situation, I feel like lying would be the right thing for my mental health. Surely, telling him the truth about my embarrassing situation would feel a whole lot worse than telling a tiny lie about what brought me here today.

"I was supposed to come here with a friend," I blurt, "but she had to cancel at the last minute for a work emergency." I clear my throat. "I bet they thought *her* cancellation was for both of us."

"That has to be it."

I look around again. "So, um, are you here alone, or . . . ?"

The man nods and leans back into the couch. "My entire extended family was here all week for my cousin's wedding, but everyone left this morning. I was supposed to leave with them, but the opportunity to play golf with an old friend came up, so I stayed for that."

Does his "extended family" include a wife or significant other? Is the "old friend" he stayed to hook up with actually a woman he's planning to bang? I'm dying to know some more details but way too shy to ask, so I take an indirect approach. "Is there anybody back home, or maybe on their way here, who's going to be upset with you for letting some random woman hang out in your bungalow for a little while?"

"Not a soul." He shoots me a sexy, lopsided grin. "What about you? Is there somebody back home who'd be pissed to find out you're hanging out with a strange man in what was supposed to be your bungalow?"

*Is he flirting with me?* Increasingly, it's starting to feel like it.

"Nope, there's nobody. I'm single, the same as you." If my assumption about his relationship status is incorrect, he'd better correct me now. Barring that, I've just made the firm decision to venture outside of my comfort zone and do my damnedest to seduce him. Admittedly, I don't know how to do that, but there's a first time for everything, and this man is too hot not to at least try.

Mr. Beautiful extends his large palm. "I'm Roman, by the way."

"Iris." I shake his offered hand, and a jolt passes through me at the point of contact. "It's nice to meet you, Roman. Sorry it had to happen like this."

"I'm not complaining." He flashes me a million-dollar smile that sends an electric current coursing through me. Okay, that smile definitely feels flirty.

"I'm not normally this frazzled," I say. "On top of being sleep deprived from stressing about my friend cancelling on me, I'm also hungover from partying with my friends last night."

"Yeah? Well, in that case . . ." Roman grabs one of the drinks from the coffee table and hands it to me with a wink. "Sounds like you could use some hair of the dog."

"Definitely. Thank you." I watch him take a long sip of his own matching cocktail, but I don't follow suit. "Sorry to ask," I say, after he lowers his glass. "But will you swap drinks with me? I promised my father when I went off to college I'd never accept a drink from a stranger, unless I'd watched it being made from start to finish, and I've never once broken that promise."

Roman doesn't seem fazed. "Your dad's a smart man. There are a lot of creeps out there."

*Yeah, I almost married one yesterday.*

We swap drinks, and Roman takes a long, greedy sip of the cocktail that used to be mine—and, holy crap, the sight of his Adam's apple bobbing is extremely sexy to me for some reason.

I follow his lead and guzzle my new drink, and fruity, spicy deliciousness awakens my taste buds. "This hits the spot. Thank you. It's delicious."

"Isn't it? I made this same cocktail for my whole family all week, and we were all obsessed." He drags his perfect teeth seductively over his lower lip. "How long ago did you make that promise to your father, by the way?" When I look at him blankly, he adds, "You said you promised your dad you wouldn't take drinks from strangers when you went off to college. How long ago was that, exactly?"

I return his wicked grin. I still get carded all the time, so I know for a fact I look much younger than my age. Could it be this sexy man is making sure I'm a full-blown adult because he's having the same kinds of naughty thoughts I'm having about me spending the night here with him?

"Is that your way of asking my age, Roman?"

"It sure is, Iris." He chuckles.

"I'm twenty-six. You?"

"Thirty-two."

*Excellent.* Kaylee once told me men in their thirties and forties generally have more confidence and skill in the bedroom than men in their twenties. She would know. Unlike me, our vivacious, carefree Kaylee's had lots of partners, of all ages, which is why I've always lived vicariously through her. Brandon's the only guy I've ever been with, and unfortunately, sex with him was never what I'd call exciting.

I've always wondered if me not being able to have an orgasm with Brandon—I can only do it when I'm alone and using my vibrator—is a "me" problem, a "Brandon" problem, or an "us" problem. And now, out of nowhere, it seems I might unexpectedly have found the perfect man to help me figure that out.

Roman's dark eyes flash. "Are you in a rush to get out of here, Iris?"

"Not at all."

"What do you think about us taking our drinks onto the deck with a plate of cheese and crackers before I start making our sandwiches?"

"That sounds great. Other than figuring out where I'm going to sleep tonight, I've got absolutely nothing to do."

"You could crash here tonight, if you're comfortable with that. There's a bed and a couch, so we'd make it work."

Well, that escalated quickly. Is he simply being polite, or is he thinking what I'm thinking? "Thank you so much. That takes the pressure off."

"Good. No stress allowed. You're on vacation."

At Roman's urging, I head onto the deck with my drink while he makes a snack plate for us, and a moment later, he joins me on a cushioned outdoor couch.

"I love the ocean," I say, gazing out at the nearby vibrant waves. "I went to the coast all the time when I lived in LA for school. I miss it so much now that I live in Denver."

"No ocean there."

"Nope. What about you? Where do you live?"

"Delaware. There's a long coastline, but it's nothing like this."

"This is heaven on Earth."

He sips his drink. "Are you originally from Denver?"

"No, I grew up in a small town in Washington State. It's about two hours northeast of Seattle."

At Roman's prompting, I tell him some details about my quaint, beloved hometown, Orchard Blossom, and all the reasons it was a perfect, magical place for a kid to grow up.

"It's right out of a movie," I say in wrap-up. "You can't walk down the street without bumping into someone who's known you forever. What about you? Where'd you grow up?"

"Pennsylvania. I left for college and then moved to Delaware for a job."

*Pennsylvania. Delaware.* I can't help noticing he's only naming states and not specific cities. Is that what people normally do when they're anticipating a one-night stand—they don't reveal too much personal information? Since I've never had one, I have no idea how they usually unfold.

We talk a bit more, until Roman holds up his empty glass and says, "I think I'm ready for a refill and a sandwich. You?"

"Sounds great."

Roman rises from the couch. "Relax. I'll handle everything."

"No, I'd like to help." I stand alongside him. "Right after I pee, that is. I didn't finish earlier for some weird reason." I snicker. "Somehow, I got hopelessly distracted."

Roman returns my snicker. "What a coincidence. I got pretty damned distracted earlier myself."

Excitement courses through me. *Lust.* I'm pretty sure it's coursing between us. Which means, if all this flirting keeps up, we definitely won't need either of us to sleep on the couch tonight.

I follow Roman through a pair of French doors, and when we're both inside the bungalow, he heads toward the kitchen, while I beeline for the bathroom.

"Don't go anywhere, Roman," I coo over my shoulder. I'm trying my best to come off as flirtatious and sultry, but instantly, I realize that was a dumb thing to say, since Roman literally just said he's going into the kitchen to make sandwiches and refill our drinks.

Luckily, Roman doesn't seem fazed by my nonsensical comment. On the contrary, when our eyes lock, he looks nothing but amused. "I'll be right here in the kitchen when you return." His smile morphs into a smolder. "If I'm being honest, Iris, at this point, I don't think wild horses could drag me away."

# CHAPTER 7
## Roman

THIS WOMAN DOESN'T know who I am.

I'm sure about that.

Add that to the list of things I'm finding intensely attractive about this unexpected gift from the universe.

We're standing shoulder to shoulder in the small kitchen. While I cut up veggies to go on top of our turkey sandwiches, Iris is methodically cutting up a pineapple for a fruit salad. To put it mildly, I'm feeling a spark with this cutie. A big one.

With Iris's sandy hair, adorable smattering of freckles, and sweet demeanor, she's got a girl-next-door quality I'd find attractive in any scenario, I think. But either way, I'm definitely feeling it while I'm here in vacation mode. So much so, I'm hoping to steer things into the bedroom, if at all possible, at some point tonight.

I probably shouldn't get ahead myself, since she's still unvetted. In theory, Iris could be another stalker like that wackadoodle in Philly. Or she could be an ambitious sports reporter who's tracked me down for an exclusive scoop after hearing rumblings about me not re-signing with the Crusaders. I can't fathom either scenario, though. Iris seems like a what-you-see-is-what-you-get type of person. A genuine sweetheart. But then again, my dick has clouded my judgment before.

Maverick's existence is proof of that. Same with the few situationships I've entertained since then, all of which quickly made me realize I'm not in the right headspace for anything serious.

"Mustard and mayo?" I ask, motioning to the two open-faced sandwiches on the counter.

"Mustard only for me." Iris makes a cartoonish face of disdain that tells me she loathes mayo as much as I do.

"I can't stand mayo, either," I say with a chuckle.

"Then why do you have it in the fridge?"

*Maverick.* That's the honest answer to the question. My son devoured turkey sandwiches slathered in mayo all week, in between wolfing down Hawaiian ices and playing on the beach outside the bungalow. But since I never talk about my son with unvetted strangers or the press, I reply with, "When my family was here for the wedding, we ate lots of sandwiches while hanging out at the beach."

"Sounds fun." She snickers. "Other than the mayo."

We both laugh.

Iris points to a bowl of fruit on the counter. "Would it be okay for me to cut up that mango for the fruit salad?"

"Go for it. There's a market down the road, so I can always get more. The fruit here is amazing. It tastes like candy."

*Taste.*

*Candy.*

The combination of those two words on my tongue makes me think about the sight that greeted me when I slid open that shower curtain again. Iris's thighs spread wide in front of me. Her head slung back as a groan escaped her. The unexpected scene would have instantly turned my dick to steel, if I hadn't been so damned shocked. Once Iris bolted away with her panties down, however, and it became clear she wasn't a stalker—that, in fact, she'd been every bit as blindsided by our unexpected encounter as me—my dick instantly started hardening. That's why I didn't immediately follow Iris outside, even though I'd thrown on my clothes. I had to wait for my hard-on to subside.

God help me, if I'd gone straight outside to greet my unexpected visitor with a massive bulge in my shorts, she might have called 911 on me. I can practically hear the frantic 911 call about me now—one that would have made the rounds on social media with my smiling Crusaders photo as the visual. I can't afford bad press like that at any time, of course, but especially not now, when Cameron is trying to convince the Thunderbolts I'm their two-hundred-million-dollar man.

We add the finished fruit salad to our sandwich plates, grab our refilled glasses, and head outside to the deck.

"It's so beautiful out here," Iris proclaims as she takes a seat next to me on the outdoor couch. "Thank you so much for letting me hang out here, Roman."

"You bet."

Iris takes a bite of her sandwich and compliments it before returning her gaze to the beach. "This is why I came to Hawaii."

I smile. "It doesn't suck."

She takes a bite of fruit, and her big, blue eyes go wide. "It really does taste like candy."

*Taste.*

*Candy.*

Images of Iris's most intimate body parts flicker across my mind again, this time coupled with the fantasy of me crawling between her legs to turn that pussy of hers into a meal. At the thought, my dick begins hardening, so I cover my rising bulge with my plate.

I shift in my seat. "So, what do you do back home?"

She lights up. "I'm a preschool teacher."

If she were vetted, I'd probably mention I've got a preschooler myself. But as things stand, I refrain and ask if she likes her job.

"I *love* it," Iris replies. "I leap out of bed to go to work every day."

"What do you love most?"

She doesn't hesitate. "The kids. They're so pure and wholesome at that age. Also, hilarious. Three- and four-year-olds can be hysterically funny. Usually, without realizing it."

Everything she's said describes Maverick to a T. "Can you give me an example of something funny a kid has said or done without meaning to be funny?"

"I just witnessed the perfect example today. This comment wasn't made to me; I simply witnessed it at the airport. But it's the first thing that popped into my head." She giggles at some memory. "While I was waiting in line for my rental car, a little boy ran out of the bathroom shouting to his grandma that he'd seen a whale in the bathroom. The kid's grandfather explained there was a mural painted on the wall—one with lots of sea creatures on it—so, the grandma asked the kid, 'What else did you see in the bathroom?' And . . ." Iris cracks up in anticipation of whatever she's going to say next. "And the little boy answered, 'My pee-pee!'"

I bust up along with her. That's *precisely* the kind of thing my son would say.

It suddenly occurs to me I've never introduced Maverick to anyone I've dated before—and certainly not to anyone I'm merely fucking. So, this topic of conversation feels like a first for me. It's not the same thing as a woman I'm attracted to actually meeting my son, of course, but hearing Iris talk with such warmth about kids Maverick's precise age feels unexpectedly exciting to me—enough to turn up the heat on my already simmering attraction.

"Do you want to know the best part?" Iris asks, her beautiful face aglow.

"There's *more*?" I retort playfully.

Iris nods gleefully. "Both grandparents belly laughed at

the little boy's cute response, rather than chastising or correcting him. I love seeing a child being raised by people with an understanding of their child's stage of development. Not to mention, by people with a fantastic sense of humor."

"That's not always the case, huh?"

Iris frowns. "Sadly, no. In my line of work, I see lots of parents and grandparents who tell their child to hush, or to stop being rude or sassy or 'inappropriate,' when the poor kid was sincerely answering a question. Kids that age are very literal and wholesome, you know? They're not trying to be subversive, for goodness' sake."

I laugh at her word choice. The idea of Maverick trying to be subversive is genuinely hilarious to me.

Iris sips her drink and continues with, "I can always tell the kids who've been chastised one too many times at home for doing something they can't help doing, versus the kids who live in an environment where they're not afraid about saying the wrong thing. A big part of my job is to make sure all the kids in my class feel like they're always in a safe space with me."

I'm impressed. If Iris worked as a teacher at Maverick's preschool in LA, I'd definitely want him to be assigned to her classroom. "The kids you teach are lucky to have you. You're not only kind and bighearted, you seem really knowledgeable about your job, too."

"Thank you so much. I've always loved kids, so I majored in child development."

"How long have you been teaching?"

"Four years. I started right after college."

For some reason, I suddenly remember the current lock screen on my phone is Maverick's smiling face. Shit. I don't want her seeing that. I touch the pocket of my board shorts and look around, but I don't see or feel my phone. Did I leave it in the kitchen? "I'm gonna get myself another drink and some more fruit. Can I get you anything?"

"I'd love both. Thank you."

I grab Iris's plate and cup and mine and head into the kitchen. Thankfully, I quickly find my phone sitting on the counter, face down. Without delay, I swap out my lock screen of Maverick for a sunset photo I snapped this week. When that task is completed, I refill both our glasses, slide the rest of the fruit onto our plates, and head back outside to Iris on the deck.

As I return to my seat, Iris asks, "So, what do you do for a living, Roman?"

Shit. I should have been prepared for that question, but I wasn't. Probably because I can't remember the last time a woman I've been hitting on didn't already know what I do for work.

My brain quickly searches for an appropriate response—a believable profession for my vacation-time alter ego. In a flash, I've got my answer when my offseason trainer's face suddenly pops into my head. "I own a specialty gym," I say smoothly. "We train professional and soon-to-be professional athletes."

"Wow. That's so cool."

I don't like lying in Iris's earnest, sweet face, but I'd hate giving up my anonymity with her even more. If this conversation eventually migrates into the bedroom like I'm hoping it will, I don't want to have to pull out my standard NDA and ruin the sexy, easy, flirty vibe. True, if Iris somehow finds out later on she slept with Roman Maguire without there being an NDA in place, she'd have a juicy story to tell her circle of friends. But that's a risk I'm willing to take, since the odds are low a preschool teacher would want to widely broadcast her sex life beyond that. Whenever I've pulled out an NDA in the past, it's definitely not been a sexy moment. But at least, in those prior instances, whatever woman I'd been seducing already knew my identity, so the NDA didn't feel like a bombshell the way it likely would for Iris.

Iris blissfully takes a bite of fruit. "It makes sense you own a gym. You look like a guy who knows a lot about working out."

I sip my drink. "Thanks. Yeah, I played football in college."

"That's so cool. Where?"

*Fuck.* "UT Austin." It's yet another lie. A necessary one, though. I'm not planning to tell Iris my last name before sending her packing tomorrow morning. So, with this clever red herring, I'm hoping I've now ensured that if Iris were to search the internet using the clues she's gathered about me thus far—Roman, college football player, gym owner, Delaware, and now, UT Austin—she won't be able to find me. Instead, she'll almost certainly get bombarded with a decade's worth of news about the amazing Chad Roman, the famed tight end who was a star for UT Austin before going on to have a stellar professional career in Minnesota. Either that, or the internet will lead Iris to some random gym owner in Delaware who happens to have Roman as his first or last name. Either way, she won't find me, and that's all that matters.

Iris cocks her head. "UT stands for University of Texas, right?"

"Correct." I hold up my index finger and pinky—the hand signal every Longhorn fan from UT Austin makes at every football game—and murmur, "Go Longhorns."

Iris laughs. "I went to UCLA, but sadly, we didn't have a cute little hand signal like that. I'm jealous." She giggles at her own comment, and I chuckle along with her, simply because she's so damned cute.

"The years you were there, you had a pretty good football team, though."

"Did we?"

"You don't know?"

Iris shrugs. "I only went to one football game in four years."

"*What?*"

"And that was only because one of my best friends was dating the star quarterback at the time."

"Who?"

"My friend Kaylee. She has a thing for athletes, and they love her in return."

I shake my head, amused. "No, who was the star quarterback your friend dated?"

"Oh." Iris giggles again before telling me the guy's name.

"I think I remember him," I say. "Vaguely, anyway." The guy wasn't a "star," as Iris just now called him. In fact, he was mediocre at best. But I guess everything's relative when you're a guy who's won the Heisman. I dig deep into the recesses of my mind. "As I recall, he did an okay job for UCLA, but he sucked ass at the NFL Combine, so his stock plummeted after that."

"What's the NFL Combine?"

"It's a yearly event where scouts from each team come to evaluate eligible college players for the upcoming draft. Players are judged based on a variety of different criteria—speed, running routes, throwing, tackling, et cetera. Whatever's relevant to their particular position. After that, all the teams decide who they want to try to draft a few weeks later."

Iris's eyes light up. "I think our quarterback got drafted!"

I can't help grinning at her exuberance. "He did, yeah. In the sixth round, I believe."

"Is that good?"

"I mean, statistically, it's amazing for a player to get drafted at all." I briefly think about my own brother, Luca, going in the sixth round during his year in the draft, and how relieved he was to make it at all. "But it's the last possible round of the draft," I add, "so in that sense, it's not great. It's not fatal to a guy having a successful career. Not at all. But it's also not an early vote of confidence, you know?"

Iris looks genuinely interested. "Did UCLA's quarterback do pretty well after he got drafted?"

I shake my head. "Sorry, no. I'm pretty sure he got cut before playing a single down in a regular season game. He might be on a practice squad somewhere at this point, if he's lucky, but I doubt it."

"Shoot. I'm so sad his big dreams didn't come true. When I was at that game—"

"That *one* game."

"Yes, during which I drank beer and didn't understand a single thing happening on the field."

"You're a monster."

She snickers. "During that *one* game, everyone around me kept saying our quarterback was going to be a superstar in the NFL one day."

"That's a tall order. It's insanely hard to get drafted at all. Even harder to nab a spot on a roster, let alone a starting spot. Even if a guy gets that far, it's hard to keep a spot for too long, because there's always someone younger, faster, and hungrier breathing down your neck. If not that, then injuries can be a major factor, so you really never know who's going to be successful and for how long." Luca pops into my head again. Man, my brother's hung in there, admirably, through all the ups and downs the League has thrown at him over the past five years.

"Wow, that all sounds really stressful," Iris says.

*You have no idea.*

Iris takes a sip of her drink. "I can't believe you remember so much stuff about UCLA's quarterback without needing to look it up. Do you follow UCLA football for some reason, or are you this knowledgeable about every college team?"

Panic flashes inside me. I need to be much more careful here if I want to preserve my anonymity with Iris. Clearly, I'm being way too obvious. "I follow college and pro football, pretty religiously, and I'm totally obsessed with the draft every year. My whole family has always loved the game—I've got two brothers and lots of friends who also played in college—so I'm kind of a football junkie." Shit. I shouldn't have mentioned my two brothers. Does Chad Roman have two brothers?

"My brother is obsessed with football, too," Iris says breezily. "He watches every Seagulls game on TV and attends every game at his school."

"Where does he go?"

"University of Washington. He's in his last year there."

"They've got a great football program there. Especially lately, they've been killing it."

"That's what Atlas keeps telling me." She snorts. "*All. The. Freaking. Time.*" Iris rolls her eyes. "Whenever his Huskies play my Bruins, my brother talks so much smack, you'd think he was one of the players on the field."

"Those are the best kinds of fans—the ones who talk smack like they're on the roster."

"Well, if that's something you like, then you'd love my little brother." Iris pops a piece of fruit into her mouth. "Did you ever think about trying to get drafted? Did you go to that Combine thingy?"

My stomach tightens. It was one thing to lie about what I do for a living, but I'm not willing to construct an entirely false, detailed persona to get laid, even if I'll never see this woman again after tonight.

"I know people who got drafted," I say lamely, trying to find something truthful to say that feels semirelevant to the question. "A lot of them are still playing today."

Obviously, I can't tell her about my experience at the Combine. Not when I've already dug myself this hole. In actuality, yes, of course, I went to the Combine. But I didn't do much there, since we all knew I'd get selected as the overall first pick of the draft a few weeks later. The team positioned to select first—the Crusaders, who ultimately drafted me first—desperately needed a quarterback, and there was no indication they'd trade their top spot away. And so, given the situation, I merely networked and marketed myself at the Combine, rather than participating in any of the evaluations.

I caught some flak from some people who don't understand football for not taking part in the dog and pony show like everyone else. But Cameron, my parents, and Coach Hardy all agreed there was zero upside to me doing a damned thing at the Combine, other than being my charming self. We all felt, and rightly so, that my back-to-back national championships and Heisman Trophy had already proved my value far better than any throwing exhibition ever could.

"Do you train any of your old friends from college?" Iris asks.

"Hmm?"

She repeats the question, and I nod, not wanting to give voice to yet another falsehood.

"That's wonderful, Roman. It must be so fun to train athletes who are longtime friends."

"Mm-hmm." I take a long sip of my drink, eager to change the subject. "So, tell me, Iris—"

"What position did you play in college?"

Fuck. Now that I've already lied and said I went to Chad Roman's college rather than my own, I guess I should tell her Chad Roman's position, too. "Tight end."

"What's that, exactly?" Iris asks with a laugh. "Sorry. I know what the quarterback does, but that's about it."

At her mention of my actual position, I have a near heart attack—but, somehow, I smile through it and then proceed to calmly explain the basics of the tight end position. As I talk, Iris listens intently, her blue eyes trained on my face like there's going to be a pop quiz about the information later on. Jesus, she's a cutie.

"I love hearing you talk about football," Iris gushes. "You're so passionate about it. Isn't it wonderful to get to do something for work that's related to something you're so passionate about?"

"It sure is." I raise my glass. "To passion."

She blushes. "To passion." She clinks my glass with hers. "I'm having such a nice time chatting with you, Roman. After the horrible day I had yesterday . . ." She pauses. "You know, with my friend unexpectedly backing out of our vacation at the last minute, I'm really grateful you're letting me hang out and relax with you."

"I'm glad you're here, Iris. I'm having a great time with you."

"You are?" She looks genuinely surprised.

I grin. "Very much so. You can't tell?"

"Honestly, I find you kind of unreadable. A bit mysterious." She waggles her eyebrows, making me chuckle.

"Well, I assure you: I'm having a blast."

Her chest heaves. "I'm so glad. So am I. It's been a long time since I've had such an easy, comfortable conversation with someone new like this. You're very easy to talk to, Roman."

"Back at you, Iris."

She bites her lip adorably. "I don't want to overstay my welcome, though, so let me know whenever you want me to leave or get out of your hair."

I hold her gaze. "I'd honestly be deeply disappointed if you left before the morning."

Her breathing halts. Her nostrils flare.

"I'd very much like you stay the whole night here with me," I add, just in case my meaning is unclear. "I mean, I'd be happy to sleep on the couch, if you want. Like I said. Whatever you want to do, Iris."

Iris shifts her position on the couch and swallows hard, her face bursting with excitement. "I'd never let you sleep on the couch. The bungalow is yours, fair and square."

I smirk, but I don't say a word. If she's game to fuck me tonight, then she's going to have to be a big girl and put herself out there a bit more than that. The last thing I want is to make her feel like sex is the going rate for a free place to sleep tonight.

The silence between us becomes thick with sexual tension and words left unspoken. Finally, with Iris's eyes locked with mine, she chokes out, "Maybe we could both sleep in the bed. Or not sleep. If you . . . know what I mean."

*Oh my fucking God. She's adorable.*

"I'd like that, but I don't want you thinking you need to share a bed with me as a requirement to stay here. Like I said, I'm more than happy to sleep on the couch."

"No, I . . . I wouldn't want you to do that."

"You wouldn't, or you don't?"

"I don't."

I lean in and hold her gaze. "What do you want, Iris? Tell me clearly."

Her cheeks burst with color. Her chest rises and falls. "*You.*"

With a satisfied grin, I take Iris's pretty face in my palms and wordlessly do the thing I've been dying to do for quite some time now—ever since I saw her naked thighs spread wide and her head slung back: I press my lips to hers. When Iris responds enthusiastically, I open her lips with mine and gently swirl my tongue with hers, making her softly moan.

In short order, our kissing ramps up into a full-blown make-out session. Until soon, I've got Iris on her back on the couch and she's got her thighs around my hips. As we kiss, we urgently grind against each other. Run greedy fingers through hair. Moan softly with arousal and anticipation. I'm sure we're both a bit tipsy by now, but I don't think that's the source of the electricity coursing between us. Rather, I think the wild, crackling chemistry I'm feeling with Iris is nothing but good, old-fashioned lust.

"Do you want to move this into the bedroom?" I gasp out hoarsely, feeling overcome by my scorching attraction.

"Yes," Iris blurts. "I need to take a shower, though. I'm covered in airplane air."

I nuzzle her nose with mine. "Take your time, sweetheart. I'll wait for you in bed."

"Naked?"

"If that's okay with you."

"It's all I want."

I chuckle. "Then that's what you'll get." I brush my lips against her ear, making her shudder. "I'm gonna make you feel so fucking good, Iris. Just you wait."

A soft moan escapes her mouth. "Do you have a condom?"

"I do."

Breathing hard, Iris chokes out, "But do you have a lot of them, Roman? Because, honestly, I want to have as much sex as humanly possible with you tonight."

# CHAPTER 8
## Iris

**Tatiana:** Where are you?

Me: In the bathroom with the door closed and the shower running. I'm supposed to be taking a shower before sliding into bed naked with him.

**Tatiana:** LOL. Iris, I say this with love, but you're overthinking this.

**Kaylee:** Tati's right. Now get into that shower and into that bed and have the best sex of your life, girlie!

Me: I'm nervous. I think I've somehow convinced him I'm a total sex kitten, and now I'm worried I won't live up to the hype.

**Kaylee:** Snort. Sweetie, I say this with love, but there's no way in hell that man thinks you're a sex kitten. Sorry. Just be enthusiastic, and I promise he'll think you're amazing in bed.

**Tatiana:** ^^ THIS!

Me: I know I've never been a seductress before, but here, I swear I'm channeling my inner Kaylee. I brazenly seduced that man!

**Kaylee:** Woohoo! How'd you do it? Tell us so we can use your techniques.

**Tatiana:** Me, anyway. I don't think you need any help, Kaylee.

**Kaylee:** Hey, it never hurts to switch things up.

**Me:** *I looked him right in the eyes and said, "I want you, Roman."*

**Tatiana:** *Atta girl! Confident, sexy, and clear. Nice!*

**Kaylee:** *\*wipes a tear of pride\* Our little girl's grown up, Tati!*

**Me:** *Except that now I'm worried my mouth wrote a check my body can't cash! What if it turns out I've never had an O with Brandon, not because he's bad at sex like you both keep telling me, but because I am?*

**Kaylee:** *Impossible. Do you want to have sex with this man?*

**Me:** *So much, I'm in physical pain.*

**Kaylee:** *Then you'll slay, as far as he's concerned. Sorry to be blunt about it, but as long as you're wet and into it, he'll think you're a goddess.*

**Tatiana:** *^^ This. Let the hottie lead the way, let loose, stop overthinking it, and I promise, you'll both have a stupendous time.*

**Kaylee:** *Now get into that shower and into that man's bed and get yourself railed and scrambled for the first time, babyyyyy!*

My hair is wet and towel dried. My skin is covered in goosebumps, despite the pleasant temperature of the bedroom. I'm doing my best to sashay confidently toward Roman's naked, prostrate frame on the bed, but as I clutch the white hotel towel wrapped around my torso, I'm pretty sure I look more like the trombone player in a marching band than a femme fatale.

Roman has pulled back the palm-tree-covered duvet and top sheet to reveal every inch of his naked, tanned skin. His abs are cut. His legs look powerful. His cock is rock-hard and straining—and so much bigger than it looked when it was hanging flaccidly between his thighs. Either Brandon was on the small side—rather than average like I've always presumed—or this guy is hung like a horse. Will that thing even fit inside me?

Roman grins as I walk toward him. "Hi there," he says, sitting up onto his elbows.

"Hi," I squeak out. "You look really good."

"And you look like an angel sent straight from heaven."

I snort. "Yeah, I bruised my tailbone when my wings malfunctioned on the way down, so please be gentle with me." Shit. I always resort to humor when I'm nervous.

"Are you nervous, sweetheart?" Roman asks, apparently reading my mind. Crap. Maybe Kaylee and Tatiana were right, and I haven't fooled this man at all.

"A little," I admit. "But that doesn't mean I don't want to do this. I do."

Roman moves into a kneeling position at the end of the bed, his cock filling the small space between our bodies. He slides a finger underneath my chin. "We can make out and do nothing more than that. We can put our clothes back on and talk again. Whatever you want to do. Like I said, my invitation to let you sleep here isn't dependent on you having sex with me."

My heart flutters, along with other parts of my anatomy. "I didn't think that. I seduced you, remember?"

Roman smiles in a way that makes me blush.

"You don't agree I seduced you?"

Roman's smile broadens. "I think you're very cute to think so."

I've been trying hard to be sexy, so the comment stings a bit, even though it was delivered with a radiant smile.

"It's a compliment," Roman says quickly. "Sorry. Whatever. Yes, you seduced me, and it was awesome. You were saying?"

I clear my throat, feeling a bit flustered. "That it would help me if you'd take the lead."

"It'd be my pleasure." He strokes my hair and whispers, "Is

this your first time, Iris?" So much for my sex kitten delusions. May they rest in peace. I'm embarrassed by the question, but I think it's a fair one, all things considered. Roman has no idea I was supposed to get married yesterday. And I have several friends my age who are still virgins, each of them for their own reasons. These days, I think it's very normal for women to be virgins well into their twenties and beyond.

"No, I've had sex before," I reply. "Lots of times." I decide to leave it at that. It's not my general habit to answer questions succinctly. I'm a compulsive oversharer by nature. But this one time, I force myself to do it to preserve at least a shred of mystery. And what woman of mystery has only had sex with one boyfriend? "I really want to do this with you, Roman," I insist. "It's just that I've never had a one-night stand, per se, so it would be helpful if you'd take the lead."

"Luckily, that's my all-time favorite thing to do—taking the lead." He skims his fingertips across the top ridge of my towel. "Can I take this off?"

My heart is racing, and my tongue feels thick in my mouth, so I nod slowly.

With hungry eyes, Roman loosens my towel, causing it to slide to the floor at my feet. Once I'm standing naked before him, his dark eyes rake over me, and his chest expands sharply before he leans in and kisses me again. When our kiss becomes passionate, his mouth travels south, at which point he kisses and laps at my breasts.

Holy crap.

As Roman's mouth becomes more and more voracious, arousal begins flooding every nerve ending between my legs even more forcefully. So much so, I can't help shivering, and then wobbling, in place with each movement of his tongue and lips. With each assured caress of his warm hands.

A tortured moan escapes my lips that surprises me. And

then, a groan that shocks the hell out of me and prompts Roman to supply one of his own.

Roman slides his warm palms to my hips and trails kisses from my breasts down my belly until, finally, he pulls me onto the bed and lays me down on my back. Once I'm lying next to him and writhing with arousal, he begins kissing my mouth again, deeply this time, while brushing his fingertips up and down between my legs. In record speed, I'm so turned on, I can't help whimpering and groaning into his mouth. I've never experienced foreplay this slow and hot. Actually, have I ever experienced foreplay at all? If this is how it's supposed to go, then the answer to that question is an emphatic *no*.

As Roman's tongue tangles with mine, he continues brushing his fingertips gently between my legs, up and down, but without ever going in for the kill. Occasionally, he lets his fingers drift to my inner thighs. To my hipbone. To my belly. But always, he returns to sweeping them up and down between my legs like he's gently coaxing a shy flower to fully bloom.

Eventually, the tactic makes me so damned wet and horny, it's all I can do not to grab his hand and shove his fingers inside me or wantonly beg him to fuck me. I've never felt this hungry to get penetrated before. This is a new sensation for me. I feel more animal than human.

Still kissing me, Roman finally slides his fingers inside me, breaching my body for the first time, and the loud, feral moan of relief and excitement that escapes me is totally foreign to me. *What was that?* I've never made a guttural, desperate sound like that in my life.

At the sound of my intense arousal, Roman groans in a way that sends goosebumps erupting across my body.

"You're so fucking wet for me," he whispers hoarsely.

"I want you," I whisper back, trembling with anticipation.

"Beg me for it," he coos.

"I want you, Roman. Please."

"You can do better than that."

"I want you inside me. Please, Roman. *Please.*"

"Better. But patience. You'll get every inch of me soon enough. But only when I say it's time."

Oh my God, this feels like a fantasy come to life. All this time, I've thought something was wrong with me. That I had a dryness problem. A passion problem. An orgasm problem. I even thought maybe I was asexual. But now, just this fast, I know I had a *Brandon* problem. I always thought I was physically attracted to him. But what I felt was nothing like this. With Roman, I feel rabid. Ravenous. Like I'd do anything to scratch the itch Roman has magically ignited deep inside me.

Speaking of magic, Roman's doing something magical with his fingers between my legs—something so delicious, it elicits loud moans from me while also making my eyes roll back. As he masterfully fingers me, he devours my lips, neck, jawline, and cheeks. He whispers into my ear that I'm hot, sexy, beautiful, a goddamned angel. That he can't wait to taste my sweet pussy. That I'm driving him crazy.

All of a sudden, I feel something seize hold of me. Something that makes my innermost intimate muscles feel like they're twisting before holding in abeyance. It's like my entire body is on the bitter cusp of unraveling. I've felt a glimmer of this sensation right before giving myself an orgasm with my vibrator, but I've never experienced it with this kind of force and magnitude—the kind that takes my breath away and makes my eyes roll back into my head.

"That's it, baby," Roman coos. "You're so fucking sexy."

"I'm close," I grit out, clutching the sheet underneath me. "Don't stop anything."

"We've got all night, baby. I'll keep going as long as it takes."

It's the hottest thing he could have said to me. With a loud groan, I grip the sheet underneath me even harder, arch my back, and let the tsunami of glorious pleasure slam into me with full force.

When the pleasure subsides, I feel like I'm under a spell—like I've been magically turned into a ravenous, horny beast. "I want you inside me," I bark out. To emphasize my point, I grip his hard dick and stroke it, and then growl with pleasure when I discover his thick tip is drenched with pre-cum. I swirl the sticky evidence of Roman's arousal around and around with my thumb, causing him to jerk and jolt, and then beg him to get his cock wrapped up and deep inside me.

"Patience," Roman coos again. But this time, when he says the word, he sounds like he's hanging on by the barest of threads. With his dark eyes blazing and his entire body quaking, Roman spreads my thighs, crawls between them, and proceeds to give me oral sex that's so fucking delicious and masterful, it quickly sends me hurtling into what can only be described as a full-bodied meltdown.

"Good girl," Roman chokes out hoarsely from between my legs, as I writhe and groan in ecstasy. Breathing hard, he grabs a condom packet off the nightstand like he's grabbing onto a lifeline. With his cock wrapped up, he climbs over my sweaty, writhing, yearning body like a panther on the prowl. When his mouth reaches mine, he feels between my legs for his target with greedy fingers before plunging his full length inside me, all the freaking way.

I cry out as Roman's thick cock stretches me and growl with pleasure as it fills me to the brim. When he begins thrusting like a beast, I grip his bare ass cheeks, reveling in the perfect fit of our bodies. How did I ever question if his dick would fit inside me, when it now feels like his body was designed specifically to fill every inch of mine?

As Roman's thrusts intensify, I wrap my thighs around his gyrating hips and dig my nails into his broad back, savoring every delicious sensation. His warm skin against mine. His musky scent. The primal sounds of his cock thrusting in and out of my wetness. I've never been this wet before. Not with Brandon. Not with a vibrator. Not even when I've woken up after a sex dream about some rock star or hot professor from college.

Our tongues are swirling in concert with the movement of our desperate bodies. We're gyrating as one by now—feeling totally connected while spiraling into ecstasy together. Suddenly, Roman's mouth breaks free of mine with a loud gasp, like he's coming up for air after spending too long under water.

"You feel so good," he grits out. "Like you were made for me."

I moan my reply, relishing the fact that the feeling is mutual—that I'm free to make whatever noises feel natural. I've never experienced a man talking during sex. I thought that was normal, so I kept quiet, too. But now, I can't get enough of Roman's dirty talk and animalistic noises. Every time this man opens his mouth, no matter what comes out, he ignites my body even more, as surely as if he were licking my clit.

"What are you doing to me?" Roman grits out. He sounds tortured. On the bitter cusp of losing it. "Your pussy is magic, baby," he growls into my ear. "You're a drug, baby. Fucking hell, what are you doing to me?"

I'm thinking he's going to lose it any second now, based on the sounds he's making and the desperation of his tone and thrusts. But to my surprise, he pulls out of me, panting, flips me over and onto all fours, and plunges himself inside me again, this time from behind. As he fucks me in this new position, I feel like he's ripping me in two—but in the best possible way. He reaches around and massages my clit as he pounds me, and . . . *Oh my God.* All of a sudden, out of nowhere, my eyes roll back into my head, my breathing halts, and a third orgasm ravages me—this one even more powerful than the prior two.

I come with a loud, keening wail, as Roman wraps a large palm over my throat and comes inside me with a loud growl of his own. As his body ripples violently inside mine, I collapse onto the bed, taking him with me, and then lie motionless underneath him, spent and breathing hard, as Roman's body quakes and shudders on top of mine with aftershocks.

When our bodies have both quieted, Roman slides off my back, turns me onto my side like a rag doll and kisses me tenderly. "Goddamn, Iris," he murmurs into my lips. "That was unexpected."

I don't know what to say in response to that, since everything about that was far more than unexpected to me—it was transformative. Transcendent. Revelatory. *Supernatural.*

Tongue-tied and exhausted, I wordlessly kiss him again, and that's what we wind up doing for a long time: kissing. We do it for so long, in fact, it eventually feels like we're having an entire conversation without words. When we finally come up for air and open our eyes, Roman wipes at my cheek with his thumb and whispers, "Those were tears of euphoria, I hope?"

*Did I cry at some point?* If so, I didn't realize it. I wipe at my cheek, and I'll be damned. It's sticky with dried tears. "I don't know what that was about," I reply honestly. "I'm definitely not feeling sad, I can tell you that. That was the most incredible, liberating, addicting thing that's ever happened to me in my life. I feel like I just walked through a secret portal into another dimension—a new world where I found a better version of myself."

Roman chuckles. "That's high praise."

"It's the truth."

"I don't doubt it." He swipes gently at my cheek again. "Something tells me you're not capable of the alternative."

Shit. Roman didn't say "Me, too" about the secret portal into another dimension thing. So, I'm thinking I've probably overshared, like I always do. In fact, now that my cringey words are hanging in the air, unmatched, I realize I should have played it much cooler with Roman. Perhaps pretended that's how sex always goes for me. Because I'm a sex kitten. But then again, I don't think I'm capable of pulling off any kind of charade, like Roman said. Especially not in this one-of-a-kind moment. I'm feeling too raw—too triumphant, alive, and powerful—to even try to put on any kind of act.

I touch Roman's stubbled cheek. "Thank you for taking so much time with me. That felt incredible."

Roman kisses my cheek. "My kink, if I have one, is getting my partner off. And the way you just got off? Jesus Christ, Iris. I feel like I've mainlined an addictive drug."

My heart quickens. That was just as good as Roman saying he walked through a secret portal, too. Maybe even better, especially when combined with the look of complete satisfaction on Roman's gorgeous face. The man does indeed look drugged—and I can't deny it turns me on to know *I'm* the source of his intoxication.

I slide my palm over Roman's bicep and bat my eyelashes at him. "Please, feel free to overdose on my body as much as you want tonight."

Roman smirks. "You wouldn't give me carte blanche like that if you knew how much I enjoyed that. It was supernatural for me, too."

Oh my gosh. This just keeps getting better and better. I open my mouth to reply, but before I get a single word out, a big yawn overtakes me.

"Thanks," Roman deadpans.

I giggle. "Sorry. I've barely gotten any sleep the last couple days."

Roman strokes my hair. "Get some sleep, then. A great orgasm will put you to sleep better than any sleeping pill."

I snicker. "And I had *three*."

"You sure did. Don't let them go to waste. Get some sleep, Iris."

I didn't know great orgasms are sleep inducing, simply because I've never had one even close to as great as the ones Roman gave me. Especially that last one. Holy crap. But I see no reason to admit any of that. I've already said too much.

I open my mouth to reply, and yet *another* yawn overtakes me, making Roman laugh again.

"Sorry to bore you," he teases this time, making me giggle again.

"Okay, maybe I'll take a short nap," I concede. "But only long enough to recharge for round two."

"Sleep as long as you can," he says gently. "I'm not going anywhere. We've got plenty of time."

I don't agree with that statement, since he's only invited me to stay for one night and I'm now craving as many rounds of sex with this man as I can get. But I can't deny the comment is a kind thing to say that relaxes me even more.

"Thank you so much," I whisper as my eyelids flutter. "I can't thank you enough."

"Sweet dreams, Iris. Whenever you wake up, I'll be here and ready to go again. But no rush."

I glance at the clock on the nightstand. It's hours before I'd normally go to bed. Granted, Hawaii is a full four hours behind Denver and three behind Orchard Blossom, so my internal clock feels hopelessly confused right now, but I can't imagine I won't wake up in a couple hours at most.

"I'll see you in an hour or two," I say with another yawn. "And then we'll go again. Oh. I'd better pee real quick." I roll out of bed and pad to the bathroom, and when I get back, there's a huge bottle of water on the nightstand and Roman is closing all the blinds in the room.

"Drink at least half of that," Roman instructs, indicating the bottle. "Flying is dehydrating, and so is good sex."

"Wow, it's almost like you're a personal trainer or something," I tease. I grab the bottle and guzzle its entire contents, eliciting a "good girl" from Roman.

"I'll get you another bottle so you'll have it if you wake up thirsty," he says. "Sleep tight."

My heart flutters. If Roman takes care of his clients in Delaware this well, it's no wonder he can afford to take a two-week vacation at a fancy resort. He's making me feel as special as a professional athlete.

"See you soon," I say coyly, resting my head onto my luxurious pillow again—and approximately three seconds later, I'd estimate, the world melts away and I'm blissfully asleep.

# CHAPTER 9
## Roman

I ENTER THE bungalow and quietly place the items I've brought back for Iris from the hotel's breakfast buffet—muffins, fruit, bacon, and coffee—onto the kitchen counter. From there, I creep into the bedroom to see if Sleeping Beauty has awakened yet, but nope, she's still dead to the world.

For a moment, I stand in the doorway admiring Iris's pretty face in repose. The way her sandy hair is splayed out on the pillow, it's like she's got a halo. Which makes sense, since it's clear she had some kind of a spiritual awakening along with her sexual one. Whatever happened for Iris last night, it was nothing short of the hottest thing I've witnessed in my life. I haven't gotten the results of the background check from Cameron yet, but I'm not the least bit concerned about it. My gut tells me Iris Benedetto is exactly the 26-year-old UCLA graduate and Denver preschool teacher she claims to be. Not to mention, one of the cutest, sweetest, most adorable people I've ever had the pleasure to meet, let alone to sleep with.

When Iris initially crashed last night, I went to the hotel bar for a couple hours to watch the basketball game. I figured Iris would be awake when I got back and ready for round two, but it wasn't meant to be. Iris was still fast asleep when I got back. And so I sat on the couch in the bungalow and scrolled on my phone.

Finally, when my eyelids got too heavy to stay open, I crashed on the couch, feeling a bit disappointed for my own horny self but also genuinely happy for Iris to get the rest she obviously needed. Man, Iris really must have let loose with her friends the night before coming here. Or maybe her friend cancelling on her at the last minute is the larger culprit—the real reason for her bone-deep exhaustion. If that's the case, then good for Iris for going outside her comfort zone to come here by herself.

Man, I'm itching to slide into that bed with Iris now, eat her out, and ask her to stay the whole week with me. Why not? She's got nowhere to go, and I've got nothing on my calendar but golf with Coach Hardy on Friday. It's not every day a guy has supernatural sex out of nowhere, and what better way to distract me from my current stressors than enjoying a scorching-hot fling in paradise?

Fuck it. I'll do it—I'll invite Iris to stay here with me. But I won't wake her up to do it. I'll let the poor girl sleep.

My mind made up, I scribble a quick note on a hotel notepad: *Going out for a run. Left breakfast for you in the kitchen.* I leave the note on the nightstand next to Iris, grab my earbuds and running shoes, and quietly slip out the bungalow door.

About an hour later, just as I'm finishing a pleasant jog along the shore, my phone buzzes with a text from Cameron. When Iris slipped into the shower yesterday, I nabbed her driver's license from her purse and sent a photo of it to Cameron with a request for a background check. *Nothing too detailed*, I wrote to Cameron. *Just make sure she's the sweet preschool teacher she appears to be.*

I'm not going to win any awards for restraint in this situation, obviously, since I went ahead and fucked Iris before getting the results back from Cameron. But considering the raging boner I had for my bungalow crasher by the time she slipped into the shower last night, not to mention the buzz I had going from those rum punches, I'm amazed I was clearheaded enough to do any due diligence at all.

*Cameron: Iris Eugenie Benedetto. Age 26. Preschool teacher at St. Luke's Preschool in Denver, Colorado, for almost the past four years. No criminal record. Strong credit score. Graduated from UCLA, summa cum laude, with a degree in childhood development & psychology. Won a bunch of Podunk regional horse-riding competitions as a teenager throughout Washington and Oregon. All in all, I'd say she's squeaky clean and a refreshing change from your usual, other than the one glaring exception which you can find at the link below. Watch the video right fucking now and then call me ASAP. And whatever you do, don't fuck her, Roman!*

I'm flabbergasted.

Is sweet, shy, angelic Iris Benedetto a *porn star*? I begin typing a reply to Cameron with anxious fingers, asking him where the fuck is the fucking link to the video he's referenced, but before I've pressed send on the message, a link magically appears underneath Cameron's text for a video entitled, "Horny Runaway Bride Destroys Cheating Groom on Wedding Day."

*Horny Runaway . . . What?*

My breathing shallow, I click on the video, and there she is. *Iris.* Looking breathtakingly beautiful in a traditional white bridal gown. She's in a church—standing with a guy in a suit who's clearly her groom, while bridesmaids and groomsmen stand on either side. What the fuck? Also, *when* the fuck?

My heart thrumming, I check the date on the video and my pounding heart stops on a dime. That can't be. If that date is accurate, then Iris was a bride mere days ago—on the same day Marco married Nicola. Could it be this is an older video that only got uploaded the other day? Either way, it's already got over a million views in a matter of hours.

I click to start the video, and Iris the Bride says to her groom, "You've always been so much better with words than me, Brandon, so I'm going to use some of your own words to express myself now." She pulls out a cell phone from her bra, making everyone in attendance titter and chuckle at her cuteness.

Unlike everyone else, however, the groom doesn't titter or chuckle. On the contrary, the second he sees the phone in Iris's hand, he looks downright panicked.

"Where'd you get that?" he blurts. "Iris, wait. Stop. *Give me that.*"

The groom attempts to grab the phone out of Iris's hand, but she whirls around and holds the device to her chest like a running back protecting the rock. In a flash, two men dressed in suits—an older gentleman and a young, fit dude—flank Iris and warn the groom to keep his distance.

"That's not mine!" the groom shouts to the crowd, pointing at Iris. "Whatever she's about to say—"

"It's Brandon's secret burner phone!" Iris shouts above him, holding up the device. "I found it last night in Brandon's toiletry bag, and—"

The person behind the camera recording, or maybe someone sitting very close to them, asks, "Is this a joke?," so I can't hear whatever Iris says next. Nor can I hear the groom, who's throwing up his arms and saying something to the two men in suits. A moment later, however, I'm able to hear Iris again, at which point she's saying, ". . . a text to a woman identified in his contacts as 'Allison with the Big You-Know-Whats.'"

A collective gasp rises up in the church, and the groom lunges at Iris again, this time shouting, "I swear, that's not my phone!"

The two men in suits physically restrain the groom while two feisty bridesmaids leap into action and stand in front of Iris, creating a human barrier between bride and groom.

"You know it's yours, Brandon!" Iris shouts. "Besides all the photos in all your dating profiles, I recognize all the photos of your privates you sent to countless women!"

A collective gasp. Chaos surrounds the person taking the video. A young man from the audience races up to help the two guys in suits. It's sheer pandemonium.

"That's enough!" the pastor booms. "Whatever's happening here, it's going to stop right now."

The young, fit man in a suit who first leaped into action with the older one yells, "Not till Iris says her piece! Go on, Iris! We've got him."

Visibly trembling, Iris faces the crowd, her beautiful face ablaze. "Brandon wrote to 'Allison with the Big You-Know-Whats,' and this is a quote: 'I'm so horny for you, baby, I practically bleep in my pants whenever I think about bleeping you!'"

The church erupts like Iris set off an atomic bomb—so much so, our trusty cameraperson loses control of their phone for a moment, causing the scene to bobble and whirl.

"And to 'Katarina from *da* Strip Club,'" Iris screams in the background of the whirling, bobbling video. "And yes, he wrote 'da' in place of 'the.' He wrote—" The scene stabilizes again. "'I got out of my meeting earlier than expected, baby, so get ready to gag on my bleep!'"

"*Enough!*" the pastor shouts. "Let go of Brandon and stop this right now!"

Whoever's recording zooms in on Iris's face at this precise point, just in time to capture an expression of such unadulterated, homicidal fury, my skin breaks out in goosebumps at the sight of her. Holy shit. She's practically engulfed in flames up there. It's heartbreaking to see. I genuinely feel terrible for her.

But I'd be lying if I didn't admit she's also hot as hell. Add Iris Benedetto looking like a murderous maniac to my list of kinks.

There's a flurry of chaotic shouting in the church, and in the midst of that, Iris defiantly holds up the phone to the crowd, like she's showing them a photo or video. I can't make out her screen, unfortunately, but whatever's on it makes a woman in the front row scream like she's been stabbed in the heart.

"How dare you bring that filth into the House of Lord!" the officiant shouts. "John, get your disgrace of a daughter out of here."

*Iris is the disgrace—not her cheating, lying, dick-pic-sending fiancé? That's rich.*

I've no sooner had the thought when one of the feisty bridesmaids shouts exactly what I'm thinking, in so many words, while the older man in a suit—Iris's father, obviously—shouts, "The only disgrace is what Brandon did to my beautiful, kindhearted daughter!"

Iris shoots a look of gratitude at her father before shouting to the crowd, "If you're one of Brandon's clients, check your bank records! There are weird bank notifications on this phone, too!"

"She's mentally unstable!" the groom shouts, pointing frantically at Iris. "She's having a mental breakdown, just like her mother did!"

Oh, shit. Iris's father loses it. With the other two guys still holding onto the groom, he stomps over to him and punches the bastard in the face, at which point pure mayhem ensues. I shouldn't do it, since I'm genuinely heartbroken for Iris, but I can't help laughing at the chaotic scene unfolding before me. No wonder this shit is going viral. It's impossible to look away.

"Screenshots of everything have been posted to my Instagram!" a bridesmaid shouts, as she and another two bridesmaids lead a sobbing Iris toward a side door. "Check it out before it gets deleted!"

With her bridesmaids flanking her, Iris shouts, "Anyone who supports me, come to the reception to celebrate me *not* becoming Mrs. Brandon Gladstone today!"

"I never wanted to marry you!" the groom screams back. His cheek is bright red from the punch he took. His eyes are wild. "My parents made me propose to you, but who would *want* to marry a frigid bitch like you?"

Iris was just about to walk through that side door when the groom dropped his final bomb. But now, without warning, she whirls around and sprints at full speed toward the groom, screaming with furious rage and flailing both arms. Luckily for the groom, one of the groomsmen intercepts Iris's rampage. He picks her up, kicking and screaming, literally, and physically drags her toward the side door again.

"Don't you dare get on that flight tomorrow!" Iris shouts to the groom. "*I'm* going on our honeymoon by myself to try to heal from all the lies you've told me!" She grips the doorframe, halting the groomsman's exit long enough to scream at the top of her lungs, "And when I get to Hawaii, guess what this 'frigid bitch' is gonna do, Brandon? She's going to get herself 'railed' and her insides 'scrambled' by some random hot stranger— someone who actually knows what he's doing in bed, unlike you, so I can finally—"

Iris doesn't get to finish her sentence before the groomsman wrangling her successfully loosens her grip on the doorframe and yanks her out the side door.

For several seconds, chaos reigns in the chapel. Until, finally, the screen goes black and the video ends.

"Holy shit," I whisper, looking up from my phone in a daze. No wonder Iris needed so much sleep last night. Mere hours before she crashed into that bathroom, she got provoked into flying into a homicidal rage, mere hours after getting her poor heart shattered into a million tiny pieces.

# CHAPTER 10
## Roman

*Damn.*

I'm still in a daze after watching that crazy video, despite sitting here staring at the ocean for a solid fifteen minutes. I know I've only known Iris for mere hours, but from what I've seen of her, I never would have guessed she was capable of that kind of fury. If that groomsman hadn't intercepted her, Iris very well might have murdered that piece-of-shit groom. It was quite a sight to see her engulfed in proverbial flames like that—equal parts heartbreaking and impressive.

I've witnessed this exact same kind of duality before. Countless times. So, I really shouldn't be surprised. Oftentimes, the most mild-mannered, quiet guys off the field are the craziest sons of bitches on it. I'm guessing that wedding was Iris's game day—her Super Bowl—and when the game was on the line, she left it all out on the field. I can respect that. Frankly, I wish a couple slackers on the Crusaders played as hard as Iris did in that video. If they did, I'd have a Super Bowl ring on my finger now.

My phone rings with a call from Cameron.

"Hey," I answer with a sigh.

"Have you seen my text about the preschool teacher?"

"Yeah, I just finished watching the video a few minutes ago."

"Why didn't you call me, right away? Are you with her now?"

"No, I'm sitting alone on the beach after a run. I needed a minute to process."

Cameron exhales with relief. "Stay away from her, Roman. You don't need her viral shitstorm splashing on you right now. Not when I'm trying to negotiate your contract."

I look out at the ocean and puff out my cheeks. "Is there really a shitstorm to splash on me, though? Iris didn't do anything wrong. Her groom did. In fact, I was pretty impressed with Iris in that video."

"Roman, she was unhinged. The entire internet is having a field day with her. That video is *everywhere*. It's all anyone is talking about."

"They're coming after *Iris*, and not the groom?"

"The groom, too. But everyone universally agrees he's a scumbag, so he's not as much fun. The lightning rod here is definitely Iris. What she said and did in a bridal gown. In a church. That thing she said at the end especially, about getting railed and scrambled—it's taking off like wildfire." He chuckles. "Oh, and the way she had to be dragged off, kicking and screaming, too. The memes are endless and savage, man. So are the comments under the video. Did you look at them?"

"No."

"Scroll through them. I'll wait."

I do as I'm told, and I'm instantly slammed with endless cruelties that make me want to commit murder, the same way Iris wanted to do in the video. *Slut. Whore. Shameless. Disgraceful. Unladylike. Trashy. Unhinged. She should kill herself out of shame. She should join her mother in hell.*

Jesus Christ. People are scary. Not to mention heartless. There are some comments praising Iris for her tenacity and courage. Also, for outing the groom's bad behavior to protect future women from him. But the positive comments are few and far between among the horrible ones.

"What a fucked-up world," I mutter. "The groom fucks anything that moves, and the world's takeaway is that Iris is a horny, shameless slut?"

"Did Iris tell you about any of this?"

"Not a thing. She said she was supposed to come to Hawaii with a friend, but the friend backed out at the last minute." I shake my head. "Poor thing. I hope she never finds out about that damned video."

"She will. It's *everywhere*. Which is why you need to stay the fuck away from her. She's a pariah, Roman. I don't want you getting sucked into the eye of her shit tornado."

"But don't you think if she finds out about that video, she's gonna need some comfort and support? She's here all alone and—"

"Roman, think with your head and not your dick. I know she's super cute and perky and you're over there with nothing to do. But you can fuck any other woman on that island this week. Please, don't choose to fuck the one who puts you at risk of getting yourself swept into her viral mania."

"Who cares?"

"The Thunderbolts might. The same kinds of people calling Iris a slut and whore and everything else buy a shit ton of football tickets and jerseys."

"Come on, Cameron. Have a heart. Who better than me to help a newbie deal with internet bullies when I've been dealing with haters on the internet, nonstop, for over a decade?"

"Roman, no. No, no, no. Don't do it. *No*."

I barely know Iris, so it's not like I owe her anything. But the thought of cutting ties with her when I get back to the bungalow pains me—especially the thought of me doing it not of my own accord, but to save myself embarrassment on the internet. Fuck the internet. And fuck the kind of people who'd attack *Iris* after seeing that video rather than cheering her on.

"Hello?" Cameron says, filling the silence.

I clear my throat. "That groom fucked around and found out, if you ask me."

"Fucking hell, Roman."

"What?"

"You already fucked her." It's a statement, not a question. Cameron knows me too well to doubt his conclusion.

"Yeah, and she's not a frigid bitch, I can tell you that." I snicker. "In the right hands—aka *mine*—that girl is a five-alarm fire."

"Jesus, Roman. What happened to waiting on the results of the background check?"

"You took too long." When Cameron grumbles, I add, "You saw her. She's sexy and cute, all at once. That's an irresistible combination."

Cameron makes a sound of extreme exasperation. "Please, tell me you had her sign an NDA, at least."

"She doesn't have a clue who I am, so why bother?"

"Roman!"

I chuckle. "Even if she eventually figures out who I am, she won't do anything with the information. She's a preschool teacher, Cam. She's not gonna sell her story for clicks."

Cameron screams, "You have the audacity to assure me, with a straight face, the unhinged, loose cannon I watched going completely nuts in that video won't do something crazy and unhinged in relation to *you* . . . simply because *you've* assured me that's the case after knowing her for mere hours?"

I sigh. "If you met her, you'd understand."

"Jesus fucking Christ."

A gentle breeze wafts off the ocean, sending a welcome coolness over the sweat clinging to my skin from my run. "Let's not forget she only flew off the handle at the end, when that asshole provoked her. What woman wouldn't fly into a rage after the shit the groom said to her? Also, how is it her father hauled off and punched the guy, but nobody's questioning his reaction? Nobody's calling him unhinged and hysterical; they're all praising him for being a good daddy."

Cameron exhales. "I'm every bit as impressed and sympathetic as you are, okay? But as your agent, it's my duty to protect you from any potential dustups while I'm working hard to get you top dollar. Please, Roman, don't see her again while you're out there. I don't care how good the sex was, there's no pussy in the world worth getting yourself involved in viral bullshit when I'm trying to convince the Thunderbolts your overall brand makes you worth two hundred million bucks."

I frown. Cameron's made some good points. But then again, he hasn't met Iris. If he met her, he'd understand she's not some kind of pariah; she's a total sweetheart. I look down at my toes burrowed into the white sand. Normally, I trust Cameron's judgment. So, why am I trying so hard to poke holes in everything he's saying?

"She's still in the bungalow," I admit. "She slept there last night. She was fast asleep when I left for my run."

"Goddammit." Cameron grunts. "Okay, well, at least, turn that lemon into lemonade, and get her to sign an NDA before you kick her out."

My spirit sinks at the thought. "Is there anything else you need to talk to me about?"

"You're gonna kick her out, right?"

"I'll decide when I get there."

"What's wrong with you? The sex couldn't have been *that* good."

"That's the thing. It was." I smirk. "It was like a portal to another dimension." I snicker with satisfaction. Without even knowing my specific assignment last night, I wound up doing exactly what Iris said in the video: I railed that woman and scrambled her insides like a champ—and in the process, wound up having the best sex of my life.

"Roman, listen to me. If someone posts a photo of you two together, everyone's going to assume *you're* the hot, random stranger Iris selected to 'rail' her."

"I am, though. So what? I'm a single man, and she's a hot, single woman in need of some TLC. No shame in that."

Cameron mutters, "Your name attached to this story would skyrocket the whole thing into another stratosphere. You know your behavior off the field drastically impacts your commercial value."

Movement in my periphery draws my attention. It's a man and woman holding hands with a kid around Maverick's age. All three are wading into the shallows of the aquamarine ocean and laughing with each passing wave. My heart pangs at the sight of them. Enough to remind me why I'm turning my life upside down. For Maverick.

"Okay," I say softly. "I'll walk away from Iris."

"Thank you."

"I won't kick her out of the bungalow, though. I'll offer her the place for the week, on my dime. It's the least I can do after what she's been through."

"Make her sign an NDA in exchange for the place."

"Would you drop the NDA thing? I'm not gonna tell Iris who I am. For the first time in a long time, I got to be with a woman without having to wonder if she only wanted to be with me because I'm Roman Maguire."

He sighs. "I'll get a new place booked for you. Do you want to fly over to Maui, since that's where Coach is staying?"

"No, he wants to play at some golf club here in Kauai."

"Okay. I'll text you the info. Thanks for listening to reason about this, Roman."

I glance at that happy family playing in the shallow waves again. I might be listening to reason about this, but that doesn't mean I'm happy about it.

# CHAPTER 11
## Roman

As I OPEN the door of the bungalow, Iris laments, "I'll never be able to leave my house again."

Shit. I quietly close the door and peek around the corner. She's lying on the couch facing away from me in the midst of a FaceTime call.

"News cycles move at the speed of light these days," one of two female faces on Iris's screen offers. The other woman on Iris's screen adds, "Give it a day or two, and the world will forget all about the viral 'Runaway Bride.'"

"The '*Horny* Runaway Bride,'" Iris says with a sniffle. "Let's not gloss over that." She sniffles again. "I can't believe the only part anyone cares about is that I said I was going get myself railed and scrambled in Hawaii. Why isn't anyone talking about Brandon being a lying, cheating piece of shit?"

"They are, honey. Lots of people are saying exactly that."

The second woman says, "I know the negative voices seem a lot louder to you, but not everyone on the internet is dragging you. Lots of people are cheering you on and calling you a badass for what you did."

Iris shakes her head. "If only I hadn't said that thing at the end about getting myself railed and scrambled. You know I was only parroting Brandon's exact words, right?"

"*We* know that, yes, but it seems that got lost in translation for anyone who hasn't pored over Brandon's phone, like we have."

Iris groans. "If Roman sees that video, I'll die of embarrassment."

I jolt at the mention of my name.

"Why?"

"If he sees it, he'll think I walked in on him in that bathroom as part of some diabolical plan."

"Was it a *plan*?" one of the women retorts. "No. But did you *manifest* that hunky man? I honestly think you did, baby."

The other one laughs. "I think maybe you're a witch."

Iris scoffs. "If I had magical powers, I assure you, a video of me at my absolute worst wouldn't be going viral."

One of the women lets out an angry grunt. "I swear, if I find out the identity of MackDaddy310, I'm going to strangle them for posting that stupid video."

"It had to be one of Brandon's fraternity brothers," the other woman says. "Or one of their plus-ones. The angle is from where they were sitting."

Iris exhales. "It doesn't matter. Identifying whoever posted it won't put the genie back in the bottle, unfortunately."

"I'm so sorry this is happening to you, honey."

Iris sniffles. "It's okay. At least I'm not Mrs. Gladstone right now. I'm trying really hard to focus on that silver lining."

"Another silver lining?" one of the women says. "You finally got to experience amazing sex for the first time. Kudos to you, Iris. Your manifestation worked like a charm."

Iris scoffs again. "If I manifested Roman, then why didn't I think to manifest that video not existing, too? Damn it! I can't let Roman see that stupid thing. Everything that happened between us unfolded in such a genuine, organic way yesterday, but that video makes it seem like I'm some kind of horny, homicidal maniac who landed in Kauai and immediately set off to find a random hot guy to rail me."

"He wouldn't think that. But if he did, why would he care, since he got some fantastic, meaningless sex out of the situation?"

I bristle at Iris's friend's word choice. Rationally, "meaningless" is an accurate descriptor for the sex that transpired last night, I suppose, and yet my body is reacting like it's been gravely insulted.

One of the women asks, "What's his last name? I'll google him."

"I don't know. I didn't ask."

"*What?* Rookie move, Iris."

"Because I'm a rookie!"

The women on the call crack up at Iris's comedic delivery, as I burst out laughing, too, without meaning to do it; but luckily, the sound of my laughter is drowned out by all three women cackling like hyenas together.

"When Roman comes back, ask if you can stay another night," one of the women says. "From what you've described, one night isn't nearly enough with a man like that."

"I can't do that, Kaylee."

"Why not? You need a place to stay, and I'm sure he wouldn't mind another night of fantastic sex."

"Fantastic sex is par for the course for a guy like him. He can get it anywhere, any time. He doesn't need lil' ol' me for that."

*No, sweetheart. The firestorm that practically burned down this bungalow last night is the rare exception, not the rule, even for a guy like me.*

"Girl, no," the same woman replies. "No matter how hot he is, scorching-hot sex like what you've described doesn't come along very often for anybody."

*Ain't that the truth.*

The other woman agrees. "Kaylee's right. I'm sorry to tell you this, but amazing sex is hard to come by, especially with someone who's also capable of carrying on an interesting conversation like Roman."

"Well, crap," Iris says. "That's terrible news. Now that I've finally experienced great sex for the first time, I don't think I can go back to living without it."

"So, ask to stay another night. Or, hell, for the whole week."

"I can't do that. At least, not without showing him the video first, which I'm not willing to do."

"Why would you have to show him the video to stay another night and fuck his brains out?"

"What if we go outside at some point—say, to the breakfast buffet at the hotel—and someone recognizes me? If they see Roman with me, they'll think he's the random, hot stranger I enlisted to have sex with me."

"Who cares if they do?"

"Roman might care."

The friend chuckles. "You're overthinking this, honey. Just ask to stay for the week, and then hunker down with him in the bungalow the whole time and enjoy an epic sex-fest."

Iris snorts. "I didn't fly all the way here to stay inside the whole time. Not even for amazing sex. Also, Roman's so nice, he'd say yes to me out of sheer pity, and I don't want to put him in that position. He's on vacation; he doesn't need to babysit some heartbroken runaway bride when he could be off having fun in paradise."

*Pity?*

*Babysit?*

I can't believe how far off the mark she is.

"So, where are you gonna go?" one of the women asks.

"I don't know yet, but I'll figure something out. There's got to be a cheap hostel or motel somewhere. God knows that's all I can afford."

"I'll send you money. I just got paid."

"No, I'll manage. Thank you, though." Iris wipes her eyes.

"I should go before Roman gets back. I want to be dressed and ready to say a quick goodbye as soon he gets here. Thank you both for telling me about the video so I didn't have to cry all by myself."

"We're so sorry this happened," one of her friends coos. "We love you so much."

"I love you, too."

"Stay off the internet this week!" the second woman calls out. "Get out there and have fun. Explore the island. Read lots of books. Take lots of naps."

"I vote she finds another hot stranger to rail her and scramble her insides."

My body zings with jealousy. *Hell to the fucking no.*

"I promise I'll have as much fun as I can this week," Iris replies. "But I'm not going to have sex with anyone else. Especially not now that I know amazing sex is rare. I'm hereby officially swearing off men for a long while."

"I didn't mean to imply Roman is your only shot at having amazing sex in your entire lifetime," one of the women says. "Look, I know you think Roman is some kind of peerless sex god among men, but since you only have Brandon to compare him to, how would you know that? Brandon set the bar really low, honey. Once you start having sex with more and more people, maybe you'll find out sex with Roman was only mediocre."

*Excuse me?*

"No, Roman's a legit sex god," Iris insists. "I don't need a basis of comparison to know that. All I need to know is he's the most gorgeous, charming man I've ever met, and I had *three* orgasms with him."

"*Three?*" both women simultaneously bellow.

"Okay, yeah, he's definitely a sex god," one of them quickly adds.

*Thank you. Fucking hell.*

Iris gasps. "Oh! I just remembered I have all those prepaid vouchers for 'adventures for two' for the week. I can do all that fun stuff by myself!"

Her friends react with enthusiasm.

"Thanks for the pep talk, ladies," Iris says. "I'd better get going before Roman gets back."

As Iris says her final goodbyes, I creep to the front door, open and close it loudly, and then stride into the room, breathing hard like I just finished my run mere minutes ago.

"Stay off the internet this entire week!" one of Iris's friends shouts, just as I appear in the living room.

Iris sees me and flushes. "Okay, bye for now." She abruptly ends the call and greets me with a bright smile. "Hey there! How was your run?"

"Good." I sit next to her. "Did you see the food I left for you?"

"I ate every bit of it. Thank you. I was famished."

"You slept a long time. How do you feel?"

"Like new. Thank you for letting me sleep. Sorry it was for so long."

"I'm glad you got what you needed." I motion to her phone. "Who were you talking to?"

"My best friends." She shifts in her seat. "They, uh, know our other friend, the one who canceled on me this week, so they wanted to make sure I'm doing okay here all by myself."

She's a terrible liar. Bright cheeks. Shifty gaze. If I keep pushing, I'm pretty sure she'll crack and tell me what's really going on. "Why did one of your friends shout 'stay off the internet this week!' before hanging up?" I playfully side-eye her. "Are you addicted to porn, Iris?"

"You caught me." She laughs. "No, my friend who said that was just reminding me to be fully present so I can thoroughly enjoy everything the island has to offer." Her chin wobbles slightly, but she quickly camouflages it with a sad little smile.

I stroke her leg and ask softly, "Have you been crying?" Her tears have dried, but her eyes and cheeks are still red, so it's believable I'd ask the question, even if I hadn't been eavesdropping.

She shakes her head. "My eyes are probably puffy from sleeping so long."

Man, she's a tougher nut to crack than expected. As I ponder my next move, there's a brief, awkward silence, which Iris fills with, "I'll get myself packed up. Thank you again, Roman. For everything." She hugs me. "I had an amazing time with you."

I'm surprised she's truly planning to leave without at least hinting about me asking her to stay longer—or, at the very least, that we should have sex another time before she heads out.

Cameron's voice pops into my head. *She's a pariah, Roman. Stay away from her, Roman.* But the words that tumble out of my mouth don't align with Cameron's instructions. "Stay here for the week," I blurt. "Stay with me."

*Oops.* In deference to Cameron, I planned to say *"on* me." Not *"with* me." As in, "You can stay here on my dime, while I leave and find somewhere else." But I guess my dick intervened and blocked the message from my brain to my mouth.

Iris's cheeks burst with color. "I would love to stay here with you." She pauses. "But I can't."

"Can't or don't want to? Come on, Iris, I'm not doing anything this week, except playing golf on Friday. As far as I'm concerned, there's no good reason for you to go somewhere else, unless that's what you genuinely want."

Iris swallows hard. "No, I'd really, really like to stay here with you, but—"

"Great. Then it's settled."

"But I really shouldn't. At least, not without showing you something first—something that might make you decide to revoke your invitation in record time."

# CHAPTER 12
## Iris

A WARM, GENTLE breeze wafts over me, and I'm hit with the fragrances of tropical flowers and sea salt. I couldn't stand to be in the bungalow as Roman watches the video, so I cued it up and staggered out here onto the patio to stare at the ocean and pray Roman won't retract his invitation for me to stay.

Movement to my left draws my attention, and when I turn to look, Roman is walking toward me with two glasses of champagne in his hands and a lopsided grin on his handsome face.

"Good for you," he says. "You sexy little baddie."

My jaw nearly clanks onto my lap. Of all the reactions I was anticipating, that wasn't one of them. "You're not totally freaked out?"

As he sits, Roman pulls a face like that's a preposterous thought. "Not at all. I'm impressed and turned on."

"*Turned on?*" I repeat, not sure I heard him correctly.

"There's nothing hotter than a woman standing up for herself." He places the two champagne glasses on a small table. "I'm sorry for what you've been through, but I'm proud of you for taking him down."

"Brandon's got everyone convinced he walks on water, so I wanted to unmask him."

"Mission accomplished." He places his large palm on my bare thigh, and his hand feels warm and comforting. "You've got nothing to be ashamed of, Iris. Your ex was a shit stain on the underpants of life, and you gave him exactly what he deserved. What you did took guts, and anyone who says any differently can eat a bag of dicks."

I can't believe he's not the least bit weirded out that I was supposed to get married mere days ago. Or, at least, put off by the raunchy thing I said at the end of the video about getting myself railed and scrambled. "Did you watch the whole thing?"

"I sure did. I liked the way you left it all out on the field, baby. Go big or go home, right?"

I'm floored. He's so unbothered by it all. "That thing I said at very end? I was parroting the exact language my ex used in some dirty texts to other women. I know this might be hard to believe, but I didn't come here planning to have sex with a random stranger."

"So what if you did?"

My lips part in surprise. "No, I . . . No shade to anyone with an agenda like that. I just . . . that's not me. I know it looks like it is, given what I said in the video and how things went down between us. But I want you to know everything that happened between us occurred naturally and not according to any master plan."

Plainly, he doesn't care either way. "If it was your master plan, then I was more than happy to be of service. If not, then same answer."

I close my eyes. "I can't believe the raunchy stuff I said in a church."

Roman chuckles. "That was my favorite part. Well, that and when you sprinted at the groom like you were going to murder him and had to be physically dragged away, kicking and screaming."

I open my eyes again. When I see Roman's broad smile, I can't help returning the gesture. "I've never done anything like that in my life. I don't know what possessed me."

"I do. He pushed you too far, and you snapped. It happens to the best of us." With a wink, he hands me one of the champagne glasses and raises the other. "To you, Iris. To your balls of steel, your heart of gold, and the debut of your sexy, murderous alter ego."

I bite my lower lip. "To you, too. To your hospitality, your impressive skills in the bedroom, and your kindhearted reaction to the video. Thank you for all of it, Roman."

I clink Roman's glass and we both take long sips of champagne. Just this fast, I'm already feeling like the weight of the world has been lifted off me, thanks to Roman's amazing reaction. So much so, I'm feeling emboldened to put myself out there.

"So, hey, no pressure," I begin tentatively. "But I have quite a few prepaid vouchers for activities for two this week. Stuff like snorkeling, parasailing, ATVing." My heart is hammering. I've never asked a man out on a date before. "I can't get my money back, so would you like to do any of those activities with me? The snorkel cruise is this afternoon, if that sounds fun to you."

Roman's forehead creases in a way that makes my spirit sink. Shoot. I shouldn't have asked him out. Clearly, I've overstepped the boundaries of whatever this vacation fling is going to be. Sex with a viral punching bag is one thing, but going on elaborate dates together out in public would be something else entirely. *Stupid, Iris.*

"Is today's snorkeling trip a group activity?" Roman asks. "You know, with a bunch of strangers?"

I nod, feeling flushed and disheartened. "Yeah, as I understand it, they take a big group out on a boat and then everyone snorkels in the same general area." My cheeks are hot. My heart is hammering. Quickly, I add, "I shouldn't have mentioned it. Let's pretend I didn't. The last thing you need is to be seen out in public with the 'Horny Runaway Bride.'"

Roman rolls his eyes. "That's not it, Iris. I just don't like being herded around like cattle when I'm on vacation. I prefer a bit more elbow room and privacy." He slides his fingertip underneath my downturned chin and raises my face to his. "What I'm saying is I'd rather book some *private* dates for us this week than use your vouchers for group activities."

*Dates?* Did I mishear that word or did Roman just now say he wants to take me out—multiple times—this coming week? "You're sure you wouldn't be too embarrassed to be seen with me in public?"

"I'd be proud to be seen with you."

My shoulders relax. "My excursions are already paid for, though."

"Don't worry about that. Everything will be my treat."

"Are you sure?"

"I am." He slides his palm across my bare thigh, causing my clit to pulse and zing. "Is it settled, then? You're staying here this whole week with me, and I'm going to show you a great time by day and night?"

I can barely breathe. "That sounds wonderful. If you're sure."

"I am. Now, come with me, my hot and homicidal little runaway bride. It feels like I've waited ten lifetimes to get inside you again. It's high time for round two."

# CHAPTER 13
## Roman

I'M STILL SWEATY from my run on the beach, so I decide to multitask and fuck Iris in the shower. She's clearly been traumatized by that viral video, fresh on the heels of being traumatized by her ex, so I'm hoping a shower might serve as a baptism of sorts for her. When Iris emerges from the hot water, I want her feeling relaxed, recharged, and renewed—and ready to jump into a week of fun and fuckery with a clean slate.

I place a condom on the bathroom counter for easy access and turn on the hot water. Pre-cum is already beading on my hard cock. My blood feels like it's simmering. Everything about this woman turns me on, but now that I know I'm the first guy to get her off, based on what I overheard of that phone call between Iris and her friends, I'm even more ravenous for her than the first time around.

We're both naked now. Steam is filling the bathroom.

I lead Iris into the blue-tiled shower and position her under the hot stream of water. As Iris gets pelted on her neck and shoulders, I run my palms over her slick, wet skin and kiss her deeply, letting the tip of my hard cock brush against her belly as my mouth devours hers. As our kiss intensifies, I stroke between her legs—and then, massage her hard, swollen clit around and around—until soon, as easy as pie, she's coming against my fingers with a loud, sexy growl.

When she comes down from her release, I guide one of her feet to rest on a tile bench, fully opening her pussy to me. And then, as hot water rakes over my back, I kneel down and devour Iris Benedetto till she's screaming my name and coming so hard against my hungry lips, I'm momentarily disoriented and dizzy with lust.

My breathing ragged, I grab the condom from the sink's ledge like a lifeline and furiously roll it on. When I return to Iris in the shower, I'm a man possessed. I smash her into the tile wall and plunge myself inside her from behind and fuck her so hard, I can't help growling with every beastly thrust.

As my pleasure spirals higher and higher, I reach around and finger her clit; the effect on her is immediate and obvious—she's unleashed.

"Oh, God, Roman," she chokes out. "Yes, yes, yes."

It takes all my willpower, but when Iris's body clamps tightly around my cock—the sensation that signals an impending orgasm—I force myself to pull out so I won't come with her, since I want to keep going for as long as possible. And thank God for that, because when Iris has an orgasm mere seconds later, it's a screaming, writhing avalanche of pleasure my body wouldn't have been able to withstand—one that sends her entire body quaking like she's having a seizure.

As Iris's orgasm fades, she turns around to face me, throws her arms around my neck, and devours my lips. As we make out passionately under the raining water of the shower, I grab her ass and pull her up, and she slams herself onto my straining cock and rides me like the world is ending tomorrow. As we fuck, Iris greedily clutches my shoulders, neck, and face. She nips at my jawline and digs her fingernails into my flesh and begs me not to stop.

"Never stop," she grits out. "Fuck me forever."

I wish. But since I'm only a man, I fuck her till I'm delirious. Till I'm drowning in as much lust and euphoria as the hot water pelting my face. I can't remember the last time I felt this unencumbered and free. Over the years, I've shamelessly enjoyed the perks of fame more than I care to admit. I've fucked my share of star fuckers and fame whores, just because I was bored and they were there. But fucking Iris is a new species of fun for me. I'm making her quiver and shudder and quake *without* the benefit of my name and the reputation that precedes me. It's a rare gift.

Out of nowhere, Iris stiffens in my arms and lets out a keening howl that's so primal and raw, so fucking gritty and animalistic, I can't stop myself from coming in response to it. As waves of bliss throttle me, Iris's intimate muscles begin squeezing and rippling around me in concert. And I swear, for a long moment, I'm convinced I'm going to literally die of pleasure. Not that I'd complain.

As my euphoria fades, I slide Iris down my body. When she's back to standing on her own two feet, I take her pretty face in my palms. "Fuck your ex," I grit out. "And fuck the internet. This week is going to be about forgetting everything and everyone and having a blast, just you and me. Okay?" When Iris nods furiously, I add, "For one glorious week, baby, we're going to make our own kind of paradise."

# CHAPTER 14
## Roman

I open the restaurant door for Iris with a wink. "After you."

After a morning helicopter tour of the island, I'm taking Iris to lunch at a restaurant recommended by our pilot—one he called a "hidden gem."

"So chivalrous," Iris replies flirtatiously, batting her eyelashes as she glides into the restaurant. Amazingly, it already feels like her factory settings have been reset. Indeed, the happy, relaxed woman practically floating past me bears little resemblance to the frazzled woman on the verge of a nervous breakdown who crashed into that bathroom yesterday.

The hostess smiles as we approach. "Do you have a reservation, sir?"

"For two, yes. I asked for a quiet table with an ocean view in the back. The name is Roman."

Iris doesn't know my last name, and I'd like to keep it that way. That's why, when I booked today's helicopter tour, I told the guy on the phone I'd throw in a thousand-dollar tip for the whole staff to split, as long as nobody uttered my last name today or asked me about football.

The tactic worked. Nobody called me anything but "sir" all morning long, and nobody said a single word about football or the Crusaders, either. Will my luck run out at some point this week? Probably, given that I'm planning to go out in public with Iris quite a bit. But I'm having so much fun being Roman the Gym Owner from Delaware, I'm determined to at least try to keep my last name out of Iris's ears for as long as possible.

"Yes, sir," the restaurant hostess chirps, looking up from her screen. "I've got a perfect table for you. Right this way."

As we follow the woman toward our table, Iris puts her head down and raises her palm to her face like she's a movie star trying to avoid paparazzi. She's so damned cute. I love that she has no idea the supposed gym owner walking behind her is exponentially more likely to be recognized than a viral flavor of the week.

We make it to our table in the back without anyone giving us a second glance. To my relief, our table is exactly as described to me on the phone: tucked away in a quiet, secluded corner with a fabulous view of the glittering sea.

"This is so romantic, Roman," Iris gushes as I pull back her chair. "You've pulled out all the stops today."

"I figured you could use a little TLC." I take a seat across from her. "The fish here is supposed to be amazing, if you like fish."

"I do, and I'm hungry."

We look down at our menus, but we both keep peeking over the tops of them to grin at each other like teenagers.

"Are you always this romantic?" Iris asks.

I'm surprised by the notion, because I don't consider myself a romantic person in the slightest. Back home, I don't have the time or inclination to invest in romance. I'm way too busy and focused on my job to allow that sort of distraction into my life. But here with Iris, I'm feeling uncharacteristically inspired to play the part of her white knight. It's only one week of my life, after all, and her excitement is infectious.

"I'm not normally as romantic as this," I confess with a smile. "I don't know what's come over me."

"Well, I'm grateful for whatever it is." She lowers her menu. "Please, don't worry that I'm misunderstanding the nature of the situation here, simply because I used the word 'romantic.' Despite all the swooning I've been doing today, I promise I'm crystal clear this is a no-strings fling."

I bite back a chuckle. "Thanks for clearing that up."

Iris blushes. "What's funny?"

"Nothing. You're just cute."

"Shoot. Do people in the midst of flinging not talk about the fling being a fling? Is that what's funny?"

I can't keep my wide grin at bay. "It's normally just kind of assumed a fling is a fling, I think. But that's okay. No harm in making it clear."

She laughs and raises her menu again. "I wish I had a handbook or something. The learning curve on this is pretty steep."

An amused smile spreads across my face. "Nah. You're doing great."

The waitress arrives, and after some back-and-forth, we order cocktails and three appetizers and agree she should come back later to take our orders for the main course.

When we're alone again, Iris and I chat about the hiking trail I'm taking her to this afternoon. But eventually, when that topic runs its course, I ask if she's always wanted to be a teacher.

"I've always dreamed of working with kids," she replies. "But not necessarily teaching in a classroom. Growing up, my best friend's family owned a horse ranch near Orchard Blossom, and I worked there every summer and on weekends, mostly giving trail rides and riding lessons to kids. That's when I started dreaming about one day combining my two passions—horses and kids—as an actual career."

"In what way?"

"One day, I'd love to provide equine therapy to kids."

I ask her to explain what that means, and it turns out

equine therapy is exactly what the name suggests: therapy administered through the care and/or riding of horses.

"Why not get a job in equine therapy now? You light up when you talk about it. Life is short."

"It's hard to break into the field, and I've already got a great job I love that pays the bills. Maybe someday. I'm still in my twenties, so I figure I've still got lots of time to work my way toward that goal."

"Of course you do."

The waitress returns with our cocktails and appetizers, and we dig in.

"What about you?" Iris asks. "Do you have any 'maybe someday' dreams you're still chasing, or is the gym your ultimate dream fulfilled?"

*Shit.* It was one thing to tell a simple lie about my profession to preserve my anonymity with a one-night stand I thought I'd never see again; but the more time I spend with this woman, the more I'm liking her as a person, which, in turn, makes lying to her harder and harder.

"I've still got some dreams I'm chasing. When a person stops dreaming, they might as well be dead. In my book, anyway."

"I agree completely." Iris looks at me expectantly, like she's waiting on me to elaborate on my big dreams. When I don't, she shifts in her seat and says, "Did you always want to own a gym and train athletes?"

*Fuck.* "No, I just kind of fell into it." I clear my throat. "My biggest dream growing up, like every other kid who played football, was to play in the NFL and win the Super Bowl."

Iris juts her lip in sympathy. "I'm sorry little Roman didn't get to experience that. But at least you got to play in college, right? That must have been pretty close to the same thing for your inner child."

I nod my agreement, feeling desperate to end this line of conversation—even though, in reality, as any NFL football player would undoubtedly agree, playing college ball doesn't compare to being in the pros and couldn't possibly fulfill any player's dream of winning a Super Bowl. I mean, the Super Bowl thing is supposition on my part, due to my own three Super Bowl losses. But Marco's won the Big Game, the lucky bastard, and I know for a fact my cousin feels like that win was the pinnacle of his long and storied career.

The waitress arrives to take the rest of our order, interrupting the current topic of conversation, thankfully. When she leaves, Iris asks, "Were you voted prom king in high school, by any chance?"

"Homecoming king. Why do you ask?"

She's got a sparkle in her blue eyes. "You played football in college for a well-known school, so I figure you must have been a superstar player at a big high school. You give off extreme big-man-on-campus energy, and I'm dying to know if I'm right."

I laugh. "Pretty close."

"That's how it always goes in movies: The star football player gets voted homecoming or prom king—although in movies, it's always the star quarterback, not the star tight end, and . . ."

She's still talking, but I'm too freaked out by her sixth sense to hear the rest. As Iris's mouth moves, I take a drink of my water and pretend to listen while trying to snuff out the pangs of guilt I'm feeling for lying.

"What about you?" I ask, when I'm able to regain my composure and it's clear Iris has finished talking. "Were you part of this Hollywood script in high school, too?"

Iris snorts adorably. "Not even close. My high school was so small, we didn't even have a football team or dances, let alone kings and queens."

"*No dances?*" I ask, like it's a mortal sin. "How are the kids supposed to know who's crushing on who, then?"

"We had festivals where we figured that out. Not the same thing, but close enough."

"Not close enough if you ask the kids, I'm sure."

Iris laughs. "That's life in a small town for you. We took what we could get."

"You must have had culture shock when you went off to UCLA."

"Oh my gosh. In the best possible way, though. I loved everything about my new, big school. Also, about LA in general."

My stomach clenches at her mention of LA, even though I know I'm the one who brought up UCLA. I've been talking to Cameron so much about wanting to make Los Angeles my new home base, I'm worried my face is now somehow giving me away.

"You certainly can't beat the weather in LA," I say vaguely, before taking a long sip of my drink.

"Thanks to the good year-round weather," she says, "there's always something fun to do. I especially loved going to the beach when I lived there."

I slide an oyster down my throat, telling myself to take a chill pill. "So, why'd you move to Denver instead of staying in LA after graduation?"

"My ex is from Denver. He wanted to work for his father's insurance firm, and since I didn't have a job lined up at the time, I followed him there."

It's plain to see the topic is taking the sparkle out of Iris's blue eyes, so I change the subject. "The great news is, now that you're single, you can move anywhere you want."

Iris nods. "My two best friends from college stayed in LA after graduation, so that's definitely a 'maybe someday' kind of place for me. For now, though, I love my job in Denver, so I'm going to keep working hard and saving money for a possible move one day."

Why is my heart sinking? Why do I care if my fun little vacation fling will live in Denver or LA or Timbuktu when she goes back to reality? I need to slow my roll and stop assuming it's a done deal I'll wind up in LA. For all I know, Cameron won't be able to get what I'm worth there and I'll wind up in Minnesota or Tampa or God-knows-where.

Also, even if I do wind up in LA, I wouldn't have time for a romantic relationship with Iris or anyone else. I'd have a new system to learn. New teammates to bond with. And most of all, my son within driving distance for the first time in his young life.

"What about you?" Iris asks, chomping on a crab cake. "Do you like living in Delaware? Is that your final destination, you think?"

*Fuck, fuck, fuck.* Delaware was a necessary lie, since even my first name, standing alone, is synonymous with Baltimore and the Crusaders. Surely, if I'd told the truth, Iris could google "Roman" and "Baltimore," and my name, face, and bio would pop right up. Just because the lie was necessary, however, doesn't mean I'm not feeling guilty about telling it.

"I've actually been thinking about moving," I admit. "Not sure where yet. That's TBD."

"Well, like you said, you certainly can't beat the weather in Southern California. But the cost of living is really high, so many not."

"Maybe. Yeah, I've still got some moving parts to figure out."

Iris pauses, apparently expecting me to provide further details. When I don't, she picks up her drink, and says, "If you do wind up moving, would you relocate your gym or open another location?"

Holy hell. My web of lies is becoming exhausting. "Not sure yet."

Iris pauses again. And when I don't say more, she takes a sip of her drink and murmurs, "Well, I hope all the moving parts work out for you, Roman. Exactly as you're hoping."

# CHAPTER 15
## Iris

AFTER OUR ROMANTIC lunch date, Roman and I quickly change into hiking gear in the restaurant bathroom before heading across the street to a small grocery store. The plan is to pick up a few snacks and sports drinks for today's next adventure: a two-hour-round-trip hike that supposedly boasts a "must-see" waterfall and jaw-dropping ocean views at its turn-around point.

According to Roman, who's done the hike before, it isn't well-known by tourists. It's more of a local's thing. So, we likely won't encounter too many hikers on the trail. That's a plus. Nobody's recognized me thus far today, and I'd like to keep it that way. I think it was so sweet of Roman to try to keep me as incognito as possibly today during our date.

"You're gonna love this hike," Roman says, taking my hand as we head toward the market. "It's one of my favorite spots on Earth." Over lunch, Roman told me about how he and some friends did this same hike a few years ago, and his obvious excitement to share it with me sent butterflies into my belly. I can't believe how much effort, time, and money Roman is putting into our amazing first date. The helicopter tour alone would have been the best date of my life—but on top of that, he also treated me to a romantic meal, and now he's taking me to one of his favorite spots on Earth, too?

*Why?*

The question pops into my head, unbidden.

*Why* is Roman pulling out all the stops like this? He's a gym owner, after all—probably not a gazillionaire. So, why spend this much money and time on a nobody he'll never see again after this week? I'm sure the dangling carrot of easy sex probably has something to do with it—and, of course, I'm more than happy to supply the easy sex, if that's all that's motivating him. But I have to think this gorgeous, charming, charismatic man could get sex any time he wants from every gorgeous woman he meets. *So why me?*

I'm not trying to look a gift horse in the mouth. Whatever's prompting Roman to act like my very own Prince Charming, I'm grateful for it. After less than a full day, I've already nearly forgotten about my troubles. But still, being grateful for something doesn't mean I'm not also confused about Roman's motivations.

We make it to the market and immediately start perusing an assortment of protein bars and trail mixes on a front rack. But before we've made any selections, a woman in her mid-forties or so practically hurls herself at Roman and screams, "Oh my gosh! Is it really you? You're my all-time favorite player, Roman!"

As the woman grips Roman's broad shoulder with excitement, he visibly stiffens. With his mouth tight and his dark eyes flickering to me, he says, "You want a selfie? Let's go over there." He gestures toward the other side of the store. "The lighting is better there."

"Thank you, Roman!"

As Roman briskly guides the woman away, he calls out to me, "Pick out a bunch of snacks for us and I'll be right back."

"My husband is going to be so jealous I met you," the

woman says breathlessly, as Roman guides her away. "He just went back to the hotel for a nap, and he's a huge Cru—"

"What's your name?" Roman asks abruptly, interrupting the woman. It's the last thing I'm able to hear of the conversation before the pair is out of earshot across the store.

I stand frozen for a long moment, watching Roman interacting with the woman with fascination. Did she attend the University of Texas, just like Roman? She must have, given that she said Roman is her favorite player. She looks to be at least ten years older than Roman, though, so she clearly didn't attend UT Austin at the same time as him. But then again, lots of people continue supporting their alma mater's sports teams long after graduation. My father still religiously watches his old college teams to this day, despite him attending school decades ago.

The cashier leaves her post to take a selfie with Roman, too, and now I'm deeply confused. Did the cashier go to UT Austin, too, or is she simply hopping on the first woman's bandwagon after hearing her gush about Roman being her favorite player? Roman is so freaking handsome, I wouldn't be surprised if the cashier simply wanted a photo with a hot guy to show her besties. *Look at this insanely hot guy who wandered into the store today!*

I strain to hear snippets of the trio's conversation, but I can only clock Roman smiling while chatting with the ladies, their words indecipherable from here.

After a few minutes, Roman side-hugs each woman before striding back to me in front of the snack rack. "Sorry about that. Did you decide on snacks?"

"Did that first woman go to UT Austin?"

Roman's jaw muscles pulse. "Possibly."

"Why'd the cashier want a photo with you, too?"

"She was just being nice, I guess. Should we pick out our snacks?"

"Did that woman's husband row on the crew team at UT?"

Roman scrunches his brow, looking deeply confused.

"She said her husband was on crew as you two walked away."

Understanding dawns on Roman. "Oh. No. I don't know what she said about that. I wasn't really listening." Roman's Adam's apple bobs as he grabs a bunch of protein bars and trail mix packs off the rack. "We should get some sports drinks." With that, he beelines to a bank of refrigerators at the far back of the store.

When I get to the refrigerated section, Roman's already holding up four different flavors to me for approval. "Good with you?"

"Great."

"Do you want anything else?"

"I don't think so. I'm still stuffed from lunch."

"Me, too." And off he goes toward the front of the store, presumably to pay for everything in his hands.

When I catch up to Roman this time, I'm expecting to find him laying down his purchases on the counter. To my surprise, however, I locate Roman just in time to witness him holding up his bounty, throwing down two hundred-dollar bills without stopping, and then calling over his shoulder, "Keep the change, Katie!"

"Thank you so much, Roman!" the cashier calls back. "*Wow!*"

Roman barrels outside, rather than stopping to open the door for me like he's been doing all morning. Thanks to his long, determined strides, coupled with my much shorter legs, I have to sprint to catch up before settling into a healthy jog alongside him.

My what-the-fuck-o-meter is screaming at me. Roman was nothing but polite and kind to both women in that store, so it's not like I'm wondering if I'm spending the day with an epic asshole who's only pretending to be a nice person around me. But still, that whole interaction felt off, like Roman couldn't get out of there fast enough. Was he worried the women might recognize me from the viral video? That's got to be it! Multiple times today, I've expressed anxiety about someone recognizing me, so I bet he was trying to protect me from embarrassment in there. The realization makes me swoon even harder. He's so thoughtful.

"Were you worried someone was going to recognize me in there?" I ask, keeping pace with Roman as he moves gracefully toward his rental car.

"That didn't cross my mind, Iris. I just don't want to chat with strangers while on a date with you."

I'm not sure if I believe the video didn't cross Roman's mind. In fact, I'd bet he's not admitting his true thought process to keep me from feeling embarrassed or anxious.

"How'd you know the cashier's name?"

"Hmm?"

"You called her Katie on the way out."

"She told me her name while we were taking a photo. I make it a habit to immediately use someone's name after they've supplied it to me. That's the kind of thing people remember, you know?"

I mean, he's not wrong. But I've never heard anyone express name recall with strangers as a conscious habit they've cultivated. Then again, I've never met a gym owner with high-profile clients before, so I bet Roman's got lots of habits and tricks that have helped him succeed in his career.

Finally, we reach Roman's car. As he reaches into his backpack for the keys, I say, "I was impressed that woman remembered you from your college playing days. You must have been a great player for her to remember you after all this time."

Roman opens and closes his mouth, but in the end, he remains silent while stuffing our snacks and drinks into his pack. As he does that, I get situated into the passenger seat of his car, and after a moment, Roman slides into the driver's seat and silently pulls the car onto the road.

I can tell Roman's feeling humble about his playing days. Which means I should let it go. But I can't seem to stop myself from probing further. "Did you do something particularly memorable on the field in college?" It's either that or the woman in the market recognized Roman solely based on his highly memorable face. Given how gorgeous Roman is, I don't think option number two is a stretch. "What's up, Roman? Come on. After everything I've been through, I can't handle any more secrets."

Roman inhales a deep breath. "I didn't ask her why she said I'm her favorite player. I have no idea why she said that." That's all I'm going to get apparently, much to my chagrin. He's stopped talking.

Over the years with Brandon, I admit I sometimes fantasized what it'd be like to be in a relationship with a classic "strong, silent type," instead of with a chatty guy who always had something to say on every topic. Well, now that I'm sitting next to one, I can honestly report: As sexy and mysterious as the type might be, they're also a tad bit frustrating.

In the silence, an idea slams into me. What if Roman was a star player in college, someone who was a shoo-in to go to the NFL, but his big dreams got snatched away by an injury? When Roman was explaining the draft to me yesterday, he said injuries can play a big part in a player's ultimate journey in the NFL. Did he base that not only on his clients' experiences but also on his own?

That would explain Roman's reluctance to talk about his college playing days. Also, why he wanted to get the hell out of that store and doesn't want to talk about it now. Because the whole situation is still too raw and painful for him to talk about. Whenever random, well-meaning people in Orchard Blossom ask me how I'm coping without my mother, I never want to talk with them about her, and certainly not about the circumstances of her self-inflicted death, so I can definitely relate to the urge to shut down and quickly move the conversation along.

"Would you mind pulling up the name of the trailhead?" Roman asks, motioning to my phone in the cup holder. "As I recall, the trailhead is a blink-and-you-miss-it kind of thing."

I salute. "You've got it, Pilot."

Roman tells me the name of the hike, and I plug it into my navigation app.

"How close are we, Copilot?"

"One point two miles."

"Keep an eye out, okay?"

"I'm on it." Am I, though? As long as I've got my phone out and Roman's laser-focused on the road, now seems like a perfect chance to search the internet using every clue I've learned thus far about Roman.

I peek at my handsome driver again, and when I'm certain he's not paying attention to me, I input everything I know: *Roman, University of Texas, Austin, tight end, football player, gym owner, Delaware.* To my disappointment, though, my search brings up some random guy named Chad Roman—a strawberry-blond dude with a goatee and light eyes who bears zero resemblance to the dark-haired, dark-eyed Adonis sitting next to me.

No shade to Chad Roman, though. Age thirty-seven. He seems like a successful guy. Apparently, he was a phenom at UT Austin who then went on to become a superstar, longtime tight end for the Minnesota Marauders, until a knee injury sadly forced him into retirement two seasons ago.

Undeterred, I search the same list of terms again, except adding "injury" and "injured," in case my hunch about Roman is correct, but my addition doesn't change the ultimate result. *Chad Roman, Chad Roman, Chad Roman.* Every link, article, and photo is about *that* particular tight end from UT Austin.

Did nobody write about Roman the Tight End for UT Austin back in the day, or has too much time passed for Roman's write-ups to remain anywhere near the top of the internet slush pile—at least, without me knowing Roman's last name?

I suppose it makes sense Chad Roman is the only one coming up. He's the player who went on to get drafted into the NFL, not Roman. He's the one who then became a superstar player in the league, while Roman faded into football obscurity and opened his gym. The thought makes my heart pang for Roman. No wonder he doesn't want to talk about his college playing days. For a kid who grew up dreaming of NFL glory, not making it into the pros, for whatever reason, must have been a tough pill to swallow.

"Hey, Copilot," Roman says. "Is that the trailhead?"

I jerk my gaze up from my phone to find Roman slowing the car and pointing to an almost imperceptible clearing in the thick rainforest alongside the highway.

As the car passes the spot Roman's indicating, I quickly swipe from my browser to my navigation app before sheepishly confirming, "Yeah, that was it. Oops."

To my relief, Roman chuckles. "You had *one* job, Copilot."

"Sorry, Pilot. My mind wandered for a minute there."

Roman pats my thigh. "No worries, sweetheart. Let your mind wander as much as you need."

My shoulders soften. *Sweetheart.* Brandon wouldn't have reacted like that if I'd messed up in the same way. He'd have chastised me for getting distracted after he'd expressly told me to pay attention.

A short distance from the trailhead, Roman parks the car, and when we exit the vehicle, he doesn't hesitate to peel off his shirt and shove it into his backpack, along with our supplies.

*My God, he looks like a god among men.* "If you're going to hike shirtless," I say, trying not to ogle him, "let me spray you with bug spray and sunscreen."

Roman snickers. "Are you a preschool teacher, by any chance?"

"Safety first," I chirp with my index finger raised, and Roman hoots with laughter.

I spray him down carefully, admiring my canvas as I do, and Roman returns the favor. But as he rubs everything into my skin, he leans into my ear and murmurs, "I hope you're happy, you sadist. I'll be starting the hike with a big ol' boner, thanks to you."

I giggle. "You won't be alone. I've got my own version of a boner."

Roman walks me two steps backward and gently pushes me against his car before pressing his hard-on into me. With a wicked grin, he says, "What can I say? I'm hot for teacher." With that, he leans in and kisses me, and we make out against the car for several delightful minutes. When it's obvious he's gotten me extremely hot and bothered, Roman slides his hand into my shorts and fingers me so deliciously, I wind up having an orgasm against the car, just as a random vehicle zips past us on the highway.

"*Shoot*," I blurt, as the car disappears down the road. "We need to be more careful. What if they recognized me?"

Roman laughs. "They were going fifty miles per hour, at least. If they saw anything, it was the blur of a horny couple kissing on the side of the road."

I exhale. "Still, I can't risk going viral again. Never again. I need to stay out of the limelight, no matter what."

Roman's smile fades. He touches my hair. "I'm sorry. I'll be much more careful from now on."

"Thank you." I bite my lip. "Also, thank you for that orgasm. That was a first for me—an orgasm in the wild." I point to the huge bulge straining behind the fabric of Roman's shorts. "What about that bad boy? Do you want to crawl into the back seat and let me take care of that for you?" I waggle my eyebrows to entice him.

Roman's dark eyes blaze as he drags his teeth over his lower lip. "It pains me to say this, but no. You're right. We should be more careful than that." He waggles his eyebrows the way I did a moment ago. "But this is a rain check, okay? I'll gladly let you 'take care of this bad boy' in the privacy of the bungalow tonight."

# CHAPTER 16
## Iris

"This hike is incredible." I have to raise my voice to be heard above the crashing of the nearby waterfall. Also, talking is hard when you're out of breath from hiking.

"I didn't overpromise?"

"Not at all." I can't believe Roman's not out of breath in the slightest. Is he even human?

Roman stops walking, so I do, too. Thank God.

"I think I remember the best viewpoint being somewhere up there," he says, gesturing toward a nearby grouping of boulders—a configuration that looks awfully steep and slippery to me.

"That looks kind of treacherous," I say warily. "I'm wearing gym shoes, not top-of-the-line hiking boots with thick tread like you." Not to mention, I'm not superhuman like him.

"I'll carry you on my back," Roman says breezily, like it's the most obvious thing in the world. "You've gotta see this view." Before I reply, he slides off his backpack, squats down, and offers his broad back to me. "Hop aboard."

With a ridiculous little giggle, I slide Roman's pack onto my shoulders and hop aboard, at which point my own personal Superman for the day grips my thighs and begins scaling the rock formation like it's an anthill.

*Swoon.*

I hate thinking about Brandon again, especially at a romantic moment like this, but I can't help it. I never minded Brandon being on the short side, and I've never found classic gym-bro-athlete-beefcakes all that attractive. But I can't deny Roman's height, brawn, and strength are insanely attractive to me. His muscles aren't for show. He didn't sculpt them in a gym simply to impress his gym-rat friends and get chicks. This man's a true athlete—that much is clear. One who plainly revels in putting his gorgeous body, and his own limits, to the test.

Roman easily reaches the peak of the large rock formation. And all of a sudden, we're treated to an unimpeded panoramic view that knocks my socks off: rainforest, waterfall, and blue skies that stretch into and blend with the aquamarine ocean beyond it all.

"It truly is paradise," I breathe out, as Roman crouches down and lets me stand on my own two feet. "Did I die, Roman? Is this heaven?"

"Heaven couldn't improve on this, that's for sure."

Mere yards away, that spectacular waterfall is thundering at full force, with so much power, it's spraying us with a gentle, cool mist—a barrage of tiny, rainbow-hued orbs that float around us and land on our skin like a gentle, ethereal embrace.

"Thank you for taking me here," I whisper, still looking around in awe. "I'll never forget it."

"Thank you for saying yes to coming," Roman replies. He slides his hand in mine, prompting me to look at him, and when our gazes meet, Roman flashes me a smile that's so panty-melting, I reflexively hurtle myself at him. We kiss for a long time, as birds chirp and flowers bloom and the waterfall thunders around us. As our passion ignites, and our lips and tongues devour, we run our hands over each other's cheeks and hair, like we can't get enough. But unlike earlier at the trailhead, Roman doesn't take things further than first base this time, which somehow makes the moment feel that much sweeter and more romantic.

After we break apart, we find a comfortable spot on a rock, where we enjoy the view, chat, and dig into our snacks and sports drinks. Mostly, though, we savor our stunning surroundings in comfortable silence.

After being left to my own thoughts for a few minutes, I'm suddenly struck with an epiphany about myself: *I'm a people pleaser to a fault.* I've always known I'm accommodating and compromising by nature. I prefer avoiding conflict, if possible. But suddenly, I can plainly see how much my natural tendencies have gotten out of control over the past several years. Ever since the shocking loss of my mother, I've taken a back seat in my own life. In terms of my relationship with Brandon, I slowly became a doormat. More intent on keeping the peace and not making waves than being happy myself. Why did I ignore so many red flags?

"What are you thinking?" Roman asks.

"Hmm?"

"You look like you're thinking deep thoughts over there."

"I am," I admit. "I just realized something. No, *decided* something." As Roman looks at me expectantly, like he's hanging on my every word, I take a deep breath and speak on my exhale. "From this moment on, I'm going to do what I want and not worry about what anyone else thinks about it."

"Atta girl. Good for you."

"As long as I'm being true to myself, that's all that matters."

"Love to hear it. Absolutely." He runs a fingertip down my forearm and smiles. "Go, Iris, go. Earn that blooming-flower name of yours to the fullest."

My heart stops. My mother always said she named me Iris in the hospital, instead of the name she'd initially planned, because she took one look at me and thought, *You're prettier than the prettiest flower.*

Roman takes my hand. "You can be anyone you want to be, Iris. Always remember, this is your life and nobody else's, okay?"

I nod, stuffing down tears. "Thank you so much for taking me here."

"Trust me, the pleasure has been mine."

I scoot toward him on the smooth boulder and press my lips against his bare, broad shoulder. "I'll never forget this day with you, Roman. Thank you." It's a true statement. But if I were feeling comfortable enough not to hold back at all, I'd probably have said it differently: *I'll never forget you, Roman.* Considering the temporary nature of this fling, though, and the way I've already overshared and said far too many stupid things, I think the incomplete truth I've admitted out loud is good enough.

I'm not going to date for a long while, once I get back to Denver. I'll take time to work on myself and become the blooming flower my name implies. But after this unforgettable day with Roman, I'm thrilled to realize I feel *capable* of loving someone again. One day. In the distant future. And that in itself, considering where I started out the day emotionally, feels like nothing short of a miracle.

# CHAPTER 17
## Roman

THE EVENING AIR is thick with humidity, floral fragrances, and the scent of my own wanton lust. I can't remember a time when I wanted a woman this badly. *I'm fucking feral.*

I open the car door for Iris, and the moment she's standing, I pull her into a passionate kiss. Instantly, a forest fire ignites between us. With my mouth still on hers, I pull Iris up by her ass, kick the car door shut, and make my way toward the bungalow with the hottest woman alive in my arms and my mouth devouring hers.

I stagger inside with Iris wrapped around me like a baby monkey, too turned on to make it all the way into the bedroom in the back. With my heart pounding, I lay Iris down on the couch, peel down her shorts and panties, and slide my hand desperately between her legs to get a read on her. She's already soaking wet and swollen for me—as ripe as a summer peach.

I don't normally jump straight to fucking. Almost always, I prefer getting my partner off first as an appetizer. But today with Iris has felt like one long, mouthwatering appetizer—a sexy slow burn of foreplay that's kept my blood at an endless simmer and my skin perpetually buzzing.

Panting with desire, I massage Iris's hard, swollen clit around and around, and then slide my fingers in and out of her slick wetness, getting her beyond ready for my aching cock. When I can't wait a second longer, when my blood feels on the verge of a rolling boil, I rip off the rest of Iris's clothes and mine, get myself wrapped up tight, bend Iris over the back of the couch, and sink myself inside her from behind.

As my body stretches and fills hers, Iris lets out a sexy growl that's nearly as loud as my own. With one hand buried in her sandy hair and the other gripping her hip bone, I fuck Iris hard, until she's making inhuman sounds and I'm dizzy and gasping for air.

As our passion intensifies even more, I grope her neck, breasts, and nipples with one hand while rhythmically stimulating her clit with the other. And the result on Iris is so plain to surmise, I'm already on the cusp of losing it.

"He's an idiot," I grit out, trying desperately to hang on. "If you were mine, I'd fuck you so often, I wouldn't have time to even think about cheating on you." *What am I saying?* It's nothing but dirty talk. The unthinking nonsense that hurtles out of a man's mouth in the heat of the moment. But damn, that's the first time that specific brand of unthinking nonsense has hurtled out of me. I need to get a grip on myself.

Or do I? Because in response to the crazy thing I said, Iris growls with ferocious intensity and releases an orgasm around my cock that rockets me into my own release on her heels. With a deep groan, I crumple over her back, gasping for air, as her innermost muscles ripple, warp, and squeeze all around me.

*Jesus.*

After catching my breath, I straighten up, pull out, and turn Iris around to face me. Rather than speaking, however, I take her face in my palms and kiss her once again. I feel addicted to this woman. I feel high. What's happening to me?

Before I manage to speak, my phone on the floor rings

with an incoming call. I've got my phone set to Do Not Disturb other than for calls from Cameron, my mother, and Maverick's mother, Vanessa—so that call's got to be from one of the three. Still breathing hard, I lurch toward the phone and make out Cameron's name as I pick it up; but with Iris here, I let the call go to voicemail.

"That was my business partner," I explain. "I need to call him back real quick."

"Okay, while you do that, I'll take a shower and get into bed to wait for round two." Iris winks. "I swear I won't fall asleep this time."

"Are you hungry?"

"Starving."

"After my call, we'll order room service."

"Yummy. Will you make me one of your famous rum punches, too?"

"You bet, baby."

Iris bats her eyelashes as she saunters toward the bedroom. "See you soon, *baby*. Don't keep me waiting too long."

As I watch her beautiful ass swish, swish, swish out of the room and disappear, I'm smiling so damned hard, my cheeks hurt. What is it about that woman that makes me feel so damned drugged? I can't remember the last time I felt like this, if ever. Even in the midst of one of the most stressful times of my life, I feel like a carefree kid when I'm around Iris. I feel light as a feather. Giddy, like a school kid with a crush.

A goofy smile still plastered on my face, I throw on my clothes from the floor and head to the kitchen first, figuring I'll make my girl that cocktail before heading outside to return Cam's call—but there's no ice in the small freezer.

"I'll be right back, baby!" I call to her. "I'm going out to grab some ice!"

With my phone in one hand and the ice bucket in the other, I head outside into the warm night to search for an ice machine while talking to Cameron. Before I press the button to place my call, however, a group of young dudes passing by loses their shit at the sight of me.

"Roman Maguire!" one of them shouts. "Holy shit! I've got you on my fantasy team!"

"Hey, guys."

"Are you gonna re-sign with the Crusaders?" one of them asks. "I heard a rumor you're shopping for a new team."

"Never listen to rumors."

They ask for selfies, and I oblige them, even though I can't wait to get away.

To my frustration, one of them begs me to sign his T-shirt before I go, so I wait for him to scurry into his nearby bungalow for a pen, and when he returns, I wind up signing not only his T-shirt, but everyone else's, too—plus a few hats.

Finally, however, I'm able to break free without coming off like a complete dick, at which point I head down to the beach to make that call to Cameron. As I walk toward the entrance to the sandy beach, I listen to Cameron's voicemail, but all he says is "Call me ASAP!" Once I've made it onto the sand, I walk a short ways, find myself a dark, secluded spot, and plop myself down.

"Hey, Roman," Cameron says in greeting.

"What's up?"

"The Thunderbolts said if you can convince Coach to come with you, they'll one hundred percent be able to meet your salary demands. They'd do a three-year deal worth two hundred mill total: a hundred-fifty in salary and another fifty in bonuses and incentives. But that's only the deal if Coach comes with you."

"I'm worth that on my own."

"I agree, but they think you're worth one-fifty total on your own. They figure they'll sell tons more season tix and merch if they market the hell out of your legendary partnership. 'Coach Hardy and Roman Maguire, together again!'"

They're not wrong about that, but Cameron knows I want two hundred mill, whether Coach comes with me or not.

"Between you and me," Cameron continues, "I can't argue with their logic. You in a Thunderbolts jersey will send shockwaves throughout the league. But you *and* Coach together again? That'd be a nuclear bomb."

I kick off my flip-flops and burrow my feet into the sand. "I'm worth two hundred mill, no matter what. If they can't meet my salary demands, they'll need to get there with more cheese on the back end in bonuses."

"It's just a question of the funding they can pull together. It's all about crunching the numbers and making sure they've got money for other players, too. You know that."

I know it, yeah. But I don't really care about the salary cap all that much. That's their problem, not mine. I've earned a record-breaking contract, if you ask me.

"Listen, Romie," Cameron says. "I know you're hell-bent on LA, but Arizona called me today and said they could do two-twenty-five to get you. They can't wait too long to close something, though. They need to lock down their number-one QB, ASAP."

"I don't want to be in Arizona, Cam. I want to be in LA *and* I want my team to pay me what I'm worth. It's not that hard."

"Phoenix to LA is only an hour and a half flight—way shorter than Baltimore to LA—so you could always—"

"The whole point is I don't want to *fly* to see my son. I want to drive a short distance to pick him up, and then I want to take him back to my house across town and tuck him into his little race-car bed in his own, permanent room. I want him to live with me part-time, Cam, and I can't do that if—"

"I know, Rome. You think I don't want that for you, too?"

"Make it happen, then. Since that's your fucking job."

"I'm doing everything in my power. If you want a guarantee you'll get everything you want, without having to compromise a goddamned thing, then convince Coach to come with you. If you do that—"

"I'm not gonna 'convince' Coach to do a goddamned thing. The man bleeds Michigan maize and blue. I'm not going to ask him to risk ruining his legacy by retiring as a Thunderbolt, instead of as a Wolverine, if he's not one thousand percent sure he's willing to take that fucking risk."

"Would it kill you to sell the man on the dream a bit, though? We both know you can sell water to a fish, so all I'm saying is—"

I exhale in frustration. "Look, I'm in the middle of something important here. Is there anything else you called to tell me?"

Cameron lets out a long exhale. "Did you check into the new place I got for you yet? I got a notification a couple hours ago you hadn't checked in yet."

*Shit.* "Oh. Yeah, about that . . . I decided to stay at the bungalow all week after all."

"The 'Runaway Bride' didn't want the place?"

I feel like a kid caught with his hand in a cookie jar. "She's staying with me. All week."

"Roman motherfucking Maguire! We talked about this, and you agreed—"

"I changed my mind."

"Goddammit. There's no pussy in the world worth—"

"There is, actually, as I've been lucky enough to find out." I snicker. "*Repeatedly.*"

Cameron gripes under his breath. And then, "Please, at least tell me you haven't gone out in public with her."

"If you want full honesty, then I can't tell you that." I give Cameron a rundown of my amazing day with Iris, and he grumbles and complains. "Look, I don't pull this card on you very often," I say, feeling intensely annoyed. "But you work for me, remember? Not the other way around. So, fine, you gave me your professional advice about what you think I should do, and I decided to disregard it. Which is my right, since this is my fucking life. Not yours. At this point, it's time for you take off your fucking agent cap and put on your best friend cap. Do that or shut the fuck up, man, because I'm done with this goddamned conversation and all your whining and bitching."

I can practically hear Cameron rolling his eyes across the phone line.

"I'd have thought you'd want me feeling as relaxed and happy as possible," I rant. "As you might recall, the 'best sports psychologist in the world' you forced me to see said me being relaxed and happy *off* the field will help—"

"Will you shut the fuck up already? You've made your point." He exhales. "Goddammit, Rome, you horny fuck. I thought you'd slowed down on the one-night stands."

"I have." There's no point in explaining my white-hot, irresistible attraction to Iris because Cameron wouldn't understand. How could he, when I don't understand it myself? Yes, I'm a horny fuck. Always have been. That's why I had sex with Iris the first time, even before getting back the results of the background check. But after that, it wasn't simple horniness that inspired me to plan a daylong romantic date today. No, I did that because Iris makes me feel something beyond simple lust. The truth is she touches my heart. She makes me laugh and feel good. She makes me feel protective, possessive, and jealous, even about hypothetical men touching her. And the best part? She makes me feel all of it without her knowing I'm Roman fucking Maguire.

"Anything else you need to talk to me about?" I bark into my phone at Cameron. "Because Iris is waiting for me back in the bungalow, and you're pissing me off."

"Where are you now?"

"Outside on the beach. I didn't want her or anyone else overhearing our call."

"Has she signed an NDA, at least?"

"There's no need."

"Fucking hell, Roman. That's your dick talking."

"Maybe, but it doesn't negate the fact that she's a trustworthy sweetheart, Cam. Trust my instincts here, okay?"

"I guess I've got no choice, huh?"

"Now you're getting it. Call me if you find out anything I should know before my golf game on Friday, or if the Thunderbolts suddenly decide to meet my demands. If it's anything other than those two things, then leave me the fuck alone to have a fun and carefree week with my horny and hot little runaway bride."

# CHAPTER 18
## Roman

When I return to the bungalow, Iris is nowhere to be found. Presumably, she's where she said she'd be: lying in bed, naked and wide awake, awaiting round two.

I stride toward the bedroom and suddenly realize I don't have the ice bucket. Did I leave it on the beach after my call with Cameron? "Hey, Iris?" I call out as I approach the bedroom. "I'll be right back. I think I left the ice bucket on the—" My words catch in my throat when I reach the bedroom doorway and spy Iris in the bed. She's not only naked and ready for me, as promised; she's a wet dream. Pleasuring herself with a vibrator with her thighs spread open and her head slung back.

I lean my shoulder against the doorframe with a smile. "Excuse me, young lady, who gave you permission to get yourself off? That's my job this week."

Iris opens her eyes and flashes me a sultry, inviting look—but she notably doesn't lift the vibrator from her sweet spot. "You were taking so long to come back, I decided to keep myself wet for you so we can jump right into round two without needing foreplay."

"I like foreplay."

She lifts the vibrator.

"No, don't stop. This is foreplay." I bite my lower lip. "Turn it to low, though. Let's draw this out."

"The lowest setting won't get me there, no matter how long I do this."

"That's perfect. Your orgasms are mine. Put it on low and take it off if you feel like you're getting really close."

Iris's blue eyes blaze. Apparently, she likes this little game, whatever it is. With a flush in her pretty cheeks, she does as she's told and the hum emanating from the vibrator becomes slower and deeper.

"Good girl," I whisper softly. I leave my spot in the doorway to sit on the side of the bed, my cock straining against my shorts. "How long does it normally take you to reach the finish line with that thing?"

"So long, I'm embarrassed to tell you. You get me there way, way faster."

The news makes my cock tingle. There's nothing I love more than being the best in every sport I attempt.

"Is everything okay?"

I slide my fingertips across her bare thigh. "Hmm?"

She lets out a shaky breath. "The call from your business partner. Is everything okay?"

"Oh. Yeah. It couldn't be better. Cameron just had a question about some numbers. Sorry the call took so long."

Iris pouts. "I missed you terribly."

"Poor baby. Let me make it up to you." I peel off my shorts, freeing my straining cock, and slide onto the bed next to her warm body. As I get situated, Iris lifts the vibrator and reaches for me, but I gently tell her to keep the vibe going. But only on the lowest setting.

When Iris dutifully returns the vibe to its home, I spread her legs wide and start feasting on her inner thighs while fingering her. From her thighs, my mouth migrates to her hips and belly before stopping to feast on her hard, pebbled nipples. From her perky tits, I trail kisses down her belly again, while running my palms up and down her torso, until, eventually, Iris lets out a guttural sound and announces, "I'm gonna come."

"Not yet." I take the vibe from her, turn it off, and set it down. "Come sit on my face, baby. I want to fuck you with my tongue before I split you in two with my cock."

Iris's eyebrows shoot up as her lips part in surprise. "I've never done that."

"All the more reason to do it now. Come here. *Now.*" I lie on my back with my head close the headboard and my hard-on straining toward my abs. "Don't think about it. Just do it. Hold onto the bed frame with one hand while you press the vibe against your clit with the other. Keep it on low, and I'll take you to heaven."

With her chest rising and falling sharply, Iris takes the vibe and begins moving into position. "Are you sure you like doing this?"

"*I love it.*" In truth, I've hardly ever performed oral sex in this position. It's the rare person who inspires me to make this kind of effort, honestly. But with Iris, all I want to do is make her feel good and come. *Hard. Repeatedly.* Rinse and repeat.

"When I squeeze your ass cheek twice," I coo, "that'll mean it's time to press the vibe to your clit. Don't do it before then." When Iris doesn't reply, I pat her ass cheek and add, "'Yes, sir.' That's what you need to say to me whenever I give you a direct order."

"Yes, sir."

I'm buzzing. This is so fucking hot. "That's it," I whisper, gripping Iris's hips and guiding her into perfect position aboard my face. With a soft sigh, she settles onto me, and what follows is a tongue-fucking so voracious and uninhibited, it quickly slingshots Iris to the very brink of ecstasy. In short order, she lets out a whimper that's so tortured, in fact, I know it's time to level up and shove her over the edge. I squeeze her ass cheek twice, and a few seconds later, the low purr of the vibe melds with the sounds of Iris's delicious torture.

Soon, I'm so blissed out underneath Iris, the entire bungalow could burn to the ground around me and I'm sure I wouldn't notice. Finally, when I'm hurtling toward the limits of my own self-control, Iris shrieks and shudders above me, and her body lets loose a squirting, writhing, screaming climax atop my face.

Practically hyperventilating, I guide her off me and onto her back. And when I've got her splayed out deliciously before me like a buffet meal, I voraciously lick up every sweet drop of my trophy from her pussy and thighs. Before this week is done, I'm going to make Iris squirt again—and even more forcefully than this. Only, next time, while my cock is buried deep inside her.

"Get on your hands and knees," I bark out, after Iris's groans have subsided and I've licked every inch of sweetness off her most intimate flesh. As she complies, I cover my length faster than I've ever performed the feat and plunge myself all the way inside her warm, wet tightness with one beastly thrust that makes both of us growl with relief and excitement.

I don't take her gently this time. I'm not gyrating with finesse. No, I'm railing this woman. Scrambling her insides, exactly like she said she wanted while dressed in pretty, perfect white. And Iris is reacting with primal sounds that tell me she's enjoying the ride as much as I am.

"Harder," Iris chokes out. "Harder, Roman."

There's no such thing. This is as hard as it gets. But I certainly appreciate the sentiment.

I'm seeing stars from pleasure, but I keep fucking her mercilessly. When I'm done with her, she won't be able to imagine fucking someone else. Not in Hawaii. Not in Denver. Not anywhere, ever again. It's not fair of me to want to ruin this poor girl for anyone else, given that I don't intend to see her again after we leave this temporary paradise, but in this moment, I don't give a shit about fairness. My body is taking what it wants and acting on instinct.

I reach around and fondle her swollen bud as I fuck her into oblivion, and pretty soon, I get what I'm after: Iris's orgasm, accompanied by a scream of ecstasy that's so unhinged, it sounds like she's birthing a demon. Is this what they call seeing God? Because I think I finally understand the expression.

As my body releases, I crumple over Iris's sweaty body, quaking and gasping for air, before eventually turning her over onto her back. When I see her face, she looks euphoric, in the true sense of the word. She looks physically high.

"That was better than any drug," she purrs softly. "Not that I'd know, honestly."

She makes me feel like a god among men. Invincible. Powerful. Immortal. *And without knowing my name.* Is this what Marco was talking about when he said Nicola makes him feel like he can do anything? I feel this way after playing a particularly good game, of course. On those rare occasions when I've gained monstrous passing yards and delivered an epic beatdown. But I've never once felt this particular sensation in a situation like this. Truly, the high Iris gives me feels like a once-in-a-lifetime sort of thing—the same kind Marco always talks about having with Nicola.

Jesus, Roman. *Stop it.* You've known this woman for a day, and this is a simple vacation fling with no possibility of becoming more. It's batshit crazy to even think about comparing your chemistry with Iris to whatever Marco feels with Nicola. His *wife*.

"I'd sure love a cocktail about now," Iris says flirtatiously.

I grimace. "I left the ice bucket on the beach."

"What? How?"

"I took it out there while I was talking to my business partner and forgot it."

Iris makes a joke comparing the "poor ice bucket" to Wilson, the volleyball from *Castaway*, and I can't help laughing along with her. It's not all that funny a joke, objectively, but whenever Iris gets going, I can't help losing it, too.

"I was gonna find an ice machine after my call," I try to explain, still laughing. "But then I forgot all about it."

Iris lays her palm on my bare chest. "It's okay. It just means you're not perfect after all. What a relief."

With a huge grin, I kiss the top of her head. I can't believe this is all happening without Iris knowing who I am. I feel like a kid on Christmas. "Hey, when's your flight home?"

She cocks her head. "Sunday morning."

"Mine, too." My heart flutters. Iris has said multiple times she's here for the whole week, but it's a relief to get confirmation her timing precisely matches mine. I would have been bummed to have to say goodbye to her a single day earlier than my own flight to LA. "I'm having a blast with you," I admit, looking into her earnest blue eyes.

"I'm having a blast with you, too. The best time ever."

My stomach tightens as I suppress the ridiculous urge to ask Iris about her work schedule back home. Would she feel open to traveling on weekends now and again if her expenses were fully covered by me?

*No, Roman. What the fuck? You can't ask her that without admitting you're not a gym owner in Delaware, remember? And you don't have time for her, regardless. So, stop.*

I slide my finger over that gorgeous curve in Iris's hip again. "I feel like I should mention . . . I've got some major moving parts in my life right now, so this week in paradise is all I can possibly offer to you."

Iris looks incredulous. "I thought you said people flinging don't talk about the fling."

"Well, yeah." I clear my throat. "Things are going really well, though, so I figured maybe I should clarify things anyway. Just, you know, to keep things crystal clear. For both of us. So nobody gets hurt."

Iris snickers. "You're not the only one with moving parts, remember?" She giggles. "As far as I'm concerned, 'What happens in Kauai stays in Kauai' is my mantra this week. That's all I can offer you, too. To put it mildly."

She's rendered me speechless. That's objectively the best possible response. The one I should want to hear. And I do. Although maybe not *that* emphatically.

"Great," I murmur. "That's good."

Iris rolls her eyes. "God knows I'm the last person who should be thinking about dating anyone, especially long-distance." She pats my arm. "I'm just using you for hot sex, baby. You saw the video and read the comments. I'm a wanton hussy. A slut. A man-eater. We're all good."

I can't help cracking up with her. Not to mention, sighing with relief that Iris seems to be taking all those horrible comments in stride so quickly. "So, listen," I say. "Besides playing golf with my friend on Friday, I'm totally free this week. I'd love to plan a bunch more dates for us, if you'd like."

"I'd love to spend as much time with you as possible, but you don't have to plan any more elaborate dates. Today was expensive, Roman. Save your money."

I resist the urge to smirk. "Don't worry about that. I want to show you a good time. But only if that sounds good to you."

Iris slides her palm onto my bare stomach. "That sounds like heaven to me."

"Good. Then it's settled." I lean in and kiss her, feeling oddly unsettled. Logically, I should be elated that went so smoothly—that there are no crossed wires or miscommunications about how and when this brief affair will end. But strangely, I find myself feeling a touch . . . what is that?

*Disappointed?* Couldn't Iris have at least pouted or frowned a bit when I expressly drew a proverbial line in the sand?

I sit up and hand Iris the room service menu off the nightstand. "While I go out to find that damned ice bucket and get us some ice, order a shit ton of food for us."

"What do you want?"

I start throwing on clothes. "Anything and everything that looks good to you. Surprise me."

"What's your budget?"

"Five hundred dollars."

She rolls her eyes. "Tell me, so I don't spend too much."

"That's not possible. Have fun. Surprise me."

After watching me for a long beat, Iris rises onto her elbows. "I'm sorry to ask a question that might ruin the vibe here, but do you promise Cameron on your phone is your work partner, and not your wife or girlfriend?"

My heart squeezes. My God, this poor girl has been through it.

I stop what I'm doing and sit on the bed. "I'm as single as a man can possibly be. I swear it on my life. Cameron's been my best friend since college, and we're in business together."

Iris visibly relaxes. "Thank you. Sorry. I'm paranoid."

"Understandably." I look around for my phone. "Do you want to see a photo of Cameron? We played golf a couple weeks ago and I think—"

"No, no, I believe you. I just got a weird feeling for a second, so I decided to be bold and ask, rather than keeping my freak-out to myself."

"Good. Never shy away from speaking your mind with me or anyone else." I find my shoes and sit on the edge of the bed to put them on. "Did I do something to give you a weird feeling?"

Iris shrugs. "Not specifically. All of a sudden, I just got this paranoid feeling you're lying to me about something. But it's fine. It's gone now. You've promised you're single, and I believe you."

Fuck.

Fuck.

*Fuck.*

Should I tell her now?

Am I doing more harm than good by keeping a low profile?

"Roman?"

"Hmm?"

"Are you okay?"

No. I can't do it. I'm having way too much fun getting to know her without "Roman Maguire" getting in the way. "Yeah, I'm great. Just trying to remember where I put the damned ice bucket."

Iris giggles again. "Well, you'd better figure it out soon, because Momma needs a spiced rum punch."

# CHAPTER 19
## Iris

I LET OUT a playful *tsk* and poke Roman in the ribs. "This isn't a *boat*."

We're walking hand in hand toward the purported "boat" Roman arranged for our snorkeling/jet-skiing/lunch-and-dinner/sunset-booze-cruise date today—and it's now abundantly clear Roman grossly understated the size of the vessel we'll be boarding today.

By now, though—at the start of our fourth full day together—I probably should have expected this kind of downplaying spin and humble generosity from Roman. I swear, he's made me feel like a princess in a fairy tale all week.

Who's my temporary Prince Charming when he's back home in his real life? I have no idea, since I still don't know his last name and he's weirdly tight-lipped about his life. Unfortunately, other than bluntly asking Roman his last name—which I'm not willing to do, since he's never asked for mine—I think I've finally reached the end of the road on all my ideas to figure him out.

After hitting a dead end with my internet searching, I thought about peeking at Roman's driver's license to get his last name. But whenever he's been in the shower or at the gym or on a run, he takes his phone with him, and since he's got one of those slim wallet things that attach magnetically to the back of his phone, he takes his license with him, too. Add to that, whenever we get back from that day's fun adventure, we always have amazing sex, followed by food and cocktails and more sex, and then, I always wind up falling asleep first, in a blissful haze of sexual satisfaction.

Once, after Roman had gone outside to talk to his business partner, Cameron, I got the bright idea to sneakily call the front desk and ask for the full name of the bungalow's registered occupant. But even though I told the hotel clerk I'd been staying here with Roman all week, he was a snippy, tight-lipped little rule follower. "Sorry, miss," he said evenly. "I can't give out that information to you or anyone, not even someone staying there with him." I was so embarrassed.

Another time, when Roman went to the gym, I searched the bungalow high and low for something with his full name on it—any receipt, boarding pass, luggage tag, or scrap of paper that might provide a clue about Roman's identity. But no such luck. Even the name tag on his suitcase reads simply: *Roman*. No last name. No address. No phone number. No email. God help the man if his luggage gets lost because then he'll undoubtedly have to buy a whole new wardrobe, wherever he might be. But to each his own, I guess.

After all my fruitless searching and conniving, I've come to accept it's probably a good thing I don't know Roman's last name. For the best. Nobody's perfect, after all. Despite appearances. I'm sure Roman's past girlfriends would attest to that fact and fill me in on a long list of his imperfections. So, given that I've got no choice in the matter, I've decided to be grateful to get to spend a week with a man who seems perfect here, in paradise, but who couldn't possibly maintain the illusion back home. God knows the last time I snooped and secretly gathered information about a man, I got far more than I bargained for and got knocked onto my ass. At this point, if

Roman isn't truly as wonderful as he appears be, I don't think my wounded, still-raw heart could handle finding that out.

"Of course, it's a *boat*," Roman retorts playfully, drawing me from my thoughts. "It's a vessel designed to float on and traverse water with passengers and/or cargo. That's the very definition of a boat."

I laugh and point at the large watercraft in our sights. "No. That, sir, is a yacht." I look down at my bikini top, running shorts, and flip-flops. "If you'd told me we'd be traveling in such style today, I would have dressed up."

Roman scoffs. "For snorkeling and lying around in the sun?" He squeezes my hand. "You look perfect, Iris. Gorgeous, as always."

My heart skips a beat. He's always saying stuff like that, like it's the most natural thing in the world. Being around Roman makes me realize how much I love words of affirmation. I told myself I didn't need them when I was with Brandon, probably out of emotional self-preservation, but now I know I do, and I'll never settle for less. Assuming I'm ever in a new relationship again, that is. At the moment, that's hard to fathom.

"Welcome," a man in uniform says as we stop in front of him. "I'm your captain for today." He introduces himself and shakes Roman's hand vigorously while telling Roman it's a pleasure to meet him.

His greeting seems particularly enthusiastic. So much so, it makes me think about that lady in the market on day one. Her eyes lit up at the sight of Roman in this same exact way. Does this captain guy remember Roman from his college playing days, too?

Roman gestures to me. "Captain, this is my date, Iris."

The captain shakes my hand. "Welcome, Miss Iris. Anything you need or want today, you let us know."

I can't help noticing the captain's greeting to me, while polite and professional, was far less enthusiastic than the one he gave to Roman. Are my Spidey-Senses correct and this man is geeked out to have Roman, specifically, spending the day aboard his yacht?

"I actually do have a question for you," I say. I motion to the vessel docked behind him. "Would you call that a 'boat' or a 'yacht,' Captain?"

Even before the man answers me, Roman throws his head back and belly laughs, which, in turn, makes me bust up along with him.

"A 'yacht,'" the captain replies. "But you can call it anything you want, miss, and nobody will correct you."

Still chuckling with Roman, I poke his arm and shoot a scathing look at him—one that communicates, "I told you so!"—and Roman breaks up all over again.

"I'm sensing I've handed Iris a win in an argument," the captain says.

"More like a friendly dispute," Roman replies. "But yes. You just handed her the win, so thanks a lot."

"A bit of advice, Roman? Never argue with a woman. If she's willing to argue about something in the first place, then that means she has good reason to be confident in her position."

"Words to live by, Captain," Roman says, his dark eyes sparkling. "I'll definitely keep that in mind."

"Are you ready to come aboard?" the captain asks.

"The 'yacht,' you mean?" I ask, innocently, and Roman laughs all over again.

Once we're aboard and standing in the main entrance room—a large space that features couches and a dining table—we're welcomed by a line of four uniformed crew members.

Down the line, all four people express obvious enthusiasm about Roman's presence, while I'm greeted, by contrast, with what feels like a far more detached, albeit pleasant, professionalism. Did someone look Roman up before our arrival today and figure out they were about to spend the day with a big-shot former college football player? I suppose that's possible, but I'm increasingly beginning to think Mr. Roman No-Last-Name from Delaware has something far more notable on his résumé than "gym owner" and "former college football player." If true, what could it be? I have no freaking idea. For all I know, my hunch is way off the mark, and my suspicions the simple by-product of me watching too many movies where royalty pretends to be a commoner to escape the rigors of their gilded cage.

One of the uniformed crew members steps forward and says, "I'm Leo, and I'll be your butler today. Would you care for some light snacks and cocktails on the upper deck while we head to your first snorkeling location?"

"Sounds great," Roman says. He looks at me, his eyebrows raised, and I agree that sounds like a fabulous plan, at which point Leo takes our drink orders and confirms the appetizers we'd like to be served.

"So fancy," I murmur to Roman. Once again, I find myself wondering how a gym owner/personal trainer can afford all these expensive, private excursions, day after day. Not to mention, all the room service Roman's ordered for us at night after we've come back from our latest fabulous adventure. I sure hope Roman hasn't been going into credit card debt to impress me, when I would have been happy with free hikes and simple picnics every day.

Roman did say he trains professional athletes, though. Surely, professionals are willing to pay exorbitant fees to get the very best trainers, given what's at stake for them. And what professional athlete with money to burn *wouldn't* want to hire a trainer who looks like a professional athlete himself?

Leo, our butler for the day, draws me from my thoughts by motioning to a younger man in uniform next to him. "This is Artemis. He'll give you a tour of the vessel while I get everything ready for you. Relax wherever you like, and I'll find you."

"Sounds good, Leo," Roman says. "Thanks."

The younger man in uniform, Artemis, steps forward and says, "Hello, Mr. Maguire. Miss Benedetto. Welcome aboard."

My heart stops.

*Maguire.*

*He's Roman Maguire.*

*Jackpot.*

I feel like every inch of my skin has burst into flames, but still, I try to keep a neutral face.

As Roman shakes Artemis's hand, I peek at Roman's face to see if he's noticed this young man announcing our last names to each other, but Roman looks as cool as a cucumber. Same as always. Either he didn't notice the comment, he doesn't care, or he's far better at keeping a poker face than me.

As Roman shakes Artemis's hand, he says, "Nice to meet you, Artemis. Please, call me Roman."

*So much for Roman not noticing.*

"Yes, sir."

"And call me Iris," I join in. But thanks to the adrenaline ravaging me, my words hurtle out in a far higher octave than normal.

"Hello, Miss Iris. Thank you. Are you ready for a tour now?"

"I could use a quick bathroom break first," I choke out, feeling physically dizzy with the need to enter Roman's full name into the browser on my phone. Is Roman feeling a similar urge, now that Artemis said my last name, too? If so, he won't find anything I haven't already told him. Unlike my mysterious and tight-lipped bungalow-mate, I've been an open book this whole week.

Artemis gives directions to the closest bathroom, and I walk calmly toward it without glancing back at Roman. I've always had a terrible poker face—hence, the reason my brother always beats me when we play—and I don't want Roman suspecting what I'm about to do.

Inside the tiny bathroom, I hurriedly close the door, pull out my phone, and search the name "Roman Maguire" with bated breath, along with "UT Austin," "football," and "tight end."

Instantly, a smiling photo of Roman pops up onto my screen. To my shock, he's wearing a purple Baltimore Crusaders' uniform and holding on to a football. The caption under the photo reads, "Roman Maguire, Quarterback."

*Roman's a quarterback? For the Baltimore Crusaders? Currently? As in, the Roman I've been having sex with, and flitting around the island with, and chatting up a storm with is a current* professional *football player—not a gym owner from Delaware?*

My brain feels like it's melting and my eyes feel like they're popping out of my head. Did Roman tell me *anything* true about himself this week? In a flash, I feel like I'm back in that horrible moment with my fiancé's secret phone: the moment I opened it and discovered nothing I'd believed about Brandon—and, by extension, about myself—was the truth.

With shaking hands, I click the link for Roman's Wikipedia page and quickly scan for the name of his college. Motherfucker! Roman went to Michigan, not UT Austin? *Why lie about that?*

I go back to the top and devour the entire write-up without breathing and discover the following:

Roman Maguire, the man I've been showering with and kissing like he's the teenage boyfriend I never got to have in Orchard Blossom, the man I've babbled my entire life story to, basically, isn't only *a* professional quarterback—he's *the* top quarterback in the NFL. An "elite" one, anyway, even according to his detractors. Also, he's the face of several major brands. A face I probably would have seen in a bunch of TV commercials if I'd ever once sat down to watch a football game on TV.

I lean against the small bathroom sink and keep reading, breathing deeply so I won't faint or barf. In college, Roman led his team—the Michigan Wolverines, *not* the Longhorns of UT Austin—to back-to-back national championships, and he also won the Heisman Trophy. I don't know much about football, but even I know all of that is a really big deal. No wonder Roman was drafted as the overall first pick. I bet *everyone* wanted to draft Roman Maguire after the success he'd had in college.

I scan the list of Roman's records and accomplishments and find out, to this day, he holds a bunch of passing records and other accolades. The one thing Roman's never done? He's never taken home a Super Bowl ring, despite making it to the game three different times. I don't know much about football, so maybe I'm wrong, but it seems to me a Super Bowl win is the *only* thing Roman hasn't accomplished in his long and storied career.

I look up from my phone, hyperventilating. Sweating. Freaking out. Why has a superstar quarterback in the NFL been romancing a nobody preschool teacher from a small town this week, when he could have been romancing any woman he wants? A supermodel or actress. A rocket scientist, brain surgeon. *Why me?*

When my stomach churns with a horrible thought, I quickly return to my phone and search: "Roman Maguire, wife, girlfriend." Thankfully, everything that comes up confirms Roman is, indeed, single. By all accounts, very, *very* single. So at least he didn't lie about that. In fact, based on the string of gorgeous women seen on Roman's arm, it seems like he's quite a player. And it's no wonder. With his options, why would Roman ever feel like he has to choose?

Trembling, I splash cold water on my face until I don't look like I've got a cattle prod shoved up my ass anymore. Yes, I still look red and blotchy, but I can now believably tell Roman that's because I'm feeling seasick, and not because I've discovered he's a goddamned football superstar with the entire world at his feet.

Shoot. I've been gone a full ten minutes. Roman and that yacht guy probably think I've fallen into the toilet or had bowel-clearing diarrhea in here.

Still quaking, I sit down and try to pee as best as I can, since returning to the bathroom in thirty minutes would probably elicit concern from Roman. And when that bit of business is done, I take a deep, steadying breath and stride through the bathroom door with my stomach in knots and a cheerful smile plastered on my blotchy, tight face.

# CHAPTER 20
## Iris

THE YACHT'S IN motion now.

We're heading toward our first snorkeling location of the day.

Roman and the yacht boy are nowhere to be found.

Still breathing hard, I wander outside the main cabin and discover the pair leaning on the railing while overlooking the sparkling ocean. As I get closer, I make out Roman's low voice. He's chatting amiably with the crew member, and whatever he's saying, he's got the crew member's undivided attention.

It occurs to me the woman in the grocery store was the same way. The cashier, too. Hanging on his every word. And now I know why. Because he's Roman freaking Maguire, not some gym owner from Delaware.

I suddenly realize a whole bunch of people have been reacting to Roman exactly like those two women in the market and this crew guy, but I've idiotically chalked it up to Roman being jaw-droppingly gorgeous or memorable, for some reason, as a college player. No wonder Roman wanted to get out of that market quickly on day one! It wasn't because he was protecting *me* from unwanted attention, like I thought. No, Roman didn't want those women unwittingly blowing *his* cover, the same way this crew member just did!

"Hey, you," Roman says as I come to a stop next to him. "Everything okay?"

"It's great. I was just feeling a little bit seasick, but I'm okay now."

Roman furrows his brow. "This fast? We just left the dock."

"It came on quick."

"Would you like some Dramamine, miss?" the crew member asks politely.

"No, I think I'm okay now. Let's do the tour."

Roman takes my sweaty palm, and we follow the crew guy, Artemis, through the vessel as he provides us with factoids about everything. Throughout the tour, Roman seems remarkably chatty and relaxed, and not the least bit suspicious of me, so I feel confident I've somehow managed to maintain a poker face for the first time in my life.

The tour ends, and Roman and I settle onto lounge chairs on the top deck to await the arrival of our cocktails and appetizers.

"I'll tell Leo where to find you," Artemis says as he departs. "Enjoy."

"Isn't this amazing?" I say brightly when the crew member is gone. "I've never been—"

"You googled me in the bathroom."

My cheeks blaze. "Hmm?"

"You heard that guy say my last name, so you ran off and googled me in the bathroom." Roman chuckles. "Don't try to deny it, Iris. It's written all over your face."

I blush. "Sorry. I couldn't resist. Did you do the same thing while I was gone?"

"Google you?" Roman shakes his head and laughs. "No need, when I already got a background check on you on day one." When my jaw hangs open, Roman adds, "I took a photo of your driver's license while you were in the shower and sent it to Cameron—my agent."

I gasp. "*Why?*"

Roman shrugs. "To make sure you weren't a reporter or a kook. A guy in my position can't be too careful."

"Cameron isn't your business partner?"

"He is, in a sense. An agent is similar to a business partner. They work on commission." Roman sighs at the sour expression on my face. "Please, don't look at me like that, Iris."

"Like what?"

"Like you don't know me at all. I'm still the same guy you've been hanging out with. Nothing's changed."

That seems like a crock of bullshit to me, but before I reply, our nice waiter, Leo, arrives with cocktails and a fancy charcuterie board, which he places on a small table between our lounge chairs.

"Can I get you anything else?"

"Nothing for now," Roman says politely. "Iris?"

"Nothing, thank you," I manage to say, even though my mind feels like it's a computer that's buffering. I don't know if it's fair or not, an overreaction or not, but I can't stop remembering the moment I cracked into Brandon's secret phone and my entire world came crashing down.

"What are you thinking?" Roman asks with a sigh.

I take a deep breath. "That you lied to me. That I don't know you at all."

"You do, though," Roman insists, his jaw muscles tight. "Better than most, I'd argue, since you've had the unique chance to get to know me as *me*."

I force air into my lungs. "Look, I get why you did it. You're a prince cosplaying a commoner to escape the stresses of your royal life. It's a tale as old as time. Or at least, as old as *Aladdin*. But understanding it doesn't mean I can easily process it, especially after everything I've been through."

"You're upset."

I ponder that. "I think I'm more . . . shocked."

He looks annoyed. "Okay, well, if you could get over that shock as quickly as possible, I'd appreciate it, because I'm excited about what's on tap for us today." He picks up one of the drinks, apparently to emphasize his determination to have fun today, no matter what. But while he sips, I continue staring at him, incredulous. He can't be serious.

"Why lie about UT Austin?" I blurt, glaring at him.

"Honestly, it pained me to do it. I bleed Michigan maize and blue. But I knew Chad Roman went to UT Austin, so I figured if you googled Roman and UT Austin, he'd come up, instead of me."

I can't help smiling at that, despite the churning of my stomach. I bite my lip, trying not to smile, but finally, I exhale and admit, "He did."

"Hmm?"

"Chad Roman. He came up on the internet when I tried to find you."

Roman bursts out laughing, and I can't help laughing, too. And all of a sudden, the situation doesn't seem quite as dire to me as it did a moment ago. True, he lied to me. But he's my vacation fling, not my fiancé.

"You tried to find me, did you?" Roman says flirtatiously. "You little sneak."

I snort. "I sure did. Every which way I could." I rattle off all the ways I unsuccessfully tried to figure out Roman's identity over the past four days, and he hoots with laughter and tells me he's duly impressed. I bat his broad shoulder. "And it turns out, that entire time, you had a background check on me in your back pocket!"

"Sorry."

He's not sorry. In fact, he's clearly deeply impressed with himself.

"You did that Longhorn thing with your hand, Roman!

You know, when you told me you went to UT Austin! Did you really have to sell the bit *that* hard?"

Roman winces. "Yeah, in retrospect, that was too much."

"Way too much."

"Guilty as charged."

"Why was it so important for me not to know the truth about you?"

"Would we be sitting here now if I'd told you my true profession from day one?"

I consider that. But there's only one honest answer. "No, I'd have been too freaked out to talk to you the way I did."

"*Bingo.*"

I shift in my lounge chair. "But still, you've told me a shit ton of lies this week, Roman, and as you can imagine, I'm particularly sensitive to being told lies of any kind at the moment."

He instantly looks remorseful. "I'm sorry, Iris. The last thing I wanted to do was throw salt on your wounds. All I wanted to do was make you feel good and help you forget your broken heart for a while." He looks and sounds sincere. So much so, I can't help patting his arm reassuringly.

"It's okay. But can you please stop telling me lies from now on, now that I know the truth about you?" We've only got three days left together, after all. It shouldn't be too much to ask.

Roman takes my hand and kisses the top of it. "Yeah, I can do that."

"Promise?"

"Promise."

I exhale. "Thank you." Now that I'm past the initial shock, it occurs to me it doesn't matter all that much to me that my vacation fling kept his football stardom a secret while also treating me to the best dates and sex of my life. If all Roman's gotten in return for all he's done for me this week was some no-strings sex and the chance to escape the pressures of his fame for a while, that seems like a reasonable exchange. Would I want to date Roman in real life, now that I know he's *this* good at lying? Hell no. But I'll happily continue having a fling in paradise with him for the remainder of my time on the island.

"Now that I've promised full honesty, I should confess something else to you," Roman says. "I'd already seen the video, when you showed it to me."

I bat his shoulder again, making him chuckle. "No wonder you reacted so calmly to it. You'd already had your freak-out in private."

"I didn't freak out the first time, either. The way I reacted in your presence was the same way I reacted when Cameron sent it to me."

"Which was when?"

"A few minutes before I came back to the bungalow from my run and you showed me the video yourself."

"Why not tell me you'd already seen it?"

"Because to do that, I would have had to admit I'd sneaked a snapshot of your license for a background check. That was simple due diligence, by the way. I never sincerely doubted you." He twists his mouth. "I should also confess: The morning you showed me the video, I actually came back from my run earlier than it seemed. While you were talking on the phone talking with your friends, I hid near the door and eavesdropped for a while before making my presence known."

"Roman!" I cover my face with my hands, remembering all the racy things I said about Roman to my friends. "I'm so embarrassed."

"Don't be. I loved everything you said." He pulls gently on my hands, making me lower them. "Everything you said made me want to invite you to stay with me for the week, even more." With a soft smile, he leans in and kisses me, and my body reacts like it always does, even though my mind is still racing. If I'd known about Roman's superstardom when I walked in on him in that shower, I never would have had the courage to stick around and talk to him, let alone flirt with him. So, in that sense, I'm grateful Roman didn't scare me off by revealing his true profession before today. On the other hand, however, did he really have to lie so freaking much—and so freaking *well*—to a woman who's recently been shredded by endless lies?

"I'm sorry I lied to you," Roman says, like he's read my mind. "I know what your ex put you through."

I exhale. "There's no comparison between what he did and what you did." It's the truth. "Like I said, I get why you concocted a fake persona. I'm sure it's been relaxing for you to be a gym owner-slash-personal trainer for a while."

"More than you could possibly know." He pauses. "But I didn't concoct a fake persona. I know I told you some lies to keep my life back home a secret, but I've been myself with you in every way that counts."

I don't see how that's possible, but I also don't see the point in arguing about it. Not when he's given me the best week of my life when I needed it most—a perfect sweet escape—and I've always known our time together would be short.

"You've been a godsend to me this week, Iris," Roman says, his dark eyes pleading for forgiveness. "I've been under a lot of stress lately, and spending time with you has made me forget all about it."

"What kind of stress?"

Roman looks around before replying, "I can't go into too much detail, but I'm going to a new team next season. That's why I keep talking to my agent, Cameron. He's trying to negotiate a big deal for me."

I bite my lip. "I'm assuming that's a good thing? Are you happy to be making a change?"

"Very happy."

"From what I read, you've done really well with your current team."

Roman lets out a long sigh. "After three Super Bowl losses, a lot of people have branded me as a choker, though. But it's a team sport, you know? I can't help it when my receivers drop balls thrown smack into their hands. Or when my kicker misses what should have been an easy winning field goal." He runs a hand through his dark hair and stares at the choppy waves of the ocean beyond the railing of the yacht. "The ownership of my current team wants me to win singlehandedly—without them shelling out money for some top-tier players to support me. But I can only do so much on my own; I need reliable targets." He grunts in frustration. "Five years ago, they brought in this head coach who's such a goddamned prick. I could go on and on about why I hate him, but suffice it to say he thinks berating me and calling me a slacker-choker-loser is going to be the magic bullet that somehow pulls the best out of me."

I scoff. "That goes against basic psychology. Nobody—I don't care if they're children or adults, schoolteachers or professional athletes—responds positively to being put down and belittled all the time. People respond best to positive reinforcement and constructive criticism from a trusted source."

Roman beams a smile at me. "I couldn't have said it better myself. I mean that literally."

I shrug. "It's the truth."

"Maybe you should be the head coach of the Crusaders. You couldn't do any worse than the current guy, and you might do a whole lot better."

I make a tipping scale with my arms. "Preschool kids, NFL players. Same-same."

"Closer than you think." With a chuckle, he sips his drink and looks out at the ocean again. "Football's a business. I know that." He returns to me with blazing eyes. "But I'm a human being, and I need the right support system around me to be happy and effective. So, that's what I'm gonna get myself. *Happy.*"

"As you should."

Roman looks down at his large hands. "I do sometimes wonder if the haters are right, though. If maybe I'm all washed up."

"No, Roman."

"What if I get to a new team and all the bullshit follows me? What if I *never* live up to all the 'Roman Maguire' hype?"

"You already have. You've broken records."

"I don't have a Super Bowl ring, though. That's the only stat that matters in my line of work."

"When you make the change to a new team, everything will click into place. I'm sure of it." I set down my cocktail and slide into Roman's lounger with him. "When you're surrounded by people who believe in you and give you what you need to succeed, I've got zero doubt you'll have your best season yet."

"Thank you, Iris," Roman whispers with a shudder. He pulls me to him and kisses me, and for the next I-don't-know-how-long, we kiss and make out on that crowded lounger like the world has melted away and we didn't get the memo.

# CHAPTER 21
## Roman

"S‍ee you in LA, Romie," Coach says in his patented low grumble.

I pat his back as he gives me a bear hug. "We're gonna take the world by storm, Coach."

"And we're gonna have one hell of a good time doing it."

It's late afternoon at the golf club. Coach and I just finished playing a life-changing round. Thanks to what we talked about today, we're about to become the first coach-quarterback duo to win a college championship *and* a Super Bowl. Wait, no. We'll win *back-to-back* Super Bowls, just like we won those two championships at Michigan.

"Hardy!" a valet yells with his hand up.

With a parting wink, Coach heads over to his rental car. As I watch him drive away, I feel like the same cocky kid I used to be under his brilliant tutelage—the hotshot with a cannon for an arm who thought the world was his bitch and nothing could keep him from achieving all his big dreams.

I crane my neck to see if my rental car will be the next one coming, but no dice. Man, I can't wait to get away from this place and call my family and Cameron—and then, to rush back to the bungalow to take Iris into my arms and tell her the amazing news. Thank God Iris found out the truth about me yesterday, so I can race back to her now and celebrate.

"Roman Maguire!" a gray-haired guy in a polo shirt booms to my left. "Great to see you again."

I look at the guy blankly, not recognizing him, so he supplies his name and reminds me we played in a foursome at Pebble Beach last year in a charity tournament.

"Oh, yeah," I say. "Hey, Frank." I only vaguely remember him. He's a CEO of something. But it's not unusual for people to unilaterally remember meeting me.

"Hey, if you're free to play here again tomorrow," the guy says, "I've got an eight o'clock tee time that needs a fourth." He name-drops the two other guys he's already playing with tomorrow morning, and they're both well-known, high-profile billionaires—guys who'd surely be able to give me some great tips on handling my business portfolio.

Normally, I'd accept the invitation. I won't be playing football forever, so I'm always trying to maximize my knowledge on the business side of things. But this time, I'm not even tempted. Tomorrow's my last day with Iris, unfortunately, and I'm not willing to miss out on a single minute with her. In fact, I've planned a spectacular horseback-riding date that's going to turn Iris into a swooning puddle.

"I'm all booked up tomorrow," I say. "Maybe another time."

"Maguire!" a valet calls out.

I say goodbye to the CEO guy, stride to my car, hand a Benjamin to the valet, and practically peel out. And the minute I make it off the golf club grounds, I turn onto a quiet side street, park my car, and place a FaceTime call to my family: my parents, my brothers, and my cousin, Marco, who pops onto my phone screen with Nicola.

"*Well?*" my father says. Everyone on this once-in-a-lifetime call knows about my golf game with Coach today, and they've been waiting with bated breath for an update.

With my heart thundering, I pause for dramatic effect before shouting, "Coach said yes! I'm going to LA, fam!"

Everyone on my screen cheers and whoops, and I proceed to tell them everything that transpired today and what it all means, based on the verbal assurances Cameron's already received from the Thunderbolts.

Mom wipes a tear. "I'm so happy for you, honey. And so happy for Maverick, too."

Luca adds, "Mav's gonna grow up with his daddy being there, just like Dad was always there for all of us."

The comment sends a lump into my throat, so I don't reply. Not verbally, anyway. Surely, my brother and everyone else on the call can see how deeply I'm feeling my brother's momentous words.

"As your cousin," Marco says, his voice laced with emotion, "I couldn't be happier for you. As a football player in the NFL, however, I can't wait to dog-walk your fucking Thunderbolt ass."

We all burst out laughing through tears. Marco's team, the San Francisco Knights, has had a storied, decades-long rivalry with the Thunderbolts.

"You've got that backwards, cuz," I shoot back, as Marco and I share a broad smile.

We chat some more, but only briefly. Soon, I tell the group, "I need to call Cameron now so he doesn't have an aneurysm waiting on me."

After another round of kind words—even from Evil Levi, who looks uncharacteristically emotional—we say our final goodbyes. But after I end the call, I feel the urgent, thumping need to see my son's face before calling Cameron. I can't tell Maverick my good news, obviously. A four-year-old can't be trusted with highly confidential information. Not to mention, Vanessa is always somewhere nearby while I'm talking to him. But even so, I'm determined to see Maverick's face and hear his voice as part of my celebration.

I place the call, and after some brief pleasantries with Maverick's mother, Vanessa, she hands the phone to our son.

The second I see Maverick's cherubic face, I tear up. "Hey, Mav," I choke out.

"What's wrong, Daddy?" Maverick asks, his dark eyebrows cinched together. "Why are you sad?"

A car passes on the quiet street where I'm parked, so I look the other way to hide my face. "I'm not sad, buddy. I'm happy because I get to see you soon and for the longest time ever." Vanessa and her husband, Jay, are going to some big wedding in Europe soon, so they've decided to do some traveling from there. When Vanessa first called to tell me about the trip, it was to inform me she was planning to take Maverick with her, but by the end of the call, I'd convinced her to let me take my son the whole time—six consecutive weeks.

"Can I bring my trains when I come to your house, Daddy?" Maverick asks. "Jay always plays trains with me before bedtime, and I want to play trains with you, too." My stomach twists. Vanessa's husband, Jay, is a solid, friendly guy who's fantastic with my kid. Also, he's never once disrespected me. Surely, a more mature man would feel nothing but thrilled to know Maverick's got such a close bond with his stepfather, but if I'm being honest, in addition to me recognizing that's a good thing for Maverick, I'm also jealous about it for myself. In fact, every time I think about Jay playing with Maverick or tucking him in at night, I feel like my hair's on fire and my skin is physically hot with the desire to get to do those things with him, too.

"You don't need to bring your trains," I say, "because you'll have all the trains you could ever want at my house."

I'm expecting Maverick to express excitement. Maybe even to thank me for wanting to make our time together this summer as fun as possible. But he simply shrugs and says, "Can I go play with Jay again?"

My heart sinks. "Sure. Have fun, buddy. I love you."

"I love you, Daddy. Bye."

There's a shuffle, and a moment later, Vanessa reappears on my screen. "He had so much fun with you and your family in Hawaii. He hasn't stopped talking about it. How many Hawaiian ices did he have per day?"

I laugh. "Two. He had everyone wrapped around his finger."

"Please, learn how to say no to him when you have him this summer, or he's going to become a little monster by the time you return him to me."

"He'll be fine."

Vanessa leans into her camera and whispers, "I saw a photo of you playing golf with Coach Hardy today. What's that about? Was it a friendly game . . . or something else?"

"Just a friendly game."

"Is Coach Hardy coming to the Crusaders?"

"It was just a friendly game, Vanessa. Tell Maverick I love him, okay? Tell him I can't wait to see him next week."

"I love you, too, Daddyyyyyyyyy!" Maverick shouts in the background, and that's all I need to tear up again.

I quickly wrap up with Vanessa and write myself a note to order every conceivable train set that's age-appropriate for Maverick, once I know where to ship them. After that, once I've composed myself, I start up my rental car, figuring I'll talk to Cameron as I make the drive back to the bungalow. *Back to Iris.* Hopefully, she's already returned from today's solo adventure, because all I want to do is take that woman into my arms the second I walk through the front door.

"What'd Coach say?" Cameron shouts maniacally after answering my call.

I cackle with glee. "He's in."

Cameron gasps. "*In*-in? With no caveats?"

"No caveats, other than them paying him what he's worth. If they do that, he said he'll sign a deal with the Thunderbolts the day after I do."

Cameron whoops. "Holy shit, you did it!"

"You think they'll offer him what he's worth?"

"And then some. They were practically jizzing in their pants when I floated the idea of you two as a package deal. Oh my God, Roman. How'd you get him to say yes?"

"I just spoke from my heart. I admitted what a shitty time I've been having in Baltimore and then segued into painting a picture of how much it would mean to end my career on a team that genuinely values me, in the city where my son lives, with *him* as my coach." I snicker. "And then, when all that failed miserably, I begged."

Cameron bursts out laughing with me. "Atta boy."

"Just kidding. I didn't need to beg him at all. Right off the bat, Coach admitted the chance to coach me again has always been a bucket list item."

"Hot damn. Let's get this locked down, ASAP. When can Coach fly to LA for a meeting with the owners?"

"He said he can fly on Monday at the earliest because he's here with his wife and kids for his anniversary. So, let's set up a three-way meeting on Tuesday."

"That's perfect. This way, we can meet with the owners first—on Sunday or Monday—to finalize your deal. I'll book a flight for you tomorrow and let them know—"

"No, not tomorrow, Cam. I'm already flying to LA on Sunday to pick up Maverick, remember?"

"You need to come tomorrow, Rome. The internet is already buzzing about you and Coach playing golf today, and we don't want anything to leak."

I shift the phone against my ear. "The thing is, I promised Iris I'd take her horseback riding tomorrow, so—"

"*Iris?*" Cameron bellows. "Please, tell me that was a joke." When I say nothing, he shouts, "I don't give a flying fuck what you promised your little vacation plaything. You're flying to LA tomorrow to reassure the owners you're worth over two-hundred-million bucks, and that's that." He proceeds to rant about all the reasons why I need to get my ass to LA, as soon as possible, and I can't deny he's making sense. As bummed as I am to miss out on one last day with Iris, clearly I'm going to need to do exactly that.

I run a palm down my face. "Okay, I'll change my ticket for tomorrow."

Cameron exhales a massive breath. "No. I don't want you flying commercial. I'll arrange a private flight so you're not bombarded at the airport with questions about why you're flying to LA a day after playing golf with Coach. The chat boards are already on fire with theories and speculation about what today's golf game meant—and some of those theories are dead-on accurate."

"I've got to go," I murmur, feeling overwhelmed. "I'm pulling in to my hotel."

After we hang up, I start walking toward the bank of bungalows before me. With each step I take, I try to shake off the disappointment I feel about my earlier-than-planned goodbye tomorrow. Today is the best day of my life, for fuck's sake. I should be feeling nothing but unadulterated elation.

As I walk, I slap my cheek. Literally. And tell myself to pull it together. My conversation with Cameron was the reality check I needed. He's right. It's time for me to focus on what matters most—being the best quarterback, teammate, and father I can possibly be—and to forget the silly fantasies I've been harboring about Iris possibly being The One.

# CHAPTER 22
## Iris

As I enter the bungalow, I glimpse Roman on the deck through an open French door. He's got his feet up and a beer in his hand. My entire body buzzes at the sight of him. As pathetic as it sounds, despite the short time I've spent with him, I missed Roman like crazy today. So much so, I physically ached for him.

I thought it'd be a nice change of pace to have some alone time while Roman played golf with his old friend, so I used a couple of my activity vouchers for two all by my lonesome. But as it turned out, even when I was having fun, I couldn't stop thinking I'd be having even more fun if Roman were there, too. Even when my cute windsurfing instructor asked me out to dinner, my only thoughts were about Roman and how much I wanted to come back here and have dinner with *him*.

"Hey there, handsome," I say, as I enter the patio.

Roman looks up and flashes me a million-dollar smile. "Hey, beautiful." He pats the cushion next to him on the couch and kisses me when I plop onto it. "Did you have fun today?"

"So much fun. I missed you, though." The minute the admission leaves my mouth, I'm worried I shouldn't have made it.

But as soon as I've had the thought, Roman, unfazed, replies breezily with, "I missed you, too. What'd you do?"

I snuggle into him and rattle off all the fun stuff I did today, wrapping things up with, "And nobody recognized me, even once!" Granted, I was wearing sunglasses and a hat all day. Also, no makeup, like all the times I've been out and about with Roman without getting recognized. But, still, I'm hoping today's uneventfulness is a sign my internet fame is already a thing of the past.

Roman squeezes my hand. "I told you everything would blow over quickly. What happens on the internet isn't real."

I hold up crossed fingers. "How was golf?"

A wide grin spreads across Roman's achingly handsome face. "It was life-changing."

"You got a hole in one?"

He laughs. "Even better. I got a new team. I know where I'm going to play next season."

"Congratulations! What team?"

"I can't tell you that yet. Everything is still on a need-to-know basis. All I can say is I'm elated about where I'm going. It was my top pick."

I pepper his face with kisses, making him belly laugh.

"I'm so happy for you. How on earth did a game of golf lead to this incredible news?"

Roman tells me the identity of his golfing partner, confidentially, and also how everything went down today and why it's such a big deal—although, once again, he emphasizes he can't divulge the identity of his new team or its city. When he's done talking, I pepper him with kisses and freak out with happiness for him. Clearly, wherever Roman is going, today's events are positively enthralling to him, and his obvious elation is a thrill for me to witness.

"This is all highly confidential, okay?" Roman repeats, even though he's already told me that, more than once. "The only people who know are my closest family members, my agent, and you."

My heart flutters to think he's trusting me so much. "I won't say a word to anyone. I promise."

"Not even to your closest family or friends. The internet is already going wild with speculation."

"My lips are sealed. How long will I be keeping this secret?"

"A week or two, maybe. You'll know when the secret is out, because there'll be a big news conference and social media will blow up. Trust me, football fans are going to go batshit crazy over this news."

I bite my lower lip. "Sounds like we've got a lot to celebrate tonight."

Roman's smile falls. "Unfortunately, my good news comes with some bad. I'm sorry, Iris. I have to catch a flight, first thing tomorrow, for a meeting with the team owners."

My heart sinks. I've always known I'd have to say goodbye to Roman, but I wasn't prepared to say it to him *tomorrow*. I know it's only a difference of a day, which really shouldn't matter to me. But whether it's logical or not, I feel gutted by this news—like a kid who's just been told Christmas has been cancelled.

Roman takes my hand. "I want you to know I tried to get the meeting pushed back, but it wasn't possible."

I put on a smile. "No need to apologize. You got your top pick of teams. Of course you need to drop everything and go to that meeting."

Roman touches my cheek. "I'm sorry to miss out on our last date tomorrow. I was looking forward to it."

I feel absurdly close to tearing up, so I take a deep breath. "We've always known goodbye was coming. Is it a bummer to miss out on tomorrow? Yes. But when it's for such a great reason, it's a paper cut."

"Thank you for understanding." He turns to look at the ocean. "I still can't believe this is happening. I've been sitting here for an hour, trying to wrap my head around how amazing this is going to be."

"I'm so happy for you."

Roman shakes off whatever he's thinking and returns to me. When our eyes meet, I plaster a grin on my face again.

"Should we order some champagne to celebrate?" I ask brightly.

Roman pulls my hand to his mouth and kisses it. "Nope. I made a reservation at the best restaurant in Kauai. I figured we'd dine in style as Part One of tonight's celebration, before coming back here for Part Two."

Crap. I'm sure the restaurant Roman's picked out is swanky and fabulous, but I'd much rather eat room service on the deck again, like we've been doing every night, so I can have Roman to myself for every minute of our last night together.

"You don't feel up to going out?" Roman asks.

"No, yes. I do. Absolutely. We should celebrate in style, like you said."

He bites his lip and looks out at the ocean again, like he's having deep thoughts. And I can't help feeling like there's something he wants to tell me—something he's holding back. But when he returns to me and our gazes lock, he smiles, winks, pats my thigh, and says, "Go on now, baby. Get showered and dressed. Our reservation is in an hour."

# CHAPTER 23
## Iris

"Bon appétit," our waiter says.

As he walks away, Roman and I greedily dig into our main courses. So far, every appetizer has been otherworldly, so we've both got high expectations for our meals.

"Mine is *incredible*," I say. "How's yours?"

"Delicious. You need to taste this."

We take bites from each other's plates and rave about everything. But when conversation about our food dies down, Roman falls silent, yet again. He keeps doing that. Going dark on me. Mostly, it seems like he's been drifting off to another place in his mind. Getting lost in his thoughts. A few times, however, it's seemed like he's actively stopped himself from saying something to me. Something that was on the tip of his tongue. The same way he did on the patio at the bungalow earlier. If I'm right about that, then I'm dying to know what he's been leaving unsaid.

Roman takes a sip of his wine. He takes another big bite of food. His Adam's apple bobs. He looks out at the ocean through the floor-to-ceiling windows of the restaurant. Finally, when he returns to me, he asks, "Do you have a contract where you work?"

"Hmm?"

"Do you have a specified amount of time you're contracted to remain at your job?"

I stare at him, too flabbergasted to answer. Where is he going with this?

"The reason I ask is, the other day, you said you'd like to move to LA 'one day,' but not any time soon because you love your job in Denver. I'm wondering if you've got a contract that'll keep you in Denver for a specified amount of time. And if so, when is it up?"

My heart is crashing. "I-I don't have a contract like that. My employment is on an at-will basis, which means I can quit at any time and they can fire me at any time." An epiphany strikes. I lean forward and whisper, "Is that where you're going?" I mouth the rest. "*LA?*"

Roman smirks and nods.

"Oh my gosh," I whisper-shout. "You're getting your favorite coach *and* the best weather in the world? No wonder you're so excited."

Roman laughs with glee. "I shouldn't be telling you this, but I know I can trust you." He looks around and then leans in to whisper, "The team has been in a rebuilding phase for its entire existence." He laughs. "But the new team owners are committed to building a winning franchise. They believe in me. And with Coach there, too, and the players they're gonna build around me, I know I'll be able to deliver in a whole new way."

"Of course you will. It's so exciting, Roman."

"And the best part is—" Roman abruptly stops talking and smashes lips together.

"What?" I prompt excitedly, leaning in, even more. "*What's the best part?*"

Roman scratches the stubble on his chin. He takes a sip of his wine. Replaces his glass.

"What is it, Roman? Don't leave me hanging, dude."

Roman leans back and exhales. "I've got a son, Iris. A four-year-old named Maverick. He lives in LA with his mother." He clears his throat. "The best part is that I'm finally going to live in the same city as my son and therefore get to be the father he deserves."

I'm floored. Speechless. Rendered mute.

Other than today, I've spent every waking and sleeping moment of the past five days with this man, and quite a few minutes of those days, Roman's had to listen to me yammering on about how much I love teaching preschoolers. *Kids the same age as Roman's child.* And he's never once bothered to mention he's the father of a four-year-old before now? How has Roman not once felt compelled to say, "Actually, that story reminds me of my own son?" Or maybe, "Wow, Iris, I know what you mean about that, because my own son does the same thing?"

Roman breaks the lengthy silence first. "What are you thinking?"

"That it's unfathomable to me you didn't mention your son before now."

"I'm not accustomed to talking about him with strangers. It wasn't personal."

I flinch. "You felt comfortable telling a 'stranger' about your new team, though?"

He rolls his eyes. "You're not a stranger now. But that's what you were when I didn't tell you about my son." At my hard stare, Roman shifts in his seat. "I suppose, looking back, there were several times when it would have made sense to mention him. But by then, it seemed too weird to bring him up for the first time, so I didn't."

I take a long sip of wine to gather myself. "Who's his mother?"

"Someone I barely dated. She's an actress and model in LA. Hence, the reason she wasn't willing to move to the house in

Baltimore I'd offered to buy for her. I bought her one in LA instead, and I've been flying across the country to see my son, as much as possible, ever since. In the offseason, that works out okay, even though it's exhausting. But during the season, I barely get to see him." He lights up. "But that's all about to change. I'm finally going to have joint custody of him."

"Congratulations," I say flatly. "That's wonderful for you both."

Another silence looms.

When Roman doesn't fill it, I do the honors.

"Do you get along well with your ex?"

Roman nods. "She's a great mother, and she's married to a good guy. We all co-parent well together."

"I'm glad to hear that."

"I don't consider her my ex, though. We had a fling, basically. It was nothing. Totally forgettable and meaningless, although it turned out to be life-changing for both of us, obviously."

Suddenly, I don't want to hear more. I've known all along Roman is a lot more experienced than me, in terms of the multitudes of people he's slept with, but suddenly, I don't want to sit here, actively thinking about him casually fucking another forgettable, meaningless fling like me and impregnating her.

Who the fuck is this man I've been sleeping with? Laughing with? Pouring my heart out to? I've always thought Roman's simply a more guarded person than me. A person who doesn't wear his heart on his sleeve, unlike me. But suddenly, I feel like Roman isn't merely guarded; he's deceptive. A con artist. It was one thing for him to keep his football superstardom to himself. I get that. But *this*? What purpose did his silence about his son serve, other than to keep his most authentic self hidden from me?

"Say it," Roman prompts on a sigh.

"What?"

"Whatever you're thinking."

I meet his gaze. "I don't understand why a gym owner from Delaware couldn't have had a son."

"What does that mean?"

"It means I get why you lied about your profession and fame. I might have done the same in your shoes. But not telling me, a *preschool teacher*, about your *preschooler* when I've talked about how much I love teaching *preschool kids* is extremely weird. Actually, no. It doesn't even matter what I do for a living. Your silence would have been extremely telling, regardless."

"Telling? In what way?"

Anger floods me. "On the yacht, you said you've been yourself with me in every way that counts, and I believed you. But that implied the gym owner was still *you*, except for all the football and fame stuff. That's not true, though. You have a child, Roman. One for whom you're rearranging your life to make a deeper connection with. Which means the gym owner wasn't you at all. Not in the ways that count."

"Football is one aspect of me, and my son is another. There's a lot more to me than either of those things."

I glare at him with skepticism. "All I'm saying is, if you were truly being your authentic self, other than about football, like you said on the yacht, then the fucking gym owner would have had a four-year-old son who lives in LA."

Roman looks pissed. But I don't care. I said what I said.

"The truth is optional, as far as you're concerned. Is that it? You tell it, sure, but only when it serves you."

He rolls his eyes.

"When I found out about your real identity, I remembered how you'd pretended to be protecting *me* and *my* identity in that grocery store, when in fact, you were only protecting yourself all along. But I shrugged it off. Well, now I know: This is just how you operate."

"Jesus, Iris."

That's all he manages in reply. Before he says more, a man and his son approach the table, and we both sharply lean back and look away, our cheeks and eyes blazing.

"Sorry to bother you, Roman," the man says. "I normally wouldn't bother you when you're on a date, but it's my son's fifteenth birthday, and he was too shy to ask for a photo. I told him I'd ask for one as a birthday present."

Roman's face is beet-red, but he manages the same smile he flashed the woman in the grocery store. The same one he flashed that crew member on the yacht, too. The false, fake, lying one he's a little *too* adept at flashing, if you ask me.

"Of course. Happy birthday." Roman takes the photo, signs the cocktail napkin offered to him, and talks to the kid about his love of football. And through it all, I feel like I'm going to scream.

The fact that Roman is a father isn't what's pissing me off. Who cares, since I'll never see him again after tomorrow? It's that the mutual connection I'd thought our souls had formed this week doesn't feel remotely possible anymore. I mean, yes, I knew it was all a fantasy on some level. But still, I feel duped. Not to the same degree as when I found Brandon's burner phone, obviously, but fresh on the heels of that fiasco, I'm still raw enough to feel like those same wounds are taking another hit.

Roman speaks, jerking me from my spiraling thoughts. "Sorry to cut this short," he says, "but like you said, I'm on a date, so . . ." He motions to me, prompting both father and son to peel their eyes off their idol and look at me for the first time during this encounter.

"Oh my God," the kid blurts, his eyes bulging. "You're the runaway bride from the video!"

Fuck.

I inhale sharply, too stunned to reply.

Why, oh why, did I put on makeup and do my hair to come

out to this restaurant? How did I not realize that simple act would break my streak of anonymity?

"She's been getting that all week," Roman says smoothly, without missing a beat. Proving, once again, he's a bit too good at lying for my taste. "I haven't seen the video," he continues, "but people keep saying the resemblance is uncanny. Happy birthday again." He pats the kid's back and then practically shoves him toward his father to make him go away, but the kid stands firm and ogles me.

"You look *exactly* like her," the kid says, eyeing me suspiciously. "I've watched the video a bunch of times."

"It's not her," Roman barks. This time, his tone isn't nearly as friendly.

The father grabs his kid's arm and pulls. "Sorry, Roman. We'll leave you alone. Go Crusaders."

As they walk away, I cover my face with my hands. "I think I might throw up."

"Iris, come on." There's unmistakable irritation in Roman's tone. "*One* person recognized you this entire week? That's pretty good odds, when you think about how many people we've interacted with or passed on the street. Plus, the kid wasn't even sure it was you." He takes a long sip of his water and places his forearm on the table. "About my son. I never talk about him with people I don't know, okay? So I was never gonna mention him to you, not in the beginning. For days, that simply wasn't an option. But I'm mentioning him to you now. And not only that, I'm sitting here telling you about my new fucking team, which is highly confidential. Don't you think that's 'telling,' too—or do I not get any credit for that?"

He's not coming across as furious. Only severely annoyed and testy. But it's enough to make me realize, once again, he's definitely not the perfect Prince Charming I've been making him out to be in my mind. "'Credit'?" I mutter. "What does that mean?"

"Never mind." He rubs his forehead, looking acutely exasperated. "Look, my son's mother and her husband are going to be traveling in Europe this summer for six weeks, so I'm taking Maverick that whole time. It's the longest I've ever had him, and I want to be fully present for him."

I stare at him. I understand his words, but I don't know why he's saying them to me.

Roman continues, "I also have to go to minicamp during the time my son will be with me, so I've hired a nanny for that small window of time. But other than that, I'll have him by myself till training camp starts in mid-July, which means I can't take on any unnecessary distractions. Football, my boy, finding myself a new home in LA. My dance card will be maxed out once I leave here."

I still have no idea why he's telling me this stuff, so I reply with, "Yeah, it sounds like you're going to be very busy."

"*Very* busy. Even when I'm not working out with the team this summer, I'll still be working hard with my personal trainer. Harder than ever. Plus, Coach and I are gonna need to construct a whole new offense. I'll need to do some team bonding stuff, too." He shakes his head. "Add my son staying with me on top of all that, and I won't have any time to pursue any kind of relationship with you."

"*What?*"

"If the timing were different, I admit I'd be tempted to give it a whirl, but—"

I can't believe my ears. "Roman, from the start, we talked about this being a fling with an expiration date. All that's happened is you've moved that expiration date up by twenty-four hours."

Roman looks flabbergasted—like what I just said to him was the last thing he could have imagined coming out of my mouth.

"Remember how I said the timing wasn't right for me to date anyone after I got back home? News flash: 'Anyone' includes you, Mr. Football Superstar. I know that might be hard for you to believe, but I didn't say that as an attempt at reverse psychology or a ploy to get you to pursue me. When I said it, I meant it, and I still do." I scoff. "Unlike you, apparently, I value total honesty."

Roman looks as indignant as if I'd physically slapped him across the face. "Okay, Miss Honesty. Tell me the truth. You genuinely have *zero* desire to date me after we leave here?"

"*Zero.*" I think that's the truth. But if by some chance I'm wrong about that and my subconscious knows something I don't, then I don't mind giving Roman a taste of his own deceptive medicine.

Roman narrows his dark, blazing eyes and his nostrils flare. Clearly, I've royally pissed him off. "You're honestly telling me," he grits out, "under oath, if I asked to date you after we leave here, if I said that to you, like expressly, you'd one-hundred-percent turn me down and say 'No thanks, Roman'?"

"Correct." As I say the words, I cross my fingers underneath the table, just in case there's a sliver of my damaged, traitorous heart that might stupidly be tempted to say yes to dating Roman, if asked.

"Why is that so hard for you to believe?" I ask, annoyed by the expression of disbelief on Roman's gorgeous face. "Is it because you think you're so irresistible, no woman could possibly turn you down, or that you think I'm so pathetic, I should leap at the chance to date any man who'd stoop to ask me?"

Roman scoffs. "Give me a fucking break, Iris. Both scenarios are ridiculous, and you know it."

"Do I? I have no idea how your mind works, Roman. Honestly, when it comes to you, I don't know what's real and what isn't."

He jerks back in his chair, like I coldcocked him. "Fucking hell, Iris."

"I know I lost my mind briefly for the entire world to see and laugh about," I huff out. "But I assure you, I'm not actually crazy. That was a blip. Temporary insanity."

"I know that. You think I don't know that?"

"So, as charming as you are, and as much fun as I've had with the *fictitious* version of you, my rational brain knows—"

"Would you please stop—"

"—that I just got out of a long-term relationship—"

"—discounting everything—"

"—that ended horribly."

"—that's happened between us? Me not telling you about my son doesn't make anything that's happened between us any less real."

We stare each other down, until, finally, I break the thick silence.

"Look, I'm sure you're normally irresistible to every woman you have flings with, but like I told you before, I'm not interested in jumping into anything with you or anyone else, so there was no reason for you to explain all the reasons you're *not* interested in ever seeing me again."

Roman's jaw muscles pulse. "That's not what I said."

"You said you don't have time to try to see me after you leave here, and what I'm saying is, good, because I don't *want* to see you. Not even if you begged me."

His eyebrows ride up. "Wow."

"It's nothing personal. How could it be, when I barely know you—if I know you at all?" I snort. "The last thing I need is to jump into a long-distance anything with a fling I don't even know when he's simultaneously starting a new, demanding job while also trying to be more present for his young child."

Roman's dark eyes are positively on fire. "Glad we're both clear."

"We are. Crystal." I put down my fork, my blood simmering.

"It's our last night together, Roman. And, suddenly, I don't want to spend it being romanced by you or getting to know you. And I certainly don't want to spend it arguing with you."

Roman's chest heaves. "How do you want to spend it? With me sleeping on the couch, I presume? Or do I need to get another room for the fucking night?"

I lean back in my chair and return Roman's molten glare. I don't know why my body is craving one last, hot-as-hell horizontal tango with this hunk of a man, when my brain feels so angry and disillusioned and deceived. But the fact remains, it is, desperately, and I'm not willing to deny my body the pleasure, no matter what other emotions I might be feeling.

"I guess you don't know me any better than I know you," I spit out. "No, Roman, I don't want to spend tonight with you sleeping on the couch or anywhere else. I want to spend it with my naked body entangled in yours, and with you giving me as many orgasms as humanly possible before it's time to say goodbye for-fucking-ever in the morning."

# CHAPTER 24
## Roman

Iris doesn't know what's "real" when it comes to me?

*How's every inch of my dick feel, for fucking real? Is the hardness of my dick for her honest enough?*

I'm fucking her with her thighs resting on my shoulders. And I'm not doing it gently. Which is why the room is now filled nothing but primal, animalistic sounds. Iris moaning. Me grunting. Our flesh slapping together with abandon. I'm determined to fuck this woman so outrageously well, she won't want to fuck anyone else after we part ways tomorrow. Yes, my brain understands the timing isn't right for Iris and me, but that hasn't stopped my body from raging at the thought of anyone else doing this to her. Not to mention, at the accusations she hurled at me at dinner. What the fuck?

Okay, yes, I can understand how it looks to her like I've lied. Like I've totally fucked up. I get that. But now, as my parting gift, I'm determined to give Iris the best night yet—one she'll never forget. One she'll hopefully look back on with regret once she realizes she'll never get fucked this good again, thanks to her decision to turn me the fuck down. Not technically, I suppose. The conversation was all hypothetical. But her words felt like a stark, acute rejection to me all the same.

"*Zero*," Iris said at dinner. She's got *zero* desire to date me, after we leave here, huh?

And to think I stupidly thought Iris would be overjoyed to find out about Maverick! Given how much she loves kids, I foolishly thought my revelation, once made, would make her like me more, not less. So much more. Hell, I actually thought she'd find out about my son and beg to visit me in LA! When I let the fact of Maverick's existence slip out, I actually thought, *Oh, shit, Roman, now Iris is gonna beg to keep on seeing you, and how are you gonna find the strength to turn her down?* Ha! I was a fucking fool.

"I'm close," Iris grits out as I continue pounding her. "*Oh my God.*"

She's already had three orgasms since we got back from the restaurant, but she's done that before, so I'm determined to surpass that number tonight. Which is why I'm fucking her without mercy. With everything I've got. Even when Iris lets out a desperate wail of ecstasy that sends goosebumps skating across my slick skin, I stay the course and continue fucking her like my life depends on it.

"*Roman*," Iris gasps out. "Oh, God. *Roman.*"

My name bursting from Iris's lips, dripping with such ragged desperation, is almost too much for me to bear. But somehow, I hang on, if only by the barest of threads. Until finally, after what feels like an eternity, Iris violently arches her back, digs her nails deliciously into my forearms, and releases a primal shriek of rapture that's so maniacal and tortured, I'm momentarily worried I've been too rough with her.

"Baby?" I blurt anxiously, gasping for air. "Did I hurt you?"

I've no sooner gotten the question out than Iris's innermost muscles begin squeezing my cock with such force, I'm hurtled into my own blissful release right along with her. Warm fluid squirts out of Iris and all over me, as I'm coming inside her, as she rides her own pleasure. *Good luck finding someone else to fuck you like this, Iris Benedetto.*

As I crumple over her body, quaking and gasping for air, Iris's name hurtles from my mouth. "*Iris.*" And as soon as the syllables leave my lips, I'm deathly afraid I've got it backward: that *I'm* the one who's not going to be able to find someone else who'll fuck me the glorious way *Iris* does.

When my body goes quiet, I lift my swirling head and gaze into her gorgeous face. She's tear-streaked and sweaty. Exhausted, for sure, but also quite obviously in a state of abject euphoria.

After taking a long, steadying inhale, I slide her legs off my shoulders, feeling unexpectedly emotional. "I'm gonna miss you," I confess, my voice strained.

"I'll never forget you," she whispers back.

I pepper her face with soft kisses, feeling like my heart is bleeding out, wishing she'd beg to come with me tomorrow, even though I wouldn't be able to say yes—and Iris holds on to me like she's holding on for dear life.

I'm probably an asshole for trying to ruin this poor woman for sex with anyone else when I know I can't make time for her in my life. But I couldn't help myself. I spent all week romancing this woman, trying to help heal her, trying to make her smile and come every which way, and what did I get for my efforts? "I wouldn't date you, Roman, not even if you begged me."

My phone on the nightstand buzzes with a call, but I ignore it. Now that Coach is locked in and the Thunderbolts and I have reached verbal terms, I'm not going to waste a single minute of the time I've got left with Iris. Even if she hates me now.

A couple seconds later, however, when Iris's phone on her side of the bed buzzes, followed by mine pinging a second time, curiosity gets the better of me. As Iris reaches for her phone, I do the same.

Shit. Cameron's the one trying to get ahold of me.
And it's not good news.

***Cameron:*** *Heads up. Some asshole teenager posted a photo of you and Iris at a restaurant tonight, and now, the internet is going apeshit with speculation about Roman "Ribbed for Her Pleasure" Maguire being the Horny Runaway Bride's railer and insides scrambler of choice.*

# CHAPTER 25
## Roman

AFTER MY SHOWER, I throw on the clothes I laid out for today's travel day and pack up my toiletries. I do a final check of the bedroom and bathroom and then head into the living room with my luggage, ready to say my final goodbye to Iris. When I enter the room, however, Iris is sitting on the couch with her phone to her ear and a look of anguish on her face.

"It wasn't a sex tape, Roberta," Iris says. "It was a photo of me on a date at an upscale restaurant."

*Shit.*

So far, that photo of Iris and me on the internet hasn't hurt me at all. In fact, despite Cameron's initial paranoia about Iris pulling me into her shit tornado, it seems the world has nothing but eye rolls for me at worst and bro-ish admiration at best when it comes to the possibility of me giving Iris what she said she wanted in that video. Since college, I've had a bit of a reputation as a ladies' man, so this new brick in the wall has only enhanced my image, I'd say, rather than tarnishing it. But after hearing only a few words of Iris's phone call, I've got a feeling Iris isn't getting quite the same treatment.

"Please," Iris pleads, wiping her eyes. "A few vocal parents shouldn't be allowed to—Yes, I know. But—" She takes a deep breath. "I'm flying back to Denver tomorrow. Let's please meet first thing Monday morning to talk about this face-to-face." Iris rubs her forehead while the person on the other end of the call speaks. After a while, Iris replies, "I understand, Roberta. I couldn't disagree more, but I understand your logic. Please, tell anyone who asks about me . . ." She chokes up. "That I really loved working there and never wanted to leave."

*Oh, fuck.*

Iris ends the call and looks at me with tears in her eyes, so I lurch toward her with my arms open and heart splintering. With a pitiful little wail, she springs up from the couch and falls into my waiting arms.

"I'm so sorry," I coo, stroking her hair.

"Apparently, I'm no longer an 'appropriate role model' for the kids."

"Tell me exactly what she said you did wrong," I command, outrage and protectiveness flooding me. I've got a team of lawyers at my fingertips. I could enlist one to send a threatening letter to the school, at the very least.

Iris sniffles. "She said going viral twice in one week was one time too many, and she can't protect me from the 'rising throng' of disapproval any longer." Iris hiccups. "She also said I'm too big a distraction—that I might even be putting the children's safety at risk."

"*What?*"

Iris nods. "She said I might attract 'internet crazies' to come to the school."

"That's bullshit."

Iris hiccups again. "My worst offense was what I shouted at the end of the video. 'In a *church*, of all places, Iris!' She said that went against the morality clause in my contract in the first place, but it's especially egregious now that it seems I'm 'brazenly following through with it' for the 'whole world to see' with a 'known womanizer.'"

"Motherfucking hell."

"She said one of the most influential parents at the school, aka one of their biggest donors—it's a private school—has been demanding to know why they hired a 'slut' to teach small children."

"This is insane. We were having dinner, not fucking on the table."

"It was the photo combined with the video combined with your reputation that did me in. She said when I chose to have dinner so publicly, with such a high-profile person, mere days after the video going viral, that showed an 'astonishing lack of judgment' that also made me look desperate to 'fan the flames of my internet fame.'" She tries to catch her breath. "The good news is, they're giving me a month's severance, at least."

"A *month*?" I shout. "That's it?" I'm enraged—wishing I could fly straight to that school and threaten to sic a team of overpriced lawyers on their ass if they don't take Iris back or pay her enough money not to care. Fucking hell. I'm the one who pushed Iris to get out into the world and ignore all the bullshit on the internet. I'm the one who told her the video would blow over and not to worry about it. And now, thanks to me and my goddamned reputation, she's lost a job she loves along with everything else she's lost over the past week.

"You know what?" I say. "Forget what we talked about last night, baby. Go pack your bags. You're coming to LA with me today."

Iris looks flabbergasted. "I'm not doing that."

"I know some lawyers there. I'll set up a meeting."

"I don't want a lawyer. I don't want to fight. I don't need the stress."

"You can't let them do this to you. You love your job, and you did nothing wrong." When she bows her head, I take her hand. "I'll have to put you up in a hotel for the first couple weeks, just so Maverick can get to know you before I—"

Iris lifts her head abruptly and pulls her hand away. "I'm not going to LA with you. I'm going to Denver to move all my stuff out of Brandon's house, as planned, and then I'm going home."

I shake my head. "I'll hire someone to get your stuff for you in Denver while you're hunkering down in LA with me and figuring out—"

"I have no desire to 'hunker down' anywhere," Iris says disdainfully. She crosses her arms over her chest. "All I want to do is get my shit out of Brandon's house and go home to Orchard Blossom for however long it takes to find a new job."

I exhale with frustration. Why is she being so fucking stubborn? "Look for a job while you're in LA. You said you've got good friends there, right? Plus, *I'll* be there."

Iris squints. "What's your endgame here, Roman?"

"I-I want to help you."

"Why?"

"You lost your job because of me."

Her mouth twitches. "Let me see if I understand. You're asking me to follow you to LA like an unemployed puppy—so I can meet with a lawyer for an hour but otherwise sit around in a hotel room and wait for you to deign to give me scraps of your valuable time in between your football and parental obligations—out of *guilt*?"

I run a hand through my hair and inhale deeply, trying to remain calm. "It's not only out of guilt. It's also because . . . Look, the bottom line is I don't know where things might lead for us. I admit that. This is horrible timing for me, but I'm willing to bring you to LA and do the best I can under some difficult circumstances."

Iris looks at me like I've gravely insulted her. "Like I said last night, I'm not interested in dating anyone right now, not even you. *Especially* not you, if I'm being honest. The last thing I want is to draw more attention to myself by being seen in public, once again, with a guy the internet calls Roman 'Ribbed for Her Pleasure' Maguire."

I let out a little grunt. "I had nothing to do with that stupid nickname. My teammates gave it to me in college as a joke, and it leaked and took off in the media like wildfire. Trust me, I've always despised it, every bit as much as you hate being called the 'Horny Runaway Bride.'"

Iris swallows hard. "The point is you haven't exactly made me an offer I can't refuse, Roman. If you think you have, then I'm sorry to inform you: You're suffering from delusions of grandeur."

I scoff. "What the fuck, Iris? I'm trying my best here."

"Don't. Please. I release you, completely." When I glare at her, she throws up her hands and bellows, "People are saying you pity-fucked me! Why would I willingly subject myself to another round of horrendous comments like that, for the mere chance to *maybe* fuck you again, at some point, in a hotel room in LA? I respect myself too much for that."

"I didn't pity-fuck you! Don't you know you're like cocaine to me? Does a man *pity-snort* cocaine?"

Iris pinches the bridge of her nose. "I'm not built for this, Roman! There are people telling me to kill myself because I'm such a disgrace and a whore. They're calling me a five out of ten! They're saying you must have lost a bet to even think about railing me."

My head is spinning. My veins are bulging with rage, adrenaline, and protectiveness. And yes, guilt, too, knowing I'm the unwitting catalyst for Iris's latest round of abuse.

"You're a perfect ten, baby," I say, touching her shoulder. "Fuck anyone who says otherwise. Also, let's not forget, nobody but you and I know for sure what we've done behind closed doors. They're speculating, yes, but nobody knows the truth."

Iris swipes at her eyes with a little whimper. "I'm a girl from a small town—one where everybody was always nice to me. I work with children who are always nice to me. My favorite thing to do is ride horses because—you guessed it—they're nice to me. Are you picking up on the theme here? I don't have thick skin, like you do. I'm not a professional athlete. I'm not a celebrity. I can't handle all these people being so mean to me all the time."

She bursts into tears, and I pull her to my chest like I did earlier. My God, my heart feels like it's being physically dragged over rusty nails.

"I'm so sorry, baby," I murmur.

"I just want to get my stuff in Denver and go home to Orchard Blossom and wait out the storm while surrounded by people who love me. That's all I want to do."

"Okay, if you won't come to LA with me, then at least go straight to Orchard Blossom and skip Denver. I don't want you risking a run-in with your ex. I'll hire someone to get your stuff shipped to you."

Iris leans out of our embrace. "I say this as a teaching moment for you, Roman, but you don't get a vote about what I do or where I go. From now on, nobody does, except me." She wipes her eyes again and gestures toward my waiting suitcase. "Please, just go. I don't want you missing your flight on my account."

I'm flying private, so they won't leave without me. But I don't think now is the best time to mention that fact. "Let me send you money every month, till you find a job," I say softly. "It's the least I can do, since it's my fault you got sacked."

"It's not your fault. Nobody could have predicted this would happen. Also, there's no reason to send me money. I'll be staying with my father in Orchard Blossom till I find a job, and he won't charge me for rent or food."

"Where are you going to look for a job?" *Please, God, let her say LA.*

"I need to see what the job market looks like. For all I know, there might not be a preschool anywhere in the country that's willing to hire an immoral, attention-seeking slut."

I gasp with an epiphany. "Why don't *I* hire you?"

Iris looks as flabbergasted as I feel. Why'd I suggest that? I don't know, honestly, but now that I've had the idea, it's rapidly gaining traction inside my head.

"Don't say no, Iris. It's a great idea. I need a nanny while Maverick's with me, remember? So, why shouldn't it be you, while you look for a job? You're more than qualified."

Iris pulls a face like I've offended her. "I don't want to be your *employee*."

"Technically, maybe," I say lamely.

Iris sighs. "Look, I appreciate that you're trying to help me in a time of crisis. But let's rip off the Band-Aid and end things cleanly, like we've always planned to do."

"Do I feel sorry for your *situation*? Yes. But I don't pity *you*."

"Whatever that distinction means, it's not reason enough for me to do something with you I'd be embarrassed to tell the world about. My mother always said, 'If you're too embarrassed to do something loud and proud and in front of the whole world, then that's your sign you shouldn't be doing it at all.' Well, sorry, I'm not ready to tell the whole world, loud and proud, I've agreed to become your wait-around side piece in LA, only a week after my failed wedding, and the day after I lost my job for being an immoral slut. On top of all that, I'm especially not willing to become a side piece for a man who'd only prolong my nightmare by attracting even more cameras and online attention to me. I can't stand the attention, Roman. I'm not like you."

My God. Are my intestines tumbling onto the floor right now, because I feel like she just fileted me from my chin to my balls.

Iris levels me with determined eyes. "I release you from all guilt, Roman. Now, please, go catch your flight. I'll never forget this amazing week with you, and I'll always root for you from afar. But it's time for us to say our goodbyes now."

My heart aches at the thought of leaving her. But my brain knows she's probably right.

"I'll never forget this week with you," I choke out. "I'll always root for you from afar, too." I peck her cheek. "Goodbye, Iris."

"Bye, Roman."

Swallowing hard, I grab my suitcase and stride through what feels like molasses to the front door. But before turning the doorknob, I turn to look at Iris's beautiful, sweet face one last time. "I'm sorry if I've added to your pain. I only meant to help."

Iris smiles thinly and nods through tears. "Thank you for everything."

With a gigantic lump in my throat, I slip out the front door and immediately start striding with purpose toward my rental car in the parking lot. I've got a whole new life awaiting me in LA—one I couldn't be more excited about. And yet, with each step I take away from the bungalow—*away from Iris*—I feel increasingly like I'm walking away from the great love of my life.

# CHAPTER 26
## Iris

"ANY MINUTE NOW," Harper, my longtime bestie from Orchard Blossom, whispers.

She's been matching my fidgety, scattered energy all day, when what I really need is for her to calm me down. It's not that Harper gives a crap about some star quarterback she's never met—especially one who doesn't play for her beloved Seagulls. It's that she cares so freaking much about me, and how much I've been second-guessing my decisions since parting ways with Roman in Hawaii, that she's vicariously feeling all my pain and regret.

The Thunderbolts have scheduled a press conference at 3:00 pm Pacific Time, so Harper and I came here—Darcy's Drinkhole, Orchard Blossom's biggest sports bar—to watch it together. Roman said football fans would have a huge reaction to today's announcement, and I want to see for myself in real time if he was right about that. Orchard Blossom is devout Seagulls country, but even so, the sports fans who congregate here tend to be diehard and knowledgeable about football in general. So I'm thinking they'll be a good barometer for the significance of today's announcement.

I'm so glad I came to Orchard Blossom to process everything that's happened to me in such a short time. Everyone has been so good to me. So supportive. Granted, everyone other than Harper thinks I've been depressed and off-kilter since I got home because of what happened with Brandon. But of course, that pathetic sack of shit hasn't even crossed my mind. No, it's Roman who invades my waking and sleeping thoughts. Roman who makes me ache, yearn, and constantly wonder, *What if?* Turning him down in Hawaii felt right in the moment. But ever since, I can't stop wondering if I'd be happier by his side in LA, even on his less-than-optimal terms.

"Two minutes," Harper murmurs.

"No countdowns, please," I mumble. "I already feel like I'm going to barf."

Her lips pursed in sympathy, Harper pats my hand on the bar while calling out to the bartender, Darcy, an Orchard Blossom fixture who loved my mother like a sister. "Hey, Darcy," Harper shouts above the din. "Will you turn up the sound on that one?" She gestures to a TV immediately above Darcy's head.

"You bet," Darcy calls back. She grabs a remote, and suddenly, the words coming out of the talking-head sports guys on TV cut through the wall of background noise in the bar.

I take a long guzzle of beer, readying myself to behold Roman. Not in past photos or videos online—but live and in real time. When I see Roman on that screen in a couple minutes, I'll know he's existing in the same moment—albeit a thousand miles away, and in a city where he doesn't think about me, even though I can't stop obsessively thinking about him.

All of a sudden, the scene on TV cuts from the talking heads to a press conference. And there he is. *Roman Maguire.* Sitting behind a long table with two older gentlemen—one with a salt-and-pepper short-cropped Afro and the other with combed-over white hair—in front of a bank of microphones. Behind the three men, the backdrop is covered in thunderbolts—the logo of Roman's new team.

I take Harper's hand and squeeze it, feeling physically ill. You'd think Roman's gorgeousness wouldn't bowl me over anymore, after all the internet stalking I've done of him over the past ten days—but seeing him on air and knowing that's *him* in the present moment is like seeing *my* Roman again. The man who rolled around with me in bed, naked, for the better part of a week. The man who generously planned date after romantic date and kindly held me close when I cried.

To this day, I don't know why Roman did all that for me, especially now that I know he was never interested in pursuing an actual relationship. But the fact remains he did, and it was swoony as hell.

On TV, the older gentleman with the white hair welcomes everyone to the press conference, while a chyron identifies him as the owner of the Thunderbolts. He makes some introductory comments about his organization's commitment to winning, to their fans, to the city of Los Angeles. *Blah, blah, blah.* Until finally, the man says the words I'm dying to hear: "Which is why I'm thrilled to introduce the Thunderbolts' new quarterback, Roman Maguire, and our new head coach, Otis Hardy."

Everyone surrounding me in the bar explodes with exclamations and reactions. People are variously clapping, hooting, booing, and cursing.

I look at Harper, and she looks taken aback by the sheer intensity and loudness of the reactions all around us. Before coming here today, I finally told another living person, Harper, the secret I've been keeping since Hawaii about Roman's new team. I also told her what Roman said about the football world losing its shit over the news. But even with that forewarning, I don't think either Harper or I could have anticipated the reactions happening around us. If a bar full of Seagulls fans in a Podunk town in Washington are reacting to Roman's bombshell news like this, I can only imagine how diehard football fans in both Baltimore and LA are reacting.

"Are you kidding me?" a guy behind us at a table booms. "How is anyone gonna beat the T-Bolts now?"

"With a solid defense," someone shoots back. "Which is exactly what we've got."

"I'm happy for Roman," a man to my right says. "The Crusaders never deserved him."

"When they brought in Coach Keller," a woman says, "that had to be the final straw for poor Roman. Who'd want to play for an egomaniac like that?"

Someone else chimes in to say, "'Poor Roman'? Please. You should be pissed the Seagulls weren't smart enough to nab him."

A man from a different area of the bar shouts, "Fuck my life. With both Roman Maguire and Coach Hardy, the T-Bolts are going to be unstoppable this season."

"No, they're not," another man spits back. "Roman's gonna choke, like he always does, whether he switches teams or not. The guy is washed up. A total loser."

Several men agree enthusiastically with that sentiment.

"Jeez," I whisper to Harper. "They're so mean."

From behind the bar, Darcy addresses one of the naysayers sitting on the other side of Harper. "No, it's not a quarterback 'choking' when a receiver fumbles in the red zone, or when a tight end can't catch a ball thrown straight into his goddamned hands to save his life."

*Thank you, Darcy,* I think. *At least someone else understands it's not all Roman's fault.*

"The buck stops with the quarterback," the guy talking to Darcy at the bar insists. "If Roman was an actual winner, he'd find a way to win when it counts most. *Period.* No fucking excuses."

Harper leans in and whispers, "How does Roman shrug it off when people tear him to shreds like this? No wonder he felt so connected to you. He understood your viral pain on a whole other level."

I freeze.

*Holy shit.*

I've never put that together before. *Roman understood my pain.* Is that why he went to such great lengths to show me a great time and help me forget my troubles?

Someone behind us says, "I've always figured Roman Maguire is all about the Benjamins over winning. Now we know it for a fact."

Harper leans into me. "They must not know about Roman's son in LA. If they did, wouldn't they talk about Roman possibly changing teams for him?"

"Roman never talks about his son in the press," I whisper back. "I'm sure they have no idea he exists."

My mind is suddenly racing. My heart, exploding with regret. When Roman told me about his son in the restaurant, I thought him not mentioning him before that moment meant his feelings for me had never evolved beyond simple lust. But now, I'm thinking my knee-jerk reaction back then might have been too harsh. Who knows what it's like to be a huge superstar like Roman? I'm sure it's incredibly difficult for him to figure out when he can safely let his guard down with anyone—especially someone new to his life.

Yes, I bared my soul to Roman, and he never returned the favor—but I was forced to do that by that stupid, viral video. If not for that, would I have kept my traumas to myself, as originally planned, and pretended to be a carefree sex kitten with Roman throughout our entire time together? If I'd done that, would I have thought of myself as the villain in the story, the same way I've been painting Roman in my mind? I doubt it. More likely, I would I have justified my actions to myself, the same way Roman justified *his* actions to me.

The team owner on TV speaks, drawing my attention back to the screen above the bar. "So, now," he says, "let's hear a few words from the man of the hour—the Thunderbolts' new quarterback, Roman Maguire!"

With the same wicked grin he wore countless times in Hawaii while looking up at me from between my bare thighs, Roman leans into the bank of microphones and says, "Hello."

Gah. At the sound of his deep, sexy voice, my body involuntarily shudders and zings with desire. In a flash, I'm barraged with memories of that same deep voice dirty-talking in my ear. Those big hands greedily caressing my naked body. Those dark eyes practically boring holes into my face, while Roman fucked me into oblivion.

"First off," Roman says, "let me say I couldn't be happier to be a Thunderbolt, and I couldn't be happier to play for Coach Hardy again." With that, off he goes, talking for several minutes about his excitement, his journey to get here, and his historic partnership with Coach Hardy.

As Roman speaks, I'm transfixed. Screaming internally at myself for not swallowing my pride in Kauai and following him to LA. True, doing that likely would have felt like compromising my integrity and turning myself into an undignified, pathetic little puppy. But so what? Seeing him now, I'm thinking it's distinctly possible I would have been happier getting to be with Roman *some* of the time in LA, however briefly and unpredictably, rather than sitting here in Orchard Blossom, watching him on TV in my present state of heartache and yearning.

Roman wraps up his remarks, and Coach Hardy, a broad-shouldered man with a twinkle in his dark eyes, is given the floor. The speech he makes echoes his star quarterback's, mostly, and as he speaks, two things become clear: One, the man has a likeable, commanding presence. And two, he absolutely adores Roman Maguire.

Eventually, the team owner invites Roman to hold up a Thunderbolts jersey for a photo op—a jersey imprinted with the number ten and *MAGUIRE* on its back. As Roman poses with the jersey, first with the team owner, then with Coach Hardy, and then on his own, flashbulbs pop from every direction. And when that display is done, the team owner invites questions from reporters.

To kick things off, a female reporter yells out, "Roman, is there something you'd like to say to all the Crusader fans cursing your name or feeling upset about you leaving Baltimore?"

Roman chuckles, like he couldn't give two shits about disgruntled fans of his former team. But what he says is, "We had a great run in Baltimore together, and I'm grateful for that. But nothing lasts forever, and this is what's best for me now." It momentarily seems he's done answering the question. But after a beat, he leans into the microphones and adds, "Also, specifically to any Crusaders fans cursing my name right now, I'd like to say . . ." He looks straight into the camera. "I can't wait to make you curse my name even more this season, when the Thunderbolts kick the Crusaders' ass."

"*Roman*," Coach Hardy chastises, shaking his head as the pod of reporters reacts loudly. But it's clear from the Coach's delighted facial expression he absolutely loves Roman's fiery words. So does the team owner. In fact, the white-haired guy is eating them up.

As someone asks Coach Hardy a question, Darcy appears in front of me. "Please, tell me you had some good, old-fashioned, naked fun with that god of a man after your famous dinner date, Iris. If not, I'm going to sob into my pillow tonight on your behalf."

I laugh breezily, even though I'm dying inside. "Sorry to disappoint you, but I had dinner with him and nothing more."

"*No*."

"Sorry, yes. Sadly, he was a perfect gentleman with me."

"Damn," Darcy grumbles. "He's got quite the reputation for burning through women like popcorn at a horror flick.

After you were photographed with him, I looked him up, and I couldn't believe all the gorgeous women he's dated. That gave me hope you'd have an extremely juicy story to tell whenever you came home for a visit."

As far as I'm concerned, my sex life is nobody's damned business, not even Darcy's. And I don't want to subject myself—or Roman—to even more online ridicule and speculation. Roman has never addressed that photo of us at dinner, so I feel like I have free rein to invent a narrative that suits me.

"Sorry to disappoint you, Darce," I say breezily. "It wasn't even a date. I happened to meet Roman that morning at the breakfast buffet at our hotel, and he recognized me from the viral video. He sweetly pulled me aside to tell me to keep my chin up and ignore the trolls, but when he had to run off for a golf game in the middle of our conversation, he offered to take me to a nice dinner that night to finish it."

Darcy looks suspicious. "He asked you out to dinner at a fancy, hoity-toity restaurant for the sole purpose of finishing a *conversation* with you?"

I nod and plaster a smile on my face. "That's what he said. And I guess he was being totally sincere about that, since he didn't make a move on me, during or after our meal."

"*Not at all?*"

I shake my head. "He didn't even flirt with me. Apparently, it was a random act of kindness. Or maybe he was simply bored that day. Who knows? All I know is we talked, had dinner, and that was it." Man, it's scary how easily I can lie about this. Probably because my fairy tale with Roman in Hawaii doesn't even feel real anymore. More like a lovely dream that never happened, except in my own mind.

"Well, damn," Darcy grumbles. "What a bummer."

Harper interjects, "Maybe Roman figured with Iris getting out of an engagement only a few days before, she wouldn't be interested in jumping into bed with him."

I tap my chin and pretend to contemplate Harper's supposedly new theory, even though I've heard it before. I've given this same fictitious account of the viral dinner photograph several times since coming home to Orchard Blossom—enough that Harper now knows exactly when to chime in to help me deflect from the truth even more and make my chaste version of events seem all the more believable.

"I hadn't thought of that," I say to Harper, even though she offered the same theory during a similar conversation yesterday afternoon at her family's horse ranch. "But it makes sense. Either way, I certainly like that theory far more than Roman simply not finding me attractive."

"Who wouldn't find you attractive?" Darcy says, waving a hand in the air. "You're beautiful. Inside and out."

"Thank you, Darcy. I'm not sure Roman Maguire would agree with you, though."

Speaking of Roman, his voice on the TV screen above Darcy draws our attention again. "No, it wasn't a hard decision for me. When someone offers you the chance to play for the best coach in the world again, you do it." Roman looks straight into the camera. "I've recently had the unfortunate opportunity to realize regret is a truly horrible emotion. Worst of all is regretting something I *didn't* do than something I *did*. That's why, whether I'm considering taking a dream job or taking a chance on a special someone, whatever it is, I'm now determined to take a risk and *do* the thing, even if it doesn't ultimately work out, so I never again have to lie awake at night in bed, wondering, 'What if?'"

# CHAPTER 27
## Iris

*Six Weeks Later*

"Does that feel good, sweet boy? You're such a big, beautiful baby. Yes, you are."

I'm cooing these words to a quarter horse named Butterscotch, a calm gelding for beginners, while brushing him in his stall after a riding lesson. His stall is one of ten lining the north side of the largest stable on Harper's family's horse ranch. During my stay in Orchard Blossom, I've helped out around here, the same way I did in high school. What else am I going to do? My job search thus far has been woefully ineffective, so at least being here and helping out is something productive to do.

"Iris."

I straighten up from brushing Butterscotch's front leg and discover the source of the deep, sexy voice. *Roman*. He's here. In Orchard Blossom, looking effortlessly cool and scrumptious in a tight-fitting T-shirt, jeans, and a baseball cap imprinted with a thunderbolt.

"Hey," I gasp out. I blink rapidly, not believing my eyes. He's standing on the other side of Butterscotch in a wide dirt walkway just outside the stall, but he might as well be licking my naked skin, based on the way my nervous system is reacting to the sight of him.

"Look at you, country girl," Roman says, a crooked grin on his face. "You're in your element."

I feel dizzy. Disoriented. This feels like two worlds colliding—my fantasy world and real life. Should I come out from around Butterscotch to hug him in greeting? If so, I'm not sure my wobbly legs will safely make the journey. Why is he here? To see *me*, specifically? If so, did he come to pursue me romantically, or to ask me to sign an NDA about our fling in Kauai? During a recent FaceTime call with Kaylee and Tatiana, Kaylee said she was surprised Roman never asked me to sign an NDA, since it's well-known that high-profile people often require them of the people in their orbits. Is that why Roman is here?

My racing mind is making it difficult to form words. But somehow, I manage to choke out, "H-how'd you find me?"

Roman's crooked smile returns. "You said you were going home to Orchard Blossom after Denver."

"No, *here*. At the ranch."

He shrugs. "I asked about you in town, and a bartender told me to look for you here. Sorry I didn't call before showing up. The number I have for you didn't work."

"I had to change it. Crazies kept calling and telling me to kill myself for being a slut."

Roman looks stricken. "I'm sorry to hear that."

"It's okay. The new number did the trick. For now, anyway." My feet still frozen in place, I lay a palm on Butterscotch's back. "So, uh, w-what, brings you to Orchard Blossom?"

Roman's dark eyes feel like they're boring into my soul. "You talked about how 'magical' your hometown is, so I figured I'd check out the magic for myself. Mandatory minicamp is over, and I've got a couple weeks till training camp, so now is the perfect time." He takes a tentative step forward. "I still owe you a day of horseback riding, remember? I know we were supposed to do it on a Hawaiian beach at sunset, but I'm hoping you'll say yes to doing it here instead."

What's happening? Why is he really here? Roman couldn't possibly have squeezed in a visit to my small hometown simply to fulfill his plan to ride horses with me.

"W-when?" I ask lamely, even though I've got zero plans for the next eighty years.

"Whenever you've got some free time over the next week. That's how long I've got my Airbnb."

*He's staying in Orchard Blossom for a full week?* "Oh, wow. Are you staying at the Claxton farmhouse?" It's the best Airbnb in the area—a large, recently renovated farmhouse on fifty acres that looks delightfully quaint but actually features tons of luxurious modern amenities and upgrades, thanks to the family's overhaul of the place after Old Man Claxton passed away. If I were a rich person staying in Orchard Blossom, that's where I'd stay, hands down. Although, if I were a rich person, I can't imagine I'd choose to stay in Orchard Blossom for a full week, when I could go anywhere in the world. Which makes me wonder, yet again, what the heck he's really doing here.

"Yeah, I think that's what it's called. It's a big, green farmhouse on the outskirts of town."

"That's the Claxton place. Good choice. It's our version of the Four Seasons." I shift my weight and run my palm down Butterscotch's back. "Have you gone down to the stream on the property?"

"Not yet. I just got in late last night."

My heart is pounding against my sternum. "You should check it out. It's teeming with rainbow trout. Some other fish, too, but mostly trout."

Roman takes two slow steps forward, but he stops when he gets just inside the small stall. "Do you know how to fish?"

I nod. "Mr. Claxton was friends with my grandpa—my mom's dad—so he used to let my brother and me go fishing on his property when we were little." I press my lips together and tell myself not to babble about fishing when all I want to know is why the heck he's here. What he wants. Why he's bothered. But when Roman doesn't speak, I can't help filling the awkward silence with, "I mean, I'm in no danger of being featured on the Fishing Channel, but I can usually catch enough fish for a nice dinner."

With a panty-melting smile on his face, Roman takes another step forward. "Maybe you can show me how to fish, while I'm here."

My breathing has turned shallow. My head is spinning. "Trout fishing is easy. All you need is the right lure and bait, and you'll be Long John Silver in no time." *Long John Silver? What the heck, Iris?*

Roman takes two more steps forward, until he's looking at me with blazing eyes from across Butterscotch's back. "Maybe you could help me pick out the right lure and bait."

It suddenly feels intolerably hot in this stable. Also, like my heart might physically burst at his sheer proximity. "I-I could certainly do that. Or y-you could go to Peterson's Bait and Tackle in town and ask for advice. Mr. P-Peterson makes these cool handmade lures that work like a charm. They're more expensive than the prepackaged cheapies, but they're totally worth it."

Roman's dark eyes twinkle and one side of his perfect mouth hitches up. "That's good to know. Thanks for the intel."

"Are there any fishing rods at the rental? If not, I'm sure my dad has one you could borrow."

Roman places his large palm onto Butterscotch's back, and the horse swishes his blond tail in reply. Not to mention, my body electrifies at the sight of Roman's big hand, resting mere inches from my chest.

"Actually," he says, his eyes locked with mine, "I think there were two rods in a closet at the Airbnb, so you'd only have to bring one for yourself if you come teach us how to fish."

My racing heart feels like it's stopped. "*Us?*" For the life of me, I can't fathom what that word means in this context.

Roman's lopsided grin returns. "I brought Maverick with me."

My jaw hangs open. "Oh. Wow." It's all my overwhelmed brain can manage.

"You said I didn't show you the real me in Kauai, so I came to show him to you here—and I realized I can't do that without introducing you to my son. He's my heart and soul, Iris. As real as I get." Roman noticeably flushes a bit. He takes a deep breath and clears his throat. "My parents are here with me, too. They came along to help with Mav this week, in case I happen to get lucky and get a date with a pretty girl while I'm here."

*Date.*

*With me?*

*Am I the pretty girl?*

My brain searches for a different meaning. A more logical one. But it can't come up with anything else. My chest heaving, I blurt, "I watched the press conference, Roman. In a sports bar. Everyone went nuts, exactly like you said." My breathing feels erratic, so I take a deep, steadying breath. "After the press conference, I heard your new Thunderbolts jersey sold out within hours of the announcement, and it's now the best-selling NFL jersey."

Roman smiles ruefully. "Yeah, we'll see how long the honeymoon phase lasts once the season starts. If I don't start racking up wins out of the gate, those same fans will start burning my jersey in effigy."

I swat at the air above Butterscotch's back to shoo a fly. "Don't worry about that. You're gonna come out of the gate winning. I know it in my bones."

He raps his knuckles to the side of his head, playfully knocking on wood. "Let's hope your bones are psychic." As he drops his hand to his side, his Adam's apple bobs. "Hey, would you be willing to come out from behind the horse so I can give you a hug?"

My knees buckle, so I grip Butterscotch to steady myself. "Yes. Of course."

"Only if you're comfortable."

"No, I am. Yes. Of course."

I inhale deeply before beginning my short journey toward Roman's opened arms, during which my knees feel rubbery and my heart feels like it's exploding in my chest. And the minute Roman embraces me and I smell the familiar, musky spice of his aftershave, I'm hurtled straight back to our magical kiss at the waterfall.

"I've missed you," Roman whispers into my ear, and my heart leaps with excitement. They're the words I've been dying to hear for over a month.

"I've missed you, too," I confess. I'm telling the truth. And yet, as soon as I say the words, another truth slams into me: I'm wary. Skeptical. Worried about getting my heart broken again. Obviously, it's exciting to realize Roman came here to Orchard Blossom to visit me—for a full week, no less, and with his family in tow. But a week isn't a long time. Not nearly long enough, anyway, for me to hope for any kind of future with Roman after he leaves and goes back to his new life in LA.

Roman leans back from our embrace to look into my eyes. "Was Denver okay? I was worried about you running into your ex."

"I didn't see him." I cock my head. "By any chance, did you send someone to watch over me in Denver? There was a dark SUV that seemed like it kept popping up, especially when I was at Brandon's house to get another load of stuff."

Roman looks sheepish. "Yeah, that was my guy. A bodyguard."

I bat his shoulder. "You should have told me! I thought human traffickers were after me."

"Your number was disconnected. Plus, you told me to rip off the Band-Aid, remember? I didn't think you'd want to hear from me."

"So you let me think human traffickers were after me?"

Roman laughs. "I didn't think you'd notice him."

"I did."

"Sorry." He bites his lower lip. "God, it's good to see you again, Iris."

"You, too."

He touches my cheek, sending shivers skating every which way across my skin. "Do you have time to meet my son?"

"When?"

"Now."

"Where?"

"Here."

"Maverick's *here*—at the ranch?"

Roman nods. "My parents, too. I left them chatting with a young woman with dark hair."

"Was her hair in braids?"

"That's the one."

"That's Harper. She's been my best friend since grade school. Her family owns the place."

Roman grins. "The minute she told me where to find you, Harper became my best friend, too."

Even as my stomach flutters with butterflies, it's also tight with anxiety. For weeks, I've been fantasizing about getting to see Roman again. In person. Just one more time. But now that he's here, I'm equal parts elated and wary.

"So, do you have a few minutes, or . . . ?" Roman asks.

"Oh. Yes." I clear my throat. As wary and nervous as I am, there's no way in hell I'd say no to meeting Roman's son and parents. "Just give me a minute to finish up here, and we'll go."

"Great." Roman steps back while I finish brushing Butterscotch. While I work, he asks, "Do you think you might have some time to put Maverick on a horse this week? He saw all the horses as we drove up and begged to ride one for his first time."

"I can saddle up a pony for him right now. Is he wearing close-toed shoes and long pants?"

Roman nods. "Sneakers and jeans."

"Perfect. We'll do it now, then. I've got the perfect pony for him. A gentle cutie named Tornado."

"Oh, man, Mav's gonna love the sound of that. Put him on a 'stallion' named Tornado, and he's gonna think you've lived up to your billing."

My heart stops. *My billing?* "Does that mean you've told Maverick about me?"

He bites back a smile. "My parents, too."

My shallow breathing is back. "W-what'd you tell them?"

He takes a step forward and his chest heaves. "That I met a special woman with a heart of gold in Hawaii. A trustworthy, kind, hilarious, sweet woman who never once failed to show me her true self." His smile drops. "But, unfortunately, I was too stupid—or maybe too scared—to let my guard down and return the favor."

*Oh my God. Seriously now, what's happening?*

"Oh," I say vaguely, as my mind races and swirls. This feels momentous. Like Roman's come here for more than a simple, weeklong visit with me. In fact, I can't help feeling like I'm Cinderella, and Roman's come to my house with a glass slipper on a pillow. But that's a crazy thought, right? The kind of thought that could get a girl's heart shattered, only even more so than last time with Brandon.

Roman sighs at whatever he's seeing on my face. "I've come to correct my mistake, Iris. Or at least try. If you'll let me."

"I . . ." I blush and clear my throat. "Honestly, I'm not sure what that means. How I'm supposed to 'let' you do anything. But you can certainly try to do whatever you came here to do, and I won't try to stop you."

# CHAPTER 28
## Iris

As Roman and I approach his group, his parents have their backs to us, but I can plainly see Harper's wide grin and Maverick's cherubic little face. *Holy crap.* Roman's son is his miniature replica. The boy is Roman's spitting image!

An intense feeling of déjà vu slams into me. Have I seen this beautiful boy before, or does he remind me of Roman so much, my brain is feeding me false memories? Before I settle on an answer, Roman's parents turn to greet us, and I'm met with a face that's instantly recognizable to me, despite the brevity of our prior encounter. *Roman's mother! She's the kind woman from the airport in Kauai.* Consider my mind officially blown.

Of course, it's wonderful to see this sweet, maternal woman again. I'd love to properly thank her for the nurturing kindness she showered me with when I needed it most. But I'd rather eat rusty nails than thank his mother in this context, and in front of Roman, thereby reminding her and Roman of the pathetic, rock-bottom state I was in upon my arrival in Kauai. It's one thing for a kindhearted mother to offer comfort to a pitiable, distraught stranger at an airport, but quite another for that same mother to approve of a pitiable, distraught stranger as a romantic interest for her beloved son. That's got to be especially true when the son in question is a world-renowned athlete with his pick of romantic partners. Not to mention, when the distraught stranger recently starred, against her will, in a mortifying viral video.

"Everyone," Roman says, his tone brimming with excitement. He motions proudly to me as we come to a stop. "This is Iris Benedetto. Iris, these are my parents, Edward and Ava Maguire, and my son, Maverick."

"Hi, everyone," I squeak out, waving and averting my eyes from Roman's mother. "It's great to meet you."

"*This is Iris?*" Roman's mother gasps out. "Iris, we've met! Don't you remember? It was at the airport in Kauai!"

*Welp. The jig is up.*

I meet Mrs. Maguire's gaze with a smile. "Of course I remember you, Mrs. Maguire. I'll never forget you. You were my guardian angel that day."

"Please, call me Ava." She pulls me into a warm hug, and I'm hit with a lovely floral scent. "You look wonderful, sweetheart. So much happier and healthier than when we met before."

"I'm like new. Even better, actually. Time heals all wounds, as they say."

"So glad to hear it."

When we break apart, I exchange an incredulous look with my bestie, Harper. One that screams, "Oh my fucking God." When I arrived in Orchard Blossom almost two months ago, Harper came over, and I proceeded to tell my lifelong best friend everything that had happened to me in Hawaii over a bottle of wine. I didn't divulge Roman's "new team" secret to Harper or anyone else, as promised—but I certainly did tell Harper the story of the lovely, elegant grandmother who'd comforted me at the airport and instructed me to indulge my every whim during my vacation.

At the time of that conversation with Harper, we both giggled and snickered to think that nice Airport Lady had given me a much-needed push to defy my inhibitions and have my first fling with a stranger. And now it turns out the Airport Lady was unknowingly giving me to permission to bang her gorgeous son? What are the odds?

"Sorry to interrupt the lovefest," Roman says with a chuckle. "But how did you two meet, exactly?"

My body seizes with preemptive embarrassment, but Ava's bubbly, happy energy doesn't shift in the least. With a smile, she links her arm in mine and breezily replies, "Iris dropped her sunglasses while waiting in line for a rental car, so I picked them up and brought them to her, and we wound up having a lovely, memorable conversation." She looks at me sympathetically, her lips pursed. "The poor baby had been through a rough time the day before, so we sat down together and she told me about it, in the most precious, darling way imaginable." She pats my arm. "I told Edward about our conversation when I got to the gate. I told him, 'I just met the loveliest girl, Edward. I swear, I'll never forget her, as long as I live.'"

"She did," Edward confirms.

Gratitude floods me. Butterflies. *Relief.* There were so many other ways Roman's mother might have described our tear-filled encounter—descriptions that would have cast me in a horribly embarrassing light. But she chose to treat me with kindness, once again. Clearly, the moment we shared in Hawaii wasn't a fluke—kindness is Ava Maguire's default setting. No wonder she reminded me of my own mother back at that airport—my mom was the exact same way. Kind and generous to her very core.

"That's so you, Mom," Roman says with a smirk. "Yet another Pop-Up Pal." To me, Roman adds, "That's what Mom calls the brief connections she always makes with people, everywhere she goes."

"I love that." I smile at Ava. "Being your Pop-Up Pal was a lucky thing for me. I needed your kind words and comfort, more than you possibly could have known." Even if it causes me embarrassment, it's only right to give the woman her due.

I look at Roman, and it suddenly occurs to me: *Like mother, like son.* Indeed, I think it's fair to say Roman did for me exactly what his mother had done at the airport, only on a much grander scale. In the beginning, I figured Roman did that for sex—but after a while, that answer wasn't good enough. Well, now I know: he was doing what he'd witnessed his own mother doing his entire life. Being kind. Going out on a limb to help someone in need. Not to mention, like Harper figured out at the bar the other day, I'm sure Roman recognized some of his own struggles in me.

"What a crazy coincidence," Roman's father says. "To think you two met at a tiny airport on an island in the Pacific, and now you're meeting again in a tiny town three thousand miles away."

"There are no coincidences," Roman's mom says ominously, her index finger raised. "Only *signs*."

"Yep," Roman agrees, with a visible squeeze of his son's little hand.

Throughout this conversation, little Maverick has been quietly holding his father's hand and shyly pressing his cheek against Roman's thick thigh. But now that my eyes have locked with his, he slides slightly behind his daddy's leg.

"Hey, Maverick," I say softly. "Your daddy told me you might like to ride a horse today. Is that true?"

Maverick gasps and looks up at his father, his little eyebrows raised to his scalp.

"You have to reply to Iris if you want to go, buddy," Roman coos. "She's the person who can make it happen for you, not me."

Maverick blushes a deep shade of crimson and his tiny body heaves with his intake of air.

"You don't have to feel shy with Iris," Roman persists, his large palm resting on Maverick's dark mop of hair. "She's the nicest person I've ever met. She's Daddy's really, really good friend, and I know you'll like her, too, if you give her a chance to be your friend."

My heart flutters at Roman's amazing words. Also, Roman's tone and body language with his son are so damned gentle and sweet, my ovaries suddenly feel like tiny pitching machines at a batting cage. *Pop, pop, pop.*

When Maverick still remains silent and blushing, I crouch down in front of him with a soft smile, the same way I do with all of my shiest students. Well, the same way I *did* with them, back when I was still an employed teacher. "I'm thinking you'd really enjoy riding a pony named Tornado. She loves taking first-timers. If you feed her some baby carrots before climbing aboard, she'll fall madly in love with you and make sure you have a wonderful first ride."

Maverick wiggles his little body with excitement and looks up at his towering father again. "Can I, Daddy?"

"It's up to Iris. Muster the courage to look at her and say, 'Yes, please. I'd love that. Thank you, Iris,' and see what happens next."

Maverick takes a deep breath and turns his dark, Romanesque gaze on me. "Yes, Irish. Tank you, pwease."

We all melt and chuckle at his cuteness—and thankfully, nobody corrects his precious pronunciation of my name.

"Good job," I say. I put my hand up for a high five, and he gives it to me. "Let's go find Tornado and get her saddled up."

I suddenly realize Harper isn't standing with the group. Apparently, my best friend drifted away at some point without me realizing it. Probably, knowing her, to give me some privacy with our unexpected guests. That would make perfect sense, actually, given how many times Harper's had to listen to me babbling about Roman and my aching heart since my arrival in Orchard Blossom almost two months ago.

After leading the group around a corner, I easily find my best friend talking to one of the ranch hands. "Hey, baby," I chirp. "Is Tornado in the north pasture? I've got a first-time cowboy who'd love to feed her some baby carrots and ride her like the wind."

Harper giggles at my sarcasm. Our beloved Tornado has

only one gear: walking very, very slowly. And everyone at this ranch knows it.

"Yep," Harper confirms brightly. "North pasture. But I'll grab her for you, while you show everyone around." To Maverick, Harper adds, "There's a bunch of horses in stalls over there who'd love to snack on carrots, if you're willing to feed them."

As Maverick whoops with excitement, I flash Harper a grateful smile. She's playing Cupid, obviously—allowing me to spend as much time as possible with Roman and his family. Otherwise, she'd surely let me run hither and yon, looking for that damned pony myself.

"Thanks, Harper. We'll meet you over at the stable."

I turn to make sure Roman and his parents are following Maverick and me, and when my eyes lock with Roman's a few feet away, my body jolts like I've gripped an electric fence. He's on fire as he stares at me. Indeed, his gaze is so intense and sexual, so damned heated, it instantly sends a throbbing ache between my legs.

I force my attention back to the sweet little boy clutching my hand. "When Harper brings Tornado to the stable, you can help me saddle her up, if you'd like."

Maverick makes a gargled sound of glee that bears no resemblance to the English language, and everyone who loves him—which I'm pretty sure already includes me—laughs uproariously at his exuberance.

"Is that a 'Yes, please, Iris'?" Roman asks from behind me, eliciting a chuckle from his parents and a swoon from me.

"Yes, please, Irish."

My chest constricts. My heart throbs. God help me, just this fast, I think I'm already in danger of falling in love with Maverick Maguire, every bit as much as I'm stupidly in danger of falling madly in love with his gorgeous, look-alike, football god of a father.

## CHAPTER 29
## Iris

"Ride 'em, cowboy!" Roman calls out to his son.

I glance at Maverick's proud daddy standing next to me and swoon at the joy on his gorgeous face. In Hawaii, I was treated to a wide range of different smiles from Roman—but not once did I witness one quite as stunning as the smile of fatherly love splitting Roman's face now.

"Go, Mavvy, go!" Roman's mother shouts, sounding every bit as proud as her son.

Roman, his parents, and I are standing outside the circular, steel rails of a corral while watching Harper slowly leading Maverick on Tornado around and around. Roman is standing immediately next to me, leaning his forearms against the top row of metal piping, while his parents stand a few feet away on Roman's other side, snapping photos, cheering, and taking endless videos.

"You look like Woody!" Roman's father yells from behind his camera, at which point Roman's mother effortlessly drops one of Woody's famous lines from *Toy Story,* the one about there being a snake in his boot. Little Maverick responds with giggles and whoops. Tornado's a small, slow-moving creature—a perfect first ride for any young child—but you'd never know her name was ironic based on Maverick's enthralled reaction to riding her.

Clearly, this kid feels like a cowboy expertly riding a bucking Shire stallion.

"Do you see me, Daddy?" Maverick shouts excitedly.

"I sure do, buddy! You're doing great!" Roman pumps his fist to emphasize his point, and when he returns his hand to the metal railing, our fingers brush. Was that an accident, or did Roman intend to touch me like that? Either way, even that slight contact simultaneously sent a flutter of butterflies into my belly and a ripple of anxiety into my veins. I'm thrilled Roman is here. Seeing him again, if only once more, is all I've been dreaming about for weeks. But now that he's here, I'm wary about reading too much into it. Like my mother always used to say, "Disappointment is merely another word for an *expectation* going unfulfilled," so I'm determined not to expect too much out of this unexpected visit.

"Are you *sure* you've never ridden a horse before?" Roman's father calls out to his grandson, jerking my thoughts back to the present.

"No, really, it's my first time ever, Grampa!" Maverick calls out earnestly, not picking up on his grandfather's sarcasm. In a flash, I recall that cute little boy (Roman's son) emerging from the bathroom at the airport in Kauai, calling out to his grandmother (*Roman's mother*—oh my God) about "what else" he saw in the bathroom. Seriously, what are the odds I felt compelled to tell Roman a cute story about his own son without realizing it? I've never been one to believe in signs all that much, like Ava apparently does, but I must admit that sure feels like one. Is there a greater power at work here—one that's been pushing me toward these specific people—or am I simply grasping at straws and believing what I want to believe?

Roman bumps my side gently and whispers, "He's having the time of his life."

My heart skips a beat at Roman's brief contact. "He's doing great," I reply. I clear my throat and shout to Maverick, "You're almost as good a rider as me, Maverick, and I've been riding horses since I was even younger than you!"

Harper agrees with my sentiment as she continues her latest slow lap around the ring. To Maverick, she adds, "See how Tornado's ears are twitching? That means she *really* likes you." As Maverick gasps excitedly, Harper shoots me a secret wink, letting me know she's as smitten with this cutie pie as I am.

"Thanks for doing this for him," Roman whispers to me. As he says it, he nudges his body against mine again, sending another round of shock waves coursing through me. "He's gonna be talking about this all week. Maybe even for months."

"It's my pleasure. He's adorable."

"Glad you think so, too." He nudges me a third time, his body language flirtatious and playful, and when I dare to look up into his face, he smiles and winks, prompting my heart to momentarily beat in an irregular rhythm.

I take a deep breath. "Do you remember that little boy from the airport I told you about?" When Roman looks at me blankly, I add, "The one who answered 'my pee-pee' when his grandmother asked what else he saw in the bathroom besides a whale painted on the wall? That was Maverick, Roman."

Roman looks flabbergasted. "Seriously? That's crazy."

"Isn't it? I can't believe it."

Roman glances at his mother, who's currently fixated on Maverick in the corral. And when he returns to me, his smile fades. Indeed, something I'd label as regret overtakes his handsome face. "If only I'd told you about Maverick when you told me that story," he says softly, "maybe things would have turned out differently for us."

I'm floored. "You not telling me about Maverick till later in the week isn't the reason we parted ways, Roman. The timing wasn't right for us back then." I hold my breath. I'm not sure if the timing is right for us now, to be honest, but as my words came out, I felt a dangerous pang of expectation seize me—the fervent hope that now could be the right time and that things might turn out differently for us this time.

Roman drags his teeth over his lower lip, mulling that over. When he speaks, his dark eyes are locked with mine. "In Hawaii," he says softly, "you said you didn't know what was real and what wasn't when it came to me. I haven't been able to get that comment out of my head, Iris. It's tortured me." He runs a large palm down his face. "If only I'd been brave enough to follow your lead—to let my guard down the way you did—maybe we could have overcome the bad timing."

*In what way? What does that mean? What does he expect to get out of this week in Orchard Blossom?* "I didn't open up to you voluntarily," I manage to say. "I was forced to do it by that stupid video, remember? If not for that, who knows what kind of mysterious femme fatale I'd have pretended to be for the entire week."

Roman snorts. "You really think you're capable of pretending to be someone you're not? If you ask me, one of the best things about you is you wear your heart on your sleeve. That's why what you said in Kauai has haunted me so much—because I never for a minute doubted what was real when it came to you. Never. The fact that you didn't feel the same way meant I messed up really, really badly."

"Okay, first of all," I say playfully, "How dare you imply I'm not capable of pretending to be a mysterious femme fatale. Granted, attempting that probably would have proved difficult for me. It maybe even would have gone against my very nature to do it. But I choose to believe I can pull off anything I set my mind to."

The side of Roman's mouth hitches up. His dark eyes are gleaming. "I stand corrected. Forgive me. I didn't mean to pick a fight."

"I forgive you. But second of all, you didn't mess up, okay? You heard your mom—there are no coincidences. Everything is happening, right on time, exactly as it should."

Roman's gaze drifts down to my lips, and the small channel of air between us suddenly feels charged. If Roman's family weren't here, would he lean in to kiss me? It feels like it. If he did, I'd surely wrap my arms around his neck and devour his soft lips like my very life depended on it.

Roman runs a finger down my forearm. "Are you free for dinner tonight?"

"Let me check my calendar. Yes."

Roman chuckles at my silliness. "I'd be happy to take you out to Orchard Blossom's finest eating establishment, if you'd like, but my mother is cooking tonight at the Airbnb, and she's a fantastic cook."

Every cell in my body jolts. Roman is inviting me to dinner with his family? "I'd never pass up a good home-cooked meal," I say, trying to sound calm and breezy, like I'm not totally freaking out.

"I was hoping you'd say that. I'd love for Maverick to get to know you while we're here. My parents, too, if that's okay with you. And I think a relaxed dinner at home with you would be a great way to try to do that."

My heart is stampeding. Racing. Thundering. An hour ago, I thought I'd never see Roman Maguire again. And now, he's here with his son and parents, and he's inviting me to a family dinner? It's too much. Too fast. Am I risking total decimation here if I take this leap of faith and say yes? Am I going to wind up with a broken heart that's even worse than the one I got with Brandon? "I'd love to get to know everyone while you're here," I manage to squeak out. "As long as that includes plenty of opportunities for me to get to know you. The real you."

"That's why I'm here, Iris." His chest heaves. "My parents are planning to babysit Mav for me all week, whenever you'll let me take you out on some dates. Would you be willing to do that?"

I swallow hard and nod. "That sounds nice." *And then*

*what?* The words pop into my head, but I quickly stuff them down and tell myself to take things one day at a time. One invitation at a time. Tonight, I'll join Roman's family dinner. For now, that's all I need to think about.

Roman's eyes drift to my lips. Once again, the air between us crackles in a way that makes me think Roman wants to kiss me. But before he moves or speaks, Maverick calls out to Roman.

"Daddy!" he shouts. "Look at me!"

Before turning his attention to his son, Roman lays a hand on mine on the railing. It's a simple gesture. A G-rated one. But it sends tingles rocketing throughout my entire body, and a certain kind of pulsing announces itself between my legs.

With his hand on mine, Roman watches his son for a long moment and cheers him on. But when Maverick's attention is drawn to something Harper is saying to him, Roman squeezes my hand underneath his, prompting me to look at him again.

"Thank you, Iris," he says softly, holding my gaze. "Thank you for giving me a second chance to show you what I'm all about."

# CHAPTER 30
## Roman

I squeeze Iris's hand underneath the dinner table. I mustered the courage to grab it about twenty minutes ago, as we all started devouring the apple pie Iris brought to tonight's dinner party, and I haven't let go of it since.

I can't believe I ever doubted my feelings for this woman. Or thought my feelings for her would fade after I arrived in LA and started my new life. Or, worst of all, that I ever thought I could find "someone like Iris" one day, whenever the timing happened to be better for me.

I was a fool for thinking all of it.

For so long now, I've ached for Iris. Dreamed about her. Kicked myself for not being brave enough to match her openness. Fantasized about including her in my new life. Indeed, with each passing day, I became more and more certain not only was I ready to follow in my cousin Marco's footsteps and settle down, but I was excited to do exactly that. The only question is whether my yearning for Iris is reliable enough to act upon. To gamble on, long-term. So, here I am in Orchard Blossom, with my parents and Maverick, intending to do whatever it takes to answer that question with certainty.

"Dinner was so delicious, Mrs. Maguire," Iris says to my mother across the table. "I'd love to get your recipe."

She's referring to the the impressive seafood pasta dish with homemade linguini my mother served this evening. It's her specialty—a time-consuming masterpiece Mom only bothers making on special occasions or when she wants to impress someone.

"Only if you give me this pie recipe," Mom replies to Iris. "It's the best apple pie I've ever tasted."

Iris blushes. "It's my mother's recipe. She grew up in Orchard Blossom, so baking and cooking with apples was a specialty of hers."

Mom palms her forehead. "*Orchard* Blossom! I didn't put it together till now there must be orchards nearby."

Iris laughs. "Lots of them. Washington produces more apples than any other state in the country. It's not prime apple-picking season yet, but some nearby orchards have perennials, so we could check them out while you're here."

"I'd love to," Mom gushes. "What about you, Mav? Do you want to pick apples off a tree with Iris?"

"Can I eat dem?" Maverick asks.

"Of course," Iris says. "An orchard has apple trees as far as you can see, so you can eat as many apples as you can fit into your belly."

"I love apples," Maverick exclaims with a grin.

"Then, let's do it," Iris says. "I'll pack us a picnic and we'll make a day of it. The countryside over there is really beautiful."

Without hesitation, my shy boy launches into an energetic conversation with Iris about the picnic episode of his favorite show, *Bluey*. And that's how I know my boy's every bit as enamored with Iris as me: He doesn't get chatty like this with everyone.

As Maverick chats excitedly with Iris, I notice Mom smirking at Dad in a way I've seen countless times. She's gloating. Nonverbally saying something along the lines of "I told you so." If I were a betting man, which I am, I'm guessing Mom predicted Maverick would fall head over heels in love with Iris. Or hell, for all I know, maybe my parents' bet was about *me*, and Mom already thinks she's won it.

When Maverick's dissertation about *Bluey* ends, Mom smiles pleasantly at me and says, "Roman, honey, take Iris outside for an after-dinner stroll, while Dad and I do the dishes and put Mav to bed. I noticed the stars are out in full force tonight."

"Let me do the dishes," Iris says. "You cooked dinner."

Mom waves at the air and tells a bald-faced lie. "No, no, Edward and I love doing dishes together." In truth, my parents have a maid who does dishes after Mom cooks. That was my Christmas present to Mom last year, since I know she loves cooking but hates cleaning up. "Now, go on," Mom says with a wwshoo of her hands. "The sky is bursting with stars tonight. It'd be rude to let them go to waste."

"Rude?" I ask, laughing.

"To God. He put them there for you to enjoy, darling. So, get out there and enjoy them."

"Your mom was right," Iris says, as we walk hand in hand down a quiet lane and look up at the night sky. "The stars are extra spectacular tonight. So beautiful."

I gaze at Iris as she continues stargazing. "Beautiful."

"When the stars are out like this," Iris continues, still looking up, "I feel so tiny—but in a good way. Feeling so tiny makes my problems feel tiny, too."

I've been dying to kiss her since I laid eyes on her in that horse stall today. She looked like a walking wet dream in those dusty jeans and boots. But other than kissing her, I'm determined to take things as slow as molasses this week. All that amazing sex we had in Hawaii? It never happened. I already know sex with Iris is a dangerous drug—the best sex of my life, by far. What I don't know, however, and what I came to Orchard Blossom to find out, is whether the intense, all-encompassing feelings I came to feel for Iris in Kauai almost two months ago, the ones that crept up on me and haven't faded over time and distance, are powered by more than my dick.

Are these feelings something I can build on, long-term? That's what I came to Orchard Blossom to figure out, with the help of my parents and Maverick, since I don't have time to slowly figure things out over an extended period of time. Training camp is in mere weeks, and then comes four preseason games, followed by a grueling, all-consuming regular-season schedule that almost never lets up. If I want to confirm Iris is The One, like I've been thinking she might be for almost two months now, then this is pretty much the only block of time I'll have to figure that out. I need clarity. Certainty. And I can't get that if I'm drunk on amazing sex with Iris.

"It's so clear tonight, I can make out all my favorite constellations," Iris says, still looking up at the starry night.

"You know enough about constellations to have favorites?"

"Stargazing is a big thing in the Pacific Northwest."

She stops walking while still looking up, so I stop alongside her.

"See that bright star there?" Iris points up with the hand not holding mine.

"Where?"

"*There.* See? That's Altair. It forms one of the corners of the Summer Triangle." As she explains further, I shift my gaze from her tutorial in the sky to her lovely profile. She's even more beautiful than I'd remembered.

"Hey," I whisper, tugging on her hand. Iris stops talking mid-sentence to look at me with blinking, blue eyes. "I don't think I can wait another second to kiss you, Iris Benedetto."

She exhales. "Oh, thank God."

With a smile, I slide my palm to her cheek and press my lips to hers—and, instantly, I'm hurtled into bliss. Our kiss simultaneously feels brand-new and nostalgic—like coming home. It feels *right*. Like a sacred gear clicking into place. How did I survive for so long without kissing these lips?

When we pull apart, Iris's chest is heaving and her blue eyes are sparkling in the moonlight. "That was a perfect kiss," she whispers. "Straight out of a fairy tale."

My heart expands in my chest. I couldn't have said it better myself, so I simply touch her cheek and kiss her again. As our tongues swirl this time, I imagine the stars above our heads swirling in concert. In a flash, I see my future in a blur. Iris in a white dress. Babies. Iris wearing the same hideous matching pajamas as the rest of us at one of our Maguire Family Christmases. I see apple pies, picnics, and pony rides for Maverick. Family days spent fishing in a stream. Moonlit nights spent impaling Iris to within an inch of her life.

The bottom line is I trust this woman. Like this woman. And I always have. Right from the start. She simply doesn't have it in her to betray me, and that's priceless. And on top of everything else, she's also great with my kid and parents, *and* sex with her is fire? Seriously now, what more could I want?

When our lips part, we stare at each other in silent awe for a long moment, both of us apparently experiencing the same loss for words.

"I'm so glad you came to Orchard Blossom," she whispers.

"So am I."

It's an understatement.

Holy shit.

I think maybe my feelings for Iris are the real deal.

I think maybe I'm in love with Iris Benedetto.

*I think it's possible I've found my future wife.*

# CHAPTER 31
## Iris

"What's your favorite flavor?" I ask Maverick.

We're standing in line with Mav's hunky daddy at Orchard Blossom's only proper ice cream parlor, deciding what to order. Sadly, it's the last full day of Roman's stay, and I have no idea what will happen next. If Roman invited me to join him in LA tomorrow, I'd say yes this time. But will he ask? And if he does, for how long would he want me to stay?

"Chocolate," Maverick says without hesitation. It's not a surprise. When I took these two to Orchard Blossom's only bakery earlier this week, Maverick picked a cookie the size of his head that was bursting with chocolate chips.

I've spent every day with Roman this week. And it's been glorious. Sometimes, with Roman alone. Other times, like today, with Roman and his adorable son. Still other times, with Roman's whole family in tow.

Early in the week, I invited Roman's entire family to Dad's house for a reciprocal dinner party. Much to my relief, everyone got along stupendously. In fact, the Maguires were so down-to-earth and easygoing when they arrived, I quickly forgot to feel insecure about our tiny, modest house.

My brother, Atlas, hilariously dropped everything at school to race home for that dinner party, by the way. Apparently,

Atlas selects Roman as his fantasy football quarterback every year, so he insisted he'd rather fail the test he should have been studying for than miss the chance to meet and have dinner with his football idol. When Atlas told me that, I wished so badly I could have assured him there'd be other chances for him to meet Roman in the future. Plenty of them. But since I have no idea what Roman is thinking about in terms of me and what lies ahead, I regrettably couldn't say that to my brother with any degree of confidence.

Fresh off that delightful dinner party at Dad's house, I took Roman's family to a nearby orchard the next morning, where we enjoyed a lovely picnic and some apple picking, as promised, much to Maverick's delight. The following day, I took everyone on a horseback-riding excursion that was so much fun, Roman, Maverick, and I went out again the next afternoon. And in the days after that, I took Roman and Maverick fishing a couple times and also, once, to Orchard Blossom's bowling alley.

In terms of alone time with Roman, we've taken a relaxed approach. One that allows us to talk a whole lot and really get to know each other. Mostly, we've taken romantic walks and hikes. Gone out for dinner at Orchard Blossom's handful of restaurants. Yesterday, Roman and I finally went on that horse-riding date we'd missed in Kauai and wound up making out like teenagers underneath the shade of a tree in a secluded meadow.

As hot and fun as yesterday's make-out session in the meadow was, I admit I felt a bit surprised about Roman's hands remaining firmly *outside* my clothes the whole time. The hotter things got between us, the more I kept expecting him to yank down my jeans and take me the way he did, so many times, in Kauai. But he never did. Before that moment, I'd assumed we hadn't had sex in Orchard Blossom yet due to simple logistics. Roman is staying with his family and I'm living with my dad, after all, so we don't have an easy place to go. Thanks to those bowling-alley photos of Roman and me that are currently swirling online, it's not like we can simply skip off to a hotel. If we did that, then the whole world would probably find out about it.

But yesterday underneath that tree, when there was nobody around and it felt like we were in our own world, I realized Roman probably wasn't yanking down my jeans in that meadow on purpose. That, in fact, the old-fashioned courtship vibe Roman's been laying down this entire week was almost certainly part of an intentional master plan. What other explanation makes any sense? We were alone underneath that tree, and all over each other, and my body language was loudly screaming, "Yes, yes, yes!"

It's all good, though. As far as I'm concerned, Roman can take the lead on the physical stuff during his visit. After all, he's the one who showed up in my small hometown unannounced, with his entire family in tow. He's the one with a decision to make, I'm guessing, since my mind has been made up since he kissed me underneath the stars on night one of his trip. I tried to hold back. Tried to fight it. But the truth is I'm now deeply smitten with Roman and willing to follow him to the ends of the Earth, if he'll have me. So, if Roman wants to take this courtship at a snail's pace, in a physical sense, no matter how badly I'm dying to jump his bones like I used to do in Hawaii, I'm going to hang back and let him do exactly that.

"What's *your* favorite flavor, Irish?" Maverick asks, looking up at me with his father's sparkling brown eyes.

"I love chocolate, too, but I think my all-time favorite is strawberry." I smile at Roman. "How about you, Daddy-o?"

Roman winks. "I like any flavor I get to enjoy with Maverick and Irish."

*Oh, my heart.* He's been saying sweet stuff like that all week.

"You have to pick," Maverick insists with a little tap on my forearm.

"Okay, well, in that case, I think I'll go with vanilla, just to round out our Neapolitan."

"Nee-nee—Huh?" Maverick says, making Roman and I chuckle at his adorableness.

We reach the front of the line, and the owner of the ice cream parlor, Wanda, gushes over Roman and his son, rather than immediately taking our order. I'm used to it by now. That's been happening all this week. Even people who've never cared about football seem elated to have a superstar of Roman's caliber in our quaint little town.

"Would you take a photo with me?" the ice cream lady asks Roman. "I'll get it printed and framed for our wall."

"You bet."

"How much longer will you be in town? I could get it printed lightning fast, so you can sign it before you leave."

"I'm leaving tomorrow, unfortunately. But I promise, the next time I'm in Orchard Blossom, I'll come in and sign it for you."

My heart seizes. Does that mean Roman is genuinely planning to come back here, or is he simply being polite with a fan, like I've seen him do countless times? And if he *is* planning to come back one day, is that a good or bad sign for *me*? If Roman is contemplating another visit to Orchard Blossom, does that mean he's *not* contemplating taking me with him to LA tomorrow? Does it mean I'm now mere hours away from unwittingly getting my heart smashed into a million pieces? It was one thing to watch this man walking away from me in Kauai, when I barely knew him and hadn't expected anything from him. But if he walks away from me now, when I've got such high hopes about continuing this amazing thing we've started here, I don't know how my heart will survive the crushing blow.

At Wanda's excited request, I snap a smiling photo of her with Roman, before Wanda finally fills our ice cream orders.

"Don't break our girlie's heart, Roman," Wanda calls out as we walk toward a window booth with our ice cream. "Iris has already had more than her fair share of heartbreak."

*Holy hell.*

"No more heartbreak for Iris," Roman shoots back pleasantly, without missing a beat. "We're both in total agreement there, ma'am."

With burning cheeks, I scoot into one side of the booth and pretend I didn't hear Wanda's mortifying comment. And a moment later, when Roman and Maverick reach the booth, Maverick surprises me by scooting into my same side, rather than his daddy's across the table, as usual.

"Sorry about that," I murmur to Roman, referring to Wanda's comment. "I'm guessing she feels duty bound to fill in for my mother."

"I think it's great how protective everyone is about you. You've obviously got a lot of people in this town who really love you."

"They loved my mother. She was practically the town mascot." In fact, when news of my mother's untimely death spread like wildfire through Orchard Blossom, it was like time stood still for everyone, not only for my family, as the entire town struggled to understand how someone as beloved and vivacious as Celeste Benedetto could succumb to the depression she'd struggled with her entire life.

"Don't sell yourself short, sweetheart," Roman says, with a little squeeze of my hand on the table. "I've been with you all week, remember? Everyone here most definitely loves *you*."

My heart skips a beat in my chest. *Sweetheart.*

"Not surprisingly," Roman adds casually, after taking a bite of his ice cream with his free hand. "To know you is to . . . adore you, Iris." When I blush, he bites his lower lip, like he's gearing up to say something. He takes a deep breath. "I've had a great time with you this week, Iris."

"So have I."

He clears his throat. "I'd really love it if—"

"Hey, Iris."

We swivel our heads toward the edge of the table and discover Brandon of all people standing there. *Oh my God.*

"Can I talk to you?" Brandon asks, looking at me.

"No, you can't," I snap, as heat flashes up my neck and into my cheeks. "What are you doing here?"

"Is this *Brandon*?" Roman grits out, like he's spitting out a curse word. Before I get a word out in reply, Roman slides out of the booth and rises to his full height, dwarfing Brandon and causing him to stumble backward with his palms raised.

"I come in peace, man," Brandon blurts. "I just want to talk to Iris for five minutes—to apologize."

Maverick's body is stiff and shaking next to mine, so I pull him closer and whisper that everything's all right. *Is it, though?*

"You've lost the privilege of speaking to Iris ever again," Roman barks out, and I can't help noticing, as he says it, he's got his right fist clenched by his muscular thigh like a spring gun.

"Who dat, Daddy?" Maverick squeaks out.

"Nobody, buddy. A big nobody." Roman looks at his son, and his nostrils flare. He glances around the ice cream parlor, at the handful of other patrons who are staring at us, slack-jawed, and I can practically see him making calculations in his head: *Exactly how much can I get away with here?* When he finally returns his dark, molten gaze to Brandon, his jaw muscles are pulsing. "Why are you still here, Brandon? Iris said she doesn't want to speak to you."

"I just need a couple minutes to—"

Roman takes a glowering step forward, and the fist by his side tightens. "My boy is here, so I'm going to be a gentleman about this, Brandon. Leave now, while your face and pride are both still intact."

Maverick snuggles even closer to me, so I give him another tight squeeze and whisper, "It's okay. They're just talking."

Brandon addresses me. "You really don't want to give me five minutes of your time to hear me apologize to you?"

"How'd you know where to find me?"

"I saw a photo of you and Roman bowling in Orchard Blossom a couple days ago. So, I asked around when I got here, and a guy told me he just saw you and Roman walking in here." He motions with exasperation to the large window adjacent to our booth and glares at Roman. "Dude, you can watch me talking to her the whole time. I'm not gonna hurt her. I'd never do that."

*Well, that's not true.* While it's true Brandon never physically hurt me, he certainly destroyed me emotionally. And now, merely being in Brandon's presence again is making me feel physically ill.

"It's your decision, baby," Roman says in a clipped voice, his jaw muscles tight. "I've got your back, no matter what you decide."

I think about it. I certainly don't need closure from Brandon, per se. That burner phone gave me all the answers I needed. But I suppose it would be nice to get to tell him to fuck off in a much calmer fashion than I managed it on our sham of a wedding day.

"I'll give you one minute," I finally say decisively. "That's all you get, though, so you'd better talk fast."

"One minute," Roman echoes, his dark eyes shooting murderous daggers at Brandon. "And if you touch her during that minute, I swear to God, mother—" He looks at Maverick and stops himself. "I won't be a gentleman anymore."

I slide out of the booth with Maverick and guide him to his father. As I gently push Maverick toward his father, he whispers to me, "Why did Daddy call him 'mother'?" It's another Maverick-ism worthy of Ava's journal. But I'm too stressed about Brandon's unexpected appearance here to smile about it.

With Maverick secured in Roman's strong arms, I march toward the front door of the ice cream parlor with my head high and Brandon trailing behind me. Once outside, I position myself in front of the window, so Roman can see everything that goes down, and then turn around in a huff to face Brandon, my hands on my hips. "One minute. *Go.*"

Brandon puffs out his cheeks. "I-I went to rehab after the wedding, and I—"

"Yeah, so you wouldn't have to go to jail for all the money you stole from clients." That's what his sister, Delilah, told me in a text—that Brandon went to rehab as part of a confidential settlement agreement brokered by their father with all his firms' clients, so Mr. Gladstone could avoid his precious son having to endure legal consequences for his bad behavior.

Brandon's face falls. "That's why I went, yes. Originally. But I've been taking it really seriously and trying to become a better person."

I look at my watch. "Thirty seconds."

Brandon shifts his weight. "As part of my treatment plan, I have to go to every person I've ever betrayed or hurt and make amends with them. You're the first person on my list."

"I should feel honored about that?"

"Just saying you're at the top of the list, that's all."

I snort. "With a list as long as yours, I'm sure the people at the bottom will die of old age before you get to them." I look at my watch. "Time's up." I glare into his eyes. "Fuck you, Brandon. Never contact me again, you lying sack of shit." I turn to go, but Brandon grabs my arm to keep me in place.

"Hang on, Iris. *Please.* Hear me out."

I jerk away from Brandon's grasp. Not because he's physically hurting me. His grip is pretty gentle, actually. But

Brandon's flesh against mine, no matter how soft his touch, feels like a violation.

Brandon opens his mouth to say more, but before he gets a word out, Roman appears out of nowhere, moving like a panther. In a blur, he picks up Brandon like he's a toddler and hurls him several feet down the sidewalk, effectively turning Brandon into Roman's human bowling ball.

As Brandon clatters onto the hard sidewalk, Roman booms, "Stay the fuck away from my girlfriend!"

*Girlfriend?* Perhaps now isn't the time to feel giddy about Roman's word choice, but I can't help myself. Does he truly think of me that way, or is he using the word to screw with Brandon, the same way I talked about getting "railed" and "scrambled" at the end of my ranting tirade in the church a lifetime ago?

Brandon raises his palms, striking a defensive posture. He doesn't seem physically hurt by his tumbling voyage onto the sidewalk. Shocked, yes. Stunned and embarrassed, definitely. But otherwise, he seems perfectly fine. "Calm down, Roman. I didn't come to fight."

Roman turns to me, his eyes aflame. "Are you okay, baby?" When I nod, he takes my hand and pulls me into him. "Do you have anything you want to say to this piece of shit before he skitters away like the cockroach he is?"

"One thing." I release Roman's hand and stride over to Brandon on the ground. "I'm not frigid, you little *bitch*. Not with the right man." I wish I could scream this petty put-down from the roof of the ice cream parlor, but I'm too battle-scarred from that stupid viral video to do anything but whisper-shout it while covering my mouth with my palm. As much as I want to release a primal, cathartic scream into the universe, it's far more important that nobody watching this spectacle—or worse, recording it—has any chance of capturing my voice or reading my lips.

"On the contrary," I add in another whisper-shout. "As it turns out, I'm a certified nymphomaniac with the right man—that man there—because he actually knows what he's doing in bed, unlike you!"

Roman snorts and hoots with glee behind me. "Atta girl."

"Never, ever contact me again," I add, practically spitting the words out. "Or I'll get a restraining order on your ass." I return to Roman and defiantly grab his hand. "Come on, baby. Let's leave the trash on the sidewalk for the trashmen to pick up."

Roman's smile is beaming and glorious—every bit as radiant and full of pride as the one he wore a week ago while watching Maverick on that pony. With a squeeze of my hand, he says, "With pleasure. Come on, baby."

As we turn to stride away, Brandon calls out from the sidewalk, "I'm gonna sue your ass for assault, Roman!"

"Go for it, you little shit," Roman tosses out, without bothering to stop walking. "I've got an unlimited budget for attorneys, and any jury would cheer me on for what I did."

When we get inside the ice cream parlor, I'm surprised to discover Maverick's not sitting in the booth any longer. Outside, I assumed Roman left him there and told him to stay put.

"Where's Mav?" I ask, as we slide into our booth on opposite sides of the table.

"In the back with the store owner. She's showing him how she makes the ice cream." He flashes me a lopsided grin. "How do you feel?"

"Fucking amazing."

He chuckles. "As you should." He reaches for my hand across the table, so I happily give it to him. "Come to LA with me tomorrow, Iris. I don't want to leave here without you."

*Hallelujah.* I've been hoping to hear those exact words from Roman for days now. But even so, I don't want him asking me only because he's currently drunk on jealousy and testosterone. I want him to want me even in the calmest, quietest of times.

"Are you sure?" I ask, even though I want to scream, "Yes, yes, yes!" "I don't want you inviting me because you're suddenly feeling territorial." By way of explanation, I motion vaguely to the window.

Roman rolls his eyes. "That's not it. I'd just mustered the courage to ask you to come with me when Brandon walked in. I swear, he interrupted me mid-sentence."

Butterflies whoosh into my belly. "You had to muster the *courage* to ask me?"

"Are you kidding me? After the way you kicked my ass in Hawaii—and rightly so, by the way—I'm scared to death about what your answer will be. Especially now, when there's so much more at stake, yes, I most certainly had to muster my courage." He inhales deeply. "Please, Iris. Come with me tomorrow. Maverick is going to his mom's house for a couple weeks when I get back to LA, so we'll have the place to ourselves."

It sounds like Roman is asking me to come for only a two-week visit, which, admittedly, isn't what I was hoping for, in a perfect world. But it's not nothing, so I decide to accept his invitation.

I open my mouth to say yes, but when I notice the pleading, waiting-with-bated-breath look in Roman's dark eyes, I suddenly realize I've got some leverage here.

"What's at stake now compared to in Kauai?" I ask, referring to his interesting word choice from a moment ago. "Answer that question to help me decide."

Roman runs a hand through his mop of dark hair, but he doesn't answer my question.

"Tell me, Roman. Explain it to me. I need to know."

After a long pause, Roman inhales deeply and answers me on his exhale. "If you say no to me this time," he murmurs softly, "I'll know it's not because of bad timing. Not because you just got out of a long-term, terrible relationship. Not because you just involuntarily starred in a traumatizing viral video." He shifts in his seat. "It wouldn't be because you haven't had the chance to get to know me. It wouldn't be because you don't know what's real." He pauses, looking intensely uncomfortable. "This time, unlike last time, you know me. The real me. You've spent time with me. With my parents and my son. And I've met your family, too." He swallows hard and his Adam's apple bobs. "This time, unlike in Kauai, if you say no to me, I'll know it's because you've decided you simply don't want me. *The real me.*" He shifts in his seat again. "And if that's your ultimate decision here, Iris . . ." He levels me with dark, blazing eyes, and his broad chest rises and falls in the brief, poignant silence. "Then that would honestly break my fucking heart."

I'm swooning uncontrollably. It's the most vulnerable—and handsome—he's ever looked. "Yes, I'll come to LA with you tomorrow," I blurt. "I can't believe you doubted my answer."

Roman looks equal parts relieved and elated. "When it comes to you, Iris, I don't take anything for granted."

We share a beaming smile. I don't know what will happen between Roman and me after my two-week stay, once it's time for Maverick to return to Roman's from his mother's. But in this moment, I don't care to think that far ahead. For now, all that matters is I'll be leaving Orchard Blossom with Roman and his family tomorrow, rather than saying goodbye to him for however long and then going home to sob into my pillow. For now, I remind myself, that's simply got to be enough.

# CHAPTER 32
## Iris

AFTER WE DISEMBARK from the private plane in LA—how is this my life?—Roman and I walk across the tarmac with Maverick between us and Roman's parents trailing behind.

"Mommyyyy!" Maverick shrieks. He breaks free of our hands and runs to the most spectacularly gorgeous woman I've ever beheld in my life. A woman so stunningly beautiful, I'm not surprised Roman threw caution to the wind and had unprotected sex with her. Who wouldn't take that gamble, when there was a possibility of creating a kid blessed with half this woman's stunning genes?

Insecurity floods me in a torrent. Roman and I had amazing sex in Kauai, but that feels like a lifetime ago, given that we didn't sleep together in Orchard Blossom. At some point during this past week, I decided that was because Roman had made some romantic decision to court me. But now, suddenly, this woman's jaw-dropping beauty is making me wonder if Roman's physical attraction to me has waned since Hawaii. Were all those internet trolls right? Was Roman "bottom-feeding" when he bothered with me in Kauai? Has he invited me to stay with him for a spell in LA to see if we might recapture some of our old physical chemistry?

"Hey, Vanessa," Roman says warmly. He gives the woman a brief side hug before gesturing to me. "This is my girlfriend, Iris. Iris, this is Maverick's mother, Vanessa, and her husband, Jay."

There it is again.

The same word he used with Brandon yesterday.

*Girlfriend.*

I exchange pleasantries with Vanessa and her husband, before Vanessa shocks me by gushing, "It's wonderful to finally meet you, Iris. During every FaceTime call this week, Mavvy talked about all the fun he was having with 'Irish.' Thank you especially for taking him horseback riding. He was over the moon about it."

I'm thrilled and relieved. Of all the ways this first encounter could have gone down, this is best-case scenario. "I've loved every minute with Maverick," I reply. "He's so sweet. You've done a great job with him."

With a smile, Vanessa runs her manicured fingers through her son's soft, lush hair. "Thank you. That means a lot coming from a preschool teacher."

I'm shocked. Roman told me he's on great terms with his baby momma, but even so, I was petrified to meet Vanessa today—terrified she might not like or trust me enough to let me continue interacting with her son. But now, I can plainly see my worst fears aren't going to materialize.

Vanessa's husband asks me a question and we chat briefly, but long enough for me to realize he's every bit as amiable and welcoming as his wife. As we're talking, Roman's parents reach the group, and another round of warm greetings ensues. There's no tension, I notice, as cheeks are kissed and words exchanged. No secret side-eyes or stilted conversations. Only love and respect. *I can feel it.*

Roman squats down in front of his son. "Bye for now, buddy. I'll see you in a couple weeks at my new house. You want to know the best part? I'm gonna pick you up in my car at your house and *drive* you to mine. No more hotels. No more airplanes. We live in the same city now."

Maverick hugs Roman. "I love you, Daddy."

Roman chokes up. "I love you, too, buddy. I've had the best time with you."

When Maverick leaves his father's embrace, he beelines to me. "Bye, Irish."

A lump rises in my throat. "Bye, Mavvy. I had fun with you this week."

Vanessa prompts, "Thank Iris for all the fun stuff she arranged for you, honey. She went above and beyond for you."

"Tank you, Irish."

"You're very welcome. I'm sure I had even more fun than you did."

Maverick squeezes my legs. "I love you," he says out of nowhere, like it's the most natural thing in the world to say—and then, as my heart explodes and my eyes prick with tears, he leaves me in the dust and traipses off to his grandparents next.

"I love you, too, Mav," I choke out, my voice cracking with emotion. "So, so much."

I look at Roman, smiling through tears, and he looks every bit as emotional as I feel. There's nothing I want more than to say those same three little words to Roman: "I love you." But, obviously, I can't say them first. Certainly not when I don't know if Roman will say them back. For crying out loud, I don't even know if Roman will invite me to stay with him in LA longer than two short weeks.

"Are you okay, baby?" Roman asks, glancing from the highway through his windshield to me.

"Hmm?"

He adjusts his hands on the steering wheel. "You seem awfully quiet over there."

We're riding in Roman's squeaky-clean fancy sports car, driving from the airport to his brand-new digs in Malibu, the affluent, oceanfront city Roman selected as his new home base in California.

"I'm just tired," I reply with a tight smile. "I was too excited about coming here today to fall asleep last night." It's the truth, but not the full truth. I am tired, yes—but Vanessa is the main reason I've been so quiet during this drive. She was so freaking beautiful, I could have stared at her for days in a trance. Also, so warm and vivacious, I'd want to be her good friend, if we'd met under different circumstances. Why didn't it work out with Vanessa and Roman? I can't understand it, especially when I think about Maverick being a big reason to give a romantic relationship a shot.

I look out the window at the passing cars on the freeway and try to wrangle my spiraling thoughts. I knew Maverick's mother would be a supernatural beauty, given how gorgeous Maverick is, but I didn't expect her to be *that* beautiful. And certainly not *that* sweet. My brief encounter with Vanessa made me realize in a visceral way that Roman truly can have literally *any* woman he wants. So, naturally, I'm now wondering how long I can reasonably expect Roman to remain interested in me, especially when he's about to be stretched to the max in every direction.

Oh, God, I don't even want to think about the horrible, mean, clickbait headlines if my romance with Roman doesn't pan out after my two-week stay in California. By now, the world has seen multiple photos of Roman and me together, both in Hawaii and Orchard Blossom. If those sightings suddenly dry up, and if Roman is suddenly seen with a new, far more beautiful woman on his arm, the internet will be brutal toward me. In fact, I'm sure the day the Runaway Bride gets dumped by Roman "Ribbed for Her Pleasure" Maguire will practically become a national holiday for my haters. A reason to pop champagne.

The navigation voice on Roman's phone draws me from my wandering thoughts.

"Turn right," the robot lady commands.

When Roman follows her instructions, he turns into a long driveway with a stunning two-story oceanfront house at the end of it.

"This is your house?" I breathe out.

"You like it?"

"Of course. It's spectacular. I can see why you picked it." In Orchard Blossom, Roman called his new digs in Malibu his "dream house," but that's all he said about it. But now I can see that Roman's dream house is a cliffside, oceanfront mansion with sleek, modern lines that could easily pass for a small, boutique hotel.

"Why so big?" I ask with a laugh.

Roman audibly shrugs as he parks his car at the end of the driveway. "This is gonna be my home for a long time. Maybe even forever. So, I figured I should get a place that's big enough to host my entire extended family on holidays."

Roman opens his car door, so I do the same on my side.

"Welcome home, Rome," a guy in a suit says, greeting us as we pile out of Roman's low-slung car.

"Hey, Mac. This is my girlfriend, Iris. Iris, this is Mac, my head of security."

*Roman's got a head of security?* "Nice to meet you, Mac."

"Likewise," Mac says. "Roman's told me some wonderful things about you, Iris."

*He has?* I look at Roman in surprise. *When? What?*

"Go on in," Mac says to Roman. "I'll get the bags and park the car in the garage for you, boss."

"Thanks. Is Cameron still here?"

"He just left. He said he'll come back tomorrow to say hi and meet Iris."

"Perfect. And Leslie?"

"She left, too. But not before stocking the fridge and pantry. She said she made a couple of your favorite meals—high protein, of course—in case you arrived hungry enough to eat a team of horses."

Roman chuckles. "She knows me well." He takes my hand. "Leslie is my private chef. Wait till you taste her food. It's even better than my mother's cooking, but don't you dare tell her I said that, or I'll deny it."

I didn't realize Roman has a team of people taking care of him in his real life. In Hawaii, he was humble and capable—always making cocktails and sandwiches for us and then running off to the market when we ran low on supplies. In Orchard Blossom, too, Roman seemed like a totally normal person. I guess it makes sense for Roman to delegate basic stuff in his daily life, though, given the intense demands on his time during the football season. He's a superstar in his real life, after all. I keep forgetting that.

"It's too bad you're seeing the house for the first time at dusk," Roman says as we approach his front door. "In full sunlight, the ocean views are spectacular."

*Is Roman nervous?* "I'll see the views in all their glory tomorrow."

Roman takes a deep breath before opening his front door and inviting me inside. "Welcome, Iris," he says, his voice brimming with excitement and nerves. "I hope you love it."

I walk inside Roman's new home and gasp. "Wow," I murmur, looking around. "This is incredible." The ceilings are high. The furnishings and décor are elegant and sleek, yet warm and homey. The general theme appears to be "Southern California, beachy elegance" mixed with "sports hero." There's abstract art on the walls in beach-evoking colors, along with framed jerseys and photos and memorabilia scattered throughout. And of course, given the house's proximity to the ocean, there are lots of large windows providing panoramic views as far as the eye can see.

"I barely know my way around the place, honestly, so it'll be the blind leading the blind here—but I'll try to give you a tour, if you'd like."

I laugh. "Lead on."

Roman takes my hand and off we go, exploring all the rooms of the sprawling house: a stunning gourmet kitchen that's so big, it needs *two* islands; a trophy room; an office; a home gym; a home theater; a darling bedroom for Maverick; a game room; several guest rooms; and on and on.

Eventually, we make our way to Roman's bedroom suite, and it's so lovely, I feel inspired to twirl across the expansive floor.

Laughing at my exuberance, Roman says, "I'm open to changing anything, if you want."

I stop twirling to stare at him. Roman's comment felt like a record scratch to me. He wouldn't have said it if he's only intending for me to stay two weeks, right?

"No, everything is absolutely perfect," I manage, even though my throat feels like it's closing up.

Roman exhales with relief. "Glad you think so, too."

I bite my lip. "If I wind up staying with you longer than two weeks, the only thing I'd change is putting a framed photo of my mother somewhere."

"*If?*" Roman looks deeply confused. "You're not already planning to stay here longer than two weeks?"

I fidget while gathering my courage. "You said Maverick will be away for two weeks, so I've been assuming . . ."

I stop talking when Roman's expression morphs into one of pure shock.

"As far as I'm concerned, you're home," he says. "I only mentioned Maverick being gone for two weeks to emphasize the point that we'd be able to settle into our new life together, at first, without him being here."

Relief floods me. And then joy. I've been feeling ready to throw my love at Roman with both hands, without an ounce of hesitation. But still, I'm not too far gone to know that's batshit crazy, given our timeline. I haven't known him all that long, even though it feels like a lifetime.

Roman steps forward. "You flew here with me, not knowing that I want you here with me for good?"

*For good.* It's a shocking phrase. One that's a synonym for *forever,* in my book. As in, Roman never wants me to go away. My brain isn't firing on all pistons right now, though, so I'm not sure if my definition of his word choice matches Roman's.

"Oh my God, Iris." Roman wraps me in a bear hug. "You're home, baby. I never want you to leave." He kisses the top of my head before leaning back and sliding his fingertip underneath my chin. "I was miserable without you. I felt like I was missing a limb."

Tears prick my eyes. "I felt the same way. Wherever you are, that's where I want to be."

"I feel the same way."

He leans down and kisses me, and sexual arousal instantly consumes me.

I take a deep breath to muster my courage and ask, "So, are we finally gonna have sex or what?"

Roman chuckles. "You noticed that, huh?"

I giggle with him. "Was it some kind of master plan or a simple matter of logistics?"

"It was a master plan, helped along by logistics."

"Why, though?"

"Going in, I knew sex with you was fire—the best sex of my life. So, I promised myself I'd hold off while in Orchard Blossom to make sure whatever decision I made came from my heart and head, and not my dick."

I raise an eyebrow. "*Decision?* About what?"

"You're here, Iris. I think that's pretty clear."

"Not necessarily." My heart is thumping. *Say it, Roman. Please. Say it first.*

His Adam's apple bobs. "You've got my whole heart, Iris, right along with my whole dick—which, by the way, is so fucking hard for you, I'm in physical pain."

It's not an "I love you." But given how horny I'm feeling, it will have to do for now.

"I'm right there with you. Let's put an end to our torture." Smiling wickedly, I pull him to me, and we kiss passionately. And a moment later, we're naked and ravenously making out in his large, luxurious bed. In record time, I'm wet and throbbing for him—aching for him to burrow inside me—and based on the river of slick wetness on Roman's tip, he's plainly aching for me in the same way.

"I'm on the pill," I whisper breathlessly. Now that I'm here to stay, I want to feel Roman inside me with nothing between us.

With a guttural groan, Roman guides me on top of him, and I take every inch of him inside me. As Roman's body stretches and fills mine, we both react loudly to the primal sensation.

He's got one hand cupping my breast and the other rubbing my clit in slow circles as I move slowly on top of him, gazing into his eyes with every gyration. In this position, he's reaching new depths inside me, literally and figuratively. So much so, I'm seeing stars. Talk about getting scrambled. *Damn.*

As my pleasure rises and my body grinds on top of his, Roman whispers all kinds of dirty talk into my ear. He tells me how gorgeous I am. How amazing I feel. He says I'm tight, warm, and wet. That he's waited a lifetime to get to feel this "heaven" again. It's all hot, hot, hot, of course. A complete turn-on. But it's what Roman says when I'm teetering on the edge of an orgasm that gets me going the most: "*I love you, baby.*"

At the sound of the words I've been dying to hear, my body

releases forcefully. "I love you, too," I grit out, as my orgasm consumes me.

As pleasure rockets through me, Roman shudders violently and releases inside me with a loud roar that sends goosebumps skating across my skin.

When his body stops quaking, Roman takes a moment to collect himself before pulling me to his face for a long, deep kiss. When our kiss finally ends, he presses his forehead to mine and smiles from ear to ear. "This house feels like a home, now that you're here." He nuzzles his nose to mine. "I love you, Iris."

Love. Elation. Joy. All of them have been slamming into me like a tsunami, ever since he said those magic words. "Even when you're not having an orgasm?" I tease.

Roman laughs. "All the time."

I kiss his cheek. "That's good, because it would have been highly inconvenient to have to stroke your dick every single time I wanted to hear you say, 'I love you.' I mean, I would have done it. Don't get me wrong. But how exhausting."

Roman chuckles and runs a fingertip down my naked back. "Trust me, you'll be hearing it a lot, every day. No dick stroking required."

I touch his stubbled cheek. "I've been dying to say it to you. I just didn't want to say it first."

"I've been dying to say it, too."

I bite my lip, trying to decide if I should risk dampening the mood by asking the question that's been on the tip of my tongue ever since I laid eyes on Vanessa at the airport. Finally, I decide there's no time like the present, especially now that we've exchanged "I love yous."

I slide off Roman and lie down on my back. "How come it didn't work out with you and Vanessa?"

Roman lies next to me and pulls me close. "Is that why you were quiet in the car—because you were wondering about that?"

I nod sheepishly.

"Why didn't you ask me then?"

"I didn't want you to think I'm jealous. I'm not. I'm confused. She's stunning and she seems nice, too—and you have a child together. So, why not at least *try* to make it work with her? Did you? If so, what happened?"

Roman strokes my hair and looks deeply into my eyes. "No, I never tried to make it work with her. Vanessa is a good person. Mostly. At her core." He chuckles. "But she's very money driven. I mean, so am I, so I guess I can't fault her for that. But . . ." He pauses to think. "I guess the easiest way to explain it is: She's not you. I didn't know it then, but I've been waiting for you my whole life, Iris. Waiting to feel like I feel when I'm with you. Somehow, my heart has always known you were out there somewhere. I just needed to be patient and wait for you to show up."

I resist the urge to roll my eyes. That was an incredibly romantic speech, but I can't help thinking it's not the full truth. And full honesty is what I'm after here so I can release any and all anxiety about this topic and hurtle myself, headlong, into my new life with Roman. Why didn't he ask Vanessa to move in with him, like he's asked me, as soon as he found out she was carrying his child? Or, hell, maybe he did, and it didn't work out?

Roman laughs at whatever skepticism he's seeing on my face. "You think I'm full of shit?"

"No, I . . . I appreciate the sentiment. That was a romantic thing to say. But I'm not looking for platitudes. I really want to understand why you didn't at least try to make it work with the mother of your child. She's gorgeous, Roman. I'm sorry to keep probing here, but if I don't ask you about this now, and get an answer that makes sense to me, I think I'll lose my nerve and always wonder."

Roman inhales a long, deep breath while running a hand

down his face. "Okay, first off, 'losing your nerve' to ask me about anything isn't an option anymore, okay? Anything that's on your mind, ask me. Don't wonder. Don't guess. I'm not Brandon, okay? I'm not a manipulative, gaslighting, insecure bastard who's gonna try to make you feel small and worthless just so I can feel big and important."

*Whoa.* He's taken my breath away. Until Roman spelled it out for me, I didn't fully understand my downward spiral throughout my long relationship with Brandon. With each passing year, he trained me to make myself smaller and smaller to avoid making waves. To keep him happy, even at the expense of my own joy. Holy crap. How did I let things go as far as they did, when Brandon's toxicity is so clear to me now?

"I love you, Iris," Roman whispers, sliding his palm onto my cheek. "Your feelings matter to me. Your questions deserve answers. This is your home, every bit as much as it's mine. That means you never have to walk on eggshells, pick your spots, or pretend. Talk to me. No matter what. And I'll always do the same, okay?"

"Okay," I squeak out.

"That's how my parents do it. And that's how my cousin Marco does it with his new wife, Nicola. They're all really happy—and it's not for show. It's real. They're partners. They're a team. They're friends. That's what I want for myself in a relationship, too. Or I don't want one at all."

My breathing hitches. "That's what I want, too. Or I don't want it at all."

Roman flashes a snarky grin. "Yeah, I know. You made that clear enough in Hawaii. Trust me, I was deeply impressed when you turned me down." He pauses to think. "Actually, I think I just answered your question. Vanessa was never going to be my teammate, and I knew it. She was never going to fully have my back. I mean, there's nothing wrong with looking out for number one. I get that we're all doing that to some degree in life. But I can't be with someone, romantically, who genuinely doesn't care about my happiness as much as they care about their own. I can't be with someone who looks into my eyes and sees dollar signs rather than my soul. You've always made me feel like you see *me*, Iris. The real me. When I'm with you—wherever we are, whatever we're doing—I feel like I can be myself, and you'll accept me. Like me. Want me for me." He strokes my arm and smiles. "Not to mention, sex with you is like a . . . what was it? 'A door to another dimension'?"

I crack up. "A secret portal into another dimension—a new world where I found a better version of myself."

"That's right." He laughs and kisses the top of my head. "Without even realizing it, maybe, I've been waiting to walk through that secret portal with the right person my whole life. And now I know you're that person. You're a needle in a haystack, Iris, and what we have is real and rare. I know that now, and I promise I'm not going to forget that."

My heart is beating so hard in my throat, I feel like I'm gagging on it. "I feel the same way," I whisper. It's all my brain will supply.

"I only had sex with Vanessa twice. I feel like I should mention that. She said she was on the pill, so I didn't wrap it up. And now, here we are. Was she telling me the truth about being on the pill? Who knows? To this day, she swears she was, but I'm not entirely sure. I wouldn't have it any other way, of course; I can't imagine my life without Mav. But you see what I mean? The fact that I don't fully trust her to this day speaks volumes about why it didn't work out for us. Right off the bat, I trusted you and told you stuff I probably shouldn't have. I didn't even make you sign an NDA, like I did with Vanessa and everyone else. But with you, there was this instant feeling of trust. This instant feeling like I could relax in your presence in a whole new way. And that feeling has grown exponentially since then."

I poke his rib. "Yeah, you trusted me so much, you secretly sent a photo of my driver's license to Cameron for a background check."

Roman chuckles. "That was simple due diligence. Trust me, if I didn't trust you, I would have asked you to sign an NDA. And I certainly wouldn't have told you about my move to LA before I was cleared to do that." He runs his fingertip down my arm. "Does that clear up your questions about Vanessa? If not, keep asking questions till you're satisfied, baby. We've got all night."

"No, I'm satisfied. Thank you."

"You're sure?"

"I'm sure. Thank you."

He looks pleased. "I'll always have love in my heart for Vanessa for giving me Maverick. That's why I'll always make sure she's well cared for, financially—because she's the mother of my child, and I don't want Maverick ever worrying about his mother. But I don't want Vanessa or anyone else who isn't you, Iris. I only want you. *I love you.*"

"I love you, too." I pull him to me for a soft kiss and whisper, "Thank you for being so open with me."

"Always." He puts his forehead to mine. "Fair warning: My life is about to get really hectic, so we won't have time for you to be thinking shit you're not saying to me, okay? And vice versa. If this is going to work, we have to make a pact now. Honesty. Always."

I nod. "Honesty. Always."

Roman grins. "Good girl. From here on out, you won't ever need to wonder how I feel, Iris. You'll know." He nuzzles his nose to mine. "It's you and me, baby. Full steam ahead."

# CHAPTER 33
## Roman

*Five Weeks Later*

Mom scans the party that's currently sprawled across my expansive living room. When she finds Iris chatting with Nicola on my couch, her eyes light up. "I knew they'd be fast friends," Mom whispers gleefully. "They're so similar."

We're in the middle of the preseason schedule with the regular season still a few weeks away, so I figured now was the perfect time to invite everyone in my inner circle to a housewarming party. At least, that's what I told Iris. In truth, I've been chomping at the bit to introduce my amazing girlfriend to everyone, so I concocted a reason. I know Iris has only been living here a month, but I'm now more certain than ever I want to wake up next to her every morning for the rest of my life.

Mom taps a manicured finger against her glass of chardonnay before shifting her gaze from Nicola and Iris to me. "Isn't it wonderful to finally have some women in our family? My God, Sofia and I have been surrounded by oceans of testosterone for far too long."

Sofia is Mom's sister. Marco's mother and my aunt. And, of course, Aunt Sofia is here today, along with everyone else who matters most to me. The only important person who's not here today is Maverick, but that's only because he was here over the weekend, and he already loves Iris as much as I do.

"It seems like things are still as wonderful with Iris as ever. Yes?"

I look around to make sure nobody's within earshot. "They're better than ever, Mom. I didn't know I could love someone like this."

Mom's dark eyes light up. "Have you told Iris that—in those exact words?"

"Keep your voice down, Mom. Jesus."

Her eyes narrow. "I was whispering, Roman."

"No, you were practically shouting."

Mom snorts. "You're insane."

"You might have been whispering with your voice, but your body language was screaming, 'Give me another grandbaby and give it to me with Iris!' I don't want Iris catching wind of that."

Mom giggles. "Why not? She's wonderful for you and a perfect fit with the family. I vote you let that cat out of the bag and let her know you love her."

"Would you take a sip of your wine and act natural, please? Your eyes are bugging out. You look like a rabid dog."

Mom shoots me one of her patented *tsks*. "If I'm a dog, then you're a son of a bitch."

"I didn't call you a dog, Mother. It was a metaphor."

Mom stares me down with those dark eyes of hers that see right through a person's soul. "I didn't appreciate the metaphor, darling."

"It was a bad choice of words. Can you please just act natural, as a favor to me? If Iris looks over here, she's gonna know something's up."

"Something's up?" Mom asks, her dark eyebrow slanted up. "What's up, Roman?"

I touch the ring box in my pocket to make sure it's still there and exhale in relief when it is. "Nothing. Never mind. Another bad choice of words."

Mom's not buying it. "Hmm," she says, while sipping her wine.

Jesus, I'm a wreck. Fuck.

When I pulled my mother over here to chat, it was because I was foolishly feeling the urge to spill my guts to her about the diamond ring that's been burning a hole in my pocket since yesterday. But now that she's being so brazenly pushy and enthusiastic about Iris, I'm realizing she's the last person to trust with my secret. Mom's normally got a fantastic poker face. She's where I got mine, actually, since God knows I didn't get it from Dad. But for some reason, when it comes to Iris, Mom can't keep a straight face to save her life.

"You still haven't answered me," Mom says. "Have you told Iris you love her or not?"

I roll my eyes. "You think I'd invite a woman to live with me, in my home, with my child, without first saying those words to her?"

"Yes."

"Well, you're right. I did. Like an idiot."

We both snort-laugh.

"But then, I figured out my mistake and said it to her during our first night here." I can't believe that was only five weeks ago. My relationship with Iris has deepened and flourished so much since then, that magical night feels like a lifetime ago.

"Did Iris say it back to you?"

I give Mom a look that says, "What do you think?"

She giggles. "I figured, but I didn't want to *assume*. Iris isn't a puppet, you know. That girl most definitely has a mind of her own."

"Ain't that the truth."

# CHASING THE RING

We both chuckle again.

I found out about Iris's "mind of her own" for the first time in Hawaii, of course. And then again in Orchard Blossom, when she stood over Brandon and told him off in the most perfect way. But over the past month, I've become acquainted with Iris's quiet strength and independent spirit in a whole new way. Once she started feeling safe and secure in her new home, and with me and our relationship, she relaxed into her new life and slowly started showing me all her glorious colors—the good, the bad, and the ugly. And that's when my love for Iris catapulted to a whole new level, because I felt safe enough to do the same.

I notice my cousin Marco walking across the room and decide he's the one I should tell about the ring in my pocket, rather than my mother. In fact, what was I thinking to even consider telling my loose-lipped, excitable mom, when Marco's the only person in this room who's recently proposed?

My gaze darts to where Iris and Nicola were chatting a moment ago. They're both still there, chatting away, but now, they've now been joined by Iris's two friends from college, Kaylee and Tatiana. *Perfect.* Whenever those two ladies come over, which they've done several times over the past month, Iris gets pulled into a marathon gab session.

"I should mingle," I say to my mother, interrupting her mid-sentence. What was she talking about? I have no idea, thanks to the ring in my pocket turning my brain to frazzled mush.

I walk toward Marco with purpose, but I'm intercepted by a couple of my new teammates along the way, so I stop to chat with them. Finally, when I make it to Marco, he's gotten pulled into conversation with my twin brothers, Happy Levi and Evil Luca, along with Cameron. It's not an ideal situation, since Luca has always been able to read my mind, for some reason, and I don't want to put this decision up to a group vote. It shouldn't be too big a stumbling block, however, if I handle pulling Marco away with finesse.

I greet the group and try to play it cool as they continue talking about Luca's new team. He doesn't have a firm spot on their roster yet. He got invited to training camp, and he's now hoping to get some good playing time in at the next couple preseason games, which he's then hoping will lead to a spot on their roster—or at least their practice squad. But however it goes for him this time, I couldn't be prouder of my little brother's tenacity and persistence. The NFL is a tough gig, man. My brother Luca, with all the ups and downs he's endured, knows that better than anyone.

During a lull in the conversation, I nudge Marco to get his attention. "Hey, cuz," I whisper. "Can I talk to you for a minute on the deck?"

"Sure thing."

Shit. As we turn to walk away, Luca grips my bicep and deadpans, "Whatever you have to say to Marco, you can say it in front of the whole class, Roman Maguire."

*Fucking hell.* How does he always read my mind? He's been able to do it since he was a toddler. "Sorry, Teacher," I shoot back playfully, trying to throw Luca off the scent. "Mrs. Teetlebaum from the office told me to come get Marco out of class. His mom is here to take him to the dentist."

Luca raises a suspicious eyebrow. Obviously, he's not buying my attempt at deflection. "Seriously, what's going on, Rome? You're sweating bullets."

I scoff a bit too loudly. "No, I'm not." I am, though. Which is crazy, since I'm known for being graceful under pressure. Even when three-hundred-pound linemen come at me with murder in their eyes, I'm unflappable. An assassin. A sniper. But slide a goddamned diamond ring into my pocket—one I'm bursting to give to the love of my life—and I fall the fuck apart.

I take a sip of my beer to emphasize what a relaxed, chill

dude I am, but Luca's still not buying it. Probably because my hand is shaking while I drink.

Luca nudges his grumpy counterpart next to him, Levi. "Back me up, brother. Rome's acting super weird, right?"

Levi shrugs. "Rome always acts weird to me. I honestly don't understand him at all."

We all laugh, even me.

"It's not a big deal," I say, realizing I've got to give Luca something, or he's never going to let it go. "I've got a business-related question for Marco. He did a deal that's similar to something I'm contemplating."

"What deal?" Cameron says, his brow furrowed.

*Fuck.* In this context, I forgot to think of Cameron as my agent, rather than my longtime best friend. My God, having that ring in my pocket is doing dastardly things to my brain.

"That was a lie," I confess on an exhale. "I need some relationship advice from Marco, and I didn't want to say that and have everyone think—"

"You're already thinking about breaking up with Iris?" Levi whisper-shouts, thereby proving the truth of his earlier statement. *He doesn't understand me at all.*

"No, dummy," Luca interjects, taking the words right out of my mouth. "He wants to *propose* to her, and he wants Marco's advice about how to do it."

Fucking Luca. I look around frantically. "Not so loud, Luc. *Jesus.*"

Luca gasps. "Oh my God. *I'm right?*"

I nod. "But don't tell anyone, especially Mom." My heart thrumming, I grab Marco's arm and drag him away, but not before throwing over my shoulder to Luca and the rest, "Nobody follow us. I don't want anyone else's opinion about this but Marco's."

Thankfully, nobody follows us. For now, anyway. Which means Marco and I are free to grab fresh beers and head into the glorious sunshine on my deck. Once we're alone, we crack open the beers, plop onto some comfy furniture, and look out at the glimmering ocean.

"Luca was seriously right?" Marco asks, incredulously.

I nod. "I've never been happier in my life. She's the real deal, man. A unicorn."

"Holy shit. When are you gonna ask her?"

"That's what I wanted to talk to you about. Initially, I was thinking about doing it on Iris's birthday next month. But now that I've got the ring—"

"*You've already got a ring?*" Marco palms his forehead. "Holy shit."

"I got it yesterday. And now that I have it, I'm not sure I can wait a month and a half to give it to her." I glance toward the party to make sure nobody is coming out here before returning to Marco. "What do you think about me doing it today, either at the party or after everyone leaves?"

Marco frowns. "Don't you think you're moving a bit fast here, Rome?"

"When you know, you know."

"Yeah, I get that. I felt the same way about Nico. But don't you think maybe you should let Iris get in the swing of the WAG lifestyle before you make her promise to love you forever? Why not ask when the season is over? By then, she'll know what she's getting into, and you'll be better able to assess if she's really—"

"She is. Whatever you're going to say, don't bother. She's the one, Marco. So, why wait? I couldn't sleep a wink last night knowing I had that ring in my safe. And having it in my pocket today is practically giving me a heart attack."

Marco's eyes widen. "You have it in your *pocket*?"

I nod. "Just in case."

"In case *what*?"

"The perfect moment presents itself."

"To *propose*?"

"That's what we've been talking about. Yes."

Marco looks stunned. "*Who are you?* The Roman I know doesn't even like to commit to lunch next week."

I look toward the party again. "I know this is uncharted territory for me, but I don't have a single doubt. Not when it comes to Iris. She's rock-solid, man. She's The One."

Marco smiles. "That's great news, man. Congratulations. But it's still early days yet, cuz. If she's The One—"

"She is."

"—then she'll still be The One in six months."

"*Six months?*" I whisper-shout. "I can't wait that long. Coach said he's gonna let me play a drive at our last preseason game in two weeks. Well, when that happens and the cameras pan to the people cheering me on in my box, I want Iris to be wearing my rock. Marco, I want the Runaway Bride to be my fiancée, my future wife, when the whole world sees her."

"Ah, so *that's* what this is really about. When you hard launch her, you want to put an immediate end to all the trolling, once and for all."

"*Exactly.* There's gonna be record eyeballs tuning in to see me in a Thunderbolts jersey for the first time, man. So, it'll be the perfect time to let the whole world know the Runaway Bride is my future wife—my family—so if anyone's got something shitty to say about her, they'd better have the balls to say it to *me*."

"Hasn't her viral fame pretty much dried up, though?"

"Yeah, but I'm guessing it's gonna spring back to life, at least somewhat, when she's seen cheering for me throughout the season." I rough a palm down my face. "If that happens, then I want to protect her, Marco. All that viral shit was tough on Iris. I can't let that happen to her again."

Marco's face softens. "I get it, Romie. But is that a good enough reason to propose *today*, when you've only known her for a couple months?"

"He wants to propose to Iris *today*?" Luca booms, barreling onto the deck with Levi and Cameron trailing behind. He plops down next to me on the couch and punches my thigh. "Don't you dare do it without a ring, motherfucker, or Mom will kill you."

"Not so loud," I hiss. I look toward the party. "I have a ring, dumbass. *Obviously.*"

"It's in his pocket right now," Marco interjects, as everyone gets settled on furniture scattered around the deck. "He's trying to decide if he should propose during the party today or right after everyone leaves."

Everyone explodes with "what the fuck" and various opinions—all of them conveying the same basic messaging. *Slow down, Roman. What's the rush, Roman? Wait till the end of the season, Roman. If she's The One, then she'll still be The One in a year, after you get to know her better.*

"Basically, he's trying to reframe the narrative from the viral video," Marco explains.

"Hmm," Cameron says. "Isn't that video a good reason *not* to propose to her so soon? A few months ago, the whole world saw Iris dressed in a wedding dress for someone else. Don't you think you should let more time pass, just to keep her from getting ridiculed for hopping from one engagement to the next?"

"Fuck," I whisper, my shoulders sagging. Fucking Cameron. He's always got a take that makes sense, even if it's not something I want to hear.

"I think Cam's got a point," Marco says softly. "Sorry, Romie."

Sensing he's making headway, Cameron adds, "Also, don't you think it's only fair to give Iris a chance to live with Regular Season Roman and the whole circus that surrounds him before she promises to love you, forever, for better or worse?"

"That's exactly what I said," Marco says. He grimaces at me. "No offense, man, but you're always a massive dick during the season."

"True, but I won't be this season, because everything that

normally turns me into a dick has been fixed." They don't believe me. I can see it in their eyes.

Levi finally speaks. "I get that you feel like a solider going off to war," he says, "so you want to propose before you go. It's a noble idea, in theory. But I think it's only fair to let her get to know Wartime Roman before you ask her to promise 'forever' to Peacetime Roman."

"Exactly," Marco says, as Cameron nods enthusiastically. "Plus, like I told Rome, I feel like Iris should get a taste of being a high-profile WAG before she's asked to commit to being one forever."

Everyone nods at that, and I can't say I blame them. "WAG" is the acronym used for the "wives and girlfriends" of players. And Cameron's got a good point: Being one, especially mine, will probably take some getting used to for Iris.

I hang my head and sigh. "Okay, fine, I won't ask her today. But I'm not willing to wait till the end of the season, like Marco said, so I'll compromise and do it on her birthday."

Levi scoffs. "Assuming she's still around and you haven't scared her off by then by being your usual dicky self during the season."

Cameron asks the date of Iris's birthday, and when I tell it to him, he shakes his head and says, "Levi's right. That's, what, six games in? Anything could happen, especially if you start icing her out, like you always do when you—"

"I told you, I'm not gonna be a dick like usual this time!" I glance toward the party again and lower my voice. "I'm a new man, guys. The new me knows that happiness *off* the field helps my performance *on* the field, so the new me therefore knows to prioritize my relationship, even during the season."

The guys look at each other, their collective skepticism on full display.

"Besides Iris, I've also got Maverick in my life now, remember? Plus, Coach on the sidelines, a city that believes in me, and some solid targets on the field. Everything's going to be different now. You'll see. By the time I propose to Iris in October, she won't hesitate to say yes to me."

Marco twists his mouth. "Maybe you should get a woman's perspective on all this before you lock in your plan. Can I text Nicola to come out here?"

"Great idea. Let's hear her out." Throughout the party, Nicola and Iris have been chatting up a storm, so I'm positive she'll side with me.

Marco taps on his phone, and a moment later, his lovely wife appears on the deck.

"Show her the thing in your pocket," Marco instructs with a nudge to my thigh.

I pull out the ring box and flip open the lid—and to my thrill, everyone on the deck goes bonkers at my selection. Nicola, especially, is swooning over the size of the diamond and its design. And, of course, over the fact that I've bought a ring for Iris at all.

"When are you going to ask her?" Nicola whispers excitedly.

"That's why I asked you out here," Marco says. "To give your opinion on that."

I start to plead my case, but Marco holds up his palm and tells me to zip it. "You're an unreliable narrator at this point, cuz." With near-surgical precision, my cousin launches into telling his wife everything she needs to know to render her expert opinion as I nervously turn the ring box around in my fingertips.

"I'm so excited," Nicola says to me, when Marco finishes his explanation. "Not only for you, but for myself. I *love* her."

"Isn't she the cutest person ever?" Luca says. "I mean, besides you, of course."

Nicola laughs. "She's way cuter than me. She's like human sunshine."

"Totally," Luca agrees. "But so are you."

"Aw."

"Can you two focus, please?" I bark out. "You need to give me some solid advice on timing."

"If you don't," Marco adds, "this dummy is gonna go out there, like a fucking bull in a china shop, and do it right fucking now."

Nicola gasps. "Oh, God, Roman, no. Don't do it *today*. She's just met all these people. Give her a minute to process before you hit her with the next thing."

"How about after everyone leaves today?" I ask hopefully.

Nicola scowls. "Roman, no. She'll be exhausted after the party."

"Okay, Plan B," I mutter, feeling disheartened. "What about me doing it on her birthday?"

I tell Nicola the date in October, and she shakes her head.

"Sorry, but I don't think you should mix her birthday with her engagement day."

"Goddammit Nicola," I say. "I only agreed to get your input because I thought you'd side with me."

Nicola juts out her lower lip. "Sorry, honey, but a woman's birthday is a national holiday. Don't deny her two separate celebrations and sets of presents."

Luca nods emphatically. "It's like those poor people who have their birthday on Christmas!"

"Exactly," Nicola agrees. "Well said, Luc."

"I'm smart like that."

"Yes, you are."

While Nicola and Luca giggle together, I stare in frustration at the glittering diamond nestled against black velvet in my hand. "She's my future wife," I murmur. "I'm sure of it. You know how much I hate waiting for something when I'm sure it's what I want."

Everyone around me offers comments that say, in essence, "Yes, we know. All too well."

"The minute I saw this ring," I continue, "I said to myself, 'That's the one. It's so Iris.' And now that I have it—"

"What's so Iris?" Iris asks, waltzing onto the deck, and I almost huck the five-hundred-thousand-dollar bauble in my hand over the railing.

Thank God clever Luca deftly hurls his body between Iris and me, thereby blocking Iris's view of the ring. "It's so Iris that everyone at this party has fallen madly in love with you, kid," Luca says brightly, wrapping his muscled arm around Iris's shoulders and guiding her back toward the house. "I was actually about to come find you, sis. I can't get that 'Baby Shark' song out of my head, ever since you taught it to Mavvy and me. It's driving me insane, so I need you to teach me a new, catchy song before I bash my head against a wall."

As Luca guides Iris back into the house, he glances over his shoulder at me, and I shoot him a look that says, "That was a close call." When they're gone, I pull the ring box out from under my ass cheek with a trembling hand and slide it into my pocket again.

"I've got to be more careful from now on," I say, wiping my brow. "If I'm sloppy like that again, she'll figure me out before the big proposal."

"Which will be when?" Nicola asks.

I shrug. "Sorry, Nico. What you said about keeping birthdays and engagements separate makes logical sense, but Iris's birthday in six weeks falls during my bye week, so it'll be the perfect time. Plus, that's definitely the longest I could possibly wait to make Iris Benedetto my future wife."

# CHAPTER 34
## Iris

*Three Weeks Later*

"Should I sit or stand?" I ask Luca, wringing my hands. We're in Roman's reserved box at his new home stadium for the first regular-season game of the new NFL season on a Thursday night. To maximize ratings and buzz, the football powers that be scheduled Roman's new team for tonight's highly anticipated matchup.

"Sit for now," Luca replies. "When the game starts, you'll sit until something big happens, at which point you'll instinctively leap out of your chair and scream."

I snort. "I think you're giving my instincts way too much credit, Luc."

"Nah. You're gonna be a natural. You'll see."

He's got far more faith in me than I've got in myself in this situation. Which is par for the course, when it comes to Luca Maguire. The man is an eternal optimist. "The whole world will be watching me," I remind Luca. "I don't want to mess this up and subject myself to endless ridicule."

Luca pats my arm and smiles. "You'll do great. And don't forget, I'll be right here next to you the whole time. I won't let you mess anything up."

He flashes me a reassuring smile, even though I'm sure

smiling is the last thing he feels like doing right now. After working his tail off throughout the short preseason with yet another new team, poor Luca wound up only making their practice squad. Which means, at least for now, it's Luca Maguire's job to practice with his team's starting lineup—the fifty-three-man roster who'll take the field every week. He's still a professional, paid football player, however, so that's the good news. But it was a gut punch for Luca to find out he won't get to play in any actual games this season, unless and until someone on the roster gets injured or traded and then his team's decision-makers choose Luca to fill whatever open slot. In other words, his odds of playing on the field one day soon this season, the way Roman's doing tonight, are pretty damned low.

"Do you want me to explain the basics to you again, now that we're here?" Luca asks, motioning to the field. At my request, Luca's been patiently teaching me about the game of football to prepare me for my life as a "WAG," which I've come to find out is my new identity—the nickname used to describe the "wives and girlfriends" of players.

"Yeah, I'd love a refresher," I say. "Thanks. Now that we're here at the stadium, everything looks big and confusing."

As Luca is pointing out the end zones, field goal posts, and some orange thingies with the chains attached for marking first downs, he continually finds ways to crack me up and put me at ease, even though I'm sure he's feeling especially low tonight. It's totally on brand for Luca. He's his mother's son, through and through.

Speaking of Luca's mother—as Luca is wrapping up his tutorial, she arrives at our seats with Edward and the rest of our group for the night: Maverick, Marco, Nicola, and Marco's parents. Roman's other brother, Levi, couldn't make it to the game tonight, unfortunately, since his team will be playing on Sunday morning across the country and he had practice today. But Marco and his family made it, since San Francisco is an easy flight to LA and Marco's team, the Knights, will be playing on Monday night this week.

Greetings and hugs ensue, all of them warm and excited.

A cocktail waitress is summoned. Apparently, when you're in the star quarterback's fancy, reserved box, you can have anything you want throughout the game, without having to stand in a long line at a concessions booth or even pay for it.

When the server gets to me, I decide to order the same thing as Nicola: a cranberry vodka with a twist of lime, even though it's not my usual drink. Nicola seems incredibly comfortable and confident in this crazy world, so I figure my best bet, at least for now, is to copy whatever she does, as much as I can. At least at first, till I get my bearings.

"Where's Daddy?" Maverick asks, looking around the massive stadium. He's sitting between his Uncle Luca and me, while Ava sits on my other side, flanked by the rest of the family down the line.

"See that tunnel down there?" Luca replies to his nephew. He rustles Maverick's dark mop and directs him toward a large, inflatable tunnel set up in a corner of the field. "Any minute now, smoke will start coming out of there and your daddy will burst out with his teammates, and the whole place will go bonkers. So, get your hollering voice good and ready, Mavvy."

"*Oooh*," Maverick says, bopping in his seat with excitement. "Dere's gonna be *smoke*?"

"Yep. It's gonna be awesome." Luca winks at me. "Get your hollering voice ready, too, Iris. Roman's gonna need all of our good juju."

"I'll do my best."

During the final preseason exhibition game last week, Roman played for only a few minutes—just long enough for the world to geek out over him passing a football in a Thunderbolts jersey—and I certainly screamed my head off for him then. But Roman told me the energy in that stadium was nothing compared to what I'll experience in a real game. In fact, he said the whole exercise at that preseason game was nothing more than a PR stunt, basically. Plus, I wasn't in a luxury box then, because that preseason game wasn't a home game, like this one. So, Roman's appearance in that stadium understandably provoked as many boos and cheers.

Luca taps my arm over Maverick's head. "Pop quiz, Riri." He's the only person who's ever called me that nickname, and I absolutely love it.

"I'm ready," I say with more confidence than I feel.

Luca motions to the field. "How many yards does a team need for a first down?"

Shoot. Luca just patiently explained this exact thing to me a few minutes ago, but, suddenly, everything he told me feels scrambled inside my brain. "Twenty?" I squeak out, just as Maverick confidently shouts, "*Ten!*"

Luca high-fives Maverick, while I palm my forehead. "I could have sworn there was something important about twenty yards."

"That's the red zone, sis."

I drag a palm over my face. "Luca, seriously, you have to promise to poke me to stand up tonight whenever something stand-worthy happens, okay? Roman told me I'll probably be on TV at some point tonight without knowing it, and I don't want to look like a fool in front of the whole world again." Roman mentioned the cameras that will likely find me throughout the game tonight not to stress me out. He told me so I wouldn't feel blindsided. He told me so I won't feel blindsided if I see myself in highlight reels later on. But nonetheless the end result is that I'm totally freaked out. I've already looked like a blazing idiot in front of the world, thanks to that stupid, viral video, and I'm determined never to do it again.

Obviously, I didn't burden Roman with my anxiety about making a fool of myself tonight on a world stage. Why add to

Roman's stress, when he's got much bigger fish to fry? Tonight, for the first time, Roman will be attempting to prove—to the Thunderbolts, the haters, and probably to himself—he's truly a two-hundred-million-dollar man. I'm sure he's feeling tons of pressure. Not that he'd admit it to me.

On the contrary, this morning over breakfast, Roman insisted he's not nervous about tonight's game at all, only confident and excited to show the world what he can do when he's on the right team—one that believes in him and gives him the right teammates. But I had a hunch he might have been willing that confidence into existence, more than actually feeling it. That's why I took Maverick into the backyard after breakfast to teach him how to do cartwheels. To let Roman do whatever pregame rituals he needed to do in peace. Luca warned me Roman can be "a cranky dickhead" throughout the season—especially on game days. "Don't take it personally," Luca told me. "Being a dickhead is how Rome gets himself pumped up and ready for battle."

To my surprise, however, not five minutes after Maverick and I started playing in the backyard, Roman appeared and joined in, dazzling us with a string of cartwheels that blew mine out of the water and made Maverick cheer and scream like Elmo himself had made a cartwheeling appearance.

"There's no need to change your usual game-day routine for me," I assured Roman. "Luca told me you prefer to be left alone on game days."

Roman scoffed. "Yeah, by *Luca* because he's annoyingly cheerful. But that doesn't apply to you and Mav. You two are my lucky charms. This season, I'll need to be around you both as much as possible before every game." To put it mildly, I swooned when Roman said that.

"And nowwwwww," a male announcer bellows through the sound system, jerking me from my thoughts—and everyone in the crowded stadium, including me, immediately bolts up from their seats and cheers. "Make some noise for your *Thunderbooooolts!*"

I cheer wildly, along with everyone else around me, and when my eyes meet Luca's, he yells above the din, "See? Your instincts are perfect, Iris!"

I flash Luca a grateful smile. Truly, I couldn't love that funny, gregarious guy more, even if he were my own flesh and blood.

Smoke begins billowing from the inflated tunnel on the field, and the announcer booms, "And now, let's hear it for number ten, your quarterback, Romannnn Maguiiiiire!"

"Daddyyyyyy!" Maverick shrieks, jumping up and down. And a second later, our beloved Roman jogs onto the field like a badass gladiator in full uniform, his golden helmet gleaming under the massive stadium lights.

I feel electrified in this one-of-a-kind moment. Also, a bit dizzy. I've seen Roman playing football in countless video clips, of course, and also, albeit briefly, in that preseason game, too. But seeing my boyfriend all geared up and inspiring thunderous applause from tens of thousands of rabid fans for a home game that will actually count—while also knowing that gladiator down there loves *me*, Iris Benedetto, above everyone else he could have picked in this world—feels surreal and amazing. Like a dream.

*Too good to be true.*

The deflating thought pops into my head, unbidden, and I quickly banish it. What's wrong with me? Ever since my mother died, dread frequently taps me on the shoulder whenever I'm feeling deliriously happy, reminding me to brace myself for the inevitable fall. Thankfully, however, by the time the rest of the team's introductions are done, I've quieted the voice of doom inside my head.

Roman and his teammates are on the sideline now, preparing for the start of the game. Roman's helmet is off, and he's talking to Coach Hardy. But when that conversation is over, he does something shocking and unexpected: He gazes up toward his box, his hand shading his squinting eyes from the stadium lights, and when his gaze finds mine, he breaks into a wide, beaming smile that sends warmth rocketing into my chest and cheeks.

"Daddy's looking at us!" Maverick shrieks, waving furiously. "Hi, Daddy!"

I blow Roman a kiss, even though I'm assuming he won't see it—but to my shock, Roman immediately blows me a kiss in reply. He can see all of us up here, clearly? And he chose *me*, specifically, out of everyone in his box, including his parents and Maverick, to communicate with? I'm swooning. Melting. Giddy. It's a stupid thing to lose my mind over, but I'm doing it, just the same. *Take that, Voice of Doom.*

As Roman turns away, every member of his family blasts me with frenzied comments, all of them amounting to the same expression of shock about Roman blowing me a happy, relaxed kiss at any time on a game day, but *especially* moments before kickoff.

"What have you done to our cranky Roman?" Marco shouts over the din.

"Whatever you did, keep doing it," Roman's mother adds.

Roman's father, Edward adds his two cents. "Roman never smiles on game days, let alone blows kisses."

Marco agrees and adds, "Romie swore he'd be a changed man this season, but I didn't believe him. I stand corrected."

"Looks like you've cast a magic spell on him this season," Luca says with a wink.

Shit. I know everyone is intending to make me feel good with all this praise, but I'm feeling a bit sick to my stomach. What if Roman has a horrible game, and he second-guesses all the smiling, cartwheels, and kiss-blowing he did beforehand?

What if he loses and blames *me* for it—for drawing him out of his usual game-day routines?

"I think he was blowing that kiss at Maverick—his lucky charm," I reply quickly, even though I don't honestly think that's true. I smile at the cutie pie sitting next to me. "Remember when Daddy said you're his lucky charm?"

Maverick smiles broadly. "He said both of us! Daddy blew dat kiss at both of us, Irish."

Ava interjects with a wink, "He sure did."

Maverick smiles angelically at his grandmother. Apparently, he's elated to share his father's adoration with me. Add that to the list reasons to adore this sweet, bighearted boy.

A country star I've never heard of sings our national anthem, and after that, there's a coin toss, followed by a kickoff—all of which Luca helpfully explains to me in real time. And a moment after all that, it's finally time for Roman to take the field with his army behind him.

When Roman heads into position with his teammates, he struts like he owns the place. Like he was born for this. In short order, he gets situated behind one of his teammates and bends over, giving me and the world a lovely view of his ass in his tight little pants. And a second later, everyone on the field from both teams begins running around like chickens with their heads cut off. Roman bounds backward, scanning the field, and when he finds his target, he unleashes a pass that makes me hold my breath as it flies through the air with impressive velocity.

Eventually, the ball lands smack into the outstretched hands of Roman's teammate, Tyrell Jenkins—a charismatic guy I got to chatting with at a team barbeque a few weeks ago. And, just like that—according to what Luca is screaming at me, anyway—Roman's first attempted pass as a Thunderbolt is a success. One for the record books. Clearly, based on the explosion of cheers and excitement happening all around me, that's a big deal.

"It's a *sign*," Ava screams, high-fiving everyone in her vicinity.

Roman's next pass connects with his target, too. And the one after that, as well. Rinse and repeat, other than one failed attempt that wasn't Roman's fault. On occasion, Roman hands the ball directly to one of his players instead of throwing it. Which, according to Luca, is par for the course. "Even with a prolific passer like Roman, the running game is an essential part of an effective offense," Luca says. "Because it helps set up the passing game." I'm not sure what any of that means, honestly, but I nod and smile and thank Luca for explaining it to me.

In the blink of an eye, we're already six minutes into the game, at which point a Thunderbolt who's not Tyrell—also not someone I met at the barbeque—is the player who catches Roman's pass in the end zone. For a touchdown. For six points. Which even *I* know is the most that can be scored at any given time in a game of football. Not to mention, it's literally the whole point of all the passes and running that came before it.

Reflexively, as the Thunderbolt in the end zone leaps and dances around in celebration, I bolt to my feet, screaming and cheering, along with everyone around me. And guess what? I do all of it—bolting up, screaming, and cheering—without Luca or anyone else needing to poke me.

For several seconds, the massive screen in the stadium displays the player who scored the touchdown. But when a different camera takes over, we're treated to Roman jogging happily toward the touchdown celebration. When he realizes he's being shown on the big screen, he leans into the camera, sticks up his pinky with one hand and three upside-down fingers with the other, and shakes both hands into the camera with his tongue hanging out and a goofy, blissful look on his gorgeous face.

"Mavvy!" I shriek, clutching my chest. "Daddy did that for you and me! That was an 'M' for Maverick and an 'I' for Iris! You and me, buddy!"

"Because we're Daddy's lucky charms!" Maverick screams. Overjoyed, he hugs me like he just won a life supply of Legos, and I squeeze him back with unadulterated glee.

By the time we break apart, I'm crying tears of joy. Partly in reaction to Roman's secret hand signal to Maverick and me. But mostly because I'm so fucking relieved Roman is having a fantastic game. He doesn't express doubt or vulnerability very often with me or anyone else. But I know those emotions are in there, somewhere, lurking. Whispering to him. Fueling him, yes. But, also, sometimes, weighing him down. Seeding doubt. Hopefully, this first touchdown as a Thunderbolt is a sign, like Ava is adamantly screaming now, of all the fantastic things to come for Roman this upcoming season.

Luca nudges my shoulder. "You and Maverick were just on TV. My buddy just texted me."

"When?"

"While you were hugging about the touchdown."

I sigh with relief. If the world was going to get a glimpse of me at this game tonight, as Roman predicted, I'm thrilled the camera caught me celebrating Roman's first touchdown as a Thunderbolt, *and* doing it with Roman's adorable son. In fact, I couldn't have orchestrated a better moment for the world to take stock of me, as Roman's girlfriend, if I'd tried.

"Commercial break," Luca says. He flops into his chair, so I do the same and take a long slug of my cocktail. A moment later, however, as I'm leaning forward to chat with Nicola and Ava down the row, someone taps me on my shoulder from behind.

"Excuse me," a female voice says.

I turn around to find a smiling, lovely woman with a little girl of about ten in the space behind my seat. "Sorry to bother you," the lady says, "but you're the runaway bride from the video, right?"

My stomach revolts. It's the first time in a long while anyone's recognized me, thanks to news cycles being lightning fast these days. I thought I was done with this.

"I hope it's okay to ask," the woman continues when my

tongue is too tied to speak. "But my daughter is hoping to take a selfie with you. I've always told her how important it is to stick up for herself, no matter what, and when we saw your video, we felt like you were a great role model of a strong woman doing exactly that."

My skin erupts with goosebumps, as my heart leaps and bounds inside my chest. Of all the things this woman might have said to me, I never in a million years could have foreseen that. "Thank you," I choke out. "That means a lot."

"I couldn't agree more," Ava pipes in, leaning into the conversation from two seats down.

"Hell yeah," Luca adds with a squeeze of my shoulder.

"Uh, yes," I say, rising from my seat. "I'd be honored to take a selfie. Thank you for asking." I don't know who she is. But if she's in Roman's box, I'm guessing she's someone important, which is all the more reason to feel relieved and excited about her request.

I get up on unsteady legs and lean in for the smiling shot, and both mother and daughter thank me profusely before giving me a hug and politely walking away and slipping out the door of the box.

When they're gone, Ava grabs me and pulls me into a hug before I return to my seat.

"That was the daughter and granddaughter of the team owner!" she whispers into my ear.

"Oh, wow. How exciting."

Ava takes my face in her soft palms. "I'm so proud of you, love. And so happy for me." When I cock my head, not understanding her meaning, Ava smiles and explains, "Happy that my son has *finally* found the perfect woman to bring into our family."

# CHAPTER 35
## Roman

*Three Weeks Later*

THE FACT THAT Iris's birthday tomorrow falls smack in the middle of my bye week is a godsend. It means I've got a few well-timed days off to celebrate the Birthday Girl.

Tomorrow, on Iris's actual birthday, I'm throwing her a dinner party with close friends, family, and teammates at a famous sushi restaurant in Malibu. Today, in advance of the official party, however, we're celebrating Iris's big day in a much quieter way: by enjoying a relaxing horseback ride and picnic with Maverick. *Or so Iris thinks.* Little does Iris know, today's also the day she's *finally* going to become my fiancée. Assuming she says yes. God help me if she doesn't.

Like I told my Council of Advisors at my housewarming party six weeks ago, I'm a new man this season. Happy and relaxed, not a dick at all. I'm still as competitive as ever on the field—as the Thunderbolts' four-and-one record thus far undeniably proves—but the difference this time around is I've managed that winning record without flogging and torturing myself, like I've always done in the past.

Even after that one loss a few weeks ago, I bounced back fairly quickly and didn't take things out on myself or anyone else, including Iris. Am I determined never to lose again this season?

Hell yes. But the point is I didn't lose my fucking mind, as usual, and make myself and everyone else around me miserable in the wake of that loss. I simply put the bad week and my contributing mistakes behind me and looked ahead, productively, to our next game, like all the sport psychologists who've ever tried to crack my stubborn walnut have always harped on me to do.

"It's perfect weather for a picnic," Iris murmurs as we get situated on our thick blanket.

When Maverick struggles to unwrap his sandwich, Iris deftly handles the task for him, at which point Maverick takes it back and attacks his lunch with gusto.

"I love it!" Maverick blurts after his first bite, prompting both Iris and me to chuckle and exchange a look of shared adoration for the kid. I've always been more than a little bit jealous that Vanessa's husband, Jay, gets to spend so much quality time with my son. And now, here I am, experiencing fatherhood the way I've always imagined and envied. Actually, sitting here now, I'd bet my entire bank account my life with Maverick and Iris is better than anything Jay's ever experienced in his entire damned life.

Not that I'm keeping score.

Except that I am.

Maverick takes another huge bite. "What is dis?"

"Turkey pesto," Iris supplies. "Isn't it fun eating something yummy after you've worked up an appetite?" The three of us just finished a long trail ride on a fifty-acre horse property in Malibu—a beach-adjacent oasis that's only five miles from our house. As in Orchard Blossom, Iris led the way like the pro she is, this time on a mare named Trixie, while I rode behind on a gentle gelding named Cheerio, with Maverick nestled safely between my thighs.

When the winding trail reached the beach, Iris galloped on Trixie for a bit, while Maverick and I stayed behind and cheered her on. Given how much Iris has been cheering me on this season, it felt good to be able to return the favor, especially in front of Maverick. I want my son growing up admiring his future stepmom's superpowers every bit as much as he admires mine. My smart momma taught me that.

"What's 'apple tight'?" Maverick asks, tilting his little head and cinching his eyebrows.

As Iris and I laugh together, she murmurs to me, "Another one for your momma's journal." To Maverick, she says, "I said 'appetite,' buddy. If you've got an 'app-e-tite', it means you're hungry."

"Oh, I've got lots and lots of apple tights!" Maverick bellows proudly. To emphasize his point, he fist-pumps the air with his sandwich in hand, prompting its turkey-pesto insides to flop unceremoniously onto the plaid blanket below.

"*Uh oh*," Maverick says, looking forlorn. "My samich got messed up."

"It's okay," Iris coos gently. "I'll fix it for you, buddy. No worries."

God, I love this woman. She's Superwoman, as far as I'm concerned. And I know Maverick feels the same way.

Reflexively, I touch the outer pocket on my backpack to make sure the ring box is still there, and when it is, I breathe a sigh of relief. In light of what Nicola told me six weeks ago, I settled for proposing to Iris today, the day before her actual birthday. But contrary to what Nicola told me, I'm going to give Iris both her birthday present *and* the ring today.

I would have preferred to give Iris her birthday gift tomorrow night, frankly, at her birthday dinner. But what I wound up getting as her gift isn't something that can be wrapped up, tied in a bow, and handed over in a restaurant. Not to mention, I'd much rather get to see Iris's reaction to my over-the-top gift in private.

I touch Iris's leg next to me on the picnic blanket. "You liked riding Trixie today?"

It's a nonsensical question that's already been answered—a question designed to prime the pump for my upcoming big surprise. Yes, Iris loved riding Trixie today, a fact I already know because she praised the horse exuberantly and repeatedly throughout our ride today. Not surprisingly, since when I made today's arrangements a month ago and I asked the woman who owned the ranch to give Iris her very best horse for an expert rider, she replied, "I'll give her Trixie. She's our best horse, hands down."

Iris pops a grape into her mouth, seemingly unfazed by the fact that my question has already been answered throughout the day. "I *loved* Trixie," she gushes. "I've never ridden a more beautiful horse in my life. Whenever we come back here to ride, I'm always going to request her."

She's cued me up perfectly. In fact, I couldn't have scripted a better segue. "There's no need for you to *request* Trixie when we come back," I say, as a shit-eating grin spreads, involuntarily, across my face. "Because Trixie's all yours, babe." When Iris stares at me blankly, I add, "Happy birthday, baby!" Iris still looks like the computer inside her head is buffering, so I add, "You're Trixie's proud owner. She'll be stabled here, and you can ride her any time you want."

"*No, Roman.*"

I laugh. "Yes, Iris."

Understanding dawns on her, as her frantic, overwhelmed expression makes clear. Shrieking with glee, she hurls herself at me across the picnic blanket and tackles me so hard, I fall onto my back with the Birthday Girl on top of me.

"Thank you, thank you!" Iris gasps out, peppering my face with manic kisses. "You're so generous! I love you so much! Thank youuuu!"

Belly laughing, I guide Iris to sit alongside me, and when I've got her face in my palms, and she seems capable of processing more good news, I move on to revealing the next birthday surprise. "I also bought Cheerio and another gelding named Pepper, so we can ride as a family, any time we want."

"*What?*" Iris shrieks. "No, Roman."

"Yes, Iris."

She assaults me again with another round of hugs and furious kisses and thank-yous. Little does she know, however, I'm just getting started.

"Your daddy got you a *horse,* Mavvy!" Iris shouts at Maverick. "Your very own horse named Pepper!"

I provide details about Pepper, reminding Iris and Maverick he's the gentle, black horse Mav fed baby carrots to when we first arrived today, and my son exuberantly leaps up, jumps around like he's on a pogo stick, and begs to go find Pepper to give him a hug right now.

"In a bit," I say with a chuckle, as Maverick wriggles and jiggles around the perimeter of the blanket.

"Please, please, Daddy! *Please.*"

"After we finish our birthday picnic, buddy." *And after I've secured myself a fiancée.*

"I can't believe you did all that," Iris gasps out. "You're insane, Roman. Absolutely insane, in the best possible way."

I shrug. "Twenty-seven is a big birthday."

Iris snorts. "No, it's not. It's totally insignificant."

"Not to me. This is our first birthday together. That's a really big deal to me."

Iris blushes. "Thank you."

"Which is why I got you *another* birthday present, on top of the three horses."

Iris waves her palms in surrender. "No more. I mean it. You have to stop now."

"I already did it, though. No turning back."

Iris shakes her head. "You've already done way too much."

I bite back a smile. "If you really mean that, then I'm in a bit of a pickle, since this next thing isn't something I can return." I flash her a playful frown. "I mean, if you're *sure* I've already done too much, then I suppose I could donate the next present to a charity without ever showing it to you . . ."

Iris swats at my shoulder and giggles. "Don't you dare. Fine. I admit it: You've called my bluff. I'm *dying* to see it."

*It's another perfect segue.* I swear, she's the perfect straight man for this particular comedy routine. "You've actually already seen it," I offer mysteriously. "In fact, you've been looking at it all day long." My comment begets another blank stare from Iris, so I motion dramatically to our surroundings. "Your final birthday present is everything you see. The whole ranch—all fifty acres and every horse, structure, and piece of equipment on it. Happy birthday, baby."

Iris looks like the hard drive in her mind is physically glitching. Shutting down. Experiencing a system-wide, catastrophic meltdown. I repeat the gist of my prior comment, and also assure Iris every word of it is true—and, finally, Iris falls into my waiting arms and sobs like a baby against my heaving chest.

"Why is Irish crying?" Maverick asks with concern. "Why doesn't your present make her happy?"

"She *is* happy," I assure him. "Sometimes, people cry when they're really, really happy." As I say the words, tears prick my eyes, effectively prove my point.

"I can't believe you did this," Iris chokes out between sobs.

I kind of can't believe it, either, honestly. It's an over-the-top birthday gift, to be sure. One that makes no logical sense, in terms of timing. But the thing is, this ranch isn't actually a birthday gift, per se. It's an engagement present. The symbol of my promise to love Iris forever. I mean, what better way to promise eternity to someone than gifting them their dream? To me, that's an even more irrevocable promise than a simple ring, which can be taken off, lost, or stolen.

Okay, I admit I'm not too far gone to realize, in a perfect

world, I probably should have waited a few years to buy Iris this ranch. For instance, it probably would have made more sense to buy it for her as a wedding gift, or maybe for our first wedding anniversary, rather than for our engagement. Surely, my jaded, hard-hearted, pre-Iris self would have been flabbergasted and disgusted to find out about *any* random guy foolishly gifting his simple girlfriend or fiancée with a present of this magnitude. And God help me, if my prior, jaded self ever discovered the foolish, over-the-top gift giver would one day be *me*, he'd need a crash cart.

But, see, that's the beauty of the whole thing. The New Roman, the guy who's in love with Iris Benedetto, doesn't give a shit what anyone else thinks. He doesn't want to play it safe. Doesn't want to hold back or create a single safety net. At least, not when it comes to Iris. With her, I only want to jump in, headfirst, with my whole heart and without a backup plan. With Iris, I'm all in, always. No reservations or doubts. And I wanted this gift to prove that to her, unequivocally.

Also, as a practical matter, I had no choice but to buy this ranch when I did. When I came down here a month ago, it was only to buy a singular horse for Iris's birthday. But that's when the owner of the ranch mentioned she was about to put the ranch on the market, so I had to act fast. Properties like this don't come up for sale very often in Malibu. Hardly ever, my real estate agent told me. If I didn't pull the trigger immediately, without overthinking it and without hesitation, I might not have had another chance in my lifetime. Literally.

So, fuck it. I followed my heart. Not my head. Not the advice of my business manager and accountant. Not the advice of Cameron, who lost his ever-loving mind. Like I told all the money managers and overseers of my life, when it comes to Iris, I'd much rather wind up regretting something I *did* out of love than something I *didn't* do out of fear.

As Iris sniffles in my arms, I kiss her cheek. "You can do

whatever you want here," I coo into her ear. "You can keep it, as is, and give riding lessons and trail rides. Or you can build a kick-ass equine therapy center. Whatever you're dreaming about doing here, tell me, and I'll make it happen."

"It's too much," Iris chokes out against my shoulder.

"Nothing's too much for you, baby. That's what I'm trying to tell you. To *show* you. I'd do anything for you. I love you more than there are stars in the sky above Orchard Blossom."

"Oh my God, Roman. You've taken my breath away."

Here we go.

This is it.

The moment I've been waiting for. As I've been planning for weeks, my mention of the stars above Orchard Blossom is my cue to pull out the ring, get down on bended knee, and launch into my planned proposal speech.

But suddenly, now that I'm here with Iris's sobbing frame in my arms and my son still jumping around impatiently and shouting about finding Pepper, it's suddenly clear it's not the right time to add even more life-changing, heart-exploding fuel to this already blazing fire. On the contrary, it feels right to savor *this* particular life-changing moment fully before moving on to the next, even bigger one. *Goddammit. Nicola was right.*

In a beat of my pounding heart, the perfect scenario for a proposal hits me like a ton of bricks. In fact, I can see it all now, like a movie. Me, in my football uniform. Iris in my arms. Cameras all around us. Why didn't I think of this perfect scenario before now? Probably because my team wasn't sitting at four and one, and only getting better with each passing week.

Okay, I'm pumped for this idea now.

Granted, making this new proposal idea happen the way I'm envisioning it isn't something I can control. No football player on Planet Earth possibly could. That's why we play the games, after all. Because anything can happen. But isn't the uncertainty of it all even more reason for me to set my sights on at least *trying* to make this once-in-a-lifetime scenario happen? Won't working toward that dream scenario only give me even *more* motivation to fulfill my ultimate professional goal? Frankly, it seems like a win-win to me. The perfect idea.

"Can we *please* go see Pepper now?" Maverick whines, flailing his arms and wiggling his little body with extreme impatience.

"And the whole ranch, too," Iris interjects. "I'd love to take a stroll around the whole property, now that I know it's ours."

*Ours.* Her word choice doesn't escape my notice. I'm pretty sure I told Iris the place is *hers.* And yet, Iris being Iris, she's converted my phrasing into something shared and co-owned. In reality, I put this place in both our names, of course. So, technically, legally, she's right: It's ours. I mean, I'm not a complete idiot. But in a practical, daily sense, it's all hers, as far as I'm concerned. From this day forward, I plan to be nothing but her angel investor.

"Let's do it," I say. "The lady who sold me the ranch said she's standing by to give us a full tour."

Iris and Maverick express excitement, and we begin quickly cleaning up the remnants of our picnic. Midway through our task, however, I touch Iris's arm, commanding her full attention.

I might not be proposing today after all, but I'm sure as hell not leaving here without Iris knowing she's my future wife. "I figured my birthday gift would make my commitment to you crystal clear," I say, a surprising tremble in my voice. "But just in case there's room for any doubt, let me say this expressly to you now: Iris Benedetto, I love you. I admire you. Like you. Respect you." I take a deep breath. "I have full faith in our love, without a single doubt. And I'm positive we're going to be together, happily, *forever.*"

# CHAPTER 36
## Iris

It's Sunday night.

An away game for the Thunderbolts.

And our opponent is Roman's former team in Baltimore: the Crusaders.

I'm seated alongside Ava and Edward for the big game in the Crusaders' stadium—the same place where Roman gave his blood, sweat, and tears to his teammates, fans, and coaches for eleven excruciating years. Mostly, Roman poured his heart out to raucous cheers and support, but, sometimes, especially toward the end of his career here, he did it to boos and jeers from turncoat "fans" who'd decided Roman Maguire hadn't lived up to his talents and potential.

Not surprisingly, Roman wants to win this game, badly. In fact, he desperately wants to deliver a beatdown of epic proportions to his former team. Can't say I blame him. I'd want to shut up all the naysayers, meanies, and haters in my old stomping grounds, too.

I look at the pregame clock underneath the big screen, and when another wave of anxiety shocks through me, I gulp my drink to calm my nerves.

As I bring my cup to my lips, Ava, sitting next to me, points at my cup. "Vodka cranberry with a twist?"

"Yes, ma'am."

"Good girl." She holds up her own cup. "Gin and tonic, of course. I'm always doing my part."

We clink and drink.

Holy mother of pearl, I'm sick to death of vodka cranberries with a fucking twist by now. But because that random, spur-of-the-moment decision to copy everything Nicola did during the Thunderbolts' dominating, crushing victory during week one, it's now inked onto the List of Things Iris Absolutely Must Do During Every Game in Support of Roman. My God, football people are superstitious motherfuckers.

I mean, vodka cranberries are pleasant enough. But they're not my favorite. Especially now that I'm not *allowed* to drink anything else during games. The good news is that when I confessed my increasing disenchantment with vodka crans to my football mentor, Luca, he assured me the "we must do everything, exactly the same as we did during the first win" clock resets, so to speak, either once we reach the playoffs or with the start of each new season. So at least I know I won't be stuck with vodka cranberries forever.

Speaking of Luca, he's not here tonight, but for a fabulous reason: He played in his team's winning game earlier today. That's right. Recently, our beloved, hardworking, keeping-his-chin-up Luca *finally* got promoted from his team's practice squad to their fifty-three-man roster—and he's been kicking ass ever since.

Levi and Marco aren't here, either, by the way, since both men played for their respective teams today. Maverick's not here, either. Although he never travels to away games anyway. In this case, however, it wouldn't have been possible regardless. Vanessa got a big job in Vancouver for the next three weeks, so Maverick traveled with his excited mommy.

"They're taking the field," Edward mutters. When he points,

it's to Roman and his teammates as they amble toward the sideline in full uniform. The visiting team never gets a fancy introduction, so it's not unusual to find them wandering onto the field unannounced. What *is* unusual, however, is the way the crowd is reacting to the opposing quarterback's appearance. At their first sight of Roman, a large smattering of the home-town crowd—the minority, I'd say—has started applauding their former star quarterback, presumably to thank him for his years of stellar service. The majority of the crowd, however, has started booing Roman. *Loudly.* In fact, as their negativity gains steam, their boos are becoming a virtual cacophony.

Roman doesn't react to crowd, of course. He's got his game face on down there as he confers with Coach Hardy on the sideline. But even if he's not bothered by the fans' lack of sportsmanship, I am. In fact, I'm livid. Ready to throw down on his behalf. How dare these people abuse my boyfriend like this, after everything he's done for them and this city! Not only on the field, but for schools and charities, too! Do these people have amnesia, or are they simply heartless and cruel toward someone who poured his heart out for them, week after week, year in and year out, for eleven freaking years?

Ava pats my hand, apparently reacting to my furious body language. "Don't worry about any of that, sweetie. Roman will use the boos to fuel his competitive tank that much more."

"*Absolutely*," Edward seconds with a decisive nod. "Romie loves proving the naysayers wrong more than anything. Trust me, he's going to enjoy shutting them all up."

*God, I hope he's right.*

"Ladies and gentlemen!" a deep-voiced announcer booms over the stadium's sound system. "Get on your feet, and let's hear it for your Crusaderrrrssssss!"

Everyone in the stadium, except for our trio and anyone else wearing Thunderbolts gear, rises from their seats and cheers wildly as the Crusaders bound into the stadium, accompanied by blaring music, plumes of smoke, and a whole lot of shaking, sparkling cheerleaders' pompoms.

As mayhem swirls around us, Ava leans into me and shouts above the din, "I can't wait to watch Roman make this place go dead silent!"

"Woohoo!" I reply. But I'm worried. Granted, I worry before every game. But this time, my anxiety is through the roof. Roman wasn't his usual, relaxed self this entire week, as he prepared for his momentous return to Baltimore. In fact, he was noticeably quiet and intense. And so, I gave him a wide berth and left him alone. Walked on eggshells whenever we were both home, which was rare. I was willing to do it, of course, given the special circumstances of this week's game, but I certainly couldn't live like that every single week. Honestly, it was exhausting.

Luckily, I know we'll reconnect after the game. After Roman's big win. Indeed, we'll snuggle in our big bed, like we always do after games, and revel in all the highlight clips on the sports channels. After that, we'll make celebratory love and belly laugh together about Roman making all these booing Crusaders' fans eat a buffet's worth of crow.

"Please rise for the national anthem," the announcer commands. And a moment later, the song is performed beautifully by a confident woman dressed in a military uniform.

The referee performs the obligatory coin toss, and it's determined Roman and his Thunderbolts will start the game on offense. That's a great sign. Roman loves to come out of the gate swinging. Several minutes later, after a commercial break and a kickoff, Roman jogs confidently onto the field, his helmet strapped on and his body language confident, as his teammates file into their designated positions on the line of scrimmage.

As always, Roman crouches behind his center to prepare for the snap, and Ava takes my hand and squeezes it in anticipation.

And we're off.

Roman's got the ball. All the players on the field are in motion. Roman takes several bounding steps backward into the pocket while looking for his target. And when he spots an open receiver, a tight end named Bradley Williams, Roman releases a perfect spiral that lands smack into Williams's outstretched hands.

Shit.

Williams immediately drops the ball during the tackle that follows his attempted catch. Crap. The pass is ruled incomplete.

"That's okay," Ava shouts, as Crusaders fans cheer wildly around us. "Roman's aim was dead-on accurate. That's a great sign."

The Thunderbolts line up again. And this time, we get a running play that doesn't do squat to advance our position on the field. No worries, though. We've still got one more chance to get a first down.

"Come on, Roman," Ava mutters, as Roman and his team line up again their opponents again.

Once again, the center snaps the ball to Roman. And once again, our Roman steps back into the pocket, looking for an open receiver. But before Roman gets the ball off, a massive, hurtling Crusader breaks through the Thunderbolts' offensive line—the players specifically assigned the duty of protecting their quarterback from exactly this sort of onslaught.

As the Crusader comes barreling at Roman, he throws the ball toward his teammate . . . and a second later, a leaping, hurtling Crusader flies through the air and catches the ball Roman intended for a Thunderbolt.

"No!" I scream. "Nooo!" But it's worst-case scenario. After making the interception, the Crusader who caught the ball evades three tackles while sprinting all the way down the field into the Crusader's end zone for a touchdown. It's a pick-six, as they say. A calamity.

The crowd around me catapults into euphoric madness, while I cover my face with my hands, feeling sick to my stomach. It's literally the worst thing that could have happened in this situation, besides Roman getting hurt.

Ava touches my arm and shouts, "It's okay. He'll use it as fuel!"

As I lower my hands from my face, Edward leans across his wife and shouts, "You'll see. Romie will come roaring back after this and have his best game yet."

Spoiler alert: Roman did not, in fact, have his best game yet.

On the contrary, it was his worst.

By far.

Not only of the season, but of his entire career.

As the clock on the big screen runs out, officially ending my torture, I hang my head and let my tears flow. As it turned out, that first, awful drive that ended in an interception and touchdown for the Crusaders was, indeed, a *sign,* as Ava always says: a very, very bad one for Roman. He was a train wreck from start to finish. And so was everyone around him on the team. As a result, the Thunderbolts just suffered more than a simple loss. They suffered a complete, faith-quaking, demoralizing catastrophe.

As Ava, Edward, and I sit in stunned silence, gleeful people wearing Crusaders jerseys are filing out of the stadium on both sides of us, all of them bopping along to the celebratory music blaring overhead in the stadium.

"Thank God we finally got rid of that loser," a guy says, as he passes by.

"Yup. Roman's definitely past his prime," his buddy replies. "Good riddance."

I feel sick. Protective. *Angry.* Anyone could see the loss

wasn't *only* Roman's fault. Every single player in a Thunderbolts' uniform ingeniously found a way to screw up royally tonight. But, of course, Roman's the one they're all going to blame. Same as ever. Same as in Baltimore.

"Come on, ladies," Edward says somberly. "Let's go wait for him."

It's what we always do after an away game: We find the designated VIP area and wait for Roman to emerge from the locker room on his way to the team bus. We always give him a big hug and tell him good game. Or better luck next time, after that one loss. And then, we head home ourselves and, in my case, wait for Roman to stride through the front door of our house and rip off my clothes.

"Do you really think Roman will want to see us this time?" I ask. This is uncharted territory for me. Yes, Roman lost that one other time this season. But not like this. Not to mention, he didn't act weird and distant the entire week before that game, either.

"We always go down to see him and hug him, win or lose," Ava says confidently. "Come on. He'll be glad to see us."

I nod meekly. When it comes to Roman and football, I always defer to his parents. They've been doing this a whole lot longer than I have, after all. And not only with Roman. With Luca and Levi, too. Earlier today, in fact, they split up to attend Luca's and Levi's games, since those games happened to be within train rides of this one.

"I wouldn't say much to him, though," Edward advises. Clearly, he's addressing me with this comment. "Just give him a hug and tell him you love him, and leave the pep talks for another time, okay?"

My stomach twists. "Got it. Thanks for the heads-up." Something in Edward's body language has me on edge, like he's giving me the one-shot dismantling code for a nuclear bomb.

We find the VIP area and show the security guard our badges, and about twenty minutes later, Roman emerges from a cement corridor, his body language tight and his face somber and gray. If I didn't know the context of this moment, I'd swear Roman just got the news of a loved one's violent death. He looks *that* devastated.

Roman heads to his mother first. Which makes sense, considering she's been comforting him after losses since his peewee football days. But even if it makes sense, it nonetheless stings a bit to watch Roman seeking comfort in his mother's arms rather than in mine. Even after that one hard-fought loss earlier this season, Roman came to me first.

I wring my hands while waiting for Roman and fight the urge to cry. And when Roman disengages from his mother, he immediately moves on to his father, who wraps his son in a bear hug for a very long time.

When Roman finally disentangles from Edward, he comes to me, slowly. Begrudgingly, it seems—like he's a political prisoner dragging his ass in front of firing squad. Although, admittedly, I might simply be paranoid, insecure, and out of my depths in this moment.

When Roman reaches me, I open my arms, and he falls into them and silently holds me tight. It's a relief to feel his body pressed, without hesitation, against mine. To smell is familiar shampoo and aftershave. To feel the beating of his heart against mine.

"I love you so, so much," I whisper. When he says nothing, I add, "I'm so sorry things didn't turn out the way you'd hoped, but I have zero doubts you'll use this game as motivation to bounce back, better than ever, next week."

Roman's body stiffens in my arms.

He pulls back, his facial expression tight and annoyed.

*Shit.* That was obviously the wrong thing to say to him. It's too soon.

He doesn't want to hear it.

"I'm sorry," I blurt. But Edward shoots me a warning look that makes me press my lips together, swallow hard, and stuff back my tears. Why'd I say that? Edward explicitly told me not to give Roman a pep talk!

"Thanks for coming," Roman says tightly. Not "I love you, too." Not "I'll see you back home, my love."

"Of course," I say lamely, wiping my eyes. I've seen Roman thank people for coming to his game many times, in many situations. But I'm the one who shares his bed every night. Not someone to politely thank for coming.

After shooting our trio a half-hearted, clipped wave, Roman turns and strides toward the waiting team bus that's parked, its engine running, about twenty yards away.

And that's that.

Roman doesn't turn and wave before disappearing through the bus door, like usual. He simply vanishes without looking back, leaving me feeling like I've majorly fucked up.

As I hang my head and cry, Edward slides his arm around me and squeezes. "It's okay, sweetheart. He's not upset with you. He's mad at himself. Give him a few days to work through his emotions, and I promise he'll be good as new."

# CHAPTER 37
## Iris

I CHANGE POSITIONS on our couch, trying, and failing, to get comfortable.

I'm watching a dishy, trashy, addicting show that's right up my alley—and yet, my eyes are glazed over. My concentration nonexistent. I'm restless. Jittery. *Lonely.*

It's been four days since the Crusaders debacle in Baltimore, and Roman is not, in fact, "good as new," as his father promised he'd be by now. On the contrary, whenever my boyfriend comes home every night from the Thunderbolts' training facility, always much later than usual, he's simply not himself. He's quiet. Distant. So intense, it's stress-inducing to be around him. I don't even know why he comes home, frankly, since all he does when he's here, besides sleeping, is watch game footage.

With Maverick still in Vancouver with Vanessa, I've kept myself busy at the ranch and with friends. Also, by bingeing shows like this one. But I can't continue like this. All I want to do is support Roman and make him feel better, any way I can—but even so, I can't allow him to ignore me *forever*. Sorry, that's not the relationship I signed on for. We haven't even had sex since the loss! Granted, that's probably mostly due to Roman's crazy schedule this week. I'm almost always asleep by the time he gets home. But is it crazy to think he might have woken me up for sex at least once this week? He's done that before, even after that other loss, so he has to know I'd happily choose sex with him over sleep.

*Too good to be true.*

The Voice of Doom is no longer whispering that horrible phrase into my ear. This week, the voice has been screaming it. Constantly. Does Roman blame *me* for that horrible loss in Baltimore? Is he second-guessing his decision to invite me to live with him? I'm well aware he's never had a girlfriend during football season before, and he's one hell of a superstitious motherfucker when it comes to football stuff. So, could it be Roman's decided I've somehow brought him bad luck or caused him to lose necessary focus?

As my thoughts spiral into another full-blown panic, Roman unexpectedly waltzes through our front door in a Thunderbolts T-shirt and gray sweats, looking freshly showered and perturbed.

"Hey," I murmur, sitting up on the couch. "You're home early."

My heart is thundering.

This is it.

I'm going to talk to Roman today and tell him everything I've been thinking about on a running loop. It might piss him off and push him away even more, but I simply can't live like this. If we're not going to make it, then I'd rather find that out now than let this drag on for the rest of the season.

"Yeah, Coach made me leave early for some 'rest and relaxation,'" Roman murmurs with a scoff. "He's forcing me to take the rest of the day off, whether I like it or not."

I clear my throat and pat the couch next to me. "Can we talk for a minute?"

Roman's features soften. "Of course." He strides over and sits down. But before I say a word, he leans in and kisses me deeply. "I'm sorry, baby," he whispers. "I've been a total dick."

My heart rate quickens. I croak out, "You blame me for the loss."

Roman pulls a face like that's the craziest thing he's ever heard. "Of course not."

Tears prick my eyes. "Then why have you been acting so pissed at me?"

"What? Iris, no." He runs a hand through his dark hair. "I didn't want to be a cranky dick around you, so I kept my distance while I worked some things out."

"If you think I prefer you icing me out and acting like you want to break up with me to you being a cranky dick, then you're sorely mistaken."

His face drains of color. "I . . . I'm sorry. There's not an ounce of me that's thinking about breaking up with you, Iris. I didn't realize that's the impression I was giving."

Tears flow down my cheeks. "You've barely looked at me, let alone talked to me. We haven't had sex. You never ask me about my day or how I'm doing. Of course I'm thinking you might be second-guessing your decision to invite me here. What else could I possibly think?"

Roman looks utterly devastated. "I thought you understood . . . I'll never, ever second-guess you. You're the best thing that's ever happened to me. Didn't the horse ranch tell you how I feel about you?"

"I mean, yes. It did. At the time. But people change their minds. Sometimes, they do something over the top without thinking it through and then regret it later on." I can't stop my chin from trembling.

"*Baby.*" Roman wraps me in a hug. "My love, I promise, what I've been going through has nothing to do with you. It's all in my own head."

"It does have to do with me, though, because I love you, through thick and thin. Because we're teammates, whether you win or lose." I lean back from our hug and look into his dark eyes. "I loved you before I knew you played football, remember? And you loved me, even when I was at rock bottom. All I want to do is love and support you through tough times, the way you did for me, but you won't let me." I wipe my tears. "If I'm being honest, I'm tired of this relationship always being a one-way street. I want to be there for you in return."

"*A one-way street?*" Roman says, like the words are unfathomable. He takes my hand. "Iris, you give me far more than I could ever give you, just by being here and being you."

I scoff. "Except when you lose a football game?"

His jaw tightens "I didn't simply lose. And it wasn't *a* football game. It was far more than that."

I exhale. "I understand that's the narrative you've been telling yourself. But there's a schedule of games, right? And it's an objective fact that was merely *one* game on that schedule. Correct?"

"It's not that simple."

"Why not? It can be, if you let it be."

He pats my thigh. "I love you, sweetheart, but you simply don't understand."

I take a deep breath to calm myself. "I don't pretend to understand football the way you do. But here's what I *do* understand: I can't continue like this. I'm fully prepared to let you have space to work through your emotions and prepare for the next game on the schedule. But giving you space and being ignored and shut out are two very different things."

"And rightly so," he mumbles. He hangs his head and sighs. "I don't know how to do this, Iris. It's all new to me—juggling a relationship and my responsibilities during the season."

"Do you *want* to juggle those two things?"

He looks up, his dark eyes wide and anxious. "Of course, I do. You truly doubt that?"

My chin trembling, I nod.

Roman looks pained. His shoulders droop. "I can't believe

I've let you doubt my feelings for you for a nanosecond. That's inexcusable. Please, forgive me, Iris." His dark eyes look downright panicked at this point. *Good.* I'm not a sadist, but Roman looks exactly how I've felt for quite some time now, and it feels good to know I'm no longer alone here.

"It's not a matter of me forgiving you," I reply evenly. "It's a matter of us figuring out a way to do this, going forward. *Together.* A way that works for both of us."

Roman nods. But a moment later, his face contorts, like he's on the cusp of losing control of his emotions. He hangs his head again. Remains silent for an eternal moment. But finally, he murmurs, "I've really been struggling. That's the truth."

*Finally.* A breakthrough. I grip his forearm. "I know you have, my love. That's been pretty damned clear. But I can't help you if you won't let me. If you don't confide in me and lean on me. Let me in, Roman. That's all I want."

Roman lifts his head, takes a deep breath, and exhales it with puffed-out cheeks. "I don't even know how to do that, honestly. I love you so much for wanting to help me, sweetheart, but nobody can. It's nothing against you, personally. I've been to loads of sports psychologists over the years, including twice this week, but there's no advice in the world that's going to help me crack this fucking nut." He bangs on his head with his knuckles, a grimace on his handsome face. "I don't know what's wrong with me sometimes. I tell myself not to let one mistake get to me; I tell myself not to listen to the negative chatter about me. But that's all easier said than done when the whole world is watching and reveling in your failure."

"You didn't *fail.* You had one bad game, along with every other player on the team. It happens."

He shakes his head. "The whole world was watching and rooting for me to fucking fail. *And I did.* And now, that game is what I'll always be remembered for, above all else. I'll be remembered as a choker." He swallows hard, clearly trying to stifle the emotion that's crept into his voice.

I squeeze his forearm in my grasp. "No, my love. The best is yet to come."

His chest heaves. "What if the haters have been right about me all along? What if I really am nothing but a loser, a choker, an overpriced, overhyped egomaniac who'll never deliver when it matters most?"

An idea strikes. With full authority and confidence, I grab his hand and hold it firmly in mine. "Go put on some jeans and sneakers, baby. I'm taking you to the horse ranch for the rest of the day."

Roman exhales. "Baby, no. I'm sorry. I need to watch some more game films and—"

"No, you don't. Coach told you to take the day off."

"I know, but—"

"No buts. Coach Hardy knows better than you. And so do I. Go on." I point toward the staircase leading to our bedroom upstairs. "Get dressed, love. You're coming with me. For the rest of the day, your ass is *mine*."

# CHAPTER 38
## Roman

"Okie doke," Iris says brightly, after tightening the cinch around Cheerio's belly. "He's all ready for you, cowboy."

I lumber over to the horse and climb aboard. But I'm not happy about it. I love Iris, though. And she was absolutely right at the house earlier: I've iced her out, thereby stupidly risking everything with her. So, whatever she wants me to do today to fix my fuckup, I'll do it.

In one fluid motion, Iris elegantly mounts Trixie nearby. "Ready?"

"Yes, ma'am."

Her blue eyes sparkle. "Notice anything different about Cheerio's tack today?"

I look around cluelessly, not sure what she means. At the reins in my hands. The stirrups at my feet. It all looks the same as always to me. "Is this some kind of a wax-on, wax-off thing? Am I supposed to find deep meaning in something mundane, or is there something really big I'm missing?"

Iris laughs. "It's a small thing. Something I think might help me make a point to you." She pauses, apparently awaiting something from me. When I don't speak, she says, "Okay, I'll tell you about it later, during the ride. That'll give you the chance to notice it on your own."

That's fine with me. I'm not in the mood for guessing games today. Not in the mood to try, and fail, to reach some divine epiphany. I just want to take in the fresh air, enjoy some alone time with my woman, and try to make things up to her, as best I can.

With a squeeze of her thighs and a clipped clicking noise from her mouth, Iris expertly signals her horse to lead us out of the barn and onto her favorite trail. And for the next several minutes, we ride in silence, the only sounds coming from the horses' hooves on the dirt and occasional rocks, mingled their soft exhales and whinnies.

"How are you doing back there?" Iris asks after a bit.

"Good." I don't how it happened or when, but it's an honest answer. I'm good. Not great, but good. My shoulders and back feel a lot less tense and tight than only a few minutes ago. My mind is clearing, too. Could it be my brilliant Iris was on to something when she commanded me here, after all?

"Have you noticed the different thing yet?" Iris asks.

I roll my eyes to myself. "Just tell me, babe. I don't have energy for guessing games today."

"There's a new piece of equipment on Cheerio's head today."

I look down at my horse's head, and I'll be damned, two square pieces of leather are abutting his eyes on either side of his head. "What are those things?"

"Blinders."

"I didn't even notice. I guess I've been distracted."

"Isn't it amazing that something can be there, all along? Just sitting there in front of your nose, but you don't even see it because your *mind* is focused on things that don't even exist?"

I chuckle. "So, this *is* gonna be a wax-on, wax-off kind of thing."

"Just saying, sometimes, you have to consciously *focus* on what's in front of you to be able to see it clearly. As I'm sure you know, Mr. I Can Do Everything Myself, the past is gone. The future hasn't happened yet. The only thing that's real is the present."

"Okay, Yoda. Go ahead and give me whatever little speech you've been cooking up in your brilliant head about blinders now. I'm listening."

She snickers. "Do you know the purpose of blinders?"

"To keep the horse from looking around, I presume."

"Correct. To keep them from getting distracted by what's to the right or the left so they can focus their full attention on what's right in front of them. They help the horse focus on the path ahead. The signals his rider is giving him. Basically, they help the horse turn off his brain and live in the moment so he can more effectively do his job."

I snort and murmur, "Wax on, wax off. I saw it coming a mile away."

"That way," Iris continues, "he can react on instinct. Without overthinking it. He can rely on all his training, power, and strength, without his brain betraying him and telling him to focus on things that don't matter—things that will only diminish his peak performance."

"That's cool, babe. I'm impressed by the metaphor. But, unfortunately, blinders aren't league-approved equipment. If they were, I'd surely give them a shot." I scoff and add, "Why not? I'll try anything at this point."

Iris sighs, and we ride in silence for a long moment.

Finally, she calls back to me, "Do you know the most important difference between you and a horse, my love?"

"Well, it's definitely not the size of our dicks, so I guess my answer is no."

Iris giggles, and to my surprise, I'm able to join her in laughing at my stupid joke.

"The most important difference," Iris says, "is that a horse can't *imagine* putting on blinders. He needs his human to do it for him. But a human being *can* imagine it. In fact, it's a scientific fact the human body reacts to everything the mind vividly tells it, whether the vision comes in a dream, as a manifestation, or whatever. That's why your heart rate increases whenever you're having a nightmare. Or you get hard or have an orgasm during a sex dream. Because your body and mind don't know the difference between what's real and what's imagined, if you focus hard enough on it."

"I have a hunch *someone* on this trail is equine therapizing me."

Iris laughs and doesn't deny it. In fact, she turns and flashes me a cute little smile over her shoulder that admits I'm spot-on. "Trust the process, grasshopper," she coos.

"You've got it, Mr. Miyagi. I'm all ears."

She motions toward a shady spot in a nearby clearing, her cheeks flushed and her eyes wide and bright for the first time in a very long time. "Let's stop for a snack, yes?"

"Whatever you say, Teacher. I'm your willing pupil today."

Iris brings Trixie to a stop, and Cheerio follows suit, as he always does. And a moment later, we're sitting underneath our favorite shady tree on the property, nibbling on apples and taking in the view, while our horses drink languidly from a nearby trough.

"Every sports psychologist I've ever seen has talked about visualization and manifestation," I say. "I did a shit ton of visualization before the Baltimore game, and look where that got me."

"Have you ever visualized yourself putting on blinders during a game?"

I laugh. "Well, no. Can't say I have."

"Then you don't know, for sure, if it would work or not. True or false?"

I smirk. "True. Technically."

"So, tell me, what do you have to lose?"

I bite my lip. "Nothing, I suppose."

"Exactly. So, here's what you're going to do on Sunday, whenever you feel like you *really* need to focus during the game. You can't wear your magic blinders all game long, but whenever—"

"My *magic* blinders?"

"Correct. That's why you can't wear them at all times during a game, because their magic might fade if worn too long. It's important you only put them on whenever you need an extra boost of focus and confidence at a critical moment. Think of them like shifting into the highest gear in a race car." Her eyebrows cinch together and a crease forms on her forehead. "Or is that the *lowest* gear?" Iris scratches her chin, contemplating her analogy, and she's so damned adorable in this moment, it's all I can do not to tackle her to the soft grass and rip off all clothes, right here and now.

"Iris, I want you to know I respect your intellect and ideas. I truly do. I also appreciate your attempt to help me. But, sweetheart, there's truly no way in hell—"

"Stop, Roman," Iris says firmly, raising her palm. "You're going to do this once on Sunday—*for me*. And you're going to do it in earnest. Without holding back. Without rolling your eyes. Without secretly thinking it's dumb. You're going all in on this, if only once. And if it doesn't work that one time, then okay, I'll never talk about this again."

I exhale. I can't argue with that. In fact, I have no desire to argue with her. Not when she's looking at me like that—like she's discovered real, true magic and wants only to share it with me, the man she loves. "Okay," I reply softly in surrender. "What, exactly, do you want me to do, love?"

She lights up. "I want you to put on your magic blinders, like this." She puts her palms on either side of her head, at her temples, mimicking the squares of leather strapped to Cheerio's head. "Once you've got your magic blinders in place, I want you to actively imagine their magic working for you, blocking out the past and future and your physical ability to think of anything that's not immediately in front of you on the field. When your blinders are on, they make it so you can only think about whatever play you've got on tap, and that's it. You can only feel with your senses. You see the receivers running their routes. You feel the ball against your hands and your cleats digging into the turf. Everything else is magically blocked out."

She's definitely using her child psychology background on me in this moment, even though I'm not a fucking child. But you know what? I can't see a downside to giving it a whirl. What have I got to lose? "Okay, Mr. Miyagi. I'll give it a shot."

"You have to believe in the magic, though. Promise me, Roman. It's like *Peter Pan*. The fairy dust won't make you fly unless you truly believe it will."

"I believe, Iris."

"Promise?"

"I *believe*!" I throw up both arms like I'm in a Baptist revival. "I believe!"

As she laughs, I take her giggling frame into my arms and kiss her deeply—and I swear, the resulting combustion feels even more earthquaking than our magical kiss in front of the waterfall in Kauai. Even more so than that life-altering kiss under the swirling stars in Orchard Blossom. She's my destiny, this woman. The best thing that's ever happened to me. And it's now clear I came *this* close to pushing her away, simply because I'm a stupid, scared, self-sabotaging idiot.

I already loved this woman before today. But my love for Iris feels like it's expanded and deepened today. Plainly, if I want to keep this once-in-a-lifetime love in my life, I'm going to have to kick Regular Season Roman to the curb, once and for all. Not only that, I'll need to commit to being vulnerable with Iris, too, like she said, even when it's hard and scary and the last thing I want to do.

"You didn't want to have sex with me this week?" she whispers against my cheek.

"I always want you, Iris. I was punishing myself."

She leans back, her breathing hitching. "By punishing *me*?"

The question hits me like a gut punch. What's wrong with me? "I'm so sorry, baby. I'll never do it again. I promise. Let me make it up to you."

I quickly get her bottom half naked, and after guiding her onto her back and spreading her thighs, I lean in and do the thing I wanted to do in that meadow in Orchard Blossom: *I eat my gorgeous woman's pussy like a starving man.* In fact, I devour Iris Benedetto with such enthusiasm, both horses start whinnying and stomping in unison when Iris eventually lets out a loud scream of ecstasy with her climax.

As Iris comes down, I yank off my shoes and jeans and pull her onto my lap. As she sinks herself onto my full length, I cradle her back and bring my forehead to hers. "I love you, Iris. I love you forever. And from this day forward, I'll always make sure you know that."

She gyrates passionately on top of me, kissing me feverishly. And when she ultimately comes, it's with a low, keening groan that sends rockets of desire shooting through me, so of course, I come on her heels.

As our bodies quiet down, we kiss passionately. And by the time our lips part again, I feel like a new man with a newfound lightness of being.

"Magic blinders," I murmur with a smile, my forehead pressed to hers.

"Magic blinders," she whispers back. "Do it for me."

"I'd do anything for you."

"Then do this. Full throttle. Without holding back. No second-guessing it."

"I will. I promise."

"Trust me, Roman. You need to go all in on this."

"I will. Because I do trust you. Completely. With all my heart and soul."

As I say the words, I realize they're true, without caveat or exception. Yes, I love Iris. But in a flash, I realize that's not enough for a relationship to withstand the ups and downs. You've got to have trust, too. Complete trust. That's what I've learned today. And now that I know it, I'm even more excited than ever to finally make this gorgeous, brilliant, kindhearted woman my wife.

# CHAPTER 39
## Iris

How much noise and vibration can the human eardrum withstand?

I'm not asking hypothetically. Not asking for a friend. I'm wondering this because my eardrums currently feel on the cusp of bursting like two little grenades inside my head.

The wall of sound, the frenetic energy, the palpable electricity in this massive stadium are unlike anything I've experienced before. And that's coming from someone who's attended every single one of Roman's loud, raucous games this season, including the hard-fought playoff games he won before making it to tonight's Big Game. Everyone told me, "Nothing compares to the Super Bowl, Iris. You'll see." Turns out, they were right.

I'm in Roman's box, which cost him a pretty penny, and I'm cheering him on with all the usual suspects and then some. Even my best friends, Harper, Tatiana, and Kaylee, flew in for the game, at Roman's generous invitation. The only usual suspects not present in Roman's box today? Marco, Nicola, and Marco's closest family members, all of whom are sitting in *Marco's* box across the stadium and rooting for *his* team, the Knights. Naturally, since Marco's team is the Thunderbolts' formidable opponent tonight.

It's a crazy thing to root against a beloved family member. But that's football, folks. At least, when you're a lucky member of the Maguire clan. In fact, we're all rooting for Marco's team to get dog-walked tonight.

It makes me feel better rooting against Marco to know he's already experienced the thrill of winning a Super Bowl, while Roman hasn't. Although, admittedly, even if the situation were reversed, I'd be rooting for Roman and his Thunderbolts to deliver an unequivocal beatdown to the Knights tonight anyway. Sorry, Marco.

Here's where things currently stand in this topsy-turvy game: The bad guys are ahead by three and there are eight minutes and six seconds left in the game. A touchdown would put the good guys ahead by four, assuming we successfully kick the point after the touchdown; a field goal would tie things up.

"Third down," Harper mutters next to me after our best running back gets tackled a yard shy of the first down. She's been watching Roman's team on TV in Orchard Blossom this whole season, along with her whole family, so she's become a bit of a diehard Thunderbolts fan. In fact, I think it's fair to say she's been rooting for the Thunderbolts even more than her beloved Seagulls this season.

I feel someone grab my free hand, and when I look, it's my beloved Luca. "Sorry in advance if I barf on you, sis," he chokes out. "I'm freaking out."

I squeeze his hand. "No need to barf. Roman's got this."

"Fuck yeah, he does," Luca shoots back reflexively. But even as he says it, I can hear the quaver of doubt in his voice. Unlike me, Luca's sat through *three* of these damned things. And each time, he's had to watch his big brother's team lose by the skin of their teeth.

I return my attention to the field and hold my breath as Roman lines up behind his center. He licks the fingers on his throwing hand, like he always does at this point, shoves his hands up his center's ass, basically, and shouts a string of gibberish that ultimately signals the center to snap him the ball.

With Roman in motion, everyone on the field follows suit and springs to life. In the blink of an eye, Roman fakes a handoff to his running back before stepping deep into an immaculate pocket. He searches for his favorite target, Tyrell—my favorite player, besides Roman. At the moment, Tyrell is in the process of running his route at full speed. And, of course, given his incredible talent, he's saddled with the usual double coverage. But even so, in this do-or-die moment, Tyrell somehow manages to elude one Knight completely and get himself a half step in front of the other.

A defender breaches the O-line and barrels toward Roman in the pocket, but as the guy rushes toward him, Roman releases the football in a perfect spiral that's headed straight for Tyrell.

*Oh my God, no.*

*No, no, no.*

I grab at my hair with both hands, disbelieving my eyes, as a Knights player leaps through the air from out of nowhere and steals the pass headed for Tyrell. Thankfully, the Knights player is immediately taken down at midfield. No yards gained on the interception. But the damage is done. The Knights now have possession of the football, which means they've got the chance to score again, in the waning minutes of the game, while Roman is forced to stand on the sidelines, watching helplessly.

"Shit!" Luca screams. "*Fuck!*"

"I can't believe it," I murmur, clutching my stomach. "That pass looked perfect."

"Fuck, fuck, fuck!" Luca bellows. "Fuck!"

My gaze shifts to Roman on the field. He's been playing like a football god throughout this entire game. That was his first mistake, if you can even call it one. If you ask me, that pass was right on target—the interception, a total fluke. At any rate, it's the first sign Roman is human, after all.

As my boyfriend marches to the sideline, his body language is tight. Clearly, he's livid with himself. He flops onto a bench and immediately throws his helmet to the ground in front of him with full force. Not a good sign. Roman never does that.

A rather brave—or stupid—player approaches Roman on the bench and attempts to mollify him. But Roman visibly shrugs the guy off with an angry wave of his hand and a turn of his shoulder. Clearly, Roman doesn't want to be coddled right now. He wants to stew in his anger and torture himself for that flukey interception. *Goddammit.*

"It's gonna be okay," Luca says on an exhale. "All we have to do is stop them from scoring on this drive, and we'll get the ball back with plenty of time." He glances at the game clock, and his handsome face tightens.

"It's gonna be okay," I murmur.

"They won't score. It'll be fine."

*God, I hope we're both right.*

There's a commercial break. One of a billion, it feels like, and through the whole two minutes, I watch Roman pacing on the sidelines, sans his helmet, like a hungry, caged lion with rabies.

Mercifully, Luca's prediction turns out to be right. During the Knights' march to the end zone following the commercial break, the Thunderbolts' relatively mediocre defense somehow forces a godsend of a fumble, which means Roman and his offense will now get the ball again, still trailing by only three points.

Commercial break.

Again.

I look at the game clock again while clutching Harper's arm for dear life.

1:04.

That's all the time left for Roman to make his dreams come true, after his long, exhausting, hard-fought first season with the Thunderbolts. For Roman to prove all the haters and doubters wrong. For Roman to work a miracle and *finally* get that elusive "W" after his *fourth* attempt at winning a fucking Super Bowl. To get that win, however, he's going to need to put that interception firmly behind him and focus on what's in front of him. That's easier said than done, I know. I've certainly never been in his shoes. In fact, very few people in the history of the world know exactly what it feels like to be Roman Maguire in this moment.

Roman huddles up with Coach Hardy, presumably going over whatever play they're cooking up next. And when the time comes for Roman to jog onto the field with his offense, he does something he's been doing for several weeks now, ever since our day of horseback riding that turned into an equine therapy session: He looks up at me in his box, raises both palms to either side of his head, and mimes putting on his magic blinders.

Nodding and smiling through tears, I clutch my heart with one hand and blow kisses with the other. *You've got this, baby. Focus on what's in front of you and nothing else.*

I've never admitted this to Roman—because why would I?—but, despite my stated confidence in those magic blinders, I honestly wasn't sure the trick would work for him. Yes, little tricks like that always worked with preschoolers, back when I was lucky enough to have a job teaching them, but I had no idea if something like that would work on a grown man. A professional athlete. A tough nut to crack, as Roman often calls himself. I figured Roman had nothing to lose, though. Plus, I figured, at the very least, he might think of *me* and our day in the meadow together while putting on those magic blinders, which then might relax him and make him smile—which then might relieve his tension and clear his mind. So why not give it a whirl? Little did I know, the trick would become Roman's secret weapon over the next several games.

Thankfully, Roman doesn't need to put on his magic blinders very often because he makes very few mistakes. But whenever he does—nine times out of ten, anyway—he slides those suckers on and becomes a new man. A focused one. A calm one. All I can hope now is this time won't prove to be part of that one-in-ten failure rate.

The teams are lined up again.

The ball is snapped to Roman.

He bounds backward, looking for Tyrell, who's once again saddled with double coverage. Despite the two defenders, however, Roman throws a spiraling dart toward Tyrell, anyway. As it sails through the air on a frozen rope—Edward always uses that phrase for a rocket of a pass, and I absolutely love it—every head in the stadium, including mine, swivels to watch its trajectory . . .

As the ball lands straight into Tyrell's hands, every Thunderbolts fan in the stadium, including me, holds their breath. And as Tyrell goes down with the ball firmly tucked in his arm, we scream and jump around in ecstasy. It's a much-needed first down—one that keeps us in the hunt for that coveted, go-ahead touchdown, baby . . .

I look at the game clock again.

There's, oh God, less than a minute left in the entire game.

"Time out, San Francisco!" a referee booms into his mic, at which point everyone in my immediate vicinity looks at each other like they're on the cusp of a collective barf-o-rama.

My eyes lock with Ava's a few seats down. She's huddled up with Roman's dad and Luca's supposedly evil twin, Levi, who's actually a sweetheart once you get to know him, and all of them look like I feel: like they could pass out at any moment from stress.

When I catch Ava's eye, I shoot her a look that says, "He's got this," which she returns. From there, I turn to look at Maverick at the back of the box. He's not looking my way, though, so I can't catch his eye. He's far too engaged in conversation with his beloved mommy, Vanessa, to look around the box.

Dare I say it, Vanessa's become my friend over the course of this football season. I see her often, since she enjoys bringing Maverick to home games, and Roman's all for it. Plus, we all joined forces to celebrate Maverick's fifth birthday, too. And sometimes, Roman and I stay and chat for a bit when we return Maverick to Vanessa's house after our allotted time with him.

Is Vanessa one of my best friends? No. Not even close. But I have to hand it to the woman, she's made a real effort, and I've reciprocated. The result is, we've formed a friendly, genuine bond that makes co-parenting Maverick a true joy.

Luca bats my shoulder, jolting me from gazing at Maverick and Vanessa behind me. "*Focus*," Luca commands. "Roman needs your good juju the most, Riri."

"Sorry," I mumble. I find Roman on the sideline and consciously send him good thoughts—good juju—as he confers with his coaches during the time-out. Roman's got his helmet on at the moment, so I can't see his face. But, even so, I can perfectly picture the game face he's wearing. Furrowed brow. Laser-sharp eyes. Tight mouth. If I know Roman, he'd rather die than leave this game as the loser, again, for the fourth fucking time.

The time-out ends.

All players on both sides line up again.

"Here we go," Luca says, taking my left hand as Harper simultaneously grabs my right.

Once he's in position and everyone is lined up, Roman looks to his left, as always, and then to his right, making sure everyone is precisely in place and ready on his side of the ball. He licks the fingers on his throwing hand, as usual. But before he shoves his hands up his center's ass crack, like he always does before the snap, Roman first mimes putting on his magic blinders. This time, without looking up at me. This time, without making it a cute thing between us. *Well, that's a first.*

With his imaginary, magic blinders in place—this time, only for himself—Roman slides his hands into position and shouts a string of gibberish signals to his teammates. And two seconds later, Roman's got the ball firmly in his large hands and he's scanning the field for an open target.

Before Roman gets the ball off, however, a Knight breaks through the O-line and barrels toward him at full speed, prompting Roman to scramble to avoid decimation.

I scream at the top of my lungs as Roman takes off running to avoid a tackle and then continues running well after he should have slid to the ground, as most quarterbacks would do in the same situation to avoid getting tackled and possibly injured.

Oh my God. He's not looking to get rid of the ball any longer! He's clearly intending to reach the end zone himself!

The entire stadium stands and screams in unison, some in support of Roman, others in support of the Knights running after him to take him down.

Three defenders close in on Roman. Based on their trajectory, he's not going to make it. He's going to go down a few yards short.

Oh my God. Without warning, Roman hurtles himself into the air and well *over* a leaping, flying, careening defender's body. And a second later, Roman comes down like a ton of bricks in the end zone. *He did it. He scored the go-ahead touchdown, all by himself.*

The nearest referee shoots both arms into the sky, signaling a touchdown, and Roman bounces up from the ground and starts celebrating like a madman with a cluster of elated teammates. Their celebration is short-lived, however, because the point after needs to be kicked. Which it is. Successfully. But with six seconds left on the game clock. Unfortunately, that's enough time for the Knights to throw a Hail Mary pass, take the lead again, and squeak out a win.

Shit. Why'd I let myself think that? *Jinx, be gone. Jinx, be gone.*

"Fucking commercial breaks," Luca mutters. He wipes his brow. "I really think I might barf this time."

"Then go stand next to Levi," I say, swatting him. "I don't want your barf on me when I go down there to congratulate Roman on his first Super Bowl *win*."

Luca claps his hands together. "Okay. I needed that, sis. I'm back. He's got this."

"Atta boy. No bad juju."

"No bad juju. I'm back."

Ava leans forward in her seat to shout at Luca and me. "We all need to send whammies to that motherfucker as a family." She's talking about the Knights' stupendous quarterback. And I'm not surprised at all by her word choice, by the way. Whenever we're at a football game, Ava Maguire turns into a swearing, violent sailor. The transformation was shocking to me at first, though highly amusing, but I'm used to it by now. In fact, elegant Ava's propensity for foul language at games is one of the many things I adore about her.

"You especially, Iris," Ava adds, wagging a finger at me. "Make those whammies extra good ones."

"Yes, ma'am." I raise my arm toward Vanessa and Maverick in the back, signaling to them. And when I finally catch their attention, they join everyone else in Roman's box in our common mission of wiggling our fingers and sending whammies to the Knights' quarterback.

My eyes drift to Roman again. He's pacing on the sideline like an angry bear at the zoo—one being teased with a steak.

# CHASING THE RING

My man did everything in his power to secure victory tonight, but now, his fate is totally out of his hands.

While I'm watching him, Roman unexpectedly looks up toward the box. His helmet is off now, so I can see his face. He's drenched in sweat and scowling, looking equal parts exhausted and pissed off. But even in this state, the second our eyes meet, he blows me a kiss and motions like his heart is beating out of his chest. I blow him a kiss and shoot him a thumbs-up, letting him know he's got this, that I've got unwavering faith in him and the Thunderbolts' destiny, and he nods his appreciation before looking away with his chest heaving and sweat trickling down his forehead.

The commercial break ends, and the ball is kicked off uneventfully. Everyone lines up, this time with the Knights on offense and Roman watching helplessly from the sideline.

The Knights' center snaps the ball to his talented quarterback, who drops back and scans the field for a miracle. Surely, he's looking for Marco, his favorite target. But it's not meant to be. The quarterback gets pummeled to the ground before releasing the ball, sending the ball skating across the turf before a Thunderbolt pounces on it and hangs on for dear life.

A referee confirms the Thunderbolts have recovered the fumble . . . and the clock runs out . . . which means the good guys, with Roman Maguire as their fearless leader, have now officially won the game!

The next few minutes are a blur of happy tears, screams, and hugs. If I weren't hanging on to Luca's arm through most of it, I'd surely pass out onto the sticky, beer-covered floor.

"Come on, Iris," Roman's father, Edward, says, grabbing my hand. "Time to go to Roman on the field."

I check to make sure Vanessa's got Maverick. When we talked earlier about a possible victory tonight, Roman said he didn't want Maverick coming onto the field in front of all the cameras and people, and we all agreed that was for the best.

My eyes meet with Vanessa's and she quickly signals she's got Maverick firmly in hand, so I take Edward's offered arm and let him pull me, along with the rest of the family and Cameron, toward a cadre of waiting security guards.

*Insanity.*

Breathtaking chaos.

That's what greets us when we make it onto the field.

There's confetti all over the ground and floating in the air. Loud, celebratory music blaring. Swarms of camera operators and reporters jockeying for position. *People, people, people, everywhere.*

Not surprisingly, a throng of reporters, cameras, and booms presently surround Roman and Coach Hardy as they exchange tearful words about twenty yards from where my group has come to a stop. Surely, those reporters are beaming out every emotional word between the pair to the world in real time.

When the short exchange between Roman and his beloved coach ends, Roman moves on to hugging Marco, who's been waiting nearby for his moment. Marco looks defeated and exhausted in this moment, but even so, he manages a wide, tearful smile for his cousin before enthusiastically embracing him. If Marco was going to lose to anyone, I'm sure he's glad it was his beloved Romie.

A tearful Nicola offers a quick peck to Roman's cheek, but soon, Roman locks eyes with our group and heads toward us as that pack of reporters moves in lockstep with him.

Before Roman reaches us, he turns to the nearest camera and shoves three upside-down fingers into its lens. Apparently, Roman wants his son to know his daddy is thinking about him, even now, in this one-of-a-kind moment.

Finally, Roman makes it through the throngs of people to

reach our group, at which point he energetically hugs both of his parents, followed by Levi and Cameron. When he gets to Luca, I can't help noticing Luca covertly handing Roman something. Something that fit neatly inside Roman's palm. What was that? Did I imagine that? I can't fathom what it could have been.

My thoughts are interrupted when Roman takes me into his arms. Suddenly, I forget all about whatever that possible handoff might have been. "You did it!" I shout into Roman's ear so he can hear me above the pandemonium. "I'm so proud of you, baby!"

"I couldn't have done it without you," Roman replies, squeezing me tight. "I love you so much." He kisses me deeply, and as he does, the world melts away. When Roman finally releases me, I'm expecting him to kiss my cheek and jog off to his next destination. But to my shock, he takes both my hands, kneels before me, and holds up a ring box displaying a massive, dazzling whopper of a diamond ring nestled in black velvet.

"Oh my God!" I blurt, as the cameras surrounding us squeeze in to capture the moment.

"Iris Eugenie Benedetto," Roman says with tears in his eyes and a tremble in his deep voice. "You're my lucky charm. My best friend. I love you, and I want to spend the rest of my life with you, as my wife. Iris, will you marry me?"

I barely get out my shrieking yes, thanks to the sob involuntarily hurtling out of my throat. But thankfully, Roman understands me well enough. With a whoop, he slides the massive rock onto my finger, rises, and takes me into his arms, crushing my sobbing frame against his chest.

When I open my eyes, there's a camera that's squeezed in so shockingly close, I feel like I'm going to pass out from claustrophobia. "Roman," I gasp out, clinging to his jersey for dear life. "Tell that guy to back up."

I don't need to ask him twice.

In a flash, Roman grabs that intrusive camera's massive lens with both of his large hands and guides it back. But he doesn't push the offending camera as far back as I'm expecting. Instead, once it's out of my personal space, he thrusts his sweaty face into its lens and bellows, "Do you see that gorgeous woman—that perfect ten over there? She's my fiancée now. *My future wife.* So, anyone who's got anything negative to say about her better come say it directly to my face—*or better yet, don't say anything at all.*"

*Swoon.*

His nostrils flaring, Roman holds up my ringed hand to the camera. "My future wife," he repeats. When he lowers my hand, he kisses me again, this time so passionately, my body goes slack in his arms, like I've been electrocuted. *Holy shit.*

Surely, Roman's proposal and that sexy little speech into the camera will spread like wildfire on the internet, far more so than my stupid runaway bride video that already feels like ancient history. At least, I genuinely hope that's the case, because hot damn: *Roman proposing to me and telling the world to shut the fuck up about his future wife is one viral video I'll be absolutely thrilled to star in.*

# CHAPTER 40
## Iris

*A Year and a Few Months Later*

AFTER PUTTING MAVERICK to bed, Roman slides onto the couch next to me, where I'm reviewing this month's payroll for my new equine therapy center.

As he gets settled, I close my laptop and grin at him. "Did he fall asleep in the middle of his first book?" We have a running bet about how quickly Maverick will fall asleep—namely, whether he'll make it through his first requested book or not. It's an especially fun game on days like today, when Maverick played especially hard.

Roman flashes me an achingly handsome smile. "He passed out on page three. You win." He motions to my closed laptop. "Finish up, if you need to."

"I'm good. It's not due till tomorrow." I slide the laptop onto the coffee table and snuggle up to him. "How was the shoot today?"

"Fun, boring, long." He waggles his eyebrows. "Lucrative."

We both laugh. After back-to-back Super Bowl wins, money seems to grow on trees for Roman Maguire these days. Sponsorships, licensing deals, brand deals, investment opportunities. He's got his pick of all of them—and they're all worth millions on top of endless millions. Hence, the top-of-the-line equine therapy facility Roman was able to build for me without breaking a sweat.

With a kiss to my temple, Roman asks, "Did you have fun shopping for wedding dresses today?"

I can't help smiling from ear to ear. "I sure did. I found the perfect dress—only the third one I tried on."

"Congrats. I can't wait to see it on my fiancée . . . and take it off my *wife*."

Today's shopping excursion was a dream come true. Totally different than the one for my stupid wedding to stupid

Brandon. Of course, knowing my groom is Roman made all the difference. That's the main thing. But it was also a pure joy to have Ava, Nicola, and Luca's beloved, Chelsea, my honorary mother and two sisters, joining me for the festivities this time, along with my besties, Harper, Kaylee, and Tatiana. Plus, having an unlimited budget was awfully fun. Not gonna lie.

The main reason today felt so different and so much better than the first time, however, aside from Roman being my groom, is the way *I* felt. When picking out a dress last time, I now realize I selected a dress to please *Brandon*. Something conservative that didn't show much skin. It was pretty, granted, but not what I truly wanted, in retrospect. Although, come to think of it, I never even stopped to wonder what I truly wanted, so I didn't understand the difference.

This time, by contrast, I picked out a dress for *myself*. A modern gown with sleek, sultry lines that made me feel beautiful and sexy and like the best version of myself. Of course, I want Roman to think I'm gorgeous when he sees me in my wedding dress. But this time around, I know my future husband will think I'm beautiful and sexy, no matter what I'm wearing, as long as it's me who's wearing the dress.

"So, hey," I say, leaning my cheek against Roman's broad shoulder. "There's a wedding detail I'd like to run past you."

"Whatever you want, the answer is yes." He's been saying that all along. Not because he's not excited about our wedding, but because he genuinely doesn't care about the details, only the end result.

"I think you might want to have a say about this one."

Roman shrugs. "I've already weighed in on the things I care about. Truly, the rest is up to you."

I twist my mouth. "I want Luca to officiate."

Roman's chuckle rumbles against my cheek. "My brother's a veritable cult leader at this point."

"Can it really be called a cult when there are only three members, though?" I shoot back, referring to myself, Nicola, and Luca's beloved, Chelsea. I snicker. "Come on. You have to admit Luca did a fantastic job for Marco and Nicola."

"How do you know that?"

"Nicola showed me some videos today. Luca killed it."

Roman snorts. "So, you're saying I've got *Nicola* to blame for this?"

"No, you've got Nicola to *thank*. She told me Luca was one of her favorite parts of the whole wedding. She said he made everything feel fun and relaxed, and that's exactly what I want." *Unlike last time.* That's the subtext here. The thing I'm not saying out loud.

Roman knows one of the most traumatizing parts of my prior wedding was the way the pastor—a man of God who's known me my whole life—bellowed at the top of his lungs to my father to "Get her out of here!" Since then, Harper told me he's been shockingly unkind about me. Apparently, he's called my behavior "deplorable" and "disgraceful" to anyone who'll listen in Orchard Blossom.

Roman kisses the top of my hand and meets my anxious gaze. "Let's do it. Luca did a great job for Marco and Nicola."

"Really?"

Roman nods and smiles. "But only if you promise not to

tell Luca I complimented the job he did for Marco and Nicola, or I'll never hear the end of it from him."

"My lips are sealed." With a laugh, I straddle Roman on the couch and kiss him. "Thank you, my love. You're so good to me."

Roman slides a palm to my cheek and kisses me passionately. And a few seconds later, after a bulge has noticeably hardened beneath his jeans, Roman rises from the couch, taking me with him in his arms, and takes me straight to our bedroom.

# CHAPTER 41
## Roman

It's my wedding day.

*Finally.*

Late afternoon on a beach in Santa Barbara.

Thankfully, the wedding gods have graced us with a perfect, temperate day.

Luca, aka our cult leader for the day, is standing next to me with his iPad in hand. My groomsmen, all dressed in tan suits, like me, are lined up alongside me: Marco, Cameron, Levi, and Iris's brother, Atlas. Mirroring my groomsmen in a line, Iris's bridesmaids, all dressed in soft, flowing blue, are Harper, Kaylee, Tatiana, Chelsea, and Nicola. And, of course, Maverick, my co-best man and ring bearer for the occasion, stands at my feet in a tan suit that matches mine, visibly aching to be of service.

When I told Maverick he'd be my co-best man at today's ceremony, along with Marco, I thought he'd be pumped to finally get a promotion from lowly ring bearer. Man, was I wrong about that. On the contrary, poor Mav broke down and sobbed at the shocking news. Apparently, my boy's watched himself performing his ring bearer's duties in videos so many times, both for his mom's and Marco's weddings, he was excited to "three-peat" at his daddy's upcoming nuptials, too.

Like father, like son. I'm looking forward to three-peating as a Super Bowl champ this upcoming season myself.

The music stops and then changes, and every guest rises to their feet in anticipation.

I look toward the end of the aisle, holding my breath, and there she is. My beautiful, blooming flower: Iris. Smiling and trembling on her father's arm.

She's as beautiful as I've ever seen her. Glowing. Ethereal. Also—am I allowed to think this?—she's hot as fuck, too. A smoke show. Her dress is elegant and classy, yes—but also downright sexy. Jesus. She's a knockout.

Our gazes meet, and Iris touches the pearl choker wrapped around her delicate neck—her mother's necklace. A lump rises in my throat. *Aw, baby.* I know how much that necklace means to her. It means a lot to me, too, especially because she saved it just for me.

When Iris reaches me, I kiss her cheek and thank her father.

"You look beautiful, baby," I whisper, taking her hand in mine. "*Wow.*"

"You look pretty *wow* yourself."

Iris's father takes his seat, and everyone in attendance sits along with him.

"We're gathered here today to celebrate two of my all-time favorite people," Luca begins. "My big brother Roman and his lucky charm, Iris. My sister from another mister. My honorary triplet. Sorry, Levi."

Everyone in on the joke laughs. We all know Levi adores Iris, too, but he always pretends to be annoyed that Luca opened up their "sacred twinship" to include an honorary third.

After scanning the crowd ceremoniously, Luca takes a deep, solemn breath and delivers his next word in a flat, somber tone. "*Mawwaige.*"

Everyone, including Iris and me, cracks up at the movie reference, the same way everyone did at Marco and Nicola's wedding. Luca's not merely recycling an old, successful comedic bit, though: Iris has always loved *The Princess Bride* as much as Nicola. And now, thanks to Iris, Maverick and I love it, too.

After Luca gives his introduction, Iris's maid of honor, Harper, steps forward to read a poem. As she speaks, I glance at my parents in the front row and exchange wide smiles with them. After that, I do the same thing with Coach Hardy and my ace receiver, Tyrell, and several of my other teammates in the second row. And finally, I look down at my beloved son and grin at his soft, dark curls and the look of deep concentration on his adorable face. Maverick's guarding that damned pillow with his life. Apparently, six-year-olds are every bit as easy to dupe as four-year-olds when it comes to attaching fake, plastic rings to pillows at weddings.

As Harper reaches the last lines of her poem, I return my gaze to my bride to find she's got moisture in her eyes. Squeezing her hands, I whisper, "I love you."

"I love you, too," she whispers back. "So much."

"And now for the exchange of vows," Luca says. When he prompts Iris to speak, she pulls out a folded piece of paper from her bra with a shaking hand, making everyone chuckle.

"Roman," Iris begins in a trembling voice. "You've taught me about true love. You're my best friend. My biggest fan. My coach and my teammate. I promise to always be all those things for you, too." Her eyes fill with proper tears, the same as mine. "Whatever passes life throws at us, I can't wait to catch them as your wife. Whatever problems might come up, we'll tackle them together. You're my endgame, Roman Maguire. Forever and always. You and Maverick and whatever babies we're lucky enough to have. I love you and Maverick—" She smiles at Mav. "And I can't wait to be your loving and faithful wife, for better or worse, in sickness and in health, till death do us part."

"Damn," Luca says. "Good luck, bro, but you can't do any better than that."

"She's a tough act to follow," I agree with a laugh. I take a deep breath and turn my attention to Iris. I'm not wearing my magic blinders right now, but I might as well be. In this moment, Iris Benedetto, the love of my life, is all I see. "Iris, for a long time, I thought I'd met you 'in paradise.' But now I know. It wasn't the place that was the paradise. It was being with you. Wherever I am, as long as I'm with you, I'll always be in paradise."

My mother lets out a little whimper in the front row, as Iris simultaneously does the same thing before me, and everyone reacts to my mother's adorableness.

I swallow hard and continue, "When Marco married Nicola, he said his Super Bowl ring could never mean as much to him as his wedding ring. And, frankly, at the time, I thought he'd lost his damned mind."

Everyone laughs, including Iris.

"But now that I've got *two* Super Bowl rings of my own—"

One of my teammates, my wide receiver, Tyrell, shouts out, "Yeah, babyyyyyy!" and everyone in attendance who isn't a Knights fan cheers and hoots loudly for a long moment.

When the disruption wanes, I return to Iris. "Sorry about that, baby. Didn't mean to get them riled up."

"It doesn't take much," Iris teases, making everyone laugh again.

"The point I was trying to make, before I got so *rudely* interrupted—" I glare with mock irritation at Tyrell, before returning to Iris with a grin. "—is that I now understand what Marco meant. Iris, loving you is better than winning any Super Bowl. Or *two*, as the case may be . . ."

Every Thunderbolt lover in attendance whoops and applauds raucously yet again, this time making Iris and me guffaw.

"*Guys*," I say with mock irritation. "This isn't a pep rally.

I'm trying to get married here." I roll my eyes playfully, making Iris giggle. "Now, where was I?"

"*I'm* paradise. Not the place."

"Right. Thank you. Actually, wait. Before I get to the rest of my vows, I feel like I should make it perfectly clear to the football gods who might be listening, nothing I might say here today should be interpreted as a lack of desire on my part to three-peat this year and get myself and my teammates *another* Super Bowl ring. Let me be perfectly clear about that. All I'm saying is, no matter how many Super Bowl rings I wind up with—whether that turns out to be two, three, four, or five—none of them will ever mean as much as the wedding ring I'm about to start wearing for the rest of my life to mark me as Iris's husband."

"Thank you for the clarification," Iris deadpans.

"It's actually a very romantic thing to say. My point is that—"

"No, I totally get it, honey. It's lovely. Thank you."

I laugh at her deadpan delivery. But a moment later, out of nowhere, seriousness settles into my chest. Moisture pricks my eyes. I clear my throat. "All kidding aside, though . . ." I take a deep breath to wrangle my emotion and take her hands again. "Iris, I love you more than I knew was possible. I trust you. I respect you. Admire and adore you. I vow to be your loving and faithful husband, forever, in sickness and in health, in good times and bad, till death takes me away from you, far too early. If I had infinite lifetimes, I'd want to spend every single one of them as your husband."

Iris wipes a tear. "That's so beautiful, Roman. I love you, too. Infinitely."

I peck Iris's lips—even though it's not technically the time to do that yet—as Luca says, "Not too shabby, Romie. In fact, that was so good, I'm not even mad I just lost a hundred bucks to Marco."

"Not enough football references for you?" I ask.

"Why didn't you make any? With all Iris's football references, I figured I was golden."

"Iris's football references don't count," Marco says. "Remember? We already agreed to that."

"I don't know if we *agreed* to that," Levi says. "I feel like we raised the idea but never really made a firm rule about it."

"Hey, guys?" I ask politely. "Can you maybe hash out the results of the bet after the ceremony is over? I'd very much like to finish getting married now."

Raucous laughter abounds.

"You've got it," Luca says. "I'll keep things moving, brother."

"Thank you."

With a chuckle, Luca beckons to Maverick. "You're up, buddy. Bring me those rings so we can officially tie this knot."

Maverick offers up his closely guarded pillow to his uncle, who quickly unties the fake rings attached to it and swaps in the real ones from his pocket. A moment after that, the rings are on our fingers and the ceremony is done and dusted.

"Time to kiss your bride, Romie!" Luca booms.

"With pleasure." As my brother pronounces us husband and wife, I lean in and gleefully lock lips with Iris. *My wife.*

"By the power vested in me by the State of California and the certificate I bought online," Luca bellows, "let me introduce to you: Mr. and Mrs. Roman and Iris Maguire!"

With a whoop and a fist pump, I grab my wife in one hand and my son in the other and bound energetically down the sandy aisle, through exuberant faces, cheers, and applause, on my way to the happy life I never even dreamed could be possible for me—a life that's sure to become our very own happily ever after.

# EPILOGUE
## Roman

*Four Years Later*

"You can't stomp around like that, Maddox," I say. "Or the fish will swim away."

"Don't you want to eat trout for dinner?" Iris adds. "You love trout."

"But I'm wearing my boots," Maddox offers, referring to the rubber boots he insisted on wearing for today's family fishing expedition, specifically because he wanted to stomp along the shallow edges of the slow-moving creek on our property.

Our little family is back in Orchard Blossom for the third time since we bought the Claxton place a year ago, and once again, we're fishing our stream for rainbow trout. Iris and Maverick are taking their fishing seriously, as usual, from a spot that's slightly upstream from Maddox, Ivy, and me. That's a good thing, given that we're hoping to feast on a dinner of freshly caught rainbow trout tonight. The Mighty Maddox started out fishing like the rest of us earlier, but after only about fifteen minutes, he got bored with the whole idea, so I'm manning his fishing rod now, along with mine, while also carrying our newborn baby girl who's strapped to my chest.

Ivy always sleeps the longest when she's being held, whether that's in our arms or in this hands-free carrier. So, she basically lives in it when we go out. That suits me fine, of course. I love having her close. If it were feasible, I'd never take Ivy off my chest, other than to ravage my wife, sleep, shower, and play with my boys. That's what the offseason has always been about for me. Spending time with my family and relaxing. Now that I've retired, I'm not sure what my life will look like, exactly, in terms of how I'll spend my time. All I know is it will include plenty of intentional, concentrated family time, just like this, no matter what business ventures might come my way.

"*Maddox*," ten-year-old Maverick pleads with his little brother when he splashes in the shallow water again. "*Chill.* I'm trying to catch a fish."

I burst out laughing, and Iris does too. That's been our family's mantra for at least a year now. *Chill, Maddox. Please.* Good lord, our three-year-old has infinite energy and zero fear. Was Maverick *this* insane when he was his little brother's age? I didn't live with Maverick full-time back then, so maybe I missed out on this same level of daredevil enthusiasm with him, but I don't think so. Now that Maverick is ten, I can confidently proclaim he's truly my mini-me in every way. Not only physically, but in terms of his demeanor and personality, too. Just like me, my older son is meticulous. Driven. Careful. Ruthlessly competitive. But Maddox? With his carefree personality and insatiable lust for adventure, he's more Luca Maguire than Roman. God help me.

When I said something along those lines to my mother this past Christmas—while all of us were wearing our matching pajamas, of course, thanks to Luca—Mom quirked an eyebrow and retorted, "Watch, Maddox will secretly become your favorite, later on."

"*Excuse me?*" I replied, given the implication of Mom's comment.

"Kidding," Mom said with a patronizing pat on my arm. But then, she waggled her eyebrows and added, "Or was I?"

"*Maddox*," Maverick snaps to my left, jerking my mind back to the present. "Chill. *Please*."

I look at Iris and we both chuckle again. It's hilarious hearing Maverick using the same tone and inflection we always do with Maddox.

"Oh! I've got a bite!" Maverick blurts, drawing our attention to his line in the water.

"Remember to set the hook before yanking back," Iris instructs calmly. "Patience, my love."

"I know, Momma."

It was never Iris's idea for Maverick to stop calling her "Iris"—or "Irish," when he was little—and to start calling her "Momma." From the start, Iris has always been extremely respectful of Vanessa. But after Maddox came along and *he* started calling Iris "Mommy" and "Momma," Maverick suddenly adopted "Momma" for Iris, without prompting, and "Mom" for Vanessa. And that's the way it's been ever since.

"Not so fast," I call out when Maverick starts reeling in the fish way too quickly.

"Dad, please. I've got this. This ain't my first rodeo."

I smile to myself. I used to say that all the time in interviews, whenever some clueless reporter asked if "the pressure and all the expectations" were getting to me.

After a little maneuvering, Maverick pulls in a medium-sized, wriggling rainbow trout and holds it up, grinning, like it's a massive marlin, and we all cheer and applaud like he's harpooned Moby Dick.

"Looks like *I'll* be feasting tonight," Maverick teases. "What will the rest of you eat?"

"*Mav*, you have to share," Maddox says, his little fists on his hips and his dark eyebrows scrunched.

"*Maddox*," Maverick shoots back, copying his little brother's inflection. "I was *joking*."

"Oh."

Laughing at their exchange, Iris snaps some photos of Maverick with his fish before helping him free the wiggling thing from its hook. While she does that, I keep an eagle eye on our holy terror, Maddox, to make sure he doesn't do something stupid. Or, at least, to keep the kid alive while he inevitably does that something stupid. The stream is shallow and slow moving where he's playing, but Maddox Maguire is exceptionally talented at finding new ways to defy physics and give us a heart attack, so we've learned to keep eagle eyes on him at all times, whenever he's not in a safely contained, Maddox-proofed environment.

In short order, the fish is nestled in our waiting cooler and Maverick's line is back into the water with new bait attached, thanks to Iris. After making sure Maddox is clomping around in a spot that's directly in Iris's line of sight, I peek underneath the floppy, flower-patterned hat covering my newborn baby girl's tiny, blonde head, and to my surprise, I'm met with two big, blue eyes staring calmly up at me.

When our eyes meet, Ivy coos and kicks happily against my abs, and my heart explodes with boundless love. "Hello there, girlie," I coo. "Did you have a nice nap?"

Ivy gurgles happily.

Iris calls out, "Was that a 'feed me' sound?"

"I don't think so. She's just looking up at me happily."

Iris snickers. "I don't blame her. I've done that myself, a time or two."

I shoot Iris a goofy grin, and she beams one back in reply.

"Let's let her hang out till she asks to be fed," I suggest. "So far, she just seems happy to be here."

Iris agrees and returns to Maddox, just in time to see him jumping from one big rock to another like a flying squirrel.

"Careful, love!" Iris calls out to him, a note of anxiety in her voice. "Those rocks are really slippery." She shoots me a look that says, "Holy hell," and I return her nonverbal message with a similar one of my own. It's useless to tell that kid to be careful. From what I can surmise, Maddox Maguire doesn't have a careful bone in his little body.

"Watch the holy terror for a second, babe," Iris calls out to me. "I think I've lost my bait."

"Got him."

I don't know how I got this lucky. I've got a wife I'm addicted to—one who loves me for me, and not for my money, fame, and accolades. I've got three children I'm obsessed with and time to spend with them. And on top of all that, I've got *three* Super Bowl rings to my name. Truly what more could a man want in this lifetime? I've got some new dreams. I'm a guy who's always dreaming. But I'm not so ambitious that I can't appreciate what I've got. How my life has turned out. And it's all thanks to Iris. Without her, I'm positive none of my final accomplishments on the field, or the insane happiness I've found off it, would have been possible.

My phone in my pocket buzzes with an incoming text. Normally, I ignore my phone when I'm on vacation with my family, but this time, I feel inclined to take a quick peek in case it's Cameron calling with an update on the negotiations with the network.

After retiring two months ago, I looked at all my options and offers and decided I'd like to join the most popular gameday broadcast every week during the season. The thing is, though, I'm only willing to sign on for a couple years to begin with, in case I find out the reality of being on TV as my actual job isn't as fun as it sounds. Also, no matter what, I'll only sign on to do it if they agree to pay me what I'm worth. Why bother otherwise?

Admittedly, I don't know what I'm worth, exactly, in this

context, but I figure I'll know it when I see it. There's no doubt I'll massively improve the show's ratings. That's the Roman Maguire effect, baby. Which means I'll improve the ratings of the show that follows. Whatever else happens, I want to get paid more than any other talking head has ever been paid on the show. I feel like that's fair, and Cameron thinks so, too.

When I peek at my phone, the text that's landed on my screen is, indeed, from Cameron. But he's not sending an update on the negotiations; he's sending me a link to some random article from *The Denver Post*.

**Cameron:** *Remember that guy in Denver I got to follow Iris around for you after Hawaii? He just sent me this, along with some details that aren't public knowledge.*

The link that follows the text is an article from two days ago. The headline reads, "Brandon Gladstone of Viral Fame Arrested for DWI After Crashing into Parked Police Car." I click on the link and scan the article, but it's not all that interesting. The only details it adds to the headline are the location of the accident and the fact that Brandon and his passenger, an unnamed woman, both suffered "non-life-threatening injuries" in the accident. The last line of the article reads, "Mr. Gladstone is presently in stable condition in an undisclosed hospital, awaiting transfer to jail after medical clearance."

Just as I'm finishing the brief article, Cameron sends another text.

**Cameron:** *One of the EMTs who arrived on the scene is buddies with our guy in Denver. Apparently, Brandon was getting a blow job from his passenger when he crashed, and upon impact, she chomped down and basically bit off the tip of his dick.*

"Oh my God," I blurt.

"What?" Iris asks, her eyebrows raised with concern.

*Shit.* "Nothing. I'm reading a text from Cam about a jerk who unexpectedly retired early." *From having a working dick attached to his body.*

I check on Maddox, and then Ivy, and when I'm sure they're both fine and Iris has eyes on our beloved daredevil, I tap out a reply to Cameron.

**Me:** *At least his dick died doing what it loved most.*
**Cameron:** *Bwahahaaa!*
**Me:** *Thanks for telling me about this. Today was already a great day, and this made it even better.*
**Cameron:** *Are you going to tell Iris?*

I glance up at my wife. She's gazing lovingly at Maddox at the moment, as he clomps around like a madman in his rubber boots. While I'm still looking at her, Iris's blue eyes find mine, and she smiles radiantly.

"Thank you for buying this place for us," she says. "I love it here so much."

"I love it, too. It's my second favorite place in the world." I don't need to name my first. Iris knows full well it's our home in Malibu. The oasis we've created with the little family we love so damned much.

"I've got so many fond memories of this place from my childhood," Iris says wistfully. "Also, from the week we spent together after you came here to *beg* me to give you a shot."

"No lies detected."

We both laugh.

"I didn't know how I was going to convince you," I add. "All I knew was I wasn't leaving OB without you."

"Don't start lying to me now, Roman Maguire. You knew from the start I'd melt into a puddle at first sight of you."

"I hoped, but I didn't know." I wink.

"A fish!" Maddox screams. "Look, Mommy!"

Iris jerks her attention to Maddox. "Where, bubba?"

"Right *dere*!" Maddox shouts, pointing frantically at the water. "Oh. He gone now."

"Gee, I wonder why," Maverick deadpans.

"He probably had to go to *school*," I say, making Iris chuckle and Maverick roll his eyes.

"Buh-dum-cha," Iris mutters.

"Momma, please," Maverick says. "Don't encourage him." To me, he adds, "Your dad jokes aren't funny, Dad."

"That's literally the whole point of dad jokes—to be so *unfunny*, you're funny." I laugh at his annoyed reaction. "Would it kill you to occasionally laugh at my jokes to make me feel good about myself?"

"I'd never do that," Maverick replies firmly. "I'll only laugh when you're genuinely funny, so you know you've truly earned it."

My heart swells with pride. *That's my boy.*

When everyone quiets down again, my thoughts drift back to Brandon and his maimed dick. Someone might tell Iris about his arrest. She's still in touch with her would-be sister-in-law, Delilah, I think. Now and again. Or God help me, some vulture of a reporter might reach out to Iris for a comment on the story. But what are the odds?

In the end, I decide not to tell Iris the news about Brandon. She's happy. Blissful, even. So, why let that motherfucker anywhere near her, even if it's only in her thoughts?

"Fish on!" Iris calls out. "Maddox, do you want to help me reel him in?"

"Woohoo!" Maddox screams, his loud rubber boots announcing every splashing step he takes toward his mother.

"Thanks, Mad," Maverick says to Maddox with a scoff. "Now every fish in the stream knows we're here."

"Not to mention, every nearby deer, fox, squirrel, and elk,"

I add with a laugh. The black bears in the surrounding woods likely know it, too, but Maverick is deathly afraid of bears, so I don't include them in my list, out of respect for his phobia.

As little Maddox exuberantly reels in the fish with Iris's deft guidance, I take videos and photos and cheer him on. But once the fish has been stowed in the cooler and everyone is distracted again, I pull out my phone and covertly send another text to Cameron.

*Me: I'll let fate decide if Iris ever finds out about this delightful news story. Until then, I'll savor the information like I'm swirling a fine red wine against my tongue. FUCKING DELICIOUS.*
*Cameron: LOL, I knew you'd be savage about this, but not THIS savage.*
*Me: Karma's a bitch, baby.*
*Cameron: Very true.*
*Me: More importantly, are there any updates on negotiations?*
*Cameron: Nothing concrete, but they're so thirsty for you, I'm positive you'll get whatever you want in the end. I'll stonewall them for a week or so, and I promise they'll cave.*
*Me: I trust you. While you're stonewalling, do you want to come hang out with us in OB? My family's coming in on Sunday for 4-5 days and Iris's brother and father will be here, too. Would love to have our star running back here so we can play a proper sequel to Fiji Bowl.*

To celebrate my third Super Bowl win, I flew everyone I care about to Fiji again for a week of fun in the sun. And of course, we wound up playing tag football on our private beach. As always, it was a family-friendly game that included everyone—men, women, and children. Pro players and former pros, as well as well-intentioned loved ones with damnnear the worst hand-eye coordination you'll ever see.

To make things fair for everyone, we decreed only women could play quarterback for either team. Also, every kid ten or younger was going to score a touchdown at some point in the game, no matter what. And finally, nobody wanted Marco and me to play on the same team, since they said that wouldn't be fair, so we wound up being our respective teams' captains again.

*Cameron:* *I'd love to come to OB. But I'll only play on your team if you promise you'll draft Iris as our star quarterback again. Your wife's got a cannon, dude.*
*Me:* *Iris is still taking it easy after Ivy's birth, but if she's feeling up to it, she'll be my first draft pick, as always. If not, then my mom can play QB for us. She's got a surprising arm and dead-on accuracy.*
*Cameron:* *I'd suggest we draft Nicola the Nuke, but Marco will obviously pick her first, and Chelsea would rather sit out than play for your team.*
*Me:* *We'll be good, either way. I promise I'll stack our roster so we take home the coconut again.*

That was our Lombardi Trophy in the Fiji Bowl. A coconut etched with an oblong shape that was meant to be a football. Not sure what we'll use in Orchard Blossom. An apple?

"Is everything okay?" Iris asks, causing me to jerk my head up from my phone.

*Whoops.* That's a surefire sign I've been on my phone for too long. It's so unlike me during family time.

"Sorry. Yeah." I sheepishly stuff my phone back into my jeans. "Cam was just giving me an update on negotiations."

"Good news?"

"It's not in the bag yet but looking good." I clear my throat. "Hey, Mad, will you come over here and hold this rod for me? I want to give Mommy a big hug."

Maddox splashes over to me through the shallows of the stream like he's on methamphetamines which, of course, causes his big brother to palm his forehead and mutter, "What the heck?"

A moment later, when I'm sure my wild child has the rod firmly in his little hand and the handle of mine is firmly wedged between two rocks, I head over to my wife and gently crush our cooing baby girl between our warm bodies. "I love you, Mrs. Maguire," I whisper. "More than I could have imagined possible."

"What brought this on?"

"Nothing. I'm feeling happy and in love, and I wanted to tell you so."

Iris's features soften. "I love you, too. Thank you for turning our life into a real-life fairy tale."

"I didn't do that. You did. I love you, Iris. So much." I kiss her cheek. "And I promise I always will."

# ACKNOWLEDGMENTS

THANK YOU TO my agent, Jill Marr. This book would not be in existence without your belief in me and your endless support and guidance all these years. Thank you, Alexandra Sunshine, my editor. Every note was pure gold, my dear. I cannot thank you enough.

Thank you to my husband, Brad, for the BIG IDEA that made the third act in this book shine. Thank you to my beautiful, brilliant, supportive daughters, Sophie and Chloe. Sophie, for title of this book and more. Chloe, for the BIG IDEA that made the first act of this book shine. Thank you to my mother for always believing in me and my writing since day one. Thank you to my best friends, Marnie, Lucy, and Lesley aka The Badass Bitches for your laughter, love, and support, and for being with me on one of our many girls trips when I found out this book would soar. You're the inspirations for Kaylee, Tatiana, and Harper.

Thank you to my book family: Sophie Broughton, Melissa Saneholtz, Sarah Kirk, and Lizette Baez. I couldn't have written this book or any others without all of you, ladies. Thank you specifically to all the readers who found me early on in my writing career and then screamed about me from every proverbial mountaintop, allowing me to continue doing this amazing job for an actual living. What a gift!

Thank you to Kensington for loving this book and for believing in my writing. I'm so grateful. Thank you to my father for having season tickets to Chargers games when I was growing up, so I could grow up as a football girlie. (The opposite of thank you to the Chargers management for deciding to take the team away from San Diego, however. I will never forgive you.) Special thanks to my husband, Brad, again, for being football-obsessed. I wouldn't have written this book without all the football in our life and all your input and support.

And last but not least, because I've saved the best for last, thank you, dear reader, for reading this particular book. I know you have an endless supply of choices, and I'm supremely grateful you chose to spend some of your valuable time with the people created inside my head. Thank you, thank you.

© Rachel McFarlin

**Lauren Rowe** is a *USA Today* and #1 internationally bestselling author of spicy, heartfelt romances. A civil litigation attorney for more than a decade, she quit practicing law the same day she was diagnosed with breast cancer and now writes novels and songs full-time. She is a lifelong football fan and San Diego native who grew up rooting for the Chargers. A UCLA alumna, she lives with her family and their dogs in San Diego, California.

LaurenRoweBooks.com

@LaurenRoweBooks